WHITE MEAT AND TRAFFIC LIGHTS

Also by Georgina Wroe

**SLAPHEAD
FLEECED**

WHITE MEAT AND TRAFFIC LIGHTS

Georgina Wroe

HEADLINE

Copyright © 2001 Georgina Wroe

The right of Georgina Wroe to be identified as the Author of the Work has been asserted by her in accordance with the Copyright, Designs and Patents Act 1988.

First published in Great Britain in 2001
by HEADLINE BOOK PUBLISHING

10 9 8 7 6 5 4 3 2 1

All rights reserved. No part of this publication may be reproduced, stored in a retrieval system, or transmitted, in any form or by any means without the prior written permission of the publisher, nor be otherwise circulated in any form of binding or cover other than that in which it is published and without a similar condition being imposed on the subsequent purchaser.

All characters in this publication are fictitious and any resemblance to real persons, living or dead, is purely coincidental.

British Library Cataloguing in Publication Data

Wroe, Georgina
   White meat and traffic lights
   1. Automobile thieves – Great Britain – Fiction
   2. Detective and mystery stories
   I. Title
823.9'14 [F]

ISBN 0 7472 6921 1

Typeset by Palimpsest Book Production Limited,
Polmont, Stirlingshire
Printed and bound in Great Britain by
Clays Ltd St Ives plc

HEADLINE BOOK PUBLISHING
A division of Hodder Headline
338 Euston Road
London NW1 3BH

www.headline.co.uk
www.hodderheadline.com

To Helma, Toby and Dan

Chapter One

I

Out of the passenger's window Patti read a multicoloured banner stretched between the Doric columns of an old church. It read: 'Jesus knows you and he *still* loves you.' Typical, was her first and only thought. She sighed deeply and shook her head in a long elaborate arc, which was how, at 11.15 a.m. on Wednesday, 31 January, she spotted the V-reg, four-by-four midnight-black Niva that would be the last car she ever stole.

For a start, the bull bars would have to come off. And the 'I Love Ladas' sticker plastered high up on the rear window, hinting at middle-class irony and possible police involvement, made it even more ominous. Then 73-year-old Emily Fricker missed the turning.

Patti leant towards her with her hand automatically on the handbrake. '*Right,* for Christ's sake, Emily,' she said. 'I told you the next available right.'

'I'm sorry, dear, it's just there's this car behind me and then another one coming towards me.'

'Welcome to driving in central London. What were you hoping for, an aerodrome?'

'No need to be sarcastic, dear,' Emily reprimanded.

'Yeah, try telling that to the examiner.' Patti's head was turned to the rear window, staring back at the Niva parked at the end of a line of cars. As she turned to face the front, inhaling a heavy sigh, she tasted a lungful of Emily's hairspray.

'Now what do I do?' Emily asked quietly.

'Well, I'll tell you what you're not going to do, you're not going to turn left.'

'OK, then,' said Emily, pluckily.

Emily was part of Patti's ten-week refresher ('Reclaim the Roads') course aimed at getting the reluctant pensioner back behind the wheel. Mostly they had specific goals: driving to their daughter's house, taking the grandchildren on outings. In Emily's case, she wanted to overcome a lifelong inability to cross a lane of traffic. Meaning she spent a weekly average of forty minutes in a five-mile network around the Bexleyheath Budgens.

Patti made a mental note of the Niva, illegally parked outside a Kentucky Fried Chicken. Movable landmarks had been a couple of six-foot teenagers in school uniform dipping into a family-sized bucket and flicking coleslaw on the pavement. It wasn't yet raining but they wore their parka hoods up, insulating them from the dismal surroundings of a wintry south London.

Patti studied Emily in the rear-view window. She tried again. 'At the next available opportunity, I want you to turn *right*.' Most of Patti's old ladies smelt of yeast infection or lily of the valley. When the Cinquecento's unsophisticated heating system warmed the car into a fug, Emily smelt of Johnson's Baby Lotion overlaced with one of those migraine-inducing perfumes from the eighties. She was given the scent by her daughters-in-law, so it was worse just after Christmas.

Patti cracked open an inch of the window. On a better day she never would have demanded the manoeuvre across Clapham High Street. But this was not a good day. Fahmy's non-specific sexual harassment had taken a physical turn. And the Australians from the moped shop (who else could it be?) had overwritten the plastic sign on top of the Cinquecento from '*L-Ability*' to read '*LIAbility*'. And this time they'd used an oil-based spray paint that Patti just knew wouldn't come off.

But she'd had sign adulteration before and Patti knew it was more than that. A fortnight before, at 8.17 a.m., her fiancé had started packing a suitcase. In the space of one sports report and a brief look at the business world he had gone. It spoke, she was forced to admit, volumes.

The traffic out of town was light for a weekday. Just past an everything-for-a-pound shop spilling bright plastic buckets onto the pavement, Patti said, 'Mirror, signal, manoeuvre. Come on,

WHITE MEAT AND TRAFFIC LIGHTS

Emily, you can do it. Pull slowly towards the middle of the road. Ignore the cars behind you.'

Emily stared hard in the mirror at a dark green Mondeo, trying to distance it with a look, then she jolted from fourth into second. 'In any case I'm not taking a test,' she said.

Patti was sitting on her hands. 'Sorry?'

Emily told her, 'You said "try telling that to the examiner". There is no examiner. I don't need to take a test.' Her tongue moved along her mouth as she concentrated.

'Sorry,' said Patti, 'I forgot.' She gave it twenty seconds then said, 'Anyway, stop changing the subject and take the next right turn.' Patti checked her watch. 'Please.'

It was almost midday and Patti was keen to get back. Twelve spelt school lunchtime with all its special problems of lobbed chip papers and footballs. And they were heading into the grey terraces of Clapham, which heralded the end of Patti's mappemonde.

'It's the buses.' Emily told her. She hadn't taken her coat off and it was thick tartan and hairy like a dog rug. At first Patti thought it was some old person's etiquette, then she realised Emily used the coat as a primitive safety suit. For much the same reason Patti kept her duffel on.

'Emily, what do we always say?' Emily stopped looking in the mirror and glanced over at Patti. Her eyes seemed to have accumulated a vat of moisture on the lower lid. Maybe tears, maybe gravity. She said nothing. The Cinquecento had been in the middle of the road for close to five minutes. Patti worried about the velocity of green-and-yellow Travis Perkins vans rattling along the inside lane. Patti gently reminded her, 'Even bus drivers were learners once. Easy does it,' she continued, watching out all the time for bicycles and motorbikes coming up unnoticed in the inside lane. Emily eased the wheel round, threading it between her black woollen gloves, her feet dancing on the pedals; straining and revving in first. Patti put a reassuring hand on the steering wheel to make sure it didn't slip.

'Now pull in on the left,' Patti told her, glancing behind. 'Look, that'll do.' She pointed ahead of her. 'Behind that Audi.' They were now a good half-mile from the Niva.

Emily protested, 'But it's a red route.'

'Treat it as an emergency stop.' Patti checked the cycle lane over her left shoulder.

'Is it?' Emily's head bobbed round nervously.

'Kind of. I need to get a lottery ticket.'

When she jerked to a halt, Patti knew congratulations were in order. But some days, most days, the praise just didn't flow.

Instead she said, 'Can I get you one?'

Emily said, 'Um, no thanks. I'm part of a syndicate.' She was using the break to apply a coat of pillar-box-red lipstick. It wasn't the nameless, part-of-the-beauty-kit type that Patti's mum tended to use, but L'Oréal's fade-resistant, stay-on-you type. Patti dug into her duffel coat to pull out a pot of Vaseline and started to smear it over her lips. In ancient Greece, lipstick was a prostitute's sign that she performed fellatio. Patti wondered what Vaseline meant. Probably more lubrication required.

Patti prised herself out of the car, which Emily had jammed up against a street light. 'How are you getting back to Bexleyheath?'

'Donald's picking me up,' said Emily. Usually her son came to collect her. Patti had never heard of Donald. 'He's from the whist club,' Emily offered unprompted.

'Do you want anything from in there?' Patti gestured to a shop called Booze, News and Food. A trestle table outside was covered in Astroturf and stacked with root vegetables from the Asian subcontinent.

Emily shrugged. 'Maybe a mineral water, please, dear.' Emily was the only person Patti knew over the age of fifty who drank mineral water. 'Badoit, if they have it,' she added.

Patti shook her head and silently tutted. Then she dodged through a break in the traffic, wondering if Emily had remembered to put the handbrake on. She resolved to get her a Ribena Light and tell her it was all they had.

At 4.10 p.m. Patti picked up a pair of clogs that were being re-heeled and at 4.35 p.m. went into Sainsbury's. Her friend Elaine would have called it multitasking, other people called it shopping. Midway down aisle twelve, cakes and pastries, she stopped and said to herself, 'Fucking Welsh faggots.'

WHITE MEAT AND TRAFFIC LIGHTS

Patti wasn't sure what suet was, but the common use of the word 'pudding' after it had made her steer her trolley – a twin carrier with unreliable nearside wheel – towards the home baking section. Shredded beef suet had thrown her, but then a lot of the evening class had had that effect. Now when people asked her which course she was on she tended to reply 'collision'. Week ten was titled, Economical Ways With Offal.

At low points, like these, whenever her mind started to veer, she forced the incident with her fiancé to the front of her brain. Her fiancé's kidney-bean-red face yanking open and slamming shut cupboard doors. Then he started picking up tins and reading the labels as if they were in Swahili. 'Heinz *baked* beans,' as if he'd never heard of them. '*Ambrosia* rice pudding.' Finally, close to exhaustion, he ripped the lid off a tupperware box.

'Most food has a shelf life. Yours has a half-life,' he'd yelled, pouring the contents into the sink. It had been a butterscotch Angel Delight to which, following the recipe suggestion on the box, she'd added a chopped-up Mars bar. Then he walked out, his Fahrenheit aftershave mingling with the metallic smell of out-of-date additives. Three days later, she signed up for Mrs Griffith's Cookery Course. It was two weeks into Lambeth's adult education autumn programme but, Patti figured, what the hell, she'd only missed Bread-Making For Beginners and A Way With Puddings.

She toyed with a packet of desiccated coconut, prodding and pummelling it like a cat on a soft blanket. The fluorescent lighting, abundance of choice, and tartrazine-filled toddlers were making her headache worse. She replaced the coconut and picked up a shopping list left in the trolley by a previous owner: 'apples, farmhouse cheddar, cheese, penne, organic butter'. She folded it up and put it in her duffel-coat pocket. It gave her something to aim for.

At the end of aisle twelve, Patti gave up on the shredded beef suet. She didn't want to replicate the sort of international incident she'd caused last Wednesday, involving three assistants and a deputy manager, when she'd asked for treacle. Instead, she headed for the meat counter for a pound of pig's liver. It was week three and not a hint of a returned call. Patti kicked the nearside wheel and made her way to the express checkout.

II

There were two good things about Winston's name. First it had the right number of syllables and, second, it made people expect a black man. Sometimes Winston even lowered his voice on the telephone and rolled his rs in what he thought was a West Indian way. On the minus side it meant most people called him Wins. Win would have made sense. Win meant victory. But add an s, rather than making it plural with a short s, it turned it into Wince.

He was the fourth in the writing class to stand up. Sometimes it went alphabetically, but tonight it was more ad hoc. People were just putting their hands up. Winston stood up and pulled down his cuffs. The evening classes posed a special sartorial problem for Winston. 'Mufti's just not my thing,' he told Douglas when City dress-down days threatened the West End. These days some bars actually banned suits the same way they used to outlaw builders' clothes or travellers. The pale grey cashmere suit he'd worn during the day would have looked out of place in a south London secondary modern. There were no curtains so the strip light reflected him in the window. Tonight he was beatnik, Left Bank, with a contemporary twist. Oxblood leather jacket with grey cords. He cleared his throat and felt the eyes of an appreciative audience. As usual he was sitting at the furthest place from the front, at the end of the back row closet to the window. It meant the others had to turn their chairs. The metal on the lino made chirruping noises. He waited for them to settle.

'The Day She Left.' He paused. It felt as if he should add, by Winston Freely, aged thirty-four.

He looked up, one hand holding his Palm Pilot, the other rooted in his trouser pocket cupping some loose change. He breathed deeply, uncurling his toes.

'The next time he'd know the signs. But you can read about how to build a relationship – how to woo her. Flowers, meals, shiny boxed gifts of jewellery. But he'd never been told anything about damage limitation, where to apply the anti-rust to stop it spreading. How to recognise when "Give me the remote" means "I don't want to sleep with you any more."'

There was a titter of recognition, though Winston hadn't meant it as a joke. He'd noticed before that any reference to sex, no matter how glancing, or a swear word, got a laugh. Outside he heard a man's shout bounce down a corridor. Winston wasn't used to reading aloud. He found a useful way to overcome his nerves was to pretend he was Fergal Keane. Fergal Keane reading Raymond Chandler.

'She started taking photos. Of them together – nothing rude. Him on a swing or a park bench. "Smile," she'd say, even when there was nothing to smile at. She even stopped a stranger to take them together next to the Serpentine on a freezing Sunday three-quarters through the football season. She grinned and put her hand to his face – part caress, but really to hide his frown. When they kissed, her lips were numb, like they'd been injected with Novocain. Spastic lips so frozen it made them dribble.' He paused and the Palm Pilot fell half an inch. Winston wasn't oversure about the dribbling bit. Or the spastic. But he'd looked it up. It was OK to use.

'It wasn't even a proper camera, it was a disposable one. The ones left on tables at wedding receptions. A camera you could only use once. After she'd gone he had figured out its purpose. She wanted a record of him. In the future, after she'd left him, she would frown and purse her lips coquettishly.

'"Boyfriends before you?" She'll smile, alluringly. "Well, you can't have thought you were the first?" She'll pretend to hide the photos at the back of her album, but still leave them close to the TV listings, knowing they'd be found.

'But he didn't know he was about to be consigned to the props cupboard. He took the camera the wrong way. Fun cameras were meant to have fun with. He wanted snapshots. He told her to dress up the way she used to. No knickers under her dress. He wanted to discover her when he came home from work. He ordered her to strip. Then knelt in front of her with one hand on the camera and one up—'

'Mr Freely, I wonder if you would be good enough to stop there.'

Winston looked up. Only the Kosovan refugee was egging him on with eye contact and approving nods.

Mr Croft scratched his temple with a Biro and loosened his collar. 'It's quite,' he paused, 'I don't know, *internal*. Wouldn't you say?'

Winston frowned. Did he mean internal as in organs? He looked around the class. Most of the women were rearranging their papers.

Mr Croft stood up. 'I mean, the monologue is very internal. You know the intention of the exercise was really, well, it was to explore anger. But you, on the other hand—'

'I haven't got to the anger bit yet,' Winston interrupted him. 'She doesn't even actually leave until page three. I'm building up dramatic tension.'

'Yeah, let the guy read more,' demanded Gentian the refugee and rocked back happily on his chair, his rangy frame made bigger by a brown leather jacket and tracksuit bottoms. He sat back on his wooden chair with his legs spread wide apart. His right hand cupped his crotch and he readjusted his legs. A fortnight ago Gentian had started winking at the elderly women in the group, anyone over thirty-five, and was rumoured to be responsible for the non-attendance of Beverley Thorpe who had been forced to leave the class due to stress. Despite the verbal and written intervention of several of the women, she had never been reimbursed. 'They only come to qualify for their vouchers,' said Beverley as she left.

Mr Croft underlined the word anger on the board. Not a blackboard, more the sort of thing sales reps projected their targets on in red felt-tip pen. 'You saw the way Harriet dealt with frustration in her piece. How everyday pent-up anger can have devastating effects.' Harriet Moffat's handwritten eight-pager centred on how an argument with an Argos customer service employee meant she missed her patchwork class the week Margaret was discovered to have had a stroke. She would never view hand whisks in quite the same way, seemed to be the moral. Though, naturally, she didn't put it quite like that.

Winston had his literary heroes: Raymond Chandler, Elmore Leonard, Walter Mosley. Like Winston, two-syllable first and second names. Freely even sounded like a member of the Mystery

WHITE MEAT AND TRAFFIC LIGHTS

Writers Guild of America. He suspected Jonathan Croft, with his corduroy elbow patches, Airware, unexpected pairs of dockers and the hint of a devoted wife was more Booker prize. Three-syllable Christian names and one-syllable surnames – Julian Barnes, William Boyd, Evelyn Waugh.

During the tea break, Winston strained to avoid the women's conversation by the drinks machine. His preferred latest method was pretending to text someone on his mobile. His head was down, his fringe curtaining the phone when someone called across to him. 'Hey, don't worry. Be happy. You story, I like.' Gentian had avoided giving his anger homework to the class. Now he lounged next to Winston, almost horizontal on a low plastic-covered seat spewing pus-coloured foam, his legs at such an obtuse angle they touched Winston's. He didn't seem to care. Winston edged gently away, casually but firmly, like pick-a-sticks. 'Women bitch.' Gentian took a swig from a taupe-coloured plastic beaker of black tea, washed it round his mouth and bit into a Twix. Winston admired his brevity.

He looked up and lowered the mobile. He said, 'Thanks. It was maybe a bit much for here, though. I mean, you know.' Winston half smiled and shrugged, suddenly worried he could be an accomplice to misogyny in a left-wing council building.

Gentian ignored him.

Winston took it that he hadn't been understood. He added, 'But I bet your story will be good. Full of anger, I mean. War, loss of family, driven from your homeland, disintegration, loneliness, asylum.' Winston didn't know much about Kosovo. From his history O level, he knew the world Balkan often appeared alongside the word belligerent.

Gentian scrunched up the Twix wrapper and kicked it towards the bin. He took his time before saying, 'Yeah, I tell you about anger.' He narrowed his eyes. 'Anger is that bastard Greek lorry driver who I pay good money to who didn't let me out at Germany. Is what anger is about. Who the fuck want Stockwell when you can have Munich?'

Winston nodded and wiped his chin with his hand thoughtfully.

'Shall we?' Harriet Moffat, still smug from her public praise, stood up. She dabbed the side of her mouth with a wet-one and pointed her court shoes towards classroom twenty-four. Winston wondered why, fifteen years on, school smells of disinfectant and glue still made him feel sick. If he inhaled hard enough it made his bowels loosen and his head swim. Then he pictured his brother Tony passing him the contents of the third-form tuck shop.

Gentian nudged him. 'I told you. All women bitch,' he repeated and winked at Winston. 'Don't worry. Be happy.'

Winston nodded weakly. He had seven months and eight days left to get a six-figure advance on a bestseller. The last thing he needed was to be in the same boat as a refugee

III

In Patti's opinion, one of Mrs Griffith's most irritating habits was starting sentences halfway through.

'From the Italian for liver, faggots are usually served with a purée of dried peas,' as if everyone knew what she was talking about. When she spoke, she lifted her arms in small circles, as though she was physically trying to disseminate information. She reeked of post-war frugality, the sort of woman you didn't get in London any more. The type who was evacuated in 1940 and never made it back. Reassured by bridge clubs and drivers who waited until you'd crossed all of the zebra before they speeded up.

All her recipes were based on leftovers. Everything needed 'eating up'. She even saved orange peel to light the fire, even though everyone knew central London was a smokeless zone. And she actually boasted how she never stacked dirty plates, thus saving washing-up liquid because she didn't have to wash both sides. That evening two more things had annoyed Patti from the start. One: how obviously Mrs Griffith was eyeing the apparent waste of material in Fazir's sari, to the point of actually asking how much material it used. Like she really ought to think about turning it into a blackout curtain or table cloth. Two: Griffith's insensitivity to the needs of a vegetarian.

'Miss Moss, why are you using chopsticks to pick up the liver?' Even the way she said 'Miss Moss' annoyed Patti. Disapproving sibilance. Criss-cross, mixed with mismatch.

WHITE MEAT AND TRAFFIC LIGHTS

Patti told her, 'Because it's disgusting.'

Mrs Griffith replied caustically, 'If you're able to eat it you must be able to prepare it.' Then added with a sigh, 'For goodness' sake.' Patti was at the station furthest from the front. In order to make the dressing-down audible to the whole group, Mrs Griffith remained rooted at the front close to the wooden podium, like an easel, from which she recited her recipes, priestlike. It wasn't a racist thing but Patti suspected she picked on the white ones more. As if they really should know better.

Patti poked the meat again. (What *were* those tubes?) Then she gave a desultory cough, like a diesel car turning over. 'But I *don't* eat it. I'm a vegetarian.'

Patti was hoping the hinted-at sense of waste would be enough to make Griffith keel over. Two middle-aged white women in trouser suits and Tony (a recently divorced gas fitter from Preston who would do anything to suck up) tutted.

Mrs Griffith visibly quivered. 'Then why, can you tell the class, are you interested in economical ways with offal?'

That was when Patti had put the chopsticks down. To avoid splashback she'd taken a leaf from Emily's book and kept her coat on. Since her fiancé had left her, Patti had presented her tupper of meat dishes to Fahmy every Thursday. Until she realised the high concentration of protein, combined with implied intimacy, was responsible for his latest bout of non-specific sexual harassment. Outside, she heard a car alarm go off. Inside, the homely sizzle of meat cooking. The windows were opaque with condensation. 'I need to learn about combination cooking,' Patti told Mrs Griffith. To Patti, anything more than opening one tin or using in excess of one packet meant combination cooking.

Either Mrs Griffith hadn't heard or she wasn't listening. 'The problem with modern cooks – Jamie Oliver, with his lazy mouth, and Nigella Lawson and her inability to tie her hair back – is that they don't understand the basics of nutrition. Food can't be cooked in an instant. It requires—'

Because she was aimlessly rhyming the word pukka in her head, Patti said, 'What's that little fucker got to do with anything?'

A hook-nosed woman in black with a smudge of flour on her cheek looked up. Mrs Griffith turned to Fazir. She said, 'Tins of soup are neither nutritional nor economic.'

Patti went on, 'That's why I'm here.' She looked down the three lines of cookers and flicked a chopstick into the sink. 'Oh, bugger off,' she said.

Mrs Griffith was walking towards her. 'I'm sorry?'

'I said, bugger offal.' Patti picked up her gloves and gave the liver a poke. 'All I need to know is how to cook. That's all. I mean it's not my fault. They go on about no one cooking or knowing grammar these days. Single parent families. As if people try to be like that. As if it's a life choice. You should spend eight years in a comprehensive.' Tony was smiling, eyes agog as though it was the best floorshow he'd ever seen. 'You know who I blame? I blame the suffragettes. If it hadn't been for frigging Emily Pankhurst I wouldn't be in this class.'

Mrs Griffith stopped six feet from her, scared to walk any further.

Patti stuck a chopstick into the liver. She said, 'But don't worry,' she looked straight at Mrs Griffith, 'next week I'm changing to pottery.'

She pushed past Mrs Griffith, leaving behind her wicker basket, her pound of pig's liver and remains of last week's cottage pie, which was going to be re-cycled after the tea break. As she tugged at the self-closing door she spun round, still red in the face and breathless from her speech. She addressed the teacher and said as flatly as she could, 'All you ever had to do was *screw* your husband.' Fazir's look of bewilderment would take some time to erase from Patti's mind.

Posters along the corridor reminded students going to college to get a meningitis jab. A cartoon arm had been defaced into someone jacking up. Patti trailed a glove along a waist-height picture rail, catching it now and again on drawing pins. She was walking pigeon-toed, which happened when she was upset, making her drag her heels. Black woolly tights stuck out of the bottom of her duffel coat. The laces on her trainers were too long. She was aware that if she had tied them the latest way, they wouldn't be. She knew trainers said a lot about a person but messages that hard to decipher didn't seem worth the effort. Not at her age. She reached in her pocket for a Curly Wurly that she'd been saving for the coffee break and ripped into it with her teeth.

In the car park she gulped in night air over the toffee and

chocolate. She dragged a cuff over her mouth, not sure if she needed to. It was just gone eight and a cover of frost was pasted over the cars like the film on a patient's tongue. An hour before the end of lessons and the car park was full. Lights from the builders' merchants next door lit up cars close to the fence. It wasn't a strip of middle managers' cars, like you found midweek outside suburban train stations. The car park was full of anything dredged up from the under-£500 classifieds. Fiestas, the odd Polo, three Opals and a rusty white Micra. Cars exerted a peaceful influence on Patti, like a row of newborns in a maternity ward. She finished the Curly Wurly, sucked the packet for any dropped slivers of chocolate and folded the wrapper this way and that, into a spring. Then she looked up. And that's where she saw it again. Second from the left in the third row. The same black 1999 Niva with the bull bars and the 'I Love Ladas' sticker. What were the chances of that? Better still, what were the chances of it being parked out of range of the street light?

Still loitering in the porch, she gave up hope of Mrs Griffith chasing after her with an apology and a written statement from the class asking her not to do pottery. She sighed and tossed the wrapper into a smokers' bin. Then she kicked at the cigarette butts stubbed out in a cluster, as close to the double doors as the smoke alarm would allow. For the second time that day, she resolved it would be the last car she ever stole.

Four hours later Patti got into bed to rewrite her obituary. Not completely rewrite it, just update it with the dates of the evening class. Her obituary was really a diary – written on separate sheets of A4 – but not one that had to be kept every day. She dumped a mug of instant forty-calorie drinking chocolate mixed with a triple shot of whisky on the Ikea bedside table next to her. Like much in the flat, the table was living on borrowed time. It was part of a stack of furniture, including the sofa, that belonged to her former fiancé. He'd paid for it while she, after arguing about the design, had stormed off to the café for a two-pound plate of tagliatelle and chips. Looking back on the relationship, as Loyd Grossman might say on *Through the Keyhole*, 'All the signs were there, if you knew where to look.' Patti pulled her hot water bottle up her legs which were encased in a pair of aged thirteen to fourteen boy's pyjamas with Starsky and Hutch on the front, hand-me-downs from her brother, scalding her thighs and praying it didn't burst.

As usual, she started the entry by rereading the whole obituary for signs where she had gone wrong. One rule was never to editorialise. She was looking for patterns. A character, she knew, best demonstrated itself through actions. Patti had started writing it the night her fiancé left. It was handwritten because she wrote it at night and since she lived alone she hadn't bothered to refill the gas canister for the heater in the study. It was too cold to sit in front of the desktop. The early life was sketchy but, as Elaine pointed out, no one – apart from Colette and Aled Jones – made much of a lasting mark before eighteen. As she wrote, the sleeve of her hand-knitted cardigan caught on the pen lid. 'Sod it,' she said, dragging her right arm out of the sleeve.

'*Born Patricia Polly Moss, September 25th 1968 in St Albans, Herts. Youngest child of Phyllis and Alan Moss and the younger sister of Alexander and Richard.*' She'd underlined the last seven words in green Biro. Didn't that speak volumes? '*In 1988, bowing to public pressure, Pat changed her name to Patti.*' That entry had been highlighted in green marker with the word '*trauma*' next to it, underlined.

'Who the hell's *Patti*?' bowl-faced Elaine had demanded two weeks into the first college Christmas holiday. Both had a bottle of Diamond Whites in the crease of their boiler suits. 'Other than a peppermint-based fondant?'

Patti (sarcastic): 'Never heard of Patti Smith? Patti Hearst?'

'No. I've heard of Patti Boulay though.'

Silence. Then Elaine said, 'Patti sounds like a poof's name.'

Patti kept quiet. Could women be poofs?

'All those names, Lizzie, Daisy, Maisy, sound so wet.' Since she'd started college, Elaine had streaked her hair and joined the women's movement.

'What do you want me to be called – *Bernard*?' Patti asked. She opened two more bottles. Elaine had started calling Diamond White working-class champagne, though it was better than champagne because it was, in fact, cider. Elaine had also enrolled in a workers' collective.

Patti went on, 'It's Patti. P.A.T.T.I.' She paused and took a gulp. 'I just don't want to be a cow pat any more,' she said.

WHITE MEAT AND TRAFFIC LIGHTS

Elaine never did call her Patti. She said it was too bourgeois. That was until one overcast June morning six months later in the Hatfield dole queue waiting to sign on. It was before automated queuing systems so the woman behind the counter had to attract their attention by shouting. Patti never forgot the day. Elaine was in a dark-blue council-issue boiler suit, with a pink triangle on her collar that everyone was ignoring, Patti in bat-wing blouse. The woman called. 'Hello, there, Miss Moss. Hellooo.' Then louder, 'Hi, Patti P. Moss.'

Elaine stopped speaking. 'Fucking hell,' she said quietly. 'It sounds like hippopotamus.'

She was right. Patti had inadvertently changed her name to a lumbering gregarious animal living in or around the rivers of tropical Africa.

By then, even if she'd wanted to change it back, Elaine wouldn't have let her. Every greeting became, 'Hi, Patti Po (shortened from Polly) Moss.' She encouraged others to do the same. A favourite, if they were going out, was, 'You're looking hip, Patti Moss.' Syntax-wise a bit had to be ironed out. But it meant Patti was the only woman in recorded history who could become enraged by the word 'Hi'. No wonder she was strident.

Patti's basement bedroom meant her ears were level with the pavement. Outside she heard the solid click of middle-aged high heels on their way home. Stilettos tended to scrape along the pavement. Especially at this time, when the wearer was likely staggering home after a lock-in at the Dog and Duck. A car door slammed. A car alarm started and then gave up.

Patti hadn't taken the Niva in the end. Her heart hadn't really been in it. Besides that, a security guard on his rounds in the builders' yard had spotted her trying the window using a couple of folded-over business cards to test the lock. She'd smiled and adjusted her clothes, embarrassed, suggesting she'd just been squatting for a pee. As Rory had told her, time and time again, nobody ever got overly suspicious of women acting out of the ordinary. Some people would have taken it was a sign she shouldn't steal the car. Patti thought the opposite.

She sank further into bed and flipped over the obituary. When her fiancé had left, she'd written, *'Differing work commitments and the strain of modern life caused an irreconcilable split and, with mutual agreement, they parted amicably.*' Now she added today's date and wrote, '*Patti decided that further cookery lessons were unneeded and terminated the course.*'

What Patti dreaded most in the world was death in unusual circumstances. Not the nature of her death (murder, car accident, tropical disease were all pretty much of a muchness) but the way she would be described afterwards. All youngish deaths ended up in some local rag somewhere. She had to keep the obituary up until her demise, maybe in her fifties, was no longer noteworthy. '*Patricia Moss, 32, a part-time driving instructor, lived on her own.*' It made her sound like such a loser. Elaine had told her having a ready-made obituary meant the lazy hack would have facts at his (or her) fingertips. Not that it'd been Elaine's idea. She'd just spoken from the authority of a media studies course.

At 1.42 a.m. Patti started awake with the radio still on, playing moody late-night lovers' stuff. She'd been halfway through a dream. She was seven and playing cricket with her brothers on the recreation ground near the station, waiting for their dad to get off the London train. They were fielding like they always did when she was batting, by standing two feet either side of her. When she asked them to move out a bit, they came so close they were almost touching her. It meant she never had a chance to score any runs and was out on the third ball.

Patti reached over to switch the radio off. Her forehead was damp and she felt a restless sense of anger. Then she pulled herself into a sitting position and switched the light on. She reached over and crumpled up the obituary and lobbed it towards the end of the bed.

'Fuck 'em,' she said and lay back down again. 'Fuck 'em all.' Then she went back to sleep.

IV

By 9.30 a.m. on Thursday, 1 February, Winston had already been in the meeting for more than ninety minutes. He couldn't help thinking, if people were that keen on selling cigarettes, why stop free enterprise? In front of him Sheila Sheepshank, ACT's PR director, was flouncing girlishly about in a grey poncho. She was the permanently man-less sort of woman who hadn't been told often enough to grow up. By middle age it was too late.

So far Winston had refused cigarettes from the silver platters dotted at intervals along the board table at the Anglo Canadian Tobacco office. Pretending he didn't smoke was a ruse. And a tactic frowned upon by Lobby Force's managing director when dealing with tobacco companies ('shared interest equals shared concern') but Winston thought it gave him the moral high ground. Even earned him a sneaking respect. Which was why when the poncho woman rasped out reasons why a link between smoking and cancer had never irrefutably been proved, he narrowed his eyes sceptically towards the pewter ashtray. The look disarmed her enough to forget her cigarette. Thirty seconds later an arc of ash scattered grey dust motes onto her brown suede lap. Excellent, thought Winston. It was always good to have them on the back foot.

In fact, for the past three years, Winston had smoked Camels. And always Camels bought in packets of ten. His intention was confusion – full tar yet only half a packet. It was a relatively new thing. For fifteen years, ever since his brother Tony had kidded that they were 'his' cigarettes, Winston had smoked his namesakes. Mainly out of loyalty – to his brother not the brand. Now he was setting the record straight.

Today Winston had been mobilised to ACT's twenty-storey all-glass office shaped like a 1970s ashtray on Victoria Embankment. His mission was to counteract an unfounded down-page report in the foreign section of an unreliable left-wing paper. 'They actually blame us for, here I'm quoting now, for "Satinclad cigarette girls targeting schools from Gdansk to Bucharest," Sheila Sheepshank spluttered. I mean it's preposterous.' She flung the paper on the table.

In her early fifties with grey-blonde hair long enough to wear in a bun, Sheila's skin was as wrinkled as dried tobacco leaves. She reminded Winston of his mother, similar ages, same clunky amber jewellery and slightly turned-up collars with frizzy hair that snagged the teeth out of combs. She ended every sentence with three nods of her chin and a slow wink with her left eye. Winston knew the trick. It hinted at confidentiality.

'Sympathy is what the tobacco industry requires,' she said.

'It's nothing new. We've been pariahs since smoking began. This whole cancer thing is nothing new. In the sixteenth century we were blamed for everything from being in league with the devil to bringing the plague. What we require, Mr Freely, is a fair crack at the whip. I mean, how do you know, positively, that lung cancer doesn't come from the tar on roads?' She let it hang.

Winston looked at the table. 'As far as I can see . . .' he kept his voice even as he snapped his Palm Pilot shut but then made the mistake of eye contact.

She interrupted him. 'Look around, see how fair, how mul-ti-na-tio-nal,' her chin bounced out the word in five nods at compass points around the glass office, 'we are. Why, our head of human resources is a Chinaman. Our head of IT is from Sene-frigging-gal.'

Winston didn't think he could get away with the term Chinaman anywhere. Not even in the *Mail*.

She collapsed against the back of her seat with a clash of vertebrae against chrome.

Winston said, 'There's no doubt . . .' he paused, 'there are several ways we could go with this—'

The woman stood up, suddenly animated. 'Ever since that bloody bugle player. I mean how can you inhale cigarette fumes through a trumpet? Nothing was ever proved. Please, Mr Freely, make a note of that. Nothing. Was. Ever. Proved.'

Winston levered his shoulders upright. Outside the glass boardroom, young marketing executives threaded their way along corridors whose carpets stored up currents of electricity. The air was thick with cigarette smoke, sales charts and statistics.

Winston pretended to write. 'And I think we made that abundantly clear at the time. In fact, I think it was even brought up in the House.' He stood to go. Leaving abruptly was one of his things. It worked on women. It worked on clients. Best of all it worked on women clients.

Walking from the lift, Winston scooped every cigarette out of every pewter dish dotted towards the front desk and stuffed them deep into his overcoat pockets, mingling with bus tickets and off-licence receipts. It was a ritual every time he visited ACT. He dropped off his visitor's pass at reception, handing it to a tiny bottle blonde so snooty you'd think she worked at Amnesty

International. The river had condensed to a low tide and smelt of the sea. Opposite him was the dull irregular symmetry of the South Bank. He let the cigarettes roll in his fingers and then dropped them one by one to leave a trail at metre intervals along the embankment wall, like place names.

It was too early for most of the homeless to be out, but come four o'clock the benches along the riverside would be a damp patchwork of greasy nylon sleeping bags and cans of Kestrel. The white trail lasted as far as Villiers Street where Big Ben dipped out of sight and Winston turned right and headed along the Strand.

The Lobby Force office was empty. At Lobby Force, staff movement was unregulated. In fact, the MD Douglas McAlistair encouraged them to be out of the office as much as possible. He was a Glaswegian, scrupulous to the point of miserly about overheads which had (unfairly) confirmed a few suspicions about the Scots. Pitch-black was the way Douglas liked to see his HQ.

'Hey, Wince, my man, how did you get on at the fag place?' Poppy with her toffee-coloured hair and unpredictable mood swings shared longevity of service with Winston. They'd both been at the company longer than the rest. She was from a south coast PR company; he a former MP's secretary who had left because the challenge wasn't stiff enough. He'd even put that on his CV.

'Same old stuff really,' said Winston. 'I'll crank that doctor out. Have a word with Reg. Get someone to discredit the *Guardian*.' He hung his coat up on the top of an opened cupboard door. The shelves were stacked with publishers' freebies – *Mobius on Emerging Markets*, *Dictionary of Political Biographies*. After Christmas the good ones had gone. Winston's mum had got a dictionary of quotations and Tony *The Alan Clark Diaries*.

The office was mostly deserted these days. It was not just the post-Christmas lull. A new Brussels branch had creamed off the most ambitious Lobby Forcers, as they were referred to collectively. In a warped exchange programme, they were currently hosting two low-grade Belgians: Rafael (with an irritating comic misuse of English) and Isobell, two ls and no e on the end.

Brussels was dangled on the recruitment section of their website in the same way 'opportunities overseas' was at ACT. Paul 'the boffin' Hoxton was in the corner hemmed in by the window to the left and a bookcase behind him. 'There's a certain irony,' Poppy said, 'that the most coveted desk, where no one can sneak up behind you, should go to him.' Poppy spent a lot of time on shopping websites which meant she'd had to rig up a mirror on top of her computer to catch people behind her.

Most of Winston's colleagues were in their early twenties, most straight from college. They were still young enough to think careers mattered. In fact at their age, if Winston remembered correctly, careers were all that mattered. At thirty-four, it was rapidly turning into a whole new ball game.

'Drink?' Poppy was texting someone on her mobile. She seemed awfully old to be texting.

'Nah, I've got to make a call, then I've got the turkey man this afternoon.' Winston switched his laptop off and opened his briefcase. A photocopied article by Stephen King entitled 'How to Write' fell out. He rammed it back in. Poppy was the last person he wanted to know about that. He pulled out the *Guardian* to see if it listed the frequency for Radio Suffolk.

'Not all the way to Kent?' Poppy said.

'No, he's near Ipswich.'

Poppy nodded and went on, 'Don't tell me you're taking that car of yours there?'

'Yes I am. As it goes.'

'If it goes.' She sent the message with a flourish of the hand. Winston ignored her.

'What is it? Salmonella? BSE? Croup in the coop?' She hugged her knees.

She thought she was funny. Winston smiled. Unlike Sheila Sheepshank, Poppy was the sort of woman who was used to having a man around. A worshipping sort of man who always let her get her own way. Two years ago Poppy had set Winston up with an old college friend of hers called Cindy.

'No, it's a weird one,' said Winston. 'He wants me to meet a pal of his.'

'It's probably a new turkey nugget formula. How fowl.'

'Maybe.' Winston stood up and reached for his coat. 'Well, let's face it, he does significantly better than your soya burger crew. How many of your lot are on the rich list?'

Poppy had tossed her hair once too often and Winston was

starting to feel claustrophobic. He was making a point. Poppy was a vegetarian. No matter what you thought of Selwyn Bates, Winston always felt a jag of pride when his scrawny two-dimensional picture with its trademark shock of white hair appeared high up the *Daily Mail* rich list. Last year he had come an impressive 203rd to the Paltry 411th of his arch turkey-farming rival from Norfolk.

Poppy shrugged and uncrossed her legs. She said, 'He's a bit of a recluse, isn't he?'

'Yeah,' Winston nodded. 'Apart from that car thing.' Six months ago Selwyn Bates went from hideaway turkey farmer to achieving celebrity status when he bought a red 1971 Ford Mustang from a serviceman at a nearby American base. The local paper dubbed him Mustang Selwyn and a day later, at the time of the petrol strikes, the tabloids branded a picture of him driving it 'the gas gobbler'.

Winston said, 'Look, the traffic's going to be murder. I'd better get going. You in tomorrow?'

Winston knew why he was driving a hundred miles out of London and it was more than the enforced leisure of getting stuck behind a lorry on the A134 or schmoozing a client. Bates had something on him: his car. Bates had told him it was a gift 'without prejudice' (in recognition of his salmonella work). According to his Lobby Force contract, and he imagined the Inland Revenue, Winston was supposed to declare gifts. But he hadn't, and the car had become Bates's and his little secret. He was also curious to meet the man Bates had described as potentially 'one of the most important men in the world' in five years' time. Like all of his clients, Bates did have an exaggerated sense of his own importance, but Winston was intrigued nonetheless. 'He could be very useful to you, young man, very useful indeed,' he'd said in that funny way of his.

As Winston got to the door, Poppy called over to him, 'Oh, I forgot to say, Cindy wants to pick up some stuff.'

'Fine, tell her to call me.' Winston heard Big Ben chime three times as he left. He tried to hit his heel on the wooden stairs at the same time. From the age of sixteen, he'd worn steel tips in his shoes to make them click on pavements as he walked. It made him feel like a movie star.

Inside his car he switched on the radio as he pulled away, only half listening, reversing round Poppy's car. He'd tuned it to Radio Suffolk to pick up the traffic news. '*Police are increasingly worried for the safety of fifteen-year-old Alan Raynham who disappeared from his Suffolk home last Friday. Alan was last heard of visiting friends in Sudbury where he was taking part in a five-a-side football tournament. According to his mother, Eleanor, a line manager for Butterballs Turkeys, Alan rarely went anywhere without letting her know. Local police, who say their task is hampered by the recent cold snap, are broadening their hunt.*'

At the mention of Butterballs, Winston had sat up.

V

Selwyn Bates was barefoot and sliding up and down a goatskin rug to the best of Dusty Springfield. In one hand he clutched a tumbler of Calvados three-quarters full. His shirt was undone and salty beads of perspiration ran in rivulets down his forehead into his eyes.

He sang, 'Life is kinda spooky with a crazy little boy like me.' Dusty was one of the best female vocalists he knew, from a turkey perspective. He'd tried others, from Ella Fitzgerald to Claire Grogan (his housekeeper Mrs King's son's suggestion). But it was always Dusty who came out trumps. He'd seen 'Down Town' calm a coop in thirty seconds. The only other thing it sometimes did was set the lurchers off but he could hardly blame Dusty for that. By rights he should have added her to his golden turkey list (now at seventeen, including Delia Smith and Keith Dellar) but he had a feeling she was dead. Or was that Lulu? He'd get Mrs King to look into it.

He felt as skittish as a young colt. He tried to calm down. He slumped into a fireside chair and separated the February edition of *Fancy Fowl* from Herbert's magazine collection. But no matter how many references were made to him as the new president of the Suffolk Poultry Society, he simply couldn't concentrate. He squeezed his elbows to his sides, clamped his buttocks together and propelled himself to his feet.

Then he raised his glass to the portrait of himself hung two feet above the fire. 'Well done, Selwyn, my boy,' he said. The Selwyn in oils clenched a 24lb frozen turkey under his left arm (Brussels or not he'd never go into kilos and they could put that on his gravestone). His left hand was in his jacket pocket to hide his missing finger. He'd insisted that the artist capture echoes of his boyhood poaching in the painting. He remembered the response. The artist had narrowed his eyes, turned his cheek quizzically, and said, '*Pooching*? Is that something to do with dogs?' The London twerp, dressed head to foot in tweed. Bates said out loud, 'Pooching my foot.' He called the painting Poacher Turned Gamekeeper. Game as in turkey, he told the artist. He was captured dressed like a squire with his beloved mansion in the background.

Right now he was thirty minutes into his Selwyn hour. Even multimillionaires need time off, he told interviewers. 'Other than that precious time, all the while I'm on the go go go.' He remembered having to repeat that to the journalist from the business pages of the *Daily Telegraph*. 'What exactly do you mean?' the jumped-up little prick had asked. 'You're *on the goo*?'

Christ Almighty, thought Bates, you couldn't switch the TV on these days without being assaulted by Jocks and Paddies, never mind the Welsh, but when did you ever hear a Suffolk accent? That's what he wanted to know.

During his Selwyn hour, staff were under strict instructions not to disturb him. Was it too much to ask? he reasoned. Sixty blasted minutes, that was all. The hour ended dead on four when the factory siren boomed the change of another shift. It was a foghorn of noise that carried miles and miles over Dedhamvale. So far, he'd once been told, you could hear it over Hadleigh way. The whole county moving to the beat of his drum. Thousands of workers bussed in from all over the county (fifteen coaches over Christmas) from your la-de-da students to family men. Every employment agency in Ipswich was booked up with his personnel requests alone. Floodlit car parks like a football game, thousands of white boiler-suited workers scurrying from pillar to post. Sometimes it reminded him of a sci-fi film. And all of them, every last man, woman and child, on that filthy minimum wage. Well, not for much longer.

At ten to four, there was a heavy knock at the door. The door was what the catalogue described as Dutch, where you could open the top bit and keep the bottom closed. Why can't they call it a stable door? he'd asked the woman on the phone, but paid the £290 plus VAT anyway. It was an excessive piece of renovation based on Mrs King's large rump and obsession with polyester trousers. Selwyn was a breast man, not a leg man, to such an extent that he didn't always have the fortitude to look at women below the waist. The stable door allowed him to compartmentalise. Now when Selwyn said, 'Enter,' all Mrs King did was open the top hatch.

'Mrs King, how many times must I tell you not to disturb—' he had almost finished the sentence before the door had swung halfway round.

'I'm sorry,' she said. 'You know I wouldn't unless it was an emergency.' She was wearing a grey polo neck and her hair was tied back. Though into her forties, almost as old as Selwyn, she wasn't a bad old bird. Plump, not too scraggy, with an ample – countrywoman's – bosom. 'It's Mr Nevski, he's on the phone, he says it's urgent.' She made it sound like an inconvenience to her, not him. What was wrong with these people? he thought.

'Fine.' He stalked over to the door, doing up his buttons as he went. He asked without looking up, 'Did you tape my programmes?'

'Nnnn,' said Mrs King, which he took as a yes.

After he picked up the phone, he used his free hand to waft shut the door. One chunky palm still over the receiver, he called out, 'I'll have my supper in here tonight.'

He heard Mrs King's mules drag down the corridor. As far as he was concerned, this latest consignment couldn't come a second too soon. He'd suffered too long. It was time he let his white hair down (for hair there was) and started behaving like a real turkey magnate.

Chapter Two

I

The fetid stench made Xenia think temperature had a smell. Throughout the factory, everywhere the smell was the worst thing, of cold dead flesh and blood. Above the steady clatter of the conveyor belt and the metronomic thud of birds landing, the whole line was talking of Alan Raynham. Everyone in cold cuts had been called in for questioning, whether they'd known him or not. For the fourth day Eleanor Raynham had called in sick. And there was a TV crew roaming the village with 'BBC Look East' painted on the side of their Range Rover, with the famous Kim Riley interviewing people in the Crown, though Pam had told everybody to say nothing.

The gossip went down the line, embellished and refined along with the turkeys. One woman in a yellow hard hat said, 'I was only speaking to him on the Saturday, he never said nothing about going nowhere.'

It was funny, because not understanding the language very well made Xenia see more. The way a middle-aged woman's eyes softened at the sight of a hook-nosed manager, the superior look of the women managers which meant they had information to pass on. The uniforms also helped – they were a leveller, so much so she couldn't always spot the foreigners on her shift. All the workers like drones in white, bloodied boiler suits, hair in nets, scraped back under a yellow hard hat (yellow for line operative, green for manager).

The bagging room was cold but not as cold as the warehouse which was three portacabins away from the main factory. But she liked it better outside where there was less chance of anyone speaking to her. Every hour, at quarter past, they all moved down a station. She went from twisting wings back (she hated the snap of the cartilage breaking) to tucking in headless necks, then down past the scales to bagging. Pricking the bags to stop them exploding (even though the eight-hour shift gave her lower backache) was her favourite job. Outside the main factory they had the radio on and some of the songs reminded her of Radio Nostalgie that she used to listen to with her brother Anton. The worst shift was plucking stubborn feathers out of the turkeys as they trundled relentlessly round the old aircraft hangar upside down on hooks, bloody gizzards trailing.

'Course, he's got family out Haverhill way,' a young woman revealed slowly, letting others on the line digest every word. She was chewing gum in an offhand way, even though it was strictly forbidden in case it ended up in a turkey and resulted in a million-pound lawsuit. She had to shout because the noise was intense. Xenia used the noise as an excuse when one of the boys lolled up to her.

'Who says?' The voice came from the other side of the conveyor belt.

A man, 'Everyone knows that. It's a half-sister or something.'

The woman told them, 'Why would he go there and not tell no one?'

'I'm not saying he did, I'm just saying.'

To Xenia they all looked the same and all sounded the same. When they erupted into laughter she half-heartedly smiled so she didn't stand out. Two of the younger ones had taken to smiling at her across the turkeys. One, called Peter, with lumpy grey skin like kasha, had given her a chocolate bar in the canteen. Now he was trying to catch her eye. She looked away, nervous. It was so far from what she'd been expecting, she couldn't even remember what she had been expecting any more. What was it Aunt Galia said? 'You're only disappointed if you expect something.' If she started to think of it her eyes began to itch and then if she really thought about it her stomach would turn over and she'd get a burst of pins and needles all over.

What would Uncle Gleb and Aunt Galia say if they could see her now?

II

It was just after eight and Patti was already in the office. Despite the weather, family-looking men were already rolling out chrome tables and chairs on pavements under awnings outside a couple of the Portuguese cafés – greasy spoons clouded over with the cigarette and tea steam fug of workmen who'd been up since five. The logjam of cars slipping in and out of first gear stretched along South Lambeth Road, halting and jolting towards the centre.

Both of her refreshers had cancelled, blaming flu. Patti understood. Outside, it was chucking it down and pensioners made fair-weather drivers. She was only hanging about herself. Mooching really because, even by her standards, 8.12 a.m. was too early to call the end of the working day. Also, she'd arranged to see Rory at midday. The office was warm from two bars of a three-bar electric fire and she had no umbrella to get home with.

She bent her head over a cup of tea and thought about herself. Her radio alarm that morning had woken her to her song. Ever since one Christmas in the early eighties, when Elaine had played *Graceland*, Elaine knew that Paul Simon had written 'roly poly little bat-faced girl' to mean her. She remembered the shock of recognition others felt on meeting their soul mate. Not that she was roly, or particularly poly. And she didn't really know what bat-faced meant other than pointed and poisonous, sort of like Björk. She just felt it summed her up. Her short black hair dangled round her mug in a fringe. She reached out for another biscuit. For Patti, custard creams, even the Happy Shopper label, were the understated prince of the biscuit barrel. Fahmy's fig rolls, on the other hand, had an exotic label. But that was one of the perks of being a boss. The tea tasted metallic because of the longlife milk. She'd also got the blue aluminium camping mug that burnt her lips.

She looked up, the steam from the tea drying cold on her face.

'Fahmy, what is it about me? Have I let myself go?' She dunked the custard cream.

Fahmy coughed, uninterested. He said without looking up, 'What you mean? Go where? You want fare?'

Her cagoule dripped rain around her thighs. The room smelt of Fahmy's Dunhill cigarettes and oily rags. An upturned can of WD-40 stood next to a tin of rat bait. In the kitchen, really a kettle standing in the sink, a radio played 'I Want to Break Free'.

Patti said, 'No. Me. Gone to the dogs.'

Fahmy closed the Property and Home section of the *Standard* with a sigh. There was a Colin-generated rumour going around VIPS (Vauxhall's Imperial Passenger Service) that Fahmy's wife had kicked him out. Fahmy half-heartedly picked up last month's edition of *Now* which promised a twelve-page pullout and keep on Madonna's wedding.

He looked straight at her legs. 'Why you wear those black woollen tights? It's not right a woman your age. Your leg not so bad.' His hooded eyes flicked up and down her lower body. Above him, too high to be easily taken down, a yellowing picture of Samantha Fox was Blu-Tacked to the wall – a pair of breasts which were almost two decades out of date and might have gone through childbirth and implants. Still, thought Patti, it was monogamy, of a sort.

'Piss off,' she said, dunking a custard cream.

'Anyway.' Fahmy made an exaggerated action of rubbing his stomach over a pair of stone-washed jeans. 'Where's my food today? Is Friday. Yesterday no food. Now where's my dish of the day?'

Patti told him, 'It was pork casserole.' No need to let on she'd been expelled from the evening class. Or at the very least expunged.

Fahmy said, 'So?'

'You don't eat pork.'

'I ruddy do. Is my all-time favourite. That's all.'

Patti said nothing. Fahmy had let her run L-Ability from his office, wedged in a damp arch under the railway line into Waterloo, for seven months since she'd put an ad in the *South London Press* wanting shared office space. She was aware that the contractual details hadn't been ironed out as such. Buying the milk and wearing a skirt tended to help. She also allowed them to use her Cinquecento if one of the boys' cars didn't start.

He fell into a dejected silence, making a sucking noise with his lips.

Patti put down her tea. She felt shut up and bored. 'Where's Titus and Colin?'

'Colin's on lates, Titus take boy to school.' Fahmy stubbed out a cigarette and took another fig roll. 'How long for Catherine Zeta Jones and Michael Douglas? What she do with old man?'

'He's loaded,' Patti told him.

'She's not short of a bob or two.' He looked at her. 'Plus, she has screen presence not seen since Ava Gardner.' He must have just read that bit.

'Is that a fact?'

Fahmy liked to be 'celebritied-up'. Depending on the award ceremonies, he bought up to eight different magazines a week. It had started so he could test Colin. Colin, with his pork pie hat and black leather driving gloves, had claimed on his handwritten CV that he had spent four years driving for an upmarket chauffeur company. Under 'other information' he added that he wasn't unused to seeing Kate Winslet in the back of his car. He claimed to have the inside scoop on everyone from Dannii Minogue to Jeremy Spake. That was why the VIPS staff studied the gossip pages in much the same way other drivers might read the Hainault car manual.

The phone went. It was a phone fax with an odd single ring. Fahmy shook his head and looked away. Rain was bad for driving lessons but good for taxis, for much the same reason. Mothers hated doing the school run in the rain. It made Patti consider what an untapped resource mothers were for L-Ability. She ought to run a new classified ad in the *South London Press*. Especially now the pensioners were drying up.

Fahmy used his phone voice. 'Hello. VIPS. How can I serve?'

Patti switched off. She was thinking of her latest escape scheme. The bottom dollop of Blu-Tack securing Samantha Fox to the wall doubled up to glue a three foot by four foot poster of Alexandria. It showed the elegant corniche stretching (according to Fahmy) twenty miles along the Mediterranean. He also boasted it was where Alexander the Great's library had been (underwater now).

Fahmy had his hand over the receiver and gnawed thoughtfully on a Biro, salivating slightly. He asked, 'You want fare?'

'No.' Patti edged the third bar of the electric fire on with her foot.

Fahmy said, 'Why not? Wandsworth Road to Victoria. Is not so far. Even for you.'

'I just don't want,' Patti told him. 'People don't like taxis with Liability written on them.' She picked up another biscuit.

Fahmy said, 'Then get your lazy arse outside and clean up the mess.'

'It's not my fault if some bloody Australians—'

Then Fahmy remembered the fare. 'Yes, madam, with you in ten minutes.' Then he added, 'Tops.' He inhaled deeply, making sucking noises with his lips and tapped his Biro against the phone. It was intended to show how tough his job was. 'Now where is my man Titus?'

Fahmy fiddled with his keys – a great Fort Knox of a set, the plastic key fob taken up by a coloured photo of an Alsatian sitting up in a field of poppies. At first Patti hoped the snapshot had come with the key ring and Fahmy hadn't realised he could change it. She wondered if that was the reason his wife had left.

She sat in silence while Fahmy tried to track Titus down. She was wearing her old school cagoule because the duffel took time to dry out and made the car smell of wet wool. Every so often she felt it to see if it was still dripping. After ten minutes, she said, 'Fahmy?'

He ignored her.

She went on, 'Is it true what they say about the Egyptian driving test?'

'What the hell you talking about?' He'd found Titus but he wasn't responding.

'Come on, you bastard boy.'

'That you only have to drive three yards backwards and three yards forwards?'

Fahmy's face was grave. He said, 'How the hell would I know? I not been to Egypt for last twenty years. Now shut up, woman, I need to concentrate.'

It was definitely worth looking into. Patti's latest plan was to open a driving school in Cairo or maybe Alexandria because she liked the idea of living by the sea. It would be like those dive holidays on the Red Sea that were advertised for £199. But rather than learning to scuba dive, you passed your driving test. Then you applied for an international one. Then before you knew it you could drive anywhere in the world, including central London.

The clincher in her advertising campaign would be no written test. Or actually, no emergency stop, three-point turn or Highway Code in general. Maybe she could incorporate it with a dive holiday. Get Rory involved, he was the rufty tufty outdoor type. Drive 'n' Dive. The more she thought about it, the better it became. Only that wasn't the best bit. She would be able to swap her woolly tights for a yashmak and be done with it.

III

The Suffolk sky seemed to go on and on in a way Winston thought only happened in jigsaws. It was unendingly flat with a strip of colour on the horizon no thicker than a brown felt-tip pen.

The wind whipping up off the land turned Bates's ruddy face redder. He didn't take his gaze from the lawn ahead of them when he said to Winston, 'You've heard of wild turkeys?' Winston had only heard of the whisky. Bates didn't wait for a reply. 'That's what I'm doin' here.'

Winston had never been in a golf buggy before. They were less robust than they looked on the TV golf courses. Bates sat with his legs wide apart, obliging Winston to strain leaning out of the buggy. A brown lurcher and a beagle hobbled alongside them. It wasn't as if the coop was miles away but Winston got the impression Bates didn't walk very far. 'Why have a dog and bark?' he'd replied when Winston told him four hours in a car had left him in need of a stroll.

In the distance to the left, swerving over a hillock edged with ornamental pines, another golf buggy trundled towards them. The effect, acted out on the sloping front lawn of Bates's luxury bungalow, built in testimony to 1970s functionality, was half space age community, half retirement home.

'That'll be Herbert,' said Bates, implying no further explanation would be required.

'Oh good,' said Winston.

'He's getting on for fifty but he still acts like a teenager.' Bates chuckled. 'Just look at 'im.'

It was difficult to gauge behaviour in a buggy but now he came to mention it, there was something careering about the way the buggy was roaming over the lawn. Bates smiled to himself. 'Looks like he's bin on the cider again.'

Selwyn Bates wasn't looking the full country squire. Truth be told, he wasn't looking the full ticket. Winston had expected Burberry and tweed, with a flat cap set at a jaunty angle. What he got was dirty trench mac held up by orange bale string and slippers. Rain threatened by the Radio Suffolk weather girl had held off, but the ground was wet from previous showers and, despite the frost, mud sloshed under tyre. The buggy jolted to a stop as if it had cut out. Bates nosed the front end towards two sizeable garden sheds back to back and got out. He said, 'It's cunning. We've knocked the sheds together with a through door.'

'Really?' said Winston and fell into step behind the wiry man. He was followed by the beagle, gasping steamy pants into the afternoon air, making its podgy girth roll from side to side.

Winston was wondering why he'd spent three hours on a B road. As they walked, the bubble of noise got louder. It sounded like a spa pool, only harsher.

'There are my lovelies,' said Bates, pausing proudly in front of the coop. There must have been more than twenty of them waddling and randomly bumping into each other like knee-high dodgems. Rambling prehistoric beasts with blood-red wattles quivering and heads like an exposed brain. The only turkeys Winston had seen were in story books or the freezer section. He watched their sudden groupings and staccato clucks, thinking he could have died happy and still not seen this. Worse than that, he'd passed on Bates's offer of Wellingtons and his handmade £300 Oliver Sweeney brogues were fast sinking in a mulch of sawdust and turkey shit.

He said, 'Well, they really are—'

'Outstanding. Exactly.' Bates stooped and started rubbing his thumb and forefinger together, making a tall one bumble over to him. 'Come to daddy,' he cooed. 'Who's a lovely girl?'

'Mr Bates,' said Winston, staying well outside his exclusion zone, 'it's not that turkeys aren't fascinating.' He made a deliberate show of looking at his watch.

Bates ignored him, hypnotised. 'Do you know how one of my girls lets a gentleman know she's ready for sex?'

'I'm sorry?'

'She just lay doon.'

'She lay doon?' Winston's interest was pricked no matter what.

'Lay doon in front of him. That's her sign that she wants him to make love to her.'

Winston thought: Did turkeys make love? 'Really?'

'And they're big brutes, you know. On the job they can inflict a lot of damage on the ladies. Not that they complain about it – you bet they don't. Spunky little ladies.'

'I can imagine,' Winston said.

'Of course it's not like that at the Big House though.' Bates called his factory the Big House. He raised a selected few turkeys free range on his lawn, but at the factory on the hill he got through thousands in a mass produced sort of way. Winston wondered how he selected which ones went to the Big House, which ones came to the coop. For the fowls in front of him it must be like living in the shadow of a turkey Belsen.

Bates scooped up a turkey and kissed it on the top of its head, clucking to it in baby talk. He gently set her down, tapping her tail feathers. 'Shall we go back?'

It was a serious ritual for Bates, taking visitors to his turkey coop. It was pride. Or maybe shame. He wanted to let people know there was more to Selwyn Bates than the industrial production of gobblers. He loved those birds.

They walked towards the buggy. 'What I'm trying to do is teach them to fly. They can, you know. Then I'm gonna hunt them like pheasants. That's what Selwyn Bates will be remembered for, just you mark my word. If nothing else, in a hundred years they'll remember me for the man who made the turkeys wild again.'

Winston didn't doubt it.

IV

Patti was on her first cappuccino after two hot chocolates by the time Rory showed up. 'What the hell kept you?' she stormed.

Rory was already annoyed. 'Keep your hair on. The Northern line was messed up and you gave me the wrong directions for this place.' He dumped a black rucksack on the table. Even above the smell of her coffee and deep-fat frying, it smelt of grass.

'I thought you cycled everywhere these days.'

'Not in this weather.'

'So how did you get here?'

'Walked,' he told her.

She was about to ask where he lived. He must have sensed it because he cut her off. 'Is there a waitress?' he asked, his neck craning around the tables

'No, you've got to go to the counter.'

He sized up her empty mugs. 'Can I get you anything?'

She shook her head. Patti had always liked the way he'd said that. Not, do you *want* anything, but could he *get* you something. It was charming really. At the counter she heard him laughing with the black-haired waitress in fishnet tights. Still in her cagoule, Patti wondered where these women got their ideas from. Then, annoyed, she called over, 'Yeah, actually can I have some patatas bravas, please.'

He came back with a can of shandy and a cheese and onion roll. He started eating before he sat down. 'She says she'll bring 'em over.' He didn't ask for any money and Patti didn't offer any. She took that as a sign.

She waited while he swallowed. 'So how are you?' she asked.

'Good. What about you? Still living with that whatshis—'

'Yes, actually.' She paused. 'Yeah, couldn't be better. What about you?'

He ripped off another mouthful, leaving a membrane of onion skin on his lower lip. He shrugged, nodded and turned his head from side to side. Which she took to mean he was seeing someone.

He swallowed and touched his lower lip, surprised. 'Playing

much pool?' He was wearing a T-shirt with lettering she couldn't read, under a tartan shirt.

'Good God, no.' Patti laughed and shook her head definitely.

He exhaled and laughed. 'You make it sound like satanic abuse. What's got into you? At one time you used to like it. If I remember correctly.'

'Yeah, well. I'm more domestic these days.'

He raised his eyebrows. There was silence. She finished her cappuccino. The chocolate had been the full milk kind they give to the infirm and she felt slightly queasy with the lactose build-up. She'd dragged the skin off the first cup with a teaspoon, covering the stainless steel in a burst brown blister.

'So?' she said. Rory never had been very good at getting to the point.

'OK, well, the bottom line is they want one more.'

'Fuck it.' She'd said it too quickly, making it sound as if she didn't really mean it. And since when did he say *bottom line*? It made him sound like a Scottish cowboy builder on a docusoap. The waitress brought over her potatoes. She picked at the biggest ones with the most sauce on them. Then she said, 'Why?'

'They just do.' Rory looked embarrassed. 'Then absolutely, definitely, that will be it.'

She stuck her tongue into her cappuccino cup. He stared at the space above her head. He knew she would do it. For a start she enjoyed it in a way neither of them acknowledged. Then Rory *had* been her first love. And because Patti believed you never stopped loving someone she did things for him. She was repaying his kindness. 'One more,' she repeated, savouring. 'Why can't you do it?'

'Oh, thanks. You know what'll happen if I get caught.'

'So it's all right for me, then.' Her voice was more petulant than strident but it still made the waitress look over. The café was empty apart from a homeless man the staff must have fed as a charity case. Two forgotten half-collapsed brollies were dripping by the door. Patti got up to go even though there were still some of the choicest chips left.

She leant her hands on the table. 'When do they need it by?'

'Next week.'

'*What?*'

Rory wiped crumbs from his shirt front, as if it meant nothing to him. He told her, 'Tuesday. Don't worry, I'll drive it up.'

'That's big of you.'

He looked at her. 'Patti, love, I'm sorry. You know how it is.' He went to squeeze her hand over the Formica but accidentally pushed her glove onto the milky spoon.

She said sarcastically, 'Whatever.' She didn't have to tell him she'd already seen the car. Even tried it once.

As she turned, he said, 'Oh, Patti?'

'What?' Now what did he want?

'You've got foam on the end of your nose.'

'*So?*' She turned away to wipe it off with her gloved hand. 'Oh, Rory.' She hated to be outdone. And now plans for her driving school abroad were long gone.

'What?'

'I doubt you even know how to scuba dive.' Then she selected the better looking of the forgotten umbrellas, tucked it under her cagoule and left.

V

Ten minutes later they were sitting in what Bates called his back parlour. Winston had the impression Bates was playing for time. The floor was covered in linoleum and the sofa was covered in dog hair. The room smelt of canine breath and wet newspaper. Winston didn't take his coat off.

The coffee was instant. Hadn't Butterballs floated last year for more than six hundred million pounds? Didn't he make the boast that, after his Norfolk rival had turned his factory private again, he was the biggest plc in East Anglia? What was Bates thinking of? Winston was wildly, unforgivably uncomfortable.

He said, provoking, 'So what's the deal with this kid that's disappeared? Didn't I read his mother worked at Butterballs?'

Bates stood up and called out, 'Biscuits, if you please, Mrs King. We have guests, after all.' There was a hatch through to what Winston guessed was the kitchen, though he couldn't see

WHITE MEAT AND TRAFFIC LIGHTS

it. Silently a tray of bourbons appeared on the strip of plastic counter.

Bates was sanguine. 'You know children, Mr Freely. They come and go.'

Winston didn't know children. Bates made them sound like taxis. 'I got the impression from the papers that—'

'Young Raynham will be back. You mark my words.'

Winston still wasn't sure why he'd been summoned to Turkey Towers. No further mention of the mysterious world dominator had been hinted at since his arrival. He tried to speed things up. 'So what is it, then, Mr Bates? Animal rights? Salmonella? Let's talk turkey.' He moved the cuff of his coat, as if the suggestion of a watch might be enough. 'It's just that it is Prime Minister's question time this afternoon.' Surrounded by the trappings of a bumpkin wonderland, Winston thought the mention of the PM made him look as if he had his finger on the pulse. He reeled off some politicians at random, including Mo Mowlam.

Bates looked him straight in the eye with an expression of non-comprehension. He took a sip of tea, swathing the cup in his fist, ignoring the handle. He said, 'What the Dickens are you going on about now, boy? Have another bourbon.'

Winston shut up. Bates said nothing. Pans clattered in the kitchen. Outside, the light was draining. Somewhere in the hall a clock ticked and he heard a dog snoring. Winston decided to finish his biscuit and go.

When the clock started to chime, Bates stood up. 'Winston, I've come to a decision.'

Winston swallowed his biscuit. The dog stopped snoring and turned over with a grunt. 'Mrs King and I would like you to spend the night with us.'

Winston nodded out of reflex and his foot involuntarily slipped from under him. He'd read in the Sunday papers about the sort of things that happened in remote Suffolk villages.

'My guest has been delayed and it would be beneficial to all if you could meet him.' Even the dog yelped. 'Now is the time to tell you that my guest is arriving from Moscow.' He made it sound like Moscoo. Bates smiled and nodded as if to an imaginary audience. It was then that Winston noticed the last digit of Bates's little finger had been severed.

VI

Elaine Peroni picked up the phone. When she'd worked at a customer call centre for a leading brand of margarine they'd been taught to smile and dial because that way you sounded affirmative. Here, though, it was the other way round, more 'grit and shit'. But she preferred it that way.

'Yes?'

'Hello. May I speak to Elaine, please?'

'Speaking.'

'Elaine, hi, it's me, Patricia.' Half-second delay while Elaine placed her.

'Well, hi, Patti Moss.'

Patti said, 'Fuck off.'

'I didn't say Po.'

Silence.

'How are you?'

'OK,' said Elaine. 'Busy though. What about you?'

'You know . . .'

Elaine heard Tracey McCloud returning. In the tiny porch she could see her taking off her cape with a flourish. Tracey thought it made her look like a DKNY Miss Marple, but Elaine knew it was why they were referred to, even in the women's charity sector, as the 'Raped Crusaders'.

'Hurry up, Patti, I'm busy.'

Patti said airily, 'I thought we could meet up for a drink.'

'Where?' Elaine's response was automatic. The crisis centre was off Dean Street but she lived in a studio flat in Stoke Newington. She didn't like hanging around after work. Her first instinct was not to travel.

'Dunno, the centre. Or I could come to Stoke Newington?'

Elaine was the serious one with no tangible problems and rarely in any need of outside assistance. Patricia wasn't known as Scatty Patti for nothing. The phone call meant something was up, which meant Patti should be the one to compromise. Elaine knew she should care more, but the last time she'd travelled on the 73 bus it had been jampacked.

'OK.' Elaine paused, doodling on a press release. 'So, really. Is anything up?'

'No, no. Good God, no.' Patti gave it a few seconds. 'Like what?'

'Well, one of those little messes you get yourself in. A boyfriend who's skipped bail – that sort of thing.'

'No, everything's hunky dory. What about you?'

Tracey walked into the office.

'Look, I've got to go. See you—'

'Tomorrow night?'

'Great. I'll call you tomorrow to fix something up.' Elaine gently put the phone down. Tracey was close to phobic about personal phone calls. She stood silhouetted against the window, with one hand on her hip and a plastic box in the other. Red neon and strip lights flashed behind her, making her look faintly *film noire*.

Tracey sighed theatrically. 'You know there's something about Pret's sushi that I just don't trust.' She looked at Elaine. 'Know what I mean?'

Elaine nodded and went back to her Iranian dictionary.

VII

During the meal (served on the stroke of five thirty – the radio in the kitchen was tuned to the local radio news) Winston found out more about Bates's turkey empire than he wanted. In Winston's book, shared knowledge spelt mutual dependency, which was why he shied away from it. In none of Winston's relationships did he ask for detail. But Bates couldn't help himself. He spoke with a child's need to tell everything. Herbert, it transpired, had worked with Bates for nearly quarter of a century. Actually he worked *for* him, though nobody put it like that. The three of them were seated, one on each side, around a square chestnut table, just far enough apart so that any conversation was heard by all. The fourth side was flush against the wall, six inches under a serving hatch.

Herbet and Bates drank cider from pint glasses and both supped from a mug of tea next to them. Winston had asked for water and got 7-Up. In the centre of the table were jars of ketchup, salad cream, HP Sauce and a squeezable low-calorie mayonnaise. There were paintings of country pursuits on the walls and a print of Saxton's map of Suffolk. On the sideboard behind were stacks of newspapers. Wedged between them were boxes of breakfast cereals, including a family-size box of Cheerios. A couple of dogs wandered in and out, sniffed Winston's leg and sloped off. Indignity was the word that most sprang to Winston's mind.

Putty-faced Herbert went all the way back to Bates's pier days. Any Butterballs customer, business student, Suffolk resident – in fact, most of the country – knew the rags to riches story of Selwyn Bates. A tale of industry and determination. How the seven-year-old had gone from selling a few chicken eggs from outside his parents' tied cottage to converting the eating habits of a nation. 'Not many people know the real truth,' Bates told Winston. 'Isn't that right, boy?' Herbert nodded, proud and shy at the same time.

The real truth was that Bates had begun his empire in the amusement arcade on Cromer pier on Silver Jubilee Day in the summer of 1977. ('I tell you, we were surprised it was open,' he spluttered.) Midway through the red-hot day, just after their chip dinner, Herbert discovered that if you wrapped a ten pence piece in masking tape, the change machine for the slot machines thought it was a fifty. 'Gave you a whopping great return, that did.'

Herbert was the bagman. Or rather held the carrier until they'd emptied every arcade along the Norfolk and Suffolk coasts. Now, of course, Bates owned several of the piers, including those at Cromer and Felixstowe. His first job had been to remove the change machines.

In those days, Bates told him, Herbert had been pretty handy with his fists. These days he still worked out twice a week at Make It Happen, Stowmarket's premier fitness centre, but he wasn't the henchman he used to be. A few years of petty theft followed until Bates got his real break smuggling cigarettes. They stacked them high in barns out back and to lend an air of authenticity put a sprinkling of turkeys out front. The fact that the birds hissed and gobbled when anyone but them tried to look in their coop was an unexpected bonus. As the smuggling empire grew, the turkey count matched it. 'It all just sorta ballooned,' said Bates with a wink. 'But now I wouldn't be without my little ladies.' A decade later and Bates's empire had diversified into a string of old people's homes, amusement arcades, eight night clubs and three factories.

The diners were chomping their way through another course of turkey toppers when Bates started to rant.

'If that blasted Kentucky man can get away with calling himself colonel, I don't see why I can't.'

'I think it's because he's fictional,' Winston told them.

Herbert belched as another course appeared at the hatch. He thumped his chest and spoke out in defence of his master. 'Why the hell can't he be a major? Or at least a flippin' captain. Who's to stop him? Why, that negro boxer from Brighton is calling himself a Lord, if you please.' He had a pair of sunglasses pushed onto the top of his bristly black hair. In the light of the bare bulb he glowed slightly orange against Bates's ruddiness.

Bates spoke with his mouth full. 'I don't see why it couldn't even *be* my name. They call people such daft blummen things these days. Why can't I change Selwyn to Sergeant? Ain't that right, Herbert?'

'You betcha,' said Herbert, finishing his third pint of cider and pouring another glass from a plastic bottle on the floor.

Winston hadn't drunk anything. He was thinking he could leave and be home in time for *Crimewatch UK*.

He was about to speak when a mobile phone chimed to the William Tell overture. Bates shook his head slightly and did a slight double blink then ripped off the greasy stained napkin tucked into his collarless white dress shirt. 'I swear that blessed woman gets lazier. She don't even come to the hatch no more.'

Herbert looked at Winston. 'Mrs King,' he mouthed to him and pointed towards the phone. Winston nodded, relieved for an excuse to lay down his turkey satay stick.

Bates said nothing but nodded and grunted once. Then he snapped his phone shut and spoke towards the centre of the table. 'Right then. That's it. He's here.' Herbert fidgeted and stopped picking his teeth. Bates said, 'Mrs King is showing him into the lounge.'

They trouped towards the lounge like sombre pallbearers in

single file, along a dark corridor, Winston straining at the rear to keep the sheen of Herbert's silk shirt in view. When Bates tugged open the door, Winston saw that Bates's guest had positioned an armchair to meet them straight on. He was wedged in the yellow velour, making it difficult to gauge his height and size. Even so he gave the impression of being swamped. He wore small round glasses with a pink tinge and his thin grey hair was gelled ineffectively into spikes. He was wearing a three-quarter length white coat with the sleeves rolled to above his elbows. He reminded Winston of one of the keyboard players of a 1980s band. In his left fist he clenched a mobile phone the size of a brick.

Bates, shod only in socks, half shimmied, half barrelled over to him and shook his hand.

'Winston, I'd like you to meet Dr Nevski.'

Winston had never met a Russian before. Sartorially he was everything he could have hoped for.

'Dr Nevski, please, this is my political front man, Winston Freely.'

Political front man? Now hang on, thought Winston.

Nevski didn't stand. His handshake was warm and flaccid. 'Mr Freely, I'm delighted to meet you.'

'Likewise,' said Winston.

Herbert was hanging back, pouring drinks.

'How was the trip?' asked Bates anxiously. The distance, from back parlour to lounge on uncarpeted floors, had caused a clammy glaze on his upper lip. He was moving in jerky anxious jabs and Winston understood how nervous he was.

Nevski waited before he replied. 'Everything is in order,' he said with a limp shrug, his palms open. Winston put his odd phraseology down to bad English. He knew the basis of English was colloquialism, which was difficult for foreigners to grasp. Besides that, he couldn't get a Flock of Seagulls song out of his head. Three of Nevski's fingers on his left hand had thick silver rings on them.

Nevski turned to Winston. 'Mr Freely, you are well-affiliated?'

Winston hitched his trousers at the knees and sat down without being asked. He stretched his legs in front of him and draped his elbows on the armrests. 'I've always thought so.'

'Good', Nevski told him, 'because we have no room for coasters.'

Herbert handed round drinks in shot glasses.

'Actually, doctor,' Bates was still standing, 'Mr Freely's not quite as up to speed with the whole thing as you might think.' He smiled confidently. 'What he does know, though, is how to get them politicians on board on this whole synthesised GM thing.'

'Ah,' said Nevski. He sat back, sagacious, and crossed one leg over the other. 'The last thing we want, the last thing we *need*, is for the GM question to blow up in our face. The type of thing Mr Bates and I are involved in could change the shape of this country,' he paused, 'maybe even the world for ever. And you do have your greens.'

For a second Winston thought he was talking about vegetables. He frowned and sipped the drink Herbert had given him. It wasn't a taste he was familiar with. 'How do you mean *change the shape of this country?*' he asked slowly. Bates and Herbert hovered by the fireplace.

Nevski said, 'Genetic engineering is the future, for turkeys, for crops. I don't think it's an exaggeration to say for the world.' He had a faint lisp on the letter s. When he came to the end of a sentence he put his fingertips together in front of his mouth. He had long manicured nails.

Bates butted in. 'The doctor is one of the former Soviet Union's foremost geneticists.'

Winston said, 'We do have a vocal minority in this country interested in green issues. But in terms of political interest, compared to big business their influence is slight.' He looked across at Bates and smiled. 'Do you feed GM food to your birds?' he asked.

'Never,' Bates told him, offendedly.

Winston didn't know that much about genetic modification. Last February, when the tabloids were awash with stories of salmon genes and tomatoes, Bates had called him in to 'ram home' (his words) the important of gene manipulation to the turkey industry. It was standard stuff, most people knew turkeys were bred in a way to maximise breast meat. Bates said his specific interest was developing meat with a longer shelf life. He was hoping to trial a Valentine's Day escalope with the slogan, 'Like your love, it'll last for ever'.

Nevski nodded. 'Well, Mr Freely, your job is to keep the lid on this green legislation. I always say let politicians pretend to run the country and let business really hold the reins.' Winston wondered how often he did actually say that. Nevski raised his glass. 'Shall we drink to success, gentlemen?'

Bates winked at Winston. As briefs went, it was a long way off comprehensive, but Winston knew what Bates was hinting at. He would get Nevski on the board of a few charities, make some donations to political parties, then haul out a couple of gene boffins and before you knew it Nevski would be the future of white meat in this country.

Genetic modification and underage smoking – Winston wondered, as he gave the Russian the benefit of his best professional smile, if he could sink any lower? Then, without standing, Nevski reached over and pulled a plastic bag towards him. He didn't so much hand it to Winston as let it spill over in his direction. A cascade of hundred-dollar bills fell onto the goatskin.

Nevski said, 'Just to ensure the rug isn't pulled from under us.' And to be fair to him, thought Winston as he exhaled, his grasp of the colloquial was spot on. Behind them Bates and Herbert beamed like parents on graduation day.

VIII

Patti fell asleep in front of the TV still wearing her donkey jacket, black leggings and gloves, though she'd taken her beenie hat off. Rory used to say it made her look like a twelve-year-old at a Bar Mitzvah. When she'd dozed off, it'd been a Channel Five programme where viewers had to vote which couples they wanted to see have sex. When she awoke, it was a *Sons and Daughters* re-run. The heating had switched off and she was low-blood-sugar frozen. It was the post-adrenaline rush that had made her collapse. She'd spent three hours wandering the streets of south London sourcing a Lada. Of all her preferred methods, this was the worst. She knew, even before she set out, she was doomed to failure. She had mentally banked the evening-class Niva, but it was a long way to go, with no guarantees it would be there next week. And that builders' yard was always going to pose a problem.

When time wasn't an issue, she'd use her lessons as an excuse to cruise the area. When she found a decent enough model, she'd three-point turn and emergency stop down its road until she'd worked out its movements. What time the woman went to the shops, when she picked the kids up in it (although almost always the Lada drivers were male and in their forties). Her happiest hunting ground was always the roads around municipal buildings, especially council offices. Better still if it was a left-wing administration.

If that failed she'd put a wanted advert in the SLP. 'Wanted Samara Lada model six.' Saying the specific model always helped. Just saying 'Lada wanted' got nothing. It simply aroused suspicion. Lada drivers were like that. Like a persecuted band, they tended to close ranks. But if you specified the model, they accepted you. In fact, couldn't do enough for you.

'I haven't got a series six, got a four if that's any help. L reg, eighty thousand miles on the clock. The clutch gets stuck. If that's still no good try this bloke in Chichester. I think he's got a series six. But you know what they say about that gear stick.'

Then there were the websites. Chatrooms where she'd sign in anonymously and mingle among them. Clubs. Really, the list was endless.

No matter how often she did it, there was always something absurd about stealing a Lada. Occasionally she'd thought about stealing another type, those Metros looked easy, just to see if she was able to. But recently the number and complexity of alarms had put her off. Hadn't she read of car thieves who used Palm Pilots to break in? No such worries with a 1500 Riva where a faulty crook lock was about as intricate a security system as you ever got. That was the joy of stealing Ladas, the most you needed was a customised clothes hanger or even a credit card. Also, from an insurance point of view, even the biggest fans were glad to get rid of them.

Which was how Rory had started her on it in the first place. He was a communist she met in a pool club in Carlisle. He was lanky with flat dark hair and the shadowy look of Lucifer to him. Not her type at all. But he was a poet who had just come down from the

Edinburgh Festival where he'd got four friends to transport him up Queen's Street in a homemade rickshaw, charging fifty pence to recite famous poems and a quid to read his own. Patti from the start thought he'd got the pricing system the wrong way round.

What she fell for in the end was his attention to detail (when his father died he changed his mother's doorbell chime to 'Auld Lang Syne') and the elegant way he arched his back to take his pool shots. He also had a fantastic bridge. Stealing Ladas was his method of global wealth distribution. According to Rory (who did, after all, sell the *Socialist Worker*) a new Lada in Russia cost $5,000 even though the average monthly wage of the Tolyatti worker in Samara was $140. That was $1,680 dollars annually; in other words, four years' wages. Put it another way, it was like the most basic Ford Fiesta retailing in the UK for £80,000. Then, said Rory, spare Lada parts in Russia were nigh on impossible to get. Whereas in the UK a second-hand Lada was barely worth a couple of hundred quid. There was a market and they were fulfilling it. Didn't every human have the right to mobility? Not to mention the seventy quid for every car they stole to be delivered to an Aberdeen dock and a five-foot Scot with blue eyes cloudy with humanitarian zeal and tipples of antifreeze and orange, and hair the colour of goldfish. At first Patti acted as lookout. Then he urged her to try it herself. She thought of them as the Borders Bonnie and Clyde supplementing their dole money by car theft and pool sharking.

And it just went to show, Ladas were more popular than you might have thought. Because there was never once a mention in the local paper about a mysterious spate of Lada thefts.

Patti pushed herself off the sofa and rubbed her eyes. She padded into the kitchen to fill her hot water bottle. One more car and that would be it. She sat up in bed, drank her hot chocolate and stared at her rail of clothes.

You'd never believe the line of mismatched outfits belonged to one person. She listed the ones she could see – two green cardigans, a pair of black leggings, a plain white shirt and a grey skirt. Underneath them a leather duffel bag spilled out a jumble of trainers and one pair of low brown lace-ups. She wondered if you couldn't synthesise it somehow, maybe on a computer programme, to produce your ideal outfit.

WHITE MEAT AND TRAFFIC LIGHTS

On her first day at primary school her mother had dressed her in a plaid grey dress, red tie and red hair band, making her prickle with embarrassment because there was no uniform and the other children wore bright dresses and stubby pairs of jeans. A boy, a fat ginger-headed kid sucking on a ten pence sherbet fountain, whose lunchbox had smelt of apples, had come up to her and told her she didn't belong there, that she should go home. She walked home alone and cried for three hours straight before her mother called the headmistress and took her back. It kickstarted a general mistrust of mates, an unnatural relationship with sweets and a cloudy feeling of alienation. All before the lunch whistle.

IX

Xenia thought, only once in St Petersburg, in February, had she felt this wet coldness. Which was ridiculous because for months at a time the thermometer in the village read minus fifteen. But it was a dry coldness, which meant the snow didn't turn to slush and stayed bright white all winter. And the skies were so blue that it was impossible not to be cheerful, no matter what they said. But here, the whole span of your eyeballs only took in grey. The weather was so heavy that it weighed your bones down and froze you from the inside out. Even in the dacha where they spent the summer weekends the rooms had been warm. And in Samara the apartment got so hot Uncle Gleb had to take off the plastic sealing round the windows to open them. Xenia couldn't imagine what it felt like to be warm. Not any more.

The top of her head felt wet. She put out her hand to touch it. And then rammed it back under the blanket. Most of them, especially the boys, slept in a hat. But if she did that it made her hair greasy. What if they came tomorrow? In that case she'd never be picked. She only had a bar of soap to wash her hair, which left a flaky residue like dandruff. And the water in the shower was cold, which was all right at the time but freezing when you got out. Also the shower floor was gritty and someone had stolen her plastic shoes. And after the men had been in there it was full of green slugs of phlegm.

Looking back, the trouble had started with her Aunt Galia and her absolute belief in anyone wearing smart clothes. She said it was in her genes. All peasants trusted men in uniforms. But it wasn't a uniform, Xenia had said. Laughed it actually, even though she'd been more impressed with the handsome strangers than her Aunt Galia. And her aunt, with her Sony TV set and half share in next door's microwave, was more avaricious than anyone she knew.

Why couldn't she just have gone to Moscow, even Samara? Why come here? When she thought of home, she felt a flutter in her stomach like a swarm of wasps. She clenched her wrists and rocked on her mattress. She heard a few of them coughing and getting up even though it was pitch-black. They must be on the early shift. She only had to get up when the dark turned a static grey like an old TV set warming up.

But who wouldn't have believed them? Uncle Gleb for one. He said they were doing nothing more than taking a quack cure to a leper colony. Then he'd poured another drink. Maybe it was her. Maybe she'd failed the test. One of them hinted (the dark one, with the sunglasses, said it looking straight at her and she knew he was talking to her. What was the dark one's name?) that not everyone would make the grade. And, of course, she never had done well at school. Could the man have known it? Was that why he was looking at her? He even set his sunglasses on his head, like a film star in an American film, to look right at her.

'They're no better than fantasy men peddling snake oil as a cure-all,' Gleb had said. Nobody really knew who had sent them or why they'd come. Touring minstrels in Cherokee Jeeps and wearing Hugo Boss suits, sunglasses and chewing gum. They preached, actually preached, their sermon. Setting up their stalls by the playground slides alongside the drunks and babushkas in the quadrangle. Or in the villages by the roadside, deliberately close to the shop to make the contrast greater when they handed round the photographs.

But the villagers were no fools. They never would have believed them if it hadn't been so obviously *them* in the grainy snapshots. The blond one bare-chested and bungee jumping down a jungle ravine. Both together, leaning into each other, on the bonnet of a seal-grey Mercedes in a street with English writing everywhere. The dark one alone, casually dressed in a T-shirt and jeans with the Eiffel Tower in the background and a can of Diet Coke in his hand. They looked so international, but something about their edginess and surprise made them Russian. What other grown men, after all, would be pictured like teenage girls, outside cinemas and in front of billboards? It was good, it made Xenia think anyone could fit in.

'Look, we're not simpletons,' said Maria Timofeyvna, 'these could be fakes. You can make things on computers. We all know that.'

'But why would I, babul?' (because Maria was in her seventies) replied the dark one, purring. 'I just want to show you what we Russians can do now. The world is vast and the opportunities are great. Not for everyone, admittedly, you might be too advanced in years to take advantage,' some of them laughed, 'but why shouldn't we make a mark? Is it only the Mafia bulls who should benefit from our suffering?'

What impressed Aunt Galia most was his manners. And his grammar was perfect, even literary. What impressed Xenia was his soft hands that smelt of geranium and the cleanness of his leather shoes. Mid-August and not even dust on them!

In two hours they were gone. Didn't even stay for a meal in the restaurant. Off to another village. Xenia already felt jealous. The dark one, with his elegant hands and half-moon nails, had handed out a couple of cards casually to no one in particular, with a mobile telephone number that no one would dare call. And that was that. Five hundred and twenty-seven villagers (though half of them would never admit it) left with a festering sense of unrest.

'Daydreamer with no real determination to succeed', was what her school report had said three terms in a row from three different teachers, which had made her think they just copied and recycled the comments, but now she wasn't so sure.

'She's flighty, that one, just like her mother,' said Gleb. 'Hasn't got her feet on the ground.' He and Galia had been coming inside after picking mushrooms in the early morning. Xenia was still in bed and they didn't know she could hear them.

'What's wrong with that?' said Galia without taking her headscarf off. 'Better to have your head in the clouds than on the twenty-fourth storey of a flat in Samara, drunk as a sow.' By that, of course, she'd meant Xenia's dad who was a bottle-a-day man.

But what was it the dark one (Pasha? Sasha? Alexei?) had said? 'Constitutionally, statistically,' (whatever that meant) 'the West isn't for everyone.'

Naturally, that had just made her want it even more.

Later, when they were sitting in the kitchen drinking tea and eating jam, Gleb said, 'That's what they want you to think.' (Since when had he been such an expert?) 'That's what they always say. That's what the bastards said when they tried to get us to move to Siberia on the oil rigs before you were even born. When your mother was still around. They gave a lecture in the House of Agriculturists. It was a KGB colonel speaking. We all had to attend it. Freezing night, it was. All of us, more than five hundred workers, all from the factory. I can still see him, built like a bathhouse, with his uniform and his stripes. He said, "Only the most excellent can perform in these conditions. You may not be chosen." Practically all of them wanted to go after that.'

Two months later the adverts started, first in the local paper and then soon after a couple of posters appeared overnight in the village like mushrooms. Xenia almost fainted when she saw them. More than a dozen applied. Even two she knew from school with young babies who'd let their relatives raise them while they were away. The opportunities were endless – dancers, waitresses, factory workers. And, when they travelled on the overnight train to Samara and waited in an empty hotel room to be interviewed, they were greeted by the dark-haired man who smelt of geraniums. Xenia felt like she was coming home.

But now, thousands of miles away (east, west, up, down, she wasn't absolutely sure she could place it on the map), she'd got to thinking. Perhaps she just hadn't been chosen. Pretty ones, the smart girls, must be siphoned off early. Only the skinny ones like her with no real sense of application came here. But maybe tomorrow she'd be chosen. She was going to look extra pretty. She still had a blue eye pencil and one of the other girls had a gloss for her lips. If they did come looking for pretty ones, she'd be ready. She'd write to Galia and Gleb and tell them all about it. And Anton. She'd even send money to Galia, to show the old bag she really could do it. Then she'd see if she couldn't send a photo to her dad. Money, at this stage, would be too much.

Xenia tried to imagine her body didn't belong to her so she

wouldn't feel so cold. She pulled the blanket round her. The room was quiet. She dug her fingernails into her palms to give her something to think about. In the mornings, before the first shift, two vacuum flasks of tea decorated with Chinese flowers appeared. Then there were chipped mugs and a plastic box of tea bags that only the early risers got.

She decided, if she still wasn't chosen in a week's time, she would see if anyone had an address for the dark-haired man. Then she would write to him (she wasn't sure quite how; did they write letters here?) and explain that there had been a terrible mistake and she wanted to go home. She was sure he'd understand.

She didn't hear the radio playing quietly in the dormitory next door. It was half past midnight. *'The parents of missing teenager Alan Raynham have appealed for help in finding their son. The fifteen-year-old has been missing from his Sudbury home for eight days. Police have already conducted extensive house to house inquiries and have started to comb rivers in the area. They are appealing for anyone with information to come forward.'*

Chapter Three

I

Fahmy blamed the racist British media for Omar Sharif not receiving the coverage owed to the international bridge player.

He was studying *Heat* magazine, forehead grooved, his hooded eyes glazed with concentration, as if he was revising it. Without looking up he told Colin, 'It's a newcomer to the market but is my celebrity magazine of choice.' He made it sound as if Colin was asking him to justify the two quid cover charge. But Fahmy was in confessional mood. Earlier that morning, just after Colin brought him his Madeira cake from the deli opposite, he'd confided to him that his wife had left him. Now Fahmy's lips moved as he read, and his tongue stabbed at his forefinger when he turned the page.

They looked up when Patti pushed herself through the door, feet sliding on a built-up pile of shiny junk mail. She swore. 'Charming,' said Fahmy. The weather was overcast with no rain forecast. A savage wind barrelled from the coast over a low Thames, flushing out the petrol fumes. Patti had two refreshers booked in. Mrs Ellis at nine thirty, a 55-year-old divorcee who'd landed a job at William Hill's as part of a government scheme for getting the nearly-retireds back to work. She had to be able to drive as far as Ascot (minimum) though her absolute goal was Aintree by the Grand National. Fanny May had a lesson at eleven. Fanny had ignored the 'Why I want to get behind the wheel again' section of the questionnaire. Patti liked Fanny. She sensed a solidarity in unfortunate names.

'Fanny May what?' Fahmy said whenever she called. 'That's

what I want to know.' He said it so often that Fanny was the only refresher Patti gave her mobile number to.

Fahmy's mouth was full. 'You want fare?' Colin was licking the centre out of a Creme Egg.

'I'd love to but I've got lessons.' Patti shrugged off her coat.

'Hey. Nice top,' Fahmy told her. 'Bright colour, look good on you.' Colin looked up.

'I'm ovulating,' said Patti as she stepped over Colin's legs and moved towards the fire.

Fahmy said, 'What the hell's that got to do with it?' Patti knew Fahmy's English lacked reproductive detail.

'It means, subconsciously, I wear bright colours.'

'What the ruddy hell for?'

'To attract a mate.' Patti took a bite out of his cake.

'You mean every woman in bright colour . . .'

Patti knew where he was going, his wife was known for her extravagant clothes. Also her Shoe Express uniform was sunshine yellow. She said, 'It's not a hard and fast rule.'

'Blimey,' said Fahmy.

'And the sperm count of my partner goes up.'

'You haven't got a partner,' said Colin.

'Cheers, Colin, thanks for pointing that out. Actually, it's any man I spend time around.' She looked at them. 'Maybe even you two.'

'Christ Almighty.' Fahmy rocked back on his chair. 'No way. I'm keeping my sperms low these days.' He shook his head and sat on his hands as if a primal urge might make him jump her. 'Very low.'

They stopped speaking. A snippet of techno beat blasted from the twenty-four-hour Dungeon Club next door every time one of the punters left in a puff of dry ice and amyl nitrate. Fahmy looked at his watch. 'That boy had a good time.' He then put his hand over his mouth and heaved with laughter.

Then he frowned, shook his head, made a noise with one side of his mouth and went back to the magazine. 'Vanessa Feltz lose weight and marriage ends. Ditto Carol Vorderman.'

'You know what I like about these magazines?' Fahmy asked. Colin was making tea. 'You miss a couple of weeks and then before you know it, they found someone else. One week split up, next week someone else. Is excellent.'

Patti guessed he was applying the theory to his own life. She went on tiptoe to burrow in the filing cabinet behind him.

Fahmy twisted towards her. 'You want chair? What you up to?' He tried to turn his head. For the first time Patti noticed he sat on one of those car seat covers of wooden balls.

'Trying to find where I left my driver's licence.'

In more organised times she used to write down and file any Ladas she saw that looked nickable. Nothing elaborate, just time, date, model and location. On average it took between eight and ten days to source and steal a car. She had until Tuesday. The Niva outside the evening class was a theft of last resort.

'What for?' asked Fahmy.

'I got done for driving without a seat belt.'

'You get fine?' Fahmy asked.

'No, just have to show my documents.' She tried to flick the conversation on with a twist of her wrists. 'Look, Fahmy, is the lock-up free at the moment? I wouldn't ask but my brother's coming down for the weekend. He's got nowhere to park.'

'Why you not get fine?'

'Dunno. I told the policeman I was menstruating and my chest was sore.'

'You think I could get away with that?'

'*No.*' She pulled the file from the cabinet and flicked through it. The list was out of date but better than nothing.

Fahmy went back to his magazine. 'You clean that ruddy car yet?'

'No,' said Patti, reading. 'I'm thinking of keeping it as Liability. At least it's honest.' She intended a dig on VIPS, Vauxhall's Imperial Passenger Service, SW8's finest taxi company, but he missed it.

'Have it your own way,' said Fahmy. 'Les Dennis and Amanda Holden. Their body language? Is very bad.' He repeated very bad to make his point and licked his finger to turn the page.

'Well,' she slammed the filing cabinet shut, 'Nigel Dempster, I'm afraid I've got work to do.'

She ripped up her spreadsheet of cars, having committed two

possibles to memory. Under the pretext of parking practice she planned to cruise Sainsbury's looking for hopefuls to at least trail during the lesson. Then she'd try the KFC on Clapham High Road.

II

Winston was first down to breakfast. His head was fuzzy and he felt mentally bunged up. After twenty minutes Bates joined him, his thin face blotchy from alcohol and anger. He stabbed at a piece of toast from the rack but abandoned it to pour himself a bowl of Cheerios. 'Blast them animal rights people,' he said. 'Like flies, they are, just come out when the weather's improving. Or at Christmas, of course. As if they don't like turkey as much as the next man. That's what get me.'

Winston reached for a triangle of rubbery white toast. 'What animal rights people?'

Bates growled, 'Bloody protesters. The flaming knit-your-own-breakfast brigade. Pasty-faced monsters.'

Winston said, 'What are they protesting about?'

'I'm buggered if I know. Herbert reckons one of the banners says "Turkeys have a right to roam". I mean, I ask you.'

Winston nodded. 'Where is Herbert?'

'He's buggied off to the front gate.'

Winston thought he said buggered until he remembered Bates used golf buggy as a verb.

Bates struggled to get a tissue out of his trouser pocket. He said, 'He reckon another one says, "One turkey, one breast."'

It sounded like a song lyric. Winston stopped buttering. 'What the hell does that mean?'

'Oh, they're having a pop at the turkey wankers.' Bates sighed. 'Again.' When he exhaled, a speck of cereal flew out and landed on the table. One of Bates's hands was underneath the table rigorously rubbing a dog.

'I'm sorry?'

'My girls have to be inseminated in an artificial way.' He said it as if everyone knew that. 'Because of the size of their breasts. They're bred to have big breasts. Double-breasted in fact. To maximise the meat. Good God, boy, don't you know nothing? It means the stags can't hop on the girls' backs.'

Winston said, 'Jeez, you mean someone's got to go around . . .' It didn't bear thinking about.

'Grow up, boy, it's only a case of stroking them.'

'Then what? Is there like a jar . . .' He winced and picked out a couple of dog hairs from the margarine. Then coughed soberly. 'Is that all they're complaining about?'

Bates said moodily, 'Who?'

'The animal rights people.'

'I'm buggered if I know. Probably not.'

Out of the corner of his eye Winston caught Mrs King lurking, pan in hand. 'It's just I ought to know what sort of thing they say. It might affect what I do, in terms of my campaign. I mean, do they get any publicity?'

'The local rag'll give 'em a show. I doubt the telly will bother, not with this kid what's gone missing. They get right up my nose.'

'Who, the media?'

'No, them protesters.' He fell into a miserable silence. 'And the media.'

Outside, clouds scudded past the window. Winston had caught a blast of S Club 7 from the kitchen. Inside, it was oppressively hot. Winston wondered if he could get away all day with wearing yesterday's boxer shorts inside out. The enamel on his teeth and his tongue were scaly. That was something he'd learned from Cindy, there was no point in brushing your teeth if you didn't brush your tongue as well.

'Look, thanks for the hospitality last night but I really ought to be getting back to London.' Winston pushed his chair out. 'I'm pretty sure the licences aren't going to be a problem.' He felt he needed to say that to justify Nevski's twelve grand outlay (he'd counted it before he went to bed). Bates looked confused. 'The GM stuff. Don't worry, I can make you seem as kosher as a . . .' he paused. 'Just look what happened with that guy who runs Iceland.'

'*Runs Iceland?*' said Bates absently. 'What the devil are you going on about?' Then he seemed to relax. 'Look, Freely, I shan't be able to go nowhere today.' Winston nodded. 'And I shan't beat about the bush. I need a favour from you.'

'What sort of favour?' Winston asked cautiously.

'With all those flying pickets about at the front gate I need you to make a delivery for me today. You are driving back to London, aren't you?'

'I guess.' He was stalling. 'What sort of delivery?' In the corridor, dogs started barking.

'Don't you worry, my boy, the very pleasantest sort. A person, actually.' He seemed to have perked up. 'Even better than that, a woman. You might get some fringe benefits, if you're nice enough.' Then Bates started laughing, staccato, shrill and unstable. When he did, his stomach vibrated underneath a polyester T-shirt which until then Winston hadn't noticed had the Butterballs' turkey logo on it.

Mrs King's head appeared through the serving hatch. She had her hair drawn back in a ponytail on top of a pink nylon overall. 'The police reckon they've found the kid's bicycle,' she said, grave but with the subdued excitement of a messenger. 'It's just been on the radio.'

A small tick appeared in Bates's left eye and to Winston he seemed to do a slight double blink. 'How the hell could they have done?' he asked. A bubble of half-eaten Cheerio appeared in the corner of his mouth.

The woman was already waiting for him in the car, hands on lap, with the impatient look all women get in the passengers' seat. Winston had to look up the address Bates had given him in the *A–Z*. She was going to her uncle's flat because she wanted to do some sightseeing in London. 'You know what these girls are like,' Bakes had said. 'Shoppin' mad.' She didn't look shopping mad. She was wearing a thin white coat on top of a flowery skirt and plain blue shirt. The nearest place he knew to the address was Brewer Street, which was a hell of a spot to get to. Usually when he visited Tony he caught the tube. If he had to drive, he parked away from Soho's one-way system which seemed to have another road-quietening scheme every week. Before he'd seen her, he'd considered telling her to find the destination on foot and dropping her at Piccadilly Circus. Then he thought better of it. After his unexpected cash injection the night before, his actions were verging on the heroic.

Winston's passenger seat window didn't shut properly and he was worried his passenger would get cold. Even worse if it started to rain. He put his foot down, feeling the engine lose revs and then pick up. He slipped it into third and started to overtake a vintage haulier's lorry that still had 01 for a London code. They drove past the dismal 1930s council houses on the edge of the village with bright plastic toys collecting rain in sodden gardens. Then it was flat strips of hedgeless fields with tufts of stumpy sugar beet. The earth was so waterlogged it made him think the country was sinking.

'I'm sorry,' Winston tried to look at her, 'but I didn't catch your name.'

'Sorry?'

'Your name. Mine's Winston. Winston Freely.' He clumsily tried to shake her hand, catching his sleeve on the gear stick.

'Xenia.' She said it like Zhenia.

Silence. They drove past a hamburger stall with a Union flag flying against the slate-grey sky. There was a fine drizzle but not enough to use the windscreen wipers.

'You've lived in England long?'

'Maybe.' She bit her lip.

Winston's hand grazed her knee every time he changed gear. Which meant he braked more often before turning corners. She was clutching a small holdall with Puma on the side in yellow and a plastic bag with 'Arbat Irish House, Moscow' written around a shamrock. He was unused to driving with a passenger. The seat belt sagged over her shoulder and was tight over her waist. Winston could see her hip bones sticking out like the knuckles of someone holding her from behind. She didn't fill the space like Cindy. Cindy was all squeezed-in shopping bags and noise. Compared to her, Xenia was ethereal.

'Where are you from originally?' he asked her.

Xenia kept her eyes focused on the dashboard. 'Samara region,' she said.

'Where?'

'Russian Federation,' she said. Then she repeated it in Russian as if to clarify it.

'Good God,' said Winston and really turned to look at her. Until yesterday, he hadn't met a Russian in his life and now the place was crawling with them.

Before they'd set off, Winston had driven into the village to buy a packet of cigarettes. The local shop turned out to be no more than a Portakabin in front of a semi-detached council house with a patchwork of handwritten adverts in the window. Inside, it smelt of Calor gas and old people's breath. Every item had a handwritten individual price tag, like when he and Tony used to play shops. It must have doubled as a post office, because the woman in front of him complained she'd never get the hang of self-adhesive stamps. Dying for a fag, Winston tutted aloud (*What was to get the hang of?*). Behind him two adolescents, underdressed for the weather, sniped at each other in low guttural voices. Winston took their dialect to be Suffolk but when their argument, over a Kingsmill loaf, came into auditory focus it sounded more like German. When he had mentioned it to Bates before he and Xenia set off, Bates had told him they must have come from Sudbury way, where no bugger could understand what the hell anyone was going on about anyway.

Winston looked at Xenia. 'What are you doing here?'

'I work with turkeys. I come in England. After advert in paper.' When she spoke she pinched her forefinger and thumb together in concentration until they went white. She gave a nervous smile. 'But today, like you see, I am chosen.'

'Really?' said Winston. He braked suddenly as a Vauxhall Cavalier swung left without indicating. 'Chosen for what?'

She frowned at him. 'For the good times, of course.'

Winston nodded. She must mean the shopping. In the distance, three magpies flew up from the bare bones of an elm tree.

She knotted her hands together. 'It's true, in this country you need papers, yes?' It was her first question and Winston felt caught out.

'Some people like the crossword,' he told her, 'but I can't say they're obligatory.'

She frowned. 'Passport, you have one?'

Winston said, 'Well, yes, somewhere, why?'

She stared out of the window. Her hair, plaited in wispy

lengths, was blown by the draught, though she didn't seem to notice the cold.

Winston asked, 'Mind if I smoke?' She shook her head and carried on shaking it when he offered her the packet.

'Are you sure you're warm enough?'

She nodded and smiled.

'Still, at least the car must remind you of home.'

Xenia nodded unsurely.

Winston went on, 'I mean the Lada, it's Russian. The Niva.' Winston indicated to come off the motorway. Beside him she smiled, but it was the sympathetic smile you gave to a simpleton.

III

Selwyn Bates still had enough alcohol chugging around his body to put him in a contemplative mood. He thought, these days, if you believed what the telly said and everything you read in the papers, everyone was on a personal journey. A quest for something extra, a new job, a new car, a new partner. 'Well, not Batesy,' he said out loud as he pushed his buttocks a bit further down the bath. A surge of hot water came up between his thighs. Of course he did have a mission, but it wasn't the sort of thing he'd like to broadcast. For example, he wouldn't like to mention it on his *Desert Island Discs,* or have Esther quiz him over it. It was a private sort of thing and really, when all was said and done, not too much to ask.

He used his big toe to lift up the Swedish-designed tap and thought back to the night before. Really, if he couldn't bed a line operative now and again, what was the point? Apart from his Selwyn hour, he was at work every hour God sent. But try telling that to Mrs King with her haughty expression every time he asked her to video *Hollyoaks.* She ought to try being a turkey magnate for a day. 'Today, Matthew, I will be Selwyn Bates.' He imagined Mrs King dressed in his clothes bursting through the *Stars In Their Eyes* doors. Because that's what he was, a star. And no one could tell him different. Of course he knew what was really jarring her off. Like a lot of the locals, she thought his recruitment methods were unfair. Only because her Darren had to go as far as Bury St Edmunds to work in the beet factory. But with so many people prepared to, *glad to*, work an eighteen-hour shift for a pound an hour, why should he pay Tony Blair's filthy minimum wage?

Well, Mrs King, that's what you call capitalism. He fed them and it wasn't like some of them didn't enjoy his attentions. For goodness' sake, his feathered girls never complained. The more of them there were in with a stag, the better it was for them. It meant they were pestered less. He was doing the same thing as the turkeys. Spreading himself about a bit. They should be grateful.

Selwyn's sexual weakness was for peasant stock. It had been ever since he lost his virginity at the age of thirteen to Bruiser Philips in a copse of silver birches, two hundred yards into the cross-country run when neither of them could make it any further. Pendulous white breasts under an aertex shirt and handfuls of cold thigh mottled with cold. Now he craved thick-stemmed young women with sturdy hips and bosoms to their waists.

Take last night. What a night. He'd waited for Freely and Nevski to go to bed and then dialled the order at ten thirty. Five minutes later, Herbert arrived with two eastern Europeans with shiny plastic handbags that sounded hollow when they put them down. Mismatched two-pieces and inappropriate shoes and no English language at all. Just how he liked them. Shorter the skirt, higher the heel. One of the girls was dark and stocky with pudgy puppy fat underneath thick denier black tights. He put on an Eminem and did his turkey rap until half past eleven when the cider ran out. Meanwhile the girls sat by impassively, ignoring everything but his family-sized bag of Cheesy Wotsits. Then Selwyn suggested a game of strip dominoes.

'Every time you knock means you take an item of clothing off,' Herbert said, pointlessly because he knew the rules and the girls didn't speak any English.

'Or we take them off for you,' said Bates.

'That's not fair.' Herbert had changed into a purple velour leisure suit. 'I'll be in the buff in a jiffy.'

'You shut your trap,' said Bates. 'Keep sitting down if you're worried about your skid marks.' He winked at the two girls.

'Anyway, who wants to see what you're keeping in your tracksuit bottoms?'

Within four games he'd stripped the dark one down to her underwear. She'd protested at first, her eyes wide like a rabbit caught in the high beam of his Range Rover. Then, when he went in for the kill, he'd told Herbert and the skinny one to bugger off.

The memory of last night and the plump one's obstinate complicance (he loved that defiant flurry of struggle – for what? – before limp resignation) and the way he'd taken her on the sofa, right underneath his portrait, was enough to half crank up an erection. She hadn't been *the* Butterballs girl, he'd known that from an early stage. But at least she hadn't been a squirmer, he couldn't abide a squirmer. Wriggling and pushing like there was supposed to be something in it for them. Why couldn't they be like his girls and just lie quietly in the coop waiting for their mate?

He reached out for a can of sweet cider by the side of the bath. The crust from a cheese and baked beans turkey toaster on a plate by his head got caught in his hair. Selwyn flexed his stomach muscles ready to haul himself out of the bath and breathed in a lungful of air.

In concentration he rubbed the crease of his mouth with his tongue. Nevski wanted to meet him out back in half an hour to see how the project was going. Though exactly what it had to do with him was anyone's guess. Thinking about his perfect mate had made him twitchy. He jiggled on the spot, standing up, and then peed in the bath. Had he been a religious man he would have offered up a prayer to find his Butterballs girl. A raven-haired, reader's wife type, with industrial-sized breasts like airships and the ability (not urge, that would be going too far) to lick dollops of butter from his testicles.

When he found her, he would love her so much, he would make her his logo.

IV

Had everything else been equal, the Millennium Club would have opened on a moonless night on 21 January, to three Asian businessmen and the tail end of a stag do from Stockton-on-Tees. They even had the black actor who used to play the doctor in *EastEnders* to cut the ribbon. Only, three days before the opening, Beaver Ciriano turned up late (due to a queue at the wholesalers) to find the sign-maker had spelt Millennium with one l.

'Start again,' he said.

'Fuck that, I've got to be in Plaistow by dinner time.'

Beaver said, 'Turn it into Mile High Club then.' Thinking on his feet and the ability to work under pressure was how he'd survived two and a half decades in the porn industry.

'It was a poxy name for a club anyway,' said the sign-maker.

'Well, it's just as well we never done it in neon,' said Beaver, who'd already made his mind up not to pay him. There were other things to consider, like the fliers. Even then the opening was already eight and a half grand over budget. Never mind the club was in a basement and prone to rats. He told the bar manager to use the job lot of silver paint, described on the tin as the 'Colour of 2001', to paint clouds on the ceiling. Then he ordered six red size-ten two-pieces from BHS and told the waitresses to go round the dance floor with an Argos hostess trolley. All of a sudden it was a theme club and when the waitresses said, 'Brandy for you, sir. Can I get you something from the trolley?' it meant he could charge a tenner a shot. He got five hundred new fliers done with a topless air hostess underneath 'Come fly with us' in eight-point Nimrod font. Cashing up after the first night (even after one stag do) Beaver sat down and drank a toast to Terry the sign-maker.

But today Beaver was wracked by a problem of a whole different kind. He wasn't a member of the real Mile High Club. His most ambitious sexual undertaking on a plane had been leaving his napkin in his lap with his flies half undone while pretending to be asleep. But halfway to Palma the crew must have changed because all that happened was a moustachioed trolley dolly handing him his number as he disembarked onto the Marjorcan tarmac.

Truth was, he'd only ever slept with one woman in his life – his first wife. He referred to her as if she was part of a sequence, though after eight and three-quarter years of bachelorhood, there was no sign of a replacement. Rita was an oral hygienist who ran off (though, by the two mugs left in the sink, it'd been a leisurely leaving) with the dentist who called himself doctor. 'Christ Almighty, Rita, he's not a doctor. It's like me calling myself Professor Beaver,' said Beaver. She just said, in that way that she did, 'Exactly, James.' She was the only person in the world who called him James. Beaver blamed the tryst on the heady atmosphere brought on by a surgery full of laughing gas. Now Beaver was most turned on by cleanliness, the smell of freshly washed hair or the way some women instinctively covered themselves when they sensed a man looking at them. That made him want to really swoon. That and the smell of soap.

Which was why, despite his lifetime in the sex business, he still wasn't sure about the whole thing. Maybe it was just the way some women did it. Like a new way of dancing. He didn't find it erotic but how many forty-year-olds were turned on by coal tar soap and long sleeves?

He took a sip of whisky and turned to his bar manager. 'Ben, don't you think it's kinda weird the way the girls dance these days?'

'Dance or strip?' said Ben.

Beaver said, 'Dance and strip.'

'Yeah, well, it's not *Saturday Night Fever* any more, grand-dad.'

'Cheeky sod,' said Beaver.

Ben had spiky dyed blond hair and a pierced left eyebrow that left staple marks when he wasn't wearing an earring. He got away with being so good-looking because punters took him to be gay. By all accounts, on his evenings off Ben had a loose sexual relationship with his sculpture lecturer who was in her thirties and encouraged threesomes.

Beaver hit his signet ring on the side of his rum and pineapple juice contemplatively. He said, 'No, there's something weird about these dancers.' Ben, checking the optics, didn't look up. 'The way they do it, the head movements, it's so, I dunno, jumpy.'

Ben carried on, his face reflected in the mirror behind the bottles. Beaver had his head down over his drink, showing his bald patch.

'I said—'

'Yeah, I heard you.' Ben looked towards the stage. 'They look all right to me. Though with tits that size I'm surprised they can stand up straight.'

On stage, one of the girls was practising her routine. It was midday and they opened at three. They were under strict instructions not to use any dry ice in rehearsals and even when performing, only sparingly. The song was upbeat and frothy, not the sort of thing Beaver thought would turn anyone on.

'Maybe that's it,' said Beaver. 'There's something like Mick Jagger about them.' He paused. 'You know what? Maybe it's a drum and bass thing. You've seen the way they dance in these clubs nowadays. Not in control of their limbs.'

The woman on stage, wearing a dancer's leggings and leotard, was twisting round a chrome pole. Her head jerked backwards and forwards.

'I think it's supposed to represent sexual ecstasy,' Ben told him.

'*Yeah?*' said Beaver, too quickly.

'Come on, you must remember what it's like when you're going at it hammer and tongs.'

'Yeah,' said Beaver. 'Course.'

Silence. Beaver used a Mile High flier to clean his nails. 'Do you think that's hygienic?'

'What, cleaning your nails?'

'Doing that with a pole. It must leave germs and that.'

Ben pulled a stool between his legs and sat down. His movements economic, he stretched himself upright, picked up a bar list and started writing on it in felt pen. Then he told Beaver, 'If you want my opinion, health and safety are the least of your worries.'

'What's that supposed to mean?'

'Nothing. I'm just saying if the immigration ever came sniffing here they'd find more illegals than a lorry park in Calais. I hope it's only the management that gets done because—'

Beaver slammed his drink down. 'Nah. That's where you're wrong. Every single one of these girls is above board. When you've got the right connections you can get round all that bureaucratic stuff. And you can quote me on that.'

'Yeah, like I would.' Ben lifted his pierced eyebrow in sarcasm and went back to the optics. 'When's the next delivery?' he asked.

When he bent over to pick up a beer mat from the floor, his jeans slipped below his hips, revealing a pair of Kangol underpants. Why didn't men wear belts these days? Beaver thought.

He said, tired, 'As it goes, there's delivery today.'

Ben looked up. 'How many?'

'One, I think.'

'Where from?'

'Same place. Some bloke's dropping her off. I'm supposed to meet them out front at twelve thirty.'

'You'd better get up there then, it's that time now,' said Ben, polishing a champagne flute in a superior sort of way. Beaver looked at him quizzically, hoping for understanding but getting haughty. Ben's eyebrow went up again, superior. Ponce, Beaver thought. No one ever had found out the sexual make-up of those threesomes.

He went upstairs to meet the arrival. To make the club look less dingy, three of the walls were mirrored and edged with fairy lights. Beaver was a sucker for small bright lights. As he walked, his shoes stuck to the syrupy puddles of lager and Campari on the plastic flooring and made a kissing noise when he lifted them. Did no one ever clean up in here? Halfway to the door he looked down. Two fluffy white feathers like you sometimes found by your pillow before they became polyester lay on the floor. His nan reckoned feathers found inside were lucky. He bent over to pick them up.

'Ben, can you tell whichever of these women is doing that Haitian voodoo routine to clean up after themselves,' he shouted over his shoulder.

Ben shook his head, shrugged his shoulders and went back to the champagne flutes, even though he couldn't remember the last time they'd ever been used.

V

By 1.50 p.m. Winston had completed two laps of the Serpentine, eaten a Cornetto and two packets of Hula Hoops, and was considering going back to work. He'd have to make his mind up by two. A couple of Euro families in primary colours fanned out across the walkway, smug, with no sense of pedestrian etiquette. On benches, lunchtime affairs crumpled their sandwich packets and reluctantly got up to leave. Winston's walk was for the dual purpose of thinking things over and trying to get the turkey shit off his shoes. Suffolk had left him unsettled and edgy. The carrier bag of money he justified (more easily than he thought he might) as nothing more or less than a late Christmas bonus. The booty meant that for a few months he could relax, though not give up, the deadline on getting an advance on his manuscript. But with what he owed (albeit by proxy), twelve grand didn't really come close.

It wasn't the thought of the money that chomped nervously at his lower intestine. There was something about that Russian girl that worried him. Just before they'd passed the sign for Colchester, he'd pulled into a service station pretending to need petrol even though the tank was half full. He knew she wanted to go to the toilet because she pressed her legs together and kept squeezing her lap the way his mother did on long journeys. Xenia walked like a woman embarrassed about her height – her knees knocked as if each step might be the last. As the car careered around the North Circular she started to gnaw her lower lip, sucking off the lipstick, making her mouth uneven and chapped.

'So, this is London,' he said.

'It's like Moscow.'

Winston didn't say anything, but since when did Russians have World of Leather?

'What's your uncle do?' he asked.

Xenia said, 'Uncle? He works at the factory, of course.'

'Of course,' said Winston. 'You know, where I'm dropping you isn't really the best place for shopping.'

She said, 'Of course not.'

Winston drove down Poland Street, past rake-thin Scandinavian boys holding hands and sour-faced runners yelling into mobiles and sauntering oblivious to the traffic. Then further past shop windows backed with red crêpe paper and piled high with pirated videos and dildos. He parked on a double yellow in the actual alley Bates had written down, next to a record shop selling vinyls. It was opposite a bookshop with Man Ray black-and-whites in the window and a handwritten sign promising an erotic selection in the basement. There was a smell of joss sticks. A neon light throbbed 'Mile High Club'.

'Great, at last you've made it.' The speaker was a compact man, five five, dressed like a model from a German clothes catalogue. Straight off Winston was annoyed because, if not early, he certainly wasn't late. Shorty ought to try driving into the West End at lunchtime, he thought.

'Yeah, well, there was an accident on the A12.'

The man ignored Xenia and went to the boot to collect her bags, automatic, like a bellhop.

'Your uncle,' suggested Winston, guessing he really wasn't. She smiled.

From the left of them came the hollow clank of metal poles as a market stallholder packed up early. Something about cold seemed to make noise travel further.

'Well, goodbye then,' said Winston, putting his hand out. 'I hope you enjoy your trip.'

The woman nodded. 'You go now?' Her bottom lip was scaly with chaps.

'Back to work, I'm afraid.' He pointed over her head. 'Over that way.' He thought about giving her his card but then reconsidered. Aside from the double yellow, the voice in his head was telling him to get the hell out.

'OK then,' she said. 'Bye bye.' Winston gave her half a hug and felt her hip bones on his waist. His arms could have encircled her twice.

'Good luck,' he said.

'Thank you.'

The man looked her up and down. 'You know, I just don't get it, they're either as skinny as rats or stacked like a wet nurse he said.' He nodded at Winston, 'Cheers anyway, mate.' He handed him a couple of fliers with a free entry to the Mile High Club on it, with a two-for-one drinks offer. 'Come back and see us sometime.' He winked at Winston. 'Closed on Mondays though.'

That was an hour ago. Back in the park he frisked his coat to find his mobile. A jogger wearing a backpack wobbled past him. Since when did all joggers strap rucksacks to their back? he wondered.

'Hi, Poppy, this is Winston.' As calculated, she wasn't back from lunch. 'Something's come up and I've got to be in the House this afternoon. Can you let anybody who needs to know? Cheers.'

Strictly speaking it wasn't a lie. He would be in the house. His house.

VI

Other than the two of them the bar was empty. It meant Elaine felt no compunction about yelling. 'What the hell are you doing?'

Patti was walking back from the bar pushing one hip out and then the other. Her head was so far back, if you were sitting down you could see her nasal hair. Elaine could only stay for a drink, so to tide her over, Patti had ordered a portion of chips and garlic mayonnaise.

Patti told her, 'Getting something to eat. What, have you changed your mind?' Elaine was on a de-tox diet.

'No, I mean, why are you walking like that?'

Patti sat down and picked up her pint of lager. 'I'm experimenting with a new walk.'

Elaine sucked on her vodka and Diet Coke. '*Why?*'

'Dunno. I've been walking in the same way for thirty years. It was scrunched up. It's easy to get stuck in a rut.' She clicked her bag strap under her chair leg, like she'd read in a crime prevention brochure.

Elaine said, 'It makes you look ready for a hip replacement.'

'Fuck off.'

'You fuck off.'

They drank some more.

Elaine was wearing a kick-pleated beige corduroy skirt, a sort of zipped-up ski jacket, and a pair of trainers. She was going for Japanese minimalism but looked like an overweight PE teacher. She also had one of those bits of ribbon pinned to her that meant she was for people with either Aids or breast cancer. She hadn't taken her jacket off, which was a sign the de-tox wasn't going well. Patti was wearing a grey knee-length skirt and her Starsky and Hutch pyjama top because she'd seen other people wearing something similar.

Patti said, 'You know, you should try it. Walking upright can shave eight pounds off you.'

'Who says?'

'*New Woman*.'

'Fuck *New Woman*,' Elaine scoffed in a Gallic sort of way. Patti knew she had to move fast before she got the 'fat is a feminist issue' speech.

She drank some lager. 'I just think I'm caught in a time trap. Like there's a look you get and you stick with it all your life. I think I got mine at sixteen. Do you know that no one wears black mascara any more? I mean absolutely no one. Or eyeliner.'

'So what?' said Elaine. 'What's the big deal? I do.'

Silence.

The bar was called O2. It was too early to be full. It had a brand-new laminated floor that smelt of glue, with two beat-up sofas along the far wall. The tables were bleached ash and the chairs rigid. In Patti's opinion, finding a full range of bar snacks was the only thing to make it noteworthy.

Patti said, 'How's work?' Elaine worked for an offshoot of Westminster Council devoted to women's issues. She was a regular on a Sunday morning discussion forum on the all-female Radio Liberty, which Patti thought sounded like a station about feminine hygiene.

'Crap,' said Elaine scowling. 'We've had our grant cut again.'

'Oh, I'm sorry.' Patti knew Elaine thought she was self-centred because she never asked much about Elaine's work. It wasn't that. Patti didn't understand enough about what other people did to be able to ask questions. She changed tack and told a story about a friend from the third year who she'd bumped into in Oxford Street. Elaine told her about a rally in Chester she was going on.

At the bar an Italian-looking man flicked through channels. The TV, jammed American-style on a special bracket, made Patti think it was a sports bar, even though the Italian hadn't stopped at either the golf or the tennis. After a while he left it on MTV with an Asian woman with pigtails and bare midriff bobbing up and down. Patti associated cable TV with the end of the world.

She said, 'Do you remember Green Shield stamps?' She'd underestimated how much lager was in her glass and spilt some down her face. 'Remember when your dad used to come out of the garage with reams of them?'

'Yeah,' said Elaine. 'Then you had to go to that place in Hemel to pick the stuff up.'

Patti said, 'Ashtrays, knives and forks. Those bedsheets. Then you went to your mate's house, who you used to think was posh, and they had exactly the same thing.'

'Janet Butcher.'

Patti nodded. 'I rest my case.'

'I suppose you get Tesco Clubcards these days,' said Elaine.

'Clubcards are not the same thing,' said Patti gravely. 'Not by a long shot.' She drank some more lager.

Elaine went to the bar to get another round and a packet of roast ox flavour crisps. Some de-tox, thought Patti. The Italian at the bar, remote in hand, brought over her chips. 'Can we have some more mayonnaise?' said Elaine. 'And salt, thanks.'

Patti swigged half her lager in one. 'It's just all so fragmented these days,' she said. 'That's what I can't stand.'

Elaine picked up the fork, staring at the plate, as if she was hypnotised by the French fries.

Patti was playing with a match in the ashtray. 'It must have been so much easier in those days. I mean, look at our parents. Why did they get married?'

Elaine gripped a chip between her teeth and was sort of panting. She shrugged.

Patti said, 'Necessity.'

Elaine tore into a sachet of tartare sauce.

Patti said, 'In those days you got married because the men needed sex and women couldn't support themselves. It made sense. Now look what's happened.'

Elaine swallowed. 'What's happened?'

'Men can get laid every day of the week and we've all got jobs.'

Elaine shook her head. 'Patti, what are you going on about?'

She rotated a chip in her fingers. 'Geoff's left me and I'm starting to feel,' she paused for the right word, 'unhinged.'

VII

Winston went to the ICA and, in a desultory sort of way, walked around an exhibition of two photographs of a man and a woman masturbating (in separate frames). He paid eight quid to see *Battleship Potemkin*, which the brochure described as a 'seminal classic', fell asleep in the auditorium and drove home. He never liked being alone in the flat, even less so since Cindy moved out, and especially not in the afternoon. Unlike houses, there was something wrong with flats in daytime.

When he got home the answer phone was beeping hard in the dark. A slow beat meant one message. But they got quicker the more of them there were. More messages, more urgency. Not that it ever worked that way. He hung his coat up, flicked the overhead light on, saw the untidy collection of newspapers, port glasses and pizza takeaway trays. Then he swivelled the dimmer switch to low. Two messages were from Cindy, asking when she could pick her ski stuff up. He stopped after two; there was only one person the other message could be from.

He skimmed a letter from a literary agent in Bath, telling him he had 'no affinity with the English language'. The agent hadn't returned the manuscript, which pissed him off. 'Fucker,' said Winston. Now he was minted he could afford to go straight to the Johnny Geller end of the literary market, hang on for the six-figure deal, not try out with halfwits in Bath. 'Since when did cretins in Bath have an affinity with anything?' he said. A letter from Lambeth Council was asking him if he still qualified for single occupancy status for payment of council tax. 'Fuckers,' said Winston.

He flicked on the TV. His plan was to eat, bathe, drink and sleep. Maybe drink first. He poured a glass of wine into a dirty glass from an opened bottle on the floor to the left of the sofa. The heating hadn't clicked on and the leather was cold. Then he played the message from Tony. On the face of it he wanted nothing. What it really meant was call him back immediately.

When Winston thought of his brother, he got the same bolus of guilt lodged in the pit of his stomach that you got thinking of elderly relatives watching daytime television alone. He took his hands-free phone into the bathroom and sat on the edge of the lavatory. Around the edge of the sink were some of Cindy's toiletries with dusty black and red lids. Winston didn't think it was possible to get dust in a bathroom.

'Tony? Hi, it's Winston.' He gave it half a second to sink in. 'Everything OK?'

'Oh, hi.' Tony sounded surprised, pretending he'd been expecting someone else. As far as Winston knew, no one used Tony's home number. Winston pictured him on the end of the phone. Thin jumper, concave cheeks, bare feet, sausage fingers with dirty fingernails clasped to the receiver. 'How ya doing?' His voice sounded too chirpy, too deliberately upbeat. In the background Winston heard a noise like furniture being dragged on bare boards and then men's laughter.

'OK, not bad. You?' He didn't wait for a reply. 'Tony, what the hell's going on there?'

'Oh, you know, just moving some stuff.'

'Shit,' said Winston. 'What do you mean moving stuff? Is someone breaking in?' It was a ridiculous thought, someone breaking into Tony's.

'No, no, Christ, no. It's like a party, man.'

'Who's there?'

'You know. The usual – Robbo, the doc was here . . .'

Winston closed his eyes and ran his hand over his mouth. 'Tony, don't move. I'll be there as soon as I can.' He hung up. 'Fuck it,' he said.

The traffic was all out of town, which was good. It only took eighteen minutes, mostly in the bus lane, past the Houses of Parliament, lit up like a cruise ship, and flat out down Whitehall, to get to Tony's.

As he drove, Winston thought what a wonderful thing it would be to have sibling rivalry – plain old anxiety about underperforming, jealousy over the best-looking girlfriend. All Winston had experienced for the last two decades was sibling guilt.

Tony's studio was the entire third floor of a late-last-century tenement so black it looked as if it'd been built next to a railway station. But it was elegant enough, so when Tony reassured his mother every Christmas that he was OK and living in a cracking house, he was only an 'ing' short of the truth. Most of the sash windows were broken, jammed half open with curtains flagging like a bomb blast.

When he swerved into the street, for a split second Winston thought it was a body being thrown out of the third-floor window, which made him feel sick. Then he realised it was Tony's dressmaker's dummy, which still made him feel pretty ill. Pieces of paper, his patterns, floated down gracefully behind it.

'Jesus Christ,' said Winston and leapt from the car, bracing himself to fly at the door which was big enough to have come from a Canadian redwood. As usual it was open. The staircase twisted at the bottom but seemed to give up after the first floor and went straight to the top by the quickest route possible.

It stank of glue and turpentine and was cluttered with stacks of free newspapers and planks of wood. Moving upwards, he got sweet blasts of marijuana from behind closed doors. A crumple-faced woman, in a brown candlewick dressing gown that looked like a waffle, slunk out of a downstairs room to see what the noise was about. She didn't say anything, looking at Winston as if he were in charge. From the second-floor landing he watched her stub a cigarette out on the bare concrete floor and look around and then go back into her room. After the second storey there was no banister. More boards, maybe old railway sidings that smelt of tar, old planks of salvaged wood, another dressmaker's dummy fallen astride two pallets. The noise of furniture being moved thudded through the house's skeleton. To his left was a toilet with the door open, seat up, and the light on.

Now he wasn't thinking about sibling rivalry; he was thinking, please, God, don't let it be the psychotic doctor from Cape Town who carried his own set of surgeon's knives. Usually Tony had the lock on – a length of cedar wood, about a foot in circumference, that he raised from his mezzanine bed with a pulley, like a drawbridge – but the door was ajar. Then there was silence.

'Jesus Christ,' said Winston almost as if he'd rehearsed it because the scene wasn't that different from normal. Tony was at his workbench, his gangling legs at random angles. His head was bent over a glass bulb. In his left hand a lighter swayed drunkenly like a teenager at a rock concert.

'Wins, what brings you here?' In the corner two men were slumped, either high or having just ended some physical exertion. One fat man strained the stitching of a cheap suit, the other looked as if he was along for the ride. Tony took a puff on a pipe as if it was an asthma inhaler. Beside him an unsmoked cigarette was turning to ash.

'How much does he owe?' Winston spoke to the one in the suit, now standing.

'Who are you, Officer Dibble?' He had pointed ears like an outsized imp and he stabbed a rollie in Winston's direction.

Winston repeated, 'Look, how much does he owe you?'

'What's it to you?' Even though, shoulders square, he was acting tough, he was the sort of man with secrets. Winston could imagine him dressing up in women's clothes. His size would have been a 22.

Winston said, 'I'm interested – what do you care who pays?'

'I like to know who I'm dealing with.'

In all of this Tony looked the most relaxed. He was wearing dungarees made out of army fatigues.

Winston was getting tired. 'Look, do you want this money or not?'

The suit told him, 'Calm down.'

'OK, fine.' Winston said. The adrenaline was wearing off and out of the corner of his eye he saw a helium-filled foil balloon sinking from the ceiling. It had a packet of green Rizlas cradled in a mesh basket.

'Hey, here come my papers,' said Tony grinning.

'Cool,' drawled a voice from the shadows.

'Christ,' said Winston, shaking his head. He really didn't need to be here. Then again, if he offloaded his brother's debts, it would give him a reason not to come back. If forensics went over his clothes, thought Winston, it'd come up with a mix of Suffolk turkey excrement and Colombian cocaine unique to criminal history.

The fat man sensed his waning interest. He said, 'He owes me two and a half.'

'Thousand, yeah?' asked Winston.

Tony was the worst drugs dealer in the West End. He ran his business as eighty per cent gentlemen's club, twenty per cent charity. Most of Tony's clients were artists. One poet, one set designer. One worked in finance (though he tended to avoid City types). It was an updated Fitzrovia set, except geographically they were a few blocks down and, inspirationally, used grade A drugs rather than alcohol. Tony only dealt with people he liked and then asked them to pay what they could afford. He had an extensive credit system akin to the Russian economy. It only took one non-payer for the whole thing to collapse like a pack of cards. Which it did three or four times a year. Unfortunately, not all of Tony's suppliers were quite as generous as he was.

Winston said, 'Look, I've got the cash.'

Tony looked up. When his spine turned, so did his legs, as if he was made of pipe cleaners. He said, 'Hey, cheers, man.'

'It's in the—' Winston tripped over an empty bottle of ammonia and an ashtray on his way to the window. He tore at the tatter of net curtain. 'Car.'

'Look, can't we all just chill,' said Tony, uninterested.

Winston breathed, 'Oh my God,' and slammed his fist on the ledge. He felt a rush of nausea. 'Shit,' he said as he watched his red taillights bob towards Charing Cross Road like a life-support machine.

VIII

Oddly enough, Patti had more qualms about driving under the influence of two and a half pints of Continental-strength lager than taking the car. At this stage she'd started to think of the Niva as hers anyway. Why else would it be trailing her around central London? Literally popping out at her as she threaded her way towards Oxford Street tube. Also it meant she saved £1.90 on a tube fare. The final sign had been the keys left in it. It was as if it was begging her to take it. She pushed herself snugly into the driver's seat. Familiar shapes – the spindly steering wheel and the unpadded functionality, the pronged pedals, took her back. It was a male interior. A man's smell of stale cigarettes and oiliness. She was glad. She hated stealing cars belonging to women who were underprivileged enough and would get such a row from their partners.

In the dark she sensed the usual jumble of papers, shiny brochures and plastic bags on the back seat. If she thought about it, this bit was like getting into someone else's skeleton, moulding herself to the frame. She switched the radio on but it was tuned to an out of London station where they were talking about the crisis in UK farming. She thought about tuning it to another station but then decided rooting around the dials of a stolen car was asking for trouble.

She used one hand to fasten her duffel and hummed 'Drinking In LA' to herself. It wasn't late. She might even go through the car when she dropped it off at the lock-up. Picking her way through the car's contents, like a beachcomber, was her favourite thing. Better than finding an abandoned shopping list in a trolley, or a house where they kept their curtains open when the lights were on. Until Rory discovered her Aladdin's cave (and went up the wall) she used to keep the treasures (once a ladies' squash kit, once a wrapped-up *Toy Story 2* jigsaw) – though most times it was just crap. Then she decided her collection wasn't only a security risk but fetishistic, like a serial killer keeping locks of hair. She imagined the Jill Dando replacement on *Crimewatch* displaying it. 'And finally, does anyone know who this lot belongs to?' she'd ask, sneering on the word 'lot' and making Patti look like a nutter.

Still, she thought to herself as she indicated left into Shafesbury Avenue, waiting for a stream of theatregoers to cross the road back to their coach, how else was she supposed to find out how other people carried on?

IX

At just after 10 p.m., Alfie Appleton started writing what he hoped would make tomorrow's front-page lead:

International turkey king, Selwyn Bates, is appealing for information to quicken the safe return of missing teenager Alan Raynham.

WHITE MEAT AND TRAFFIC LIGHTS

Bates, head of the multimillion-pound empire Butterballs, is the employer of the fifteen-year-old's mother, Eleanor.

Speaking today, Mr Bates, whose mansion is close to the Suffolk village from where Alan disappeared, said: 'I am asking anyone who knows the whereabouts of young Alan to come forward. His mother is in a terrible state and we are all worried about the lad.'

He added that Alan was from a close knit community and everyone had been affected by his disappearance.

Police have widened their search for Alan, who was last seen on 25 January as he left his Sudbury home, into Essex.

Alfie supped from a Starbucks styrofoam cappuccino placed out of reach of the keyboard of his Apple Mac. Writing Bates up in a positive light went against the grain, but news was news, and it was a fresh angle on a story that was losing its legs. Library cuttings on the Butterballs empire, trawled from the business to lifestyle section, were scattered by his left elbow. How quickly news aged, thought Alfie. Even last month's clippings were starting to look as old as the Dead Sea scrolls. Top of the pile was a photo of Bates handing over a cheque to a woman in a wheelchair (even though the editor had long since banned pictures of money presentations). Young Alfie Appleton used his coffee beaker to obliterate Bates's grinning face. He even went as far as removing the plastic lid so the foamy drips could run all over it.

Chapter Four

I

The woman called Helena flicked her chin savagely towards a woman on a camping bed, flush against the far wall. She hissed, 'Ignore that one, she thinks she owns the place.' There was a pecking order to the room. The best-looking girl, a Lithuanian whose thighs had a ten-centimetre gap between them at the top, took the bed. When Xenia had got up to pee, just as the light was starting to solidify the shapes in the room, she'd made out her white-blonde hair fanned out on her pillow like a halo, or a princess in a fairy tale – even though she snored like a cat. Xenia's brain still fizzed from the music in the club, so that she had to grind her teeth when she tried to sleep. The room stank of cheap perfume and boxed-in breath. Helena told her, by way of comfort, she'd be used to it in a week. Xenia said she wouldn't be there in a week. Helena told her that's what they all said.

Helena whispered, 'What are you going to do, grow wings and fly back home? You need to work here to get your passport back. The sooner you start, the better.' Helena's real name was Oxana. She was no taller than one metre sixty, a chunky Ukrainian, pockmarked with measles scars, who had failed the audition for the Kighiz National Ballet and answered an advert in a Moscow paper to join a foreign dance troupe. She said caustically, 'What a mug, the ad even said "no experience required". Then I paid five hundred bucks for the privilege. Can you believe it?' She cleared her throat in a way that made Xenia think she was going to spit.

Helena was from a village called Bratkovichi in western Ukraine. Her clothes smelt of stale sweat and underneath Xenia recognised the tinny odour of cheap day-old vodka. Xenia was wedged between Helena and another girl. Her hips ached from sleeping on a concrete floor even though she'd jammed her skirt underneath her. A Nigerian girl muttered to herself – according to Helena, they all did that. In the far corner the taller of the Baltic girls reorganised her belongings, putting piles of clothes in plastic bags and then taking them out again. She hummed a tune to herself and rocked backwards and forwards.

'What's up with her?' Xenia asked.

Helena put a finger to her temple and said brazenly, 'Loco. Don't lose sleep over that one. She's a proper cow.'

Xenia nodded. If she breathed inside her sleeping bag, it warmed up. She said, 'How long have you been here?'

Helena said like a boast, 'Nineteen weeks and three days.'

Xenia's insides did a backflip. 'That long?' What scared her most was what Aunt Galia used to say about the prison camps: 'In time, people get used to anything.'

'Sure,' said Helena as if it was nothing.

Xenia waited as long as she could before asking, 'How long before they make you . . . ?'

'Do tricks? That depends.' She glanced at the door. 'How much do you owe them?'

Xenia gulped. '*Owe them?*' She rubbed her feet together, nervously.

Helena said, 'Yeah, they charge us twenty pounds a night lodging and then there's your travel costs and food.'

'They haven't said anything.'

Helena said, '*Yet*, they haven't said anything yet. You've got to pay up before you get your passport back. Me, they said ten thousand, UK. But you never know, you could be lucky, It happens, you know.'

'Like what?'

'Well, one girl got married to a client. Old guy, crazy, said this girl reminded him of his niece. Polish, she was. And they let her out. That was a big surprise. Another got cancer of the cervix and was sent back. They thought she might pass it on.' Xenia could hear in her voice that Helena was smiling. 'That's who I got Boris off,' she said. 'I inherited him.'

'Whoever is Boris?' asked Xenia, not really concentrating.

'My snake, of course,' Helena told her. 'I use him in my act.'

Xenia felt the jaw ache that meant she wanted to cry. She said, 'I want to go home.'

'How you gonna do that, no passport, no money, no nothing? This country is an island, remember, what you going to do – swim?'

Xenia's head flopped on the concrete. 'I don't want to do that with men, though. I never did.' Xenia knew the worst thing she could do was start to cry, especially with Helena so hard, like the whole thing was no worse than Pioneer Camp. 'What if we just refuse?'

Helena gave a deliberately hollow laugh meant to menace (Whose side was she on? thought Xenia). 'Then they kill you. Forget it. If you run away, they go looking for your family back in . . . Where are you from?'

'Volga region.'

'You haven't got kids, have you, back home?'

'No,' said Xenia.

'That's good,' Helena told her. 'Remember, don't take anything that the girls offer you. It's bad enough being a *prostitutka* without being a *narkotika* as well. That way you'll never get out.'

Xenia felt panic bubble up in her insides. The thought of going through the last few hours again made her writhe. Pushing that trolley, handing out drinks and being paid with greasy, sour-smelling money. Men looking like they'd just spent four days on the train from Tblisi, with their dark hair, greased and shiny like billiard balls, and underneath, eyes hypnotised in a leer.

She had felt so ridiculous with her shirt off – more a child than a grown-up. Then they'd look at her and make a face as if they couldn't believe it either. And she felt ashamed because she didn't really have breasts like other girls her age. Aunt Galia used to make jokes about it. How Xenia looked like a farm boy. She didn't even wear a bra. Helena said not to worry because some men liked tits like that. For the first two hours she covered herself with her hair but the men just lifted it up, like a curtain, and peered underneath. Then a black man in a grey uniform stopped them, by which time she'd decided to wear her hair back in any case.

At midnight Helena gave her 250 grams of vodka. It made her head spin and when the strobe came on for one of the dancers, she felt so dizzy she had to get some air, or faint. But the black man clamped his arm in front of her like a railway barrier and spun her round back into the club with words she didn't understand.

As she was nodding off, Helena leant over. 'You'll need another name. They don't like Russian sounding ones. Go for something English.'

'Like what?' The only English woman Xenia had heard of was Margaret Thatcher.

'That'll do. Call yourself Maggie.'

'Will they mind that?'

'What do you care?' said Helena. 'Remember, they are nothing but varmints. Now sleep.'

She had a point. To stop herself crying Xenia bit her cuticles until they bled.

II

At 5.02 a.m. Winston's mobile rang. He was halfway through a dream where Cindy was on her knees, pleading with him to take her back. She said she realised how wrong she'd been to leave him for a travelling Pilates instructor who kept a metre-wide red exercise ball in the front seat of his Honda Civic. In the background, the Pilates man was astride the ball when it punctured, launching him into an orbit from which he never returned. Winston told Cindy he could never take her back. Then she went down on him but she was on her knees anyway. On waking, it occurred to Winston, even though half asleep, that there was an undeniable testicular motif throughout the dream. He wondered, did Cindy's current partner have huge balls?

Groggy, he grabbed the mobile. 'Hello?'

'Freely?'

'Speaking.'

'Freely, you pillock, you've gone and driven off with something that belongs to me.'

The only light in the room came from Winston's phone.

WHITE MEAT AND TRAFFIC LIGHTS

Outside, the hum of a milk float made Winston dimly aware you could still get milk delivered in London.

'Mmmmm. Maybe. What exactly do you mean?' He washed his face with his hand. He was still thinking of Cindy's head bobbing up and down in front of him. 'The girl?'

Bates said acidly, 'No, not the blasted girl.'

'What then. Not the car?'

'No, not the bloody car. That simpleton girl picked up the wrong bag when she left. She's made off with important things belonging to our friend Mr Nevski. He's left with a bag full of nonsense.'

'Made off with? You make it sound like she did it deliberately. What was in the bag?'

'That's for me to know and you to find out,' Bates told him.

Winston wasn't in the mood for playground games. He had a sense of unreality brought on by exhaustion. Pacifying Tony's visitors had taken till past midnight. He'd only managed to get away after Tony's offer of free lines to his creditors (Winston didn't point out that was what had got them there in the first place). Winston snorted a couple and left, promising he'd get the money over in a couple of days. In Soho, there'd been an impromptu demonstration the length of Old Compton Street to commemorate a gay bloke who'd been killed in a pub bombing, which meant he couldn't get a cab. He wasn't being what Cindy called minority minded, but at this stage he was past caring. Not only had the Niva contained his sack of cash but his Palm Pilot (with the only version of his eighty-two-thousand-word manuscript) was locked in the glove compartment. Had Cindy still lived with him she would have said, firstly, why didn't you take the money out of the car and, secondly, why didn't you back the book up on a disk? It was times like this when he was glad he lived alone.

'Can't this wait until morning?' he asked Bates.

Bates sounded slightly wired, as if he'd been up all night. 'It is morning, boy.'

Winston said, 'You know what I mean. A decent time. Like after nine.'

Bates said, 'I'll tell you why, because Mr Nevski is sitting here with a bagful of ladies' cosmetics and women's fashion items, which are a long way from what he should be sitting here with.'

'Oh dear,' said Winston.

Bates spelt it out. 'So that means the bag's either with the young lady, or it's in the back of your car.'

Winston's stomach went kerplunk, the hairs on the back of his neck stood up and he elbowed himself into a sitting position. 'The where?'

'Christ, boy, the back of your car, unless you've had some sort of car-boot sale.' He made boot sound like boat.

'Yeah, well, I've been having some problems with a gammy clutch so it's in for a service.'

Bates said, 'Well, I suggest you get it out. I want that bag immediately.' In the background Winston heard a low growl that he hoped wasn't Nevski. 'You might think Herbert is the extent of my security,' Bates went on. 'If you do, you are making a very grave error, Mr Freely. Herbert's for old times' sake. My real boys could make a Rottweiler look like a puppy. Twenty-four hours. Do I make myself clear?'

'As crystal,' said Winston, and hung up.

He levered himself out of bed and flicked on the bedside lamp. It was too early for the heating to be on, so he threw a dressing gown over his shoulders, which was too cold to put his arms into. To preserve body heat, he covered the bed with the duvet. Bare boards painted white were as cold as an ice floe. He swore. Cindy had been behind the hessian in the hall, jute in the bathroom and generally carpetless interior. Left to his own devices, Winston was much more a shag pile man.

Burrowing in the inside pocket of his winter coat he came up with a cinema stub for the ICA, the receipt for the Cornetto and Hula Hoops that he planned to claim on expenses, and the fliers that Xenia's maybe uncle had given him. They read, 'Come fly with me' with the 'come' in bold red letters. A woman in a severe red jacket with a mountainous cleavage was sucking the top of an Airfix model Spitfire. Given the context it made very little sense but, he guessed, contextual detail wasn't the point. The club opened at three. Winston resolved to be there at two and slumped back into bed.

III

So far in his four-month journalistic career, Alfie Appleton had only received one piece of advice when it came to door-stepping. Always take a packet of tissues. When they start to cry, say nothing and pass them one. It was a gesture to show you cared.

'But I do care,' Alfie had said.

'*We* know that,' said the news editor. Ralph Betts was a baby-faced fifty-year-old who, because he'd always looked young, had the vocal habit of lowering his sentences at the end. The result was you rarely questioned him. His skin was as thick as a dinosaur and his lack of people skills made him friendless but an excellent journalist. He said, 'But *they* may not.' He clipped a pencil behind his ear. 'If they refuse to see you, tell them you're doing a tribute piece. If they still say no, tell them they either talk to the local paper or the tabloids. That usually does the trick. If they *still* refuse, start crying and say if you don't get the story you'll lose your job.' He scratched his earlobe. 'It's the mother you're seeing, right?'

'That's right. Eleanor. But I can't tell her we're doing a tribute piece. He's not even dead.'

Betts said, 'True, officially he's not dead, but remember to ask a few "what if" questions we can use when the body turns up. "What if it turned out your son had been murdered, Mrs Raynham, how would you feel?" That sort of thing. Get his dreams for the future, you know the gig.'

After he left school Alfie had had the opportunity to work in his uncle's abattoir near Halstead on a two-year apprenticeship. Sometimes he wished he had done. For a start it paid better and secondly it would have been less bloodthirsty. But Alfie had always been inquisitive; loved finding out things. Even aged seven he used to pretend his mixed-race action man was Colin Powell and put on Desert Storm press conferences balancing Colin on the toilet cistern.

Halfway up the Raynhams' garden path he felt a tingle of excitement mixed with a feeling of remoteness. The tingle of being in the presence of unimaginable grief and then the power of feeling none of it. It was vicarious emotion and, if he thought about it for too long, not very laudable. From the cuts, he knew Alan was an only child Mrs Raynham must have had late in life, which explained the name. Even in Suffolk no one called kids Alan any more.

It was a semi-detached council house from the fifties, with its front made of slabs of overlapping concrete, the middle of one of a group of four clinging to the village just beyond the signpost. Two were painted village colours and two, like this one, were bare. The skeleton of a rusty Morris Minor mixed with the rain and bled an unnatural orange onto the concrete. Woman reporters usually got the doorsteps, because they were more sensitive. But this was in recognition of today's page lead (the first Alfie Appleton by-line) and the fact that Jeanette and Pauline were doing a BSE special in Wisbech. Alfie also had a connection to Mrs Raynham. Before she joined Butterballs, she'd been a dinner lady at Alfie's brother's middle school. Also, Alfie was small and the news desk reasoned no one could take offence at questions asked by a midget.

'Mrs Raynham?' Alfie looked up at a woman who would have stood at nearly six foot if she hadn't been buckled over. 'I'm Alfie Appleton from the *Eastern Angle*. I said I'd be popping in at about this time. Is it convenient?' Alfie was expecting a policewoman to be there, sitting erect with her hips forward on a dining-room chair, with a painted-on expression of sympathy, but the house was empty.

'Come in. Ricky, my husband, he's gone round his sister's. He can't bear the wait, but someone's got to be here. In case he calls.' In the background he heard the music of a daytime chat show trying too hard to sound carefree but important. It surprised him, hearing the noise, but then he guessed grief wasn't all sitting in dark rooms. There was a pile of wellingtons by the back door and a smell of birdseed. Alfie saw the initials A.R. written in black marker on the side of a boot. It would make a good picture, he made a mental note. As he moved into the house it smelt less of stale shoes and more of unwashed dogs' bowls.

Alfie had never seen such a tall woman close up. She was like an Iceni tribeswoman with a long dark plait snaking down her back. The crown of Alfie's head made it as far as her breasts. He delved into his bag for his reporter's notebook. Then he had to ask for a pen. He said, 'No news then?'

'Nothing.'

Alfie said, 'You know they got his bike. It turned up over Halstead way.'

She said without looking at him, as if she was engaged in an act of betrayal, 'Of course I know.'

Alfie said softly, 'What would he be doing over there?'

'I don't know.' She looked at him, eyes pleading him to stop. 'I've told them I don't know what he was doing there. He's such a good boy.' She started to snivel and Alfie passed her a tissue. Alfie's skin wasn't dinosaur thick. Clearly, now was not the time for 'what if' questions.

'Selwyn Bates has put out an appeal for information,' he said. 'Are you hopeful that will encourage people to come forward?'

'People,' she said venomously. 'What people? You make it sound as if he just wandered off into the back of beyond. People round here were his friends. Christ, he was related to half of 'em.'

'But what about Mr Bates?' The very least he could get was her angle on Bates's appeal.

'Course it's good of him but . . .' she bit her lip.

Alfie prompted, 'But?'

'But it's the least he could do'. She spoke bitterly. 'Alan so wanted to be a gamekeeper when he grew up. He spent half his time on that estate one way or another.'

'Did he?' asked Alfie, writing. 'Did Bates know?' He was trying to find out politely if it'd been more than poaching.

'Christ, yeah,' said Mrs Raynham, looking up. 'He was with him half the time. Or if not him, his mate. Used to come home full of it. Turkey this, turkey that. I used to say, "Christ, boy, I see enough of them bloody birds during the day, without you goin' on about them all night."' Then she started to sob. Alfie passed her another tissue and, as his news editor would say, made a note.

IV

When the room started to stir, grumpily, some time after midday, Xenia knew she had to escape. Before, it had been an abstract idea.

Now, with the watery grey light leaking into the room through stained velour curtains, she was definite. And she knew she would do better to start straight away. She didn't want to get used to this. When her resolve began to wobble, she pictured Uncle Gleb sitting at the kitchen table with his eyes narrowed and lips lifted, not smiling, but saying I told you so. She couldn't find her cosmetics but that didn't matter. Cosmetics had got her here in the first place. For toiletries Helena said she could borrow hers.

'Only don't take any Tampax.' She said the word in English. 'They're like gold dust in here. They're the only thing they let us go out and buy and they're expensive.'

At one thirty Xenia crept downstairs. She kept her shoulder to the wall, hoping it would absorb some of the noise of her shoes on the bare boards. One door led to the basement and the club, the other to outside. She had her hand on the latch when a black man put his hand on her shoulder. It rooted her to the spot like a lightning bolt. She smelt him before she saw him, a sickly sweet smell of aftershave.

'Oh no you don't, young lady.' It was the same man from last night, not in uniform but a green tracksuit. 'My, my, aren't you the slippery one.'

'Why? I must.'

His teeth were as white as piano keys. 'Well, it's not safe out there for young ladies to walk about with no documents, comprenez?'

Xenia said, 'Of course.'

When she looked at him, he said, 'Where do you think you're going anyway? You got any money?'

'Money I have,' Xenia told him definitely.

'How much?'

'Four pounds, maybe more. I need things. It's my every month thing.' The man looked away for a half-second.

'Are you sure?' He exhaled and his broad rib cage fell.

Xenia tutted impatiently. 'Yes, of course.'

He said, 'You're not going anywhere on your own.'

Xenia said, 'Please, I must.'

'What about the other girls?' He nodded his head towards the stairs.

Xenia looked blank.

He said slowly, each word a sentence, 'The girls give you some.'

'They say no, they hate me,' said Xenia. 'Come if you don't believe my monthly.'

'Oh no, I believe you.' The guard shook his head and made a clicking sound in his cheeks. 'Wait here. You'll need to go with one of the others.'

Xenia slumped against the wall while the man disappeared. She had only seen black people on the television and thought, until then, they were either American or African. His thighs bulged out of slim hips and he walked like a cowboy to stop his legs rubbing together. Galia would have said he probably got through a lot of pairs of trousers.

The sullen-faced woman he brought was chewing on the skin of a fruit Xenia didn't recognise. Her left hand swayed drunkenly with a carton of milk shake that sounded empty when she sucked on the straw. She was puffy-eyed and looked as if she'd been dragged away from something. Her blue jumper had milky stains down the front, as if she was lactating.

'Ten minutes,' said the man and flashed both fists with fingers outstretched as if he was dancing. He pointed at his watch. And then raised his hand, meaning he'd hit them if they were late.

Outside, the coldness caught Xenia off guard. She breathed in several times as if she was flushing out all the air from the brothel. Her companion walked staring straight ahead, unseeing, like a sleepwalker. Xenia felt too tall. For the first ten meters the woman grabbed Xenia's coat sleeve but at the end of the road she relaxed. She ambled as if her upper body was in a barrel. 'What's your name?' Xenia asked. She repeated it in English. The woman said nothing, just kept barrelling along, impassive.

Xenia knew everyone was looking at her. So much so she bent over to look at her reflection in a car wing mirror to see what was wrong with her face. Nothing. In that case they must all know, she thought. Know that she was the one who took her shirt off in public. Then she remembered the photograph the dark man from the Cherokee Jeep had handed around the village, of himself standing in a European back street, just like this one. And the way Maria Timofeyvna had shown off, saying they could have been done on a computer. Well, that's what it was; Xenia Malakova, aged nineteen, walking along a made-up street in a made-up place. When she thought of it like that, she felt a whole lot better.

Even on autopilot, her minder nudged Xenia round a mishmash of streets, steering her imperceptibly. After five minutes she stopped outside an empty shop with a yellow logo and pushed Xenia inside. There were no security men on the door, as there would have been in Samara, and no one there to take your bag (even though Xenia's was under her coat), just three aisles of food. Big deal, thought Xenia. Galia used to say she once met a woman who had passed out when she visited a shop in Paris due to the choice of tinned vegetables. What a thing to faint over, Xenia remembered thinking at the time.

She picked up the smallest box of Tampax, because she didn't need them and she had to preserve her money. Then she thought, with her guard outside she didn't even need to do that. She glanced at the Indian lady behind the cash register who was showing a young boy how to open and shut the till. Every time they did it, the register pinged and the boy laughed. Xenia shut her eyes and adjusted the bags under her coat. When it got to her lucky number seven, she'd do it.

V

Tracey McCloud had always been passionate about the exploitation of women. So much the better that she, too, belonged to that underprivileged caste. In an ideal world she would have been black, but she realised you couldn't have everything. On the other hand, because of her surname (even though her family had lived in Cheltenham for three generations) Tracey claimed descent from the Scots who, everyone knew since *Braveheart*, yearned for their freedom. When pushed, Tracey could even trace her lineage on the distaff side back to an impoverished turn-of-the-century Gorbals tenement. Why else would she develop a Scottish accent when drunk? And what else but a rogue Scottish gene could explain her love of tartan? Well, at least Burberry.

Tracey knew her co-worker Elaine – whom she preferred to call assistant (she didn't believe women should be barred from power structures just because they were patriarchal) – felt the same way. Elaine was one of her type, a true believer, at a time when so many young women seemed to have forgotten feminism and just seemed to be getting on with their lives. 'Thank God for Jenni Murray,' said Tracey on more than one occasion, even though she disapproved of the way she spelt her name. 'Where would we be without *Woman's Hour*?'

She was almost at the end of her cleansing programme. She took up her 'ready to rub' stance, knees bent, cape flicked back over both shoulders, and body square to the back of the booth (slightly Maori-esque). With one hand she got ready to flick the fliers and with the other she sloshed detergent on a brush and scrubbed. At first she used to be intrigued by the cards, '40 DD Brazilian, new to town, will make you come', 'Young Thai girls fulfil *all* your needs', 'Busty Russian Lolita will spank you hard', but now she was just intrigued by the methods used to stick them there. Laminated, Sellotape, UHU, Super Glue it was only a matter of time before they were engraved in the telephone boxes.

She had considered petitioning BT to get rid of the booths altogether. After all, now everyone had mobiles, phone boxes were nothing more than a public lavatory. And a showcase for smut.

'You finished in there, lady?' A short man in a thin pinstripe and distinguished half-glasses, like a classics lecturer, tapped on the side.

'Piss off,' said Tracey. Then she thought, he could be a Westminster councillor who would report her. He looked the type and Westminster Council could be so Stasi in their information gathering. 'I'll be right out.' She smiled and flicked her cape coquettishly.

'Is that your bucket?' he asked.

She froze. Maybe she was contravening the latest health and safety diktat. She said quickly, 'Yes, no, I mean it's not official business. I just like to clean.' Her neck flushed.

'You like to clean,' repeated the man. 'Truly?'

'Tracey nodded, turned her back on him and thought: how spooky.

In any case, it was her last box of the morning. She took up her throw-the-bucket position, with legs spread and perched on her Ellesse pumps. Then she tossed the bucket of soapy water and disinfectant and watched it wash the men's filthy urine clean away.

As she left the booth she spotted one of them, lurking under the awning of an Italian deli, in army fatigues (how fitting, she thought) with a stack of fliers under his arm. Waiting like a vulture to put them up again. She thought she recognised a Thai man scurrying between two cars. He was another one. One who should know better. No sooner had she cleansed a box than it was time for them to start polluting it again. Well, if they wanted a war, she muttered, they could have it. Tracey adjusted her Burberry headscarf, meaning business. The look was supposed to be All Saints, though Elaine called it more Dana. 'That sweet Irish singer?' replied Tracey wistfully. 'No,' Elaine told her, 'Dana International.'

Tracey left the box.

Watching her walk away from inside the box, Beaver Ciriano inhaled hard the smell of Eau d'Issey and citrus fruits. He wanted to steep himself in it; he wanted to steep himself in her. The deeper he breathed in, the more he knew it. He was in love. Well, if not love in the strictest Romeo and Juliet sense of the word, at least advanced lust (with mutual respect). When he thought he could fill his lungs no more, he said to himself, 'Time for business.' There was work to be done and it would be a shame if the Mile High fliers didn't get pride of place.

VI

Winston dodged lunch with Poppy at the Glass Blowers Arms, claiming the whole smoking lobby was about to blow. He walked to the Mile High Club – the flier even had a segment of map on it, with a phallic arrow pointing at the entrance. The weather was milder but the air felt charged. Winston felt like a barometer with the mercury rising. He tried to remember the last time he had had sex. Certainly before Christmas. Before bonfire night? It had to be after the FA Cup final. Towards the end, Cindy had been most unresponsive. Best not to think about it, thought Winston. But, all of a sudden, sex was all around him: leather maids' outfits, red whips, PVC face masks. Videos of men, videos of women, men and women, women and animals, builder men, Asian women, Asian men, pregnant women, the subject of lewd and furious scrutiny. What selection process did men use to choose a video? Probably the same one to choose a woman – the certainty of instant gratification and the promise of something more.

It was just gone one. Too early for the club. He got a table outside Bar Italia, under a mushroom gas heater, and ordered a mozzarella, basil and tomato toasted ciabatta from one of the cow-eyed snake-hipped waiters. At right angles to him, a dark girl with a sleek bob was writing in a notebook, keeping an eye on a bike chained to a lamppost. She wore a ring with a black stone, which nodded up and down as she wrote, like a prawn's eye. She didn't have that twitchy look women had waiting for someone. Winston guessed she wanted to be picked up. Then again she could just be hungry.

Since he'd got up, Winston had been trying to figure out the bigger picture. This was how he looked at it. Bates employed immigrant labour in his factory. That, in itself, was not illegal. Winston had spent forty minutes that morning on the phone to Pete Harriman, a chap he knew at the Home Office who played in the same five-a-side league in which Lobby Force had a team. He'd called them gang masters. Winston said they sounded like something out of Hardy.

'Yeah, I guess they kinda are,' said Pete. Pete was from the West Country. He had a natural storyteller's voice. 'In the old days you used to get gangs of labourers who went around the country working as they were needed. Yeah? Picking hops in Kent, sugar beet in East Anglia. They were organised by gang masters. It still happens now, only the cheapest labour comes from abroad, mainly Eastern Europe. They work on the land, in factories.'

'It's not illegal then?' asked Winston.

'Not as such, they can get work visas, or even student visas. Why do you want to know?'

'No reason,' Winston said. 'Cindy and I were in Suffolk last weekend, walking. Some of the accents we heard. You'd have thought we were in the Russian steppes. I just wondered, that's all.'

'It's big business.'

'Like what?'

'Think about it. What's the minimum wage these days? Four quid? They pay less than a pound an hour for an eighteen-hour shift, most of which goes back to the gang masters in rent or travel expenses.'

'Why don't they go back home then?'

'The gang masters take the passports. If they try to speak out, well, put it this way, it's not that difficult to dispose of an illegal immigrant who's most probably travelling under a false name.'

'So it's dangerous?' Winston tried to sound noncommittal.

'Yeah,' said Pete. 'At least that's what I've heard.'

'But that's all they do, is it, work on the land?'

Pete said, 'Pretty much, why?'

'No reason,' Winston said again.

'I hear your mate Poppy's split up from her boyfriend,' said Pete.

'Really,' said Winston and hung up.

The thought of implied violence meant Winston couldn't finish his sandwich. Not all of them stayed picking parsnips or plucking turkeys, some came to London. Damn it all, he'd driven one of them. And what did penniless illegal immigrants who wound up in Soho do? In a second he had Xenia servicing twenty clients a night. Then he thought, what if she just had a job as a barmaid or was hoping to work in a sandwich shop, take up a language course? She didn't have to be a stripper. As if to prove a point, the Italian waiter slapped a bill for £4.20 on the chrome table and told him to pay inside. Then Winston found himself disappointed. He hadn't realised how much he'd been looking forward to seeing her naked.

VII

Bates was playing croquet with Herbert. He always started the Thursday afternoon tournament with the phrase, 'Okey dokey, let's play croquet.'

The weather wasn't the best, but a couple of days without rain had dried out most of the lawn. And besides, said Bates, it just meant you had to give it more wellie. In the old days, the pier days, it used to be crazy golf but croquet was Bates's concession to sophistication. That, his boxed set of *I Claudius* and his Andrew Lloyd Webber CD collection. Usually Mrs King acted as referee, or made up a four with the manager in cold cuts, but she was laid up with a bad ankle.

'Most likely foot and mouth,' said Herbert.

'Hussy,' Bates said. 'She only do it to dodge doing any work. I s'pose I'll have to video my own programmes now.'

Herbert clobbered his ball. The unaccounted-for gradient of the lawn meant it ended up in the ornamental bush at the end of the garden.

'Christ, boy, you don't know your own strength,' Bates told him. Herbert flexed his muscles. Bates went back to practising with his mallet on an invisible ball.

'You seen Oddjob today?' Herbert asked. Oddjob was Herbert's name for Nevski.

'No, I haven't, confounded man,' Bates said, irritated.

'Any word from Freely?' Herbert asked.

'Not a dickie bird, not since this morning. He reckon the car's in for a service.'

'What did you tell him?'

'That he had twenty-four hours to deliver that bag back here, otherwise there'd be trouble.' As Bates spoke, the mallet scudded against the lawn, making a clod of earth fly up. He swore.

'It'll be curtains if it all got out, wouldn't it?' said Herbert sheepishly.

'Christ, boy, not half.' Bates whacked his ball. It missed the hoop by half a foot, and ended up next to Herbert's. Herbert told him if it had been bowls it'd have been an excellent shot. Bates told him to shut up. They mooched towards their balls in silence.

Halfway down the lawn, Bates said, sagely, 'All it is, is that the world's just not ready for Project X.'

'What if Freely don't get them papers back?' Herbert asked.

Bates watched his friend crouch down. 'Let's worry about that when it happens.'

VIII

Winston's forehead was banged against the wall, which effectively stopped him from moving any part of his body, apart from his lips. 'What was she? the bouncer repeated. 'Your girlfriend?' They were at the bottom of a short flight of stairs below pavement level.

'No, I just gave her a lift here.' The brick was surprisingly sharp on his brow. Cindy would have called it a good exfoliant. 'Look, could you let up?'

'Where is she?' the bouncer asked grimly.

'Who?'

'The Russian bird.'

'How the hell would I know?' pleaded Winston. 'I'm looking for her as well. What do you think I'm doing here?' He felt a couple of spots of water on his forehead – rain, he thought, or perspiration.

The bouncer was cautious. 'Why?'

'She's got something that belongs to a friend of mine.'

Maybe it was the shared predicament, maybe his arm ached, but the bullyboy released his grip. He said, 'I ought to have gone with her, but you've got to watch these tarts twenty-four hours a day. They're more slippery than a bucket of eels.'

It made Winston less and less sure he was dealing with a sandwich-making outfit. And if Xenia had done a bunk, he was in big trouble.

'Where could she have gone?' he asked desperately. Above them, passers-by walked by oblivious. Winston heard a mobile go off.

'Haven't a clue,' the bouncer said. She's got no money, no passport, she'll end up whoring, just for a different outfit.'

Winston thought of Xenia's profile in the car and the way her hair curled outwards just above her collar. 'You're joking.'

'Do I look like Russ Abbott?'

Winston said, 'Did she leave anything behind?'

'Like what?'

Winston shrugged unconvincingly. 'I dunno. A bag maybe. Some sort of case?'

The bouncer looked at Winston. 'It's not the bleeding Italian Riviera, these girls travel light.'

Winston reached into his pocket for a Camel. He offered the packet to the bouncer and said, 'Can I look in her room?'

The bouncer ignored the cigarettes. 'No, I think I've had

enough of you.' He spun Winston round and shoved him in the base of his back hard enough to propel him a shop length. Winston turned round. The idea of angry Bates's face loomed in the front of his brain. He put his hands out to show he was defeated.

'Please, mate,' he said, 'I need to know, did she leave any stuff behind?'

The bouncer shrugged his coat collar up. 'What's it to you?'

'Please.' Winston slumped his back against the wall, going for sympathy.

'No.' The bouncer spat on the concrete, saliva mixing with spots of rain. 'She didn't leave anything. By all accounts she even nicked one of the sink plugs and a bog roll. That's gratitude. Bloody tart.'

It didn't seem to Winston that Xenia had a hell of a lot to be thankful for. He stopped outside a Japanese kitchenware shop to check his phone. Most times he kept his mobile switched off and used it more as a messaging service. Four messages, one a text from Poppy asking him if he wanted to go to a gallery opening at the Haymarket. Winston wondered if she was angling for some sort of affair. One from Cindy demanding her ski wear, one from Sheila Sheepshank at ACT, warning him that the anti-tobacconist lobby was a smoking gun about to go off, then, from Selwyn Bates, delivered in his peculiar Suffolk brogue. 'Freely, I have to remind you that unless you deliver that bag in the next twelve hours you'll be for it. Remember, we know where you live.'

As far as Winston could remember Bates didn't know where he lived but it wasn't the sort of message you questioned. Winston stretched his shoulders out to check for damage to himself or the silk lining of his jacket. There was none to either. As a precaution he licked the palm of his hand and rubbed it over his forehead to get any brick dust off. He ambled away from the club. Two minutes later, as if moved by an inner force, he found himself in an off licence that specialised in Czech imports. Three minutes later he slipped into a shop called Hard and Fast. All in all, less than five minutes after his encounter with the Mile High bullyboy, Winston started for home with a half-bottle of absinthe the colour of snooker baize, and a selection of adult literature. 'Nothing kinky,' he told the man when he paid, 'just women.'

If he only had twelve hours to live, he might as well make the most of them.

IX

Fahmy was on his own, which, in the words of his favourite singer, was not unusual. Colin was at his karate lesson and Patti was on a date. 'Liar,' he'd said to her as she left. 'Fuck you,' she'd replied. 'At least Western women have a clitoris.' Fahmy didn't know what was the matter with English ladies these days. When he was growing up, women were supposed to be the epitome of gentleness and grace. 'Fragrant blossoms' was what his father called the ones that went to the Saqqara Country Club. Now, if they weren't throwing up in the back of his car they were strutting around with next to nothing on, swearing and giggling. He'd like to get a few of them across his knee, he really would.

'VIPS, how may I serve you?' He made a point to pick up before the fourth ring. He looked at the wall clock behind him: 7.10 p.m. Egyptian pound to a penny it was a call from a pub. A quick after-work drink that had got messy.

'Hello.' Straight off he'd got it wrong. It was a woman.

'Yes, madam, how can I help you?'

'L-Ability?' Young girl, say seventeen, foreign and hesitant.

Fahmy said, 'Madam, I must stop you there. You need to speak to my associate Miss Patricia Moss, she's not presently—'

'Where are you situated?'

'Me, madam, we are just off South Lambeth Road.' He gave the address.

'Is far?'

'Well, that all depends where you are. Most times we recommend a car. But then we're a taxi firm, innit?' He started to laugh and banged his fist on his chest.

She said, 'Of course.' Then she hung up.

Bloody females, thought Fahmy and flicked a page. It was eleven days since his wife had left him. In celebrity circles he'd

WHITE MEAT AND TRAFFIC LIGHTS

already have been seen out with two starlets, possibly dating one of them. In real life it wasn't that easy.

X

Patti tried to elbow herself off the sofa. She was watching last week's videos of *Through the Keyhole* and eating Sherbet Dib Dabs. She'd already eaten the lolly that came with it and was now using a traffic light that, until she'd spotted them in a newsagents in Landsdowne Road, she hadn't thought you could still find. The lolly started off red but as you sucked, it went through amber and ended up a bright green nugget. She considered it an appropriate sweet for a driving instructor.

Problem was, Toyah Wilcox played up to the crowd every time. After each round Patti would exhale in annoyance and cover her Whipsnade Zoo sweatshirt in a fine yellow dust. It made her mad. Everyone knew the audience would clap at anything. Wilcox couldn't guess the Queen if Loyd Grossman was standing outside Buckingham Palace.

Apart from the footballers, most times Patti got it wrong. Sometimes she didn't even get the right sex. Her worst ever guess was Lester Piggot when it turned out to be the couple who made Diana's wedding dress. Everything had seemed so small and she'd been thrown by the coloured silk.

One more episode and then she'd walk down to the lock-up and make a start on that Niva.

'Mo Mowlam,' said Patti aloud, confident after spotting the wig on the dresser and a Riverdance video.

'Will you come through the keyhole please, Mr Leo Sayer,' said Sir David Frost.

'Shit,' said Patti.

Even Wilcox looked put out.

XI

Because of her height, Xenia had worn flat shoes since childhood. Cheap Byelorussian imports with no support, which would make her arches collapse, but at least she didn't loom half a metre over everyone else. Now she was glad of them. She had the address and she went into a food shop to ask the way. Twice she was told to leave if she wasn't buying anything, then an old Chinese man, in a vegetable shop, looked it up in a book and drew her a map. He must have known his writing wasn't clear because he drew pictures. Houses of Parliament, Big Ben, the Thames.

In her primary school a stylised picture of London had hung above a map of the former Soviet Union, as if in judgement, she always thought. She'd said to Helena earlier, 'What sort of a country starts with the word Former, when others start with the word Great?'

'You're lucky,' Helena told her. 'The Ukrainian national anthem starts "Not defeated yet".'

Was it any wonder they'd left?

Xenia knew if she could find the river she'd be all right. A river was a lifeline, Gleb said. But he meant it for fishing for carp in the Volga. Keep going, she told herself. She was hungry. When was the last time she ate? Yesterday, in the car, a chocolate bar that the tall man had given her. Her stomach rumbled and her head ached. When she stepped out to cross the road, cars flew from all directions. Some hooted, men in vans whistled at her even though it was dark and she was no more than a streak in a raincoat. She put her head down and pretended she was just walking back to the apartment in Samara, past the Peace statue and along Dnieper Street.

XII

After three more episodes, when Patti had acquainted herself with the interiors of Ryan Giggs, Max Clifford, a darts player she'd never heard of, Peter Tatchell, Mary Peters and the bassist from Ultravox, Patti knew she wouldn't do the Niva that night. The sugar high from the sherbet had worn off, leaving her restless and irritated. At least if she got her obituary up to date she'd have got somewhere. (She'd already written the epitaph to her TDA career in her head: '*Patti realised it was time to move on and abandon the girlhood dream of global motoring equality.*')

She ran a bath and put a Crystal Gayle CD on. Which was why she didn't hear her phone ring. It was Fahmy. 'Moss, get your lazy arse over here pronto. There's a girl here with your card who wants to see someone. I tell her come back tomorrow but she say she's nowhere to go. Now she cry.' Fahmy held the receiver towards a gulping sound by way of verification. 'Moss, I'm warning you, get your—'

The answerphone cut out.

XIII

'Did you hear from that Freely yet?' Herbert was doing leg lifts in front of the TV.

'Herbert, for the love of God, how can I concentrate on the telly with your bloody leg wafting up and down like that.' Bates was watching a video of the *Hollyoaks* omnibus. He told Mrs King and Herbert he watched it to keep up to date with trends in the junior palate but really it was because of the very hippy, almost beefy look the wide-angle TV gave to the teenage girls. 'They look good enough to eat,' he said to Herbert, though what he really meant was they looked good enough to eat him.

Silence. Herbert moved off the rug away from the TV, went on all fours and started leg raises.

'To think you were going to give freely a Golden Turkey award for services rended,' Herbert said in a short gaspy way.

'Rendered, you pillock,' Bates told him. He dug down the side of the sofa for the remote and flicked the off button. 'Try as I might to avoid Nevski, I bumped into him this afternoon coming out of the test zone. I do believe Mrs King grassed me up, but that's another story.'

Herbert was counting to himself.

'For Christ's sake, man,' bellowed Bates, 'will you stand up? I can't talk to your arse.'

Herbert sat on his knees, beetroot.

'Nevski told me in no uncertain way that if those papers fall into the wrong hands it'll be the end. He's blaming us for the loss and if we don't get our hands on them soon we'll be history.'

Herbert said, 'Bloody Oddjob, who do he think he is?'

Bates ignored him. 'And as I haven't heard from Freely, I've only got one course of action. I'm going to have to go to that filthy city and flush him out. I'll wager he know exactly where that Russian slag is. As they say, Herbert, *cherchez la femme*.'

Herbert didn't know anyone who said that.

Then Bates looked at him square in the eye, unblinking, which over the years Herbert knew was shorthand for straight talking. 'Herbert,' he said gravely, 'we leave at dawn.'

Herbert who had, unbeknown to Bates, been practising pelvic floor exercises, exhaled loudly. 'Can't we send the boys?' he said. 'We're a bit old for that sort of caper.'

'No, Herbert,' Bates told him. 'I've had it with people not carrying out my wishes. Besides that, Nevski's as mad as a ferret down a hole. I'd prefer to be out of the picture.'

They heard the scrunch of tyres on the gravel drive. Dogs awoke and yelped, more annoyed than fierce. The turkeys in the nearest coop went off like a short blast of machine-gun-fire.

'What the hell? It's a bit late for visitors,' Herbert said.

'That'll be the camera crew.' Bates looked at his watch: 9.26 p.m. 'They're late, but what can you expect from the media?'

'What are they up to?' asked Herbert, feverish from exercise and excitement.

Bates said, superior, 'My appeal, Herbert, didn't I say? It's live for the late evening news, though they'll repeat it tomorrow. Might even get a show in the nationals.' Show sounded like shoe.

'What?'

'I'm putting up a ten grand reward for the return of the Raynham lad,' Bates told him casually.

'But I thought we decided the sooner they thought he was dead—'

'Tut tut, Herbert. Who says he's dead? No, this is going to be the best publicity this place has ever had. It'll stop those bloody animal rights people dead.'

Herbert nodded just as Mrs King brought a young woman with a clipboard into the lounge.

XIV

After three ignored messages, in the end Cindy came round to pick up her ski stuff. Winston ignored the first two knocks in case it was Bates or his henchmen. Then, just when he thought the visitor had left, and he got back down to it, she used a key.

'Winston!' Her angry silhouette was a familiar sight framed in the doorjamb. Not so the Pilates teacher behind her, toned and loitering. Winston had his trousers round his ankles and the February edition of *Babes In Uniform* opened at firefighter Ffiona doing spectacular things with a hose attachment. The half-drunk bottle of absinthe was fighting for space on the coffee table stacked with the detritus of singledom.

'Cindy, hi. I was just thinking about you.'

'I bet you were.'

'No, the ski stuff, I got your message. It's in the cupboard, I looked it out, it's all—'

She reddened to the colour of her polo neck. In her log book of past lovers he'd probably scrubbed up pretty well. Affluent lobbyist and would-be writer. Now all of a sudden she was a woman who dated wankers.

They went into the bedroom while Winston pulled his trousers up. To deflect his embarrassment he flicked the TV on to *Newsnight* and threw a copy of the *Economist* over *Babes In Uniform*. When Cindy re-emerged clutching a black bin bag and goggles, she acted as if nothing had happened. The Pilates man was wearing a green ski jacket. True, he looked muscular and blond but he had a hooked nose like a parsnip past its sell by date. Winston's face was a study in concentration. He even nodded when Jeremy Paxman hinted the country was about to be taken over by asylum seekers. What he was really thinking was that he'd blown all chances of reconciliation sky high.

XV

'She's on a date.' Fahmy put the phone down, smiled at the girl and offered her another fig roll. She drank her tea without milk and ate the biscuit in one go. For a skinny thing she sure did have a big appetite. 'You know how you girls are,' he said, 'man crazy.'

She nodded.

Fahmy thought twenty-four years in the cabbying business had made him an expert on human beings. He narrowed his eyes and looked at the girl, surveying her.

'You want lesson, innit?'

'I look for man.'

'Now listen, sweetheart, I don't know the operation Moss is running—'

'He work here?' she asked.

Next door, music from the dungeon reverberated through the floor. The woman smiled and Fahmy saw she was quite beautiful: what would happen if the pages got stuck together and you got a cross between Christina Ricci and Kate Moss.

Then she said, 'Please, I need bathroom.'

Fahmy stood up and pointed down the corridor. When she was out of the room he picked up the phone, pressed redial and hissed into the receiver.

'Moss, get your behind here now. This woman crazy, she want a man. Thanks to you, my sperms is up today. You get her out of here, now.'

He spoke to the answer machine. Patti was still in the bath, sucking on a traffic light, so when she sang the chorus to 'Don't It Make Your Brown Eyes Blue' she dribbled red saliva into the water.

XVI

His strippers were still doing that monkey dance thing. Sticking their tits out and strutting around the stage. When he put it like that, it sounded ridiculous – like a man complaining his wife was too good in bed. Weren't strippers supposed to do that? He took a swig of whisky and tried to blend into the background. It was busy – the horny remnants of a delayed Christmas office do and a bunch of drowsy Middle Easterns waiting for the casinos to get going. Two of the girls were making the rounds with the hostess trolley and (beset as he was with worries) Beaver couldn't help wondering how a saucy pilot outfit might go down.

'Where do you think she's got to?' Ben asked him. When the trolleys were going round, trade at the bar was always slow. He was flicking through a sculpture magazine.

'Who knows?' Beaver said.

'You're too soft on them.'

Beaver looked at him, sarcastic. 'Right.'

'OK, fine,' said Ben, 'sorry I even mentioned it.'

On nights like this Beaver wondered what would have happened if he'd refused to take over his dad's chain of strip clubs. Gone into landscape gardening like he'd always said he would. But as his dad always said, people who look backwards walk into dogs. It was something like that. His dad was a Greek Cypriot and a lot of his sayings lost something in translation. The girl on the stage was dancing to Duran Duran and using too much dry ice. It was expensive but on the other hand it did make the punters drink more.

'You've never seen a woman round here cleaning telephone boxes, have you?' Beaver said, casually.

Ben looked up. 'What, the raped crusader? Are you kidding?'

Beaver looked blank.

Ben went on, 'Wears tartan, yeah?'

Beaver nodded half-heartedly, as if he wasn't sure.

Ben said, 'Yeah, course I know her. She's a one-woman anti-porn mission. Got a thing about prostitutes.' He looked at the stage. 'And strippers. Works for some leftie council. Why do you want to know?'

Beaver looked embarrassed. 'No reason. I caught her yanking our fliers out of phone boxes. It pissed me off, that's all. Fliers cost a bomb.' He took a swig of his drink and said as if it was an afterthought, 'What would she be, in her thirties?'

'No idea,' said Ben. He looked at Beaver. 'Now hang on, boss, you're not telling me you've got the hots for her?'

Beaver rolled his eyes to the ceiling, 'Nah. Course not. What do you take me for?'

The truth was he hadn't been able to stop thinking of that bucket all day.

XVII

When Eleanor Raynham sat down to watch the late local news she clasped an old teddy bear that used to belong to Alan. She corrected herself. *Belonged* to him, even though he was much too old to play with it. Ricky was still at his sister's or at the pub. Not that she considered it fitting for him to be out. He told her he needed to unwind. As if she didn't. The news item was the first up. Read out by a breathless girl, no more than a teenager, who put the emphasis on all the wrong syllables.

'*Suffolk turkey millionaire Selwyn Bates is tonight offering a ten thousand pound reward for information as to the whereabouts of missing teenager Alan Raynham. Our reporter is live at Bates's home close to the Butterballs factory. Nigel.*'

The next shot was inside a whitewashed room, bachelor style, not cosy. The TV flashed a red 'live' logo in the corner.

'*Hello, Judy. Yes, I'm live with turkey multimillionaire Selwyn Bates. Mr Bates, what would you like to say?*'

His face was unshaven and potato lumpy, red and shiny, red like a Desiree. His white hair was scraped over his crown. He wasn't even wearing a tie.

'*The disappearance of young Alan has been a bitter blow to the community. He was a well-liked young lad and well known in the vicinity.*' Then he looked hard into the camera. '*I'm imploring anyone who know something about where he's got to to come forward. In fact anyone what bring information what mean we can get him home, I'm offering ten thousand pounds reward.*'

The report ran background clips that she'd seen before. She switched off the set and caressed the teddy bear's ear, thoughtfully. Without realising it, she had started sobbing again.

Chapter Five

I

'Why you never answer your phone, Moss?' Fahmy's voice stung. 'No wonder your business go downhill.'

'No it hasn't,' Patti snapped.

Fahmy said, 'What you mean, you got less clients than a whore with herpes.'

'I have not.' She was about to list them. But that was straying from the matter in hand.

'Look, she's not my responsibility,' she said. 'I don't even know any Russians. Why does she want me?'

'How the hell do I know?' Fahmy had his feet crossed on the desk. The dark rings under his eyes were a bruised purple. For comfort he cupped his genitals. 'She had one of your cards is all I know. Then she say, she's after a man. My marriage is rocky choppy enough as it is at the moment. Is why I put her there.'

Patti said, 'Where?'

'In the lock-up, where else? I have to sleep in the office now. You have problem with that?' Patti didn't. 'Then all I say is, it's my ruddy office.'

Patti had wondered about the monkish truckle bed that had gone up in the corridor outside the bathroom with a pea-green sleeping bag with a flowery lining. For a big man Fahmy travelled Bedouin-light, with only a Timotei shampoo by the sink and a pair of slippers that shimmied along on ballbearings of dust.

Most times, Patti's problems, like her sexual urges, went away of their own accord if she left them long enough. They might resurface later, in which case she ignored them all over again. But Patti had identified this as a concern that was unlikely to go away without direct action. She snatched a spare key to the lock-up on her way out and grunted towards Fahmy who was going through a ledger.

She'd been caught out by yesterday's warmer weather and was wearing a cow-print-edged bomber jacket over a pair of leggings which gave her a middle-aged toddler look. Maybe the leggings emphasised her bum as she walked because she was aware of a tinny boy racer (Ford Escort?) driving towards her from behind in a sexually frustrated way, straining the engine quickly from first to third and then relaxing into fourth as if he'd ejaculated just as he passed her. It was the motoring wolf whistle. She flicked a V sign as the car passed her. Tomorrow, she'd go back to the duffel. Then she saw the Peugeot wasn't driven by a teenage boy but by a shaky old dear whose head hardly showed above the seat. Immediately Patti tried to turn the V sign into an elaborate hair movement but it was too late. Sometimes Patti forgot that it wasn't all about her.

Further down the road she got to thinking. The only possibility that occurred to her was that the woman waiting for her was from her evening class. Patti had surreptitiously dotted half a dozen L-Ability cards around the domestic science module (in drawers, under grills, even in ovens) like an Easter egg hunt. But nothing could explain a desperation to get back on the road that included a twenty-four-hour vigil. Maybe the mystery refresher would have left by the time she got there. This was unlikely, bearing in mind Fahmy had locked her in. ('I can't leave lock-up open overnight, maybe she thief,' he said. Then, 'And, by the way, who the hell does that bloody Lada belong to?' 'I said,' Patti told him truculently, 'it's my brother's. You said it was OK.')

The Russian was lying on the workbench near the door when Patti unchained it. The scene reminded her of those family graves where everyone had their own shelf. Patti inhaled the comforting smell of sawdust and oil. The bare bulb must have been on all night, which would thrill Fahmy. Patti clattered intentionally, hoping to wake her. By now she'd decided the woman was a deranged drug user who had seen her advert in the *South London Press*. It did happen. And more often than the classified advertising rates took account of.

'Hello there,' said Patti, jaunty and businesslike. 'Can I help at all?' The lock-up was under the same railway track as VIPS, only further towards Waterloo. It was a cavern of a place with room enough for seven or so vehicles. Fahmy's dream was to turn it into the second VIPS office, when things picked up. The Lada was at the far end, as far into the curve of the roof as she could park it.

The girl was swathed in a rust-coloured tarpaulin and had a travel rug round her head. 'Mr Farid said you wanted to talk to me,' Patti went on. 'I'm Patti Moss, executive director of L-Ability.'

What happened next was unexpected, even for the most forthright of Patti's refreshers. The woman swivelled her hips and let her feet fall to the floor. She had a monkey wrench in her left hand that she smashed onto the bench, causing a cavalcade of screws to shower onto the concrete floor. For a split second, Patti was struck by the unusual cut of the girl's fringe. Then she realised it was the tassels from the travel rug.

'Not you,' she said low, even and menacing. 'The man I want.'

'What man would that be exactly?' Patti said calmly.

'His car here.' She stabbed a finger out of the tarpaulin towards the Niva.

Patti said, 'Oh shit.'

II

Selwyn and Herbert set off in a spirit of fiesta. Bates wore a green worsted suit and Herbert put on his best leatherette trousers. 'We're not taking the Ford Mustang, Herbert. It's the devil's work to drive it around London.' Instead they boarded the 10.10 from Ipswich. They were later starting off than he'd hoped for, but as Bates pointed out, London could have been taken over by Martians in the time it took for Mrs King to come up with a couple of bacon butties. Bates was a great devotee of Anglia Railways, even more so after they named one of their first-class carriages after him. (What a day that had been. A junior minister for transport had turned up to watch Selwyn cut the ribbon. According to Mrs King, he'd propositioned her in the economy toilets. Bates told her, 'In your dreams.') What an honour. What an accolade to have a train carriage named after you. He loved being sandwiched between Delia Smith and Benjamin Britten, he told Herbert, in the rolling-stock sense. 'It really makes me feel like I've arrived.'

'Well, that's a sight more than half these damned trains do,' Herbert, who loved the Ford Mustang, sulked.

They ordered two honey-roast ham and pickle sandwiches for Bates and a healthy eater roll for Herbert and eight large cans of Strongbow from the buffet carriage. Not that the slip of a girl behind the counter even recognised him. When Herbert told her 'turkey magnate', she thought it was a new type of roll. 'For pity's sake,' said Bates and Herbert had to agree.

Now, as Selwyn used his tongue to tease sesame seeds from between his teeth, he found he was fretting. He was worried that his overnight suitcase trolley was too close to the radiator. For research purposes (because he never knew where he might find his Butterballs girl) he travelled with half a pound of 'I Can't Believe It's Not Butter' in a tupper. He used ICBINB because of its spread-straight-from-the-fridge quality. Now, though, he was certain it would have melted. It never was quite the same when it solidified. There was a health and safety issue. After all, he was only thinking of the girls.

Bates stopped wondering – dash it all, the tupper was sealed tight – and picked up his book. Herbert was bent over a 100-page puzzle pamphlet while Bates skimmed a novelette on the making of the TV programme *Popstars*. Five minutes out of Whitham, Herbert took a break and asked, 'Where is this Lobby Force place situated anyway?' Five empty cans of Strongbow lurched from corner to corner of the table.

'Hang on.' Bates fumbled in his pocket for the card. 'Somewhere near Victoria.'

'Where's that?'

'Christ, boy, I don't know. What do you take me for, Judith Chalmers?' He sat back with his chin up, signalling the conversation was over.

Chastised, Herbert went back to his anagrams. The countryside flashed by them in a colourless blur. Bates studied his reflection in the window. He decided he preferred it to a mirror. It showed the overall shape but without any actual definition and colour.

Suddenly Herbert looked up. 'Oddjob see us go?'

'No, he's been in the test zone all morning and best part of last night. He reckon he's struck a problem.'

'Not a serious one, is it?'

Bates said, irritated, 'Christ alive, now I'm supposed to be Albert Einstein. Will you, please, rap up?'

Herbert had no concept of the difficulties Selwyn's life encompassed. Sometimes Selwyn wondered if he was there just for the ride. He studied him with vague hostility. Herbert made perfect sense in the context of the farm (backing up his anti-Mrs King campaign, letting him win at croquet, helping jump-start the golf buggies) but now he wasn't so sure about him. Did any men of his age wear plastic trousers? And the patchy way his fake tan had gone on was making him look jaundiced.

In a flash Bates felt guilty. Truth was, once he found his Butterballs girl, he was thinking about giving Herbert the old heave-ho. But not just yet.

Bates said in the spirit of reconciliation, 'I see one of them Popstars is a local girl from Frinton way. What say we give her a Golden Turkey award?'

Retaining was what you did with old retainers.

III

'Do you wish to carry on holding?'

Before Patti could answer, the receptionist flicked her back onto a pop tune she didn't recognise but could narrow it down to the easy listening section. It surprised her, she expected a left-wing council to be more world music than Matt Munro, but then everyone knew the political climate was changing.

She looked at the LCD monitor on the phone. She'd been on the line for thirteen minutes, being bounced around the building from the Sanitary Department to the Press Office. After fourteen minutes twelve seconds a woman's voice said, 'This is Emily Embargo speaking.' Patti missed the surname but it sounded like embargo.

'Is that the Education Department?'

'It's Learning Needs.' Disapproval reverberated down the line with her disembodied voice.

'Does that mean education?'

'We call it learning needs now.'

Patti said, 'Oh,' and weighed up the information. Maybe it was because of her size but, unless she had to deliberately speak like a grown-up, most people took her to be a child on the phone.

Silence.

Emily Embargo snapped, 'Can I help you?'

Patti fortified herself by the £156 monthly council tax direct debit. 'Actually, you can. I am an HND student of demographics at the University of Battersea.' Patti waited a split second for any objections, then said, 'I wonder if you might be able to help. You see, my dissertation is on the efficacy of adult learning within the context of an urban framework.'

'Have you tried Information?'

'Information told me to try Education.'

Emily Embargo said scratchily, 'There is no Education. What about the Press Office?'

'They told me to try Information.'

Silence. Patti thought she must have hung up. 'Hello, hello?'

Emily Embargo said tiredly, 'What?' In Patti's experience only very ugly or very beautiful people were this unhelpful.

'I'm conducting research into evening classes,' Patti told her.

Embargo didn't speak.

Patti said, 'But my specific interest can be narrowed down.' She paused. 'You see, I'm interested in classes specifically conducted at secondary schools. In the South Lambeth Road area.'

Silence. Patti looked across the road. She had as long as it took for Fahmy to get to the deli, queue, order his elevenses slice of cake, chat up the waitress and get back. Then she remembered Fahmy was in self-imposed exile from women. That sliced three minutes off his estimated time of arrival. She had to hurry.

'In essence, I need the names and addresses of attendees at classes at Wycliff Secondary School on, say, Wednesday, the thirty-first of January?' She kept her voice even and raised the intonation at the end, hoping to carry Embargo with her on a wave of enthusiasm. 'From seven to nine o'clock?' Patti tried to sound confident.

'What for?'

'Research.'

'I'm sorry, you need our How Can We Help You Desk,' said Embargo and hung up.

Patti made a note to herself to vote for whichever party promised the most council cuts in the next local election.

Fahmy walked in as Patti was cursing. He had his arms clamped round himself. 'I never get used to this bloody weather—' He looked at Patti. 'What are you doing in my chair?'

'There was a call, but they hung up.'

Fahmy narrowed his eyes in suspicion. Last November, his phone bill itemised a forty-three-minute call to a premium rate chat line. Collectively, and in his absence, the VIPS staff had blamed Colin.

Fahmy threw his coat on the back of his chair and fumbled for the cake. 'What happened with that girl? You find out how she know you?'

Patti was waiting for this. She spoke in a so-what voice. 'Oh, nothing much, turns out I'd met her before. Her boyfriend kicked her out and she'd nowhere to go.' Patti smiled. 'She's foreign,' she added as if that explained it all.

Fahmy shooed her out of the chair. 'You're joking, right?'

Patti said, 'Why would I joke about that?'

'Because she was a bonkers girl.'

Patti said, wistfully hoping to strike a lovesick chord, 'Yeah, love can make you that way.'

'True,' said Fahmy. He finished the Madeira cake and wiped the crumbs off his cardigan. 'Where she is now?'

'Still at the lock-up.'

Fahmy jabbed his forefinger at her. Even though she was six feet away she noticed its nicotine tip like the rubber thimbles bank tellers used. He said, 'If you think she can stay there you got another think coming. No way. It's council tax and all sorts.'

'You don't pay council tax for staying in a lock-up.'

'Who are you, all of a sudden, Ken Ruddy Livingstone? I tell you, Moss. Get her out.'

Patti mooched restlessly. Then she told Fahmy not to talk to

115

her. She needed time to think. First of all how the Russian had come to be there in the first place. It had taken her thirty minutes of broken English and a trip to the deli for two double espressos and four pain au chocolats two hours earlier to work it out. This was how she figured it. The girl Xenia had picked up the L-Ability card from the floor of the Niva, when some bloke was giving her a lift from Turkey. (It sounded like a hell of a long way and not a journey to be undertaken in a Lada, but Patti let it go.) The man's name was Winston. Patti didn't know any Winstons but maybe the Russian had got that bit wrong.

On the second pain au chocolat it came to her. The time she'd tried to nick the Niva a week or so ago, when it was parked outside the evening class. She didn't remember the details, but sometimes the adrenaline made it like that. But she knew that, in the absence of anything harder, she sometimes used a couple of business cards wedged together to slide the lock (it only worked on a Lada). Somehow one of them must have fallen into the car. As she was working this out, the girl's refrain had got louder. 'I want Winston, I want Winston.' Finally Patti told her to shut up before she strapped her to the bottom of a Eurostar bound for Paris and deported her. 'Hear that?' she said as a train rumbled overhead. 'I tie you to underneath and bye-bye, baby.' She sort of acted it out to make herself understood. But when she got to the waving bye-bye part, the girl started to cry.

Besides that, the stolen Niva part of the equation put Patti on a very sticky wicket vis-à-vis the authorities. She had two options. The first was to find the bloke called Winston (she didn't have to mention the car, just throw them together and run off). That was why she'd tried to get the names from the evening classes. Now she was stumped and it looked as if she was going to have to fall back on Option B. Call Elaine Peroni.

IV

It was one of those days when, on balance, the reasons to stay in bed outweighed those to get up like cartoon scales with a ton weight one side and a feather the other. Not even firefighter Ffion was enough of a lure for Winston to cross the Arctic landscape of his bare boards. He had a hangover from the absinthe that had dehydrated him so much he felt the fluid deserting his eyeballs, mobilised for duty elsewhere in his war-torn body. But then, if he was going to make the call, he should do it now. While the dark shadow of last night's tar still rasped in his throat.

He groped for his mobile without moving his head above the duvet. Overnight he'd notched up two more messages. One from Sheila Sheepshank wanting to know how the tobacco campaign was going. Winston reached across his chest, slowly, to his bedside table for a Camel. The second was from Cindy telling him she'd never been more embarrassed in her life. In the first minutes of semi-conciousness he'd forgotten about that. He flushed red on his throat. Then thought, uptight cow.

Winston knew that at 10.50 a.m. Poppy would leave her desk and spend three minutes buying her tuna nicoise bap from the sandwich man. It was a risk. New Year diets might have made business light and the trolley early. But it was the only window of opportunity he might have that would guarantee he got her voice mail.

The phone rang three times, then, 'Hello, Poppy Blanchard speaking.'

Winston thought, shit. He tightened his neck muscles and croaked, 'Hi, Poppy, it's Winston.'

'God, Winston, you sound terrible.'

'I feel awful. I think it's the flu. I'm not going to make it in today.'

'No, I should think not. You stay there and get better.'

'Who's in?'

'Don't worry, it's quiet. Listen, Winston, don't speak, your voice sounds so rough.'

'OK then, just say I'll be in whenever.'

He was about to hang up when Poppy said. 'Oh, Winston, did you get my message about the gallery thing?'

'Poppy, I don't think, what with my throat like this, I'm probably—'

'Don't worry,' said Poppy, trying to hide her disappointment. 'Another time.' Then she said, 'Christ, Winston, I nearly forgot, there was someone looking for you earlier.'

'Who?'

'Well, I'm no expert, but one of the French exchange guys recognised him. Selwyn Bates was after you.'

Winston gulped.

Poppy said, 'Yeah, God, he's quite creepy in the flesh, isn't he?'

Winston said drily, 'Is he?' and hung up. He pictured Poppy standing there, phone in hand, worrying if it was something she'd said or if she was being too pushy.

Bates on the loose in the city was another reason not to get up. Like any animal, away from his natural habitat, he had the potential to be very dangerous. Winston smoked his Camel to beyond the filter and nipped it out with his fingers, swallowed three Neurofen with spittle his mouth could ill afford to lose, and went back to sleep.

V

At midday when Fahmy disappeared to the loo with a rolled-up copy of *Hello!* under his arm, Patti made the call. There was a wedding day special on Rick Wakeman's son that Patti, optimistically, thought might slow Fahmy down. She couldn't put it off much longer. It was getting complicated, not to mention costly, keeping the Russian in the lock-up. She needed feeding and taking to the loo. Patti was already down a savoury beef Pot Noodle, albeit one that had stayed on the shelf since the BSE crisis. Maybe she ought to have invited the girl home, but then she really would have been lumbered. Patti sometimes read the *Daily Mail*. Give a foreigner an inch and before you knew it truckloads of them appeared claiming asylum.

On the first ring it was picked up. 'Elaine? It's Patti.'

'Oh, hello. How are you feeling?' Straight off Patti smelt a rat. It wasn't like Elaine to ask after her.

'Er, OK, I think,' said Patti nervously. 'What about you?'

'Never better.'

'Really. Why?'

Elaine lowered her voice. 'She's next door, so I can't say too much, but it's Tracey, you remember Tracey?'

'Mad bint who wears a poncho?'

'It's a cape actually, but yes, her.'
'What about her?'
'Well, she's decided to run for Westminster Council. It means she's out of the office a lot more instead of breathing down my neck. She's running on a Women for Freedom of Information/Clean up London/No More Phone Boxes sort of ticket.'
Patti said, 'Quite broad, then.'
'Anyway, what can I do for you?'
Patti said, 'You know about women, don't you?'
Elaine said guardedly, 'Mmmm.' Patti heard her keyboard clunking in the background.
'Immigrants and that. Asylum seekers?' It was such an odd way of putting it. Something about the word 'seek' that hinted at promise. Seek and you shall find. Paradise seekers, New Seekers. It should be more of a get-what-you're-given word. Like asylum hopers.
Elaine stopped typing. 'I suppose.'
'Well, I seem to have one in my lock-up.' Patti paused. 'A Russian one. Teenage girl. At least I think she's Russian.'
Elaine said nothing for a moment. 'You've got a Russian teenage girl immigrant in your lock-up?' She lowered her voice. 'I hope Tracey isn't listening to this.'

Until she heard Elaine's phone ring, Tracey had been going through the spring Katherine Hamnett catalogue. Lunchtime was always the slack time of day for women's issues. Domestically harangued women had been re-housed, overnight complaints from other departments had been dealt with. For a big-boned woman Tracey moved quietly, almost stealthily around the office, which was why Elaine didn't hear her creep towards her. And because Elaine had her back to the room, she didn't see her make the lunge until it was too late. It was a boxer's lunge, precise and well-aimed. Elaine was only aware of a well-tailored arm jut at her from behind.
Patti was speaking when she heard Elaine's wail, outraged and then indignant. Then Tracey came on the line.
'Hello, my name is Tracey McCloud and I am the prospective Westminster councillor for Charing Cross ward. I am

an independent, campaigning for the rights of women everywhere.'

Patti said uncertainly, 'Oh, good.'

'I understand that you may be harbouring an asylum seeker in your garage.'

Instinctively Patti hung up. McCloud must have 1471'd her because the phone rang back immediately. She threw the receiver towards Fahmy, who was returning from the bathroom, as if it was molten steel. He yelped and Patti screamed, 'Quick, Fahmy, fare.'

Fahmy said, 'Idiot girl.' Then he put the receiver to his mouth. 'VIPS. How may I be of service?' He frowned as he listened. 'Immigration? Garage? You ruddy bonkers. I here twenty-four years of paying taxes, now fuck off.' He hung up. 'Wrong number,' he said to Patti.

VI

According to Bates, eating in the Pompeii Pastahouse should guarantee everything was burnt to a cinder. Herbert said he liked his steak well done so they decided to give it a whirl. When it came to it there was no steak so they both ordered *pollo surpriso*, which – when they asked – the waitress said was the same as chicken Kiev, as if she'd already been asked the question a thousand times that day. 'Yeah, the *surpriso* is the price,' Bates told her. 'Fourteen quid for a little lump of chicken. Christ alive.'

He wasn't happy with the starter either. 'I can't stand this foreign muck,' he said, prodding strands of a congealing green pasta with his fork. 'I wouldn't feed it to cattle.'

As far as Herbert's farming knowledge went, you fed chopped up cattle to cattle. He kept quiet.

They wallowed in silence while a waitress whose tiny apron was longer than her skirt, so that from the front it looked like as if she had nothing on, took a family's order.

Then Herbert said dolefully, 'I don't know how they stand it.' To curry favour he added, 'No turkey on the menu nowhere.'

'Not even no cider.' Bates used a bread stick to clean his ear.

A kid at a table opposite did the same and grouched when his father yanked it away.

Herbert said, 'I don't know what's happening to this country.'

Italian waiting staff in the mêlée beyond the double doors yelled in excited voices. Bates said, 'The women are skinny, not a decent pair of breasts between them. I don't know if I can tolerate much more.'

'Now come on, Selwyn,' said Herbert, 'it's not like you to get downhearted.'

'Yeah, well, we haven't seen sight nor sound of that Freely.'

Herbert tried to be upbeat. 'Well, to be fair, we've only tried one place. Cor, I say,' he said excitedly, thinking back, 'that one was a witch.' Herbert used his thumbs and forefingers to pull out his sweatshirt to simulate breasts. He flicked his fringe back and then, in a faux Sloane accent, impersonated Poppy Blanchard. 'I'm sorry, gentlemen, but it is impossible to give out that sort of information. In our line of work we must protect our employees.'

'Our line of work, my foot,' said Bates acidly. 'Stuff her. We'll find that boy, you mark my words.' He downed his house red in one and in the same movement polished off his cup of tea. He thumped his chest and Herbert thought of the pernicious mixture falling down his boss's oesophagus. Bates belched.

'Shouldn't we try the place he was taking the girl?' Herbert suggested. 'Chances are she's still got the bag. Where was it she was going?'

'I'm blessed if I know. They take 'em all over. Mrs King organises that side of it. There's so darned many of 'em these days.'

Herbert said, 'Needle in a haystack job, is it?'

Sometimes, Bates thought, Herbert could sway too easily to the side of pessimism. All of a sudden he felt his mood darken (red wine never served him as well as cider). He was moody and low, and at the same time restless and jumpy, like a turkey in the autumn of its life. He self-diagnosed acute situational anxiety, the type that sometimes struck when he left East Anglia. For that reason he had never left the country and rarely strayed out of his home county.

Sitting around was no good. He said, 'Come on, Herbert, I

reckon it's time we lived a little. Showed this town what Suffolk boys are made of.'

They paid up, left a £1.50 tip, put their coats on and made their way to the matinee of *Starlight Express*.

VII

A good month before the campaign trail was due to start, Tracey McCloud was in a savage frame of mind. 'It's well within my rights to know that sort of information,' she insisted grimly.

Tracey was so close to her that Elaine could see the remnants of her spicy crayfish and rocket wrap between her teeth. 'No, it's not.'

'But you were using a company telephone. Whatever you say is, ipso facto, my business.'

Elaine chuckled hollowly. 'I think you're talking about emails, not speech, and besides, what happened to the freedom of information part of your manifesto?'

Tracey stamped her foot. Then tried cajoling. 'Look, Elaine. We've come a long way, haven't we?'

But Elaine knew the tactic of old, unnerving her with her good cop, bad cop routine. She ignored Tracey and went back to translating an invitation for a repeat smear test into Farsi.

'Imagine how it would be if I really did get into politics,' Tracey wheedled. 'You could be my first lady.'

'Cheers,' said Elaine caustically. 'Anyway, Westminster Council is hardly the White House. It'll be pooper scoopers not cruise missiles.'

When Tracey started to think hard, Elaine imagined she could see the synapses crackle, pulling her face at unexpected angles. Tracey kicked the side of Elaine's desk with her Manolo Blahnik slingbacks. Now her expression reminded Elaine of the faces painted on the tip of Japanese WWII bombers – all teeth and scrunched-up eyes.

'You know what I mean,' Tracey went on. 'If I could get hold of one decent female asylum case, it could be the making of me. If she's young, so much the better. We'd show the truth behind the traffic in young women. It'll knock the right-wing press for six. It's a cast-iron vote winner.'

Suddenly, the thought of Tracey in political office, any office – even hers – terrified Elaine. 'I'll think about it,' she said with a look intended to wither. 'And please, make sure you close the door on your way out.'

Now who was top dog of the patriarchal power structure? After checking the sodium content, Elaine happily munched a celebratory handful of Japanese crackers.

VIII

Like a biblical fisherman, Winston threw out his towel to trawl a different section of the paper towards the bath. So far he'd netted only personal finance and a new pull-out called *You and Your Shed*. The task was made more difficult by the lit cigarette in his left hand, which added fire hazard to the equation. Winston instinctively shied away from matters of savings and pensions, of which he had neither. Which left him *You and Your Shed*. He picked it up with a low level of expectation. An A4 sheet of paper advertising an omega four-based miracle cure for obesity drifted into the bath. In bold letters across the top it asked, 'Have you ever wondered why fish don't get fat?' Winston never had; hadn't occurred to him even to try. For a startling moment he thought of all the other things he hadn't wondered about. Why trees didn't speak French, why dogs couldn't play ping-pong. Then he felt slightly nauseous, hurled the fat cure to the floor and submerged his body.

Easy come, easy go was how Winston viewed the money Bates had given him. Sure, it would have been a relief to pay off some of Tony's debts but then there was comfort in some debts hanging over him. It defined their relationship. Maybe he didn't want to even things out. Maybe on a karmic level that was why the car and the money had been stolen. Maybe he still had some absinthe in his system.

He felt fairly unequivocal about the car too. He'd never earned it, never really needed it and the thought of reporting it stolen just activated a bureaucratic tic in his inner ear. Legally, his ownership would be difficult to prove. But he did object to losing the manuscript. And it surprised him how much. Winston squeezed out a sponge on his head. He'd always kidded on that the reason he wanted an advance on a book was to square up with Tony. Now he was thinking it was more than that. More than an excuse to skive at work or lock himself away when Cindy wanted an opinion on hand-woven Ethiopian rope rugs.

Winston lobbed his cigarette butt at the lavatory and thought about his homework: two thousand words on an emotion of your choice. He hauled himself as far as the mirror. He wiped condensation off it and stared at himself as he went through the alphabet of emotions. Anger, boredom . . . he got to cowardice and stopped.

IX

While Alfie Appleton was waiting for the door to be opened, he jotted down some background notes. Two cars in the drive. A series six black BMW (leather upholstery, right-hand drive), a blue Orion estate and two golf buggies (?). He did it slowly and with the tip of his tongue poking out of the left-hand corner of his mouth. Longhand would have done, but a good reporter knew how to take a note. Of all his new found skills, Alfie loved shorthand the best. A secret code that dazzled everyone from the girl at the cats' home (who had actually asked if he was Arabic) to his Uncle Keith at the abattoir, even though he'd blown it by having to write 'spinal cord' out in full.

'No more bloody animal rights stuff,' Ralph Betts had told Alfie as he was about to get on his bike. 'Try to remember this is a local paper in a *rural* area. We tend not to give a stuff for animal rights.' Betts was mad that *Look East* had scooped them to the Bates appeal. 'Has no one got a contact left in this godforsaken county?' he bellowed across the newsroom. Then he'd turned to Alfie. 'It's your story. Get up to Butterballs and don't bother coming back till you've got something.'

Dogs barked but no one came to the door. Alfie bent over and pulled his cycle clips off, at the same time thinking: wasn't Bates the name of the bloke in *Psycho*? Then he chained his bike out of habit and set off round the back. It was still a good three hours off lighting-up time but a mid-afternoon February gloom had crept up on Alfie the way it does when you're outside. The sky was mud-grey. Inside, he'd have flicked on an overhead light, in a temporary way, expecting to switch it off again. But no lights appeared. It was still eight minutes before the factory klaxon blared out the end of a Butterballs shift. Alfie was catlike on his feet so the gravel didn't crunch underneath him. Ten metres from the door a security light clicked on, making him jump. Unwashed milk bottles with a cloudy sediment circled a foot scraper at the back door. Alfie could very nearly inhale the fishy breath of dog biscuits and dehydrating apples seeping out of the crack under the door. His scrutiny meant he didn't see the light flicker on behind him. When he turned round to face the back of the forecourt, the light was already on, shining round the barn door like an extraterrestrial landing.

In the best tradition of investigative reporters, Alfie followed the tip of his retroussé nose. If it was the gardener, at least he'd know where Bates was. Closer to the stable door the discordant blast of turkey gobble masked his footsteps, soft as they were. Alfie felt he couldn't just barge into the stable. He skirted round the back, past cracked buckets and acidic bags of disused fertiliser. He stopped to pick up a used cartridge and halfway to his knees saw a hole in the stable wall. The wall was unpainted creosote so that the grain of the wood circled it in contours, turning it into an eyehole.

Hunched over with his tiny gymnast's spine all twisted, Alfie took a look. The light was a cold blue, the kind you got from a strip light, and for a split second it reminded him of a fridge. Something about the bars, white and plastic-coated like freezer shelves, instinctively made him shiver.

Right then the Butterballs siren went off and for a microsecond Alfie imagined it was the noise of blood shooting through his brain. He dropped his pencil but in a reflex clutched his notebook hard. He ran as fast as his little legs could carry him, scrambling on the stones to catch up with his body, like a cartoon. His mind was fuzzy and numb as if it had pins and needles. The only thought in his head was why had he bothered to use his bike lock? He didn't realise that from inside the house someone was watching him.

X

Mr Jaycroft didn't tell them to write about what they knew, he told them to write about what they were interested in. Winston's two current concerns were running neck and neck. First, the type of revenge the turkey millionaire might extract for losing the bag when he caught up with him. And second, when was the next time he could reasonably expect to have sexual intercourse? As parallel themes in a bestseller they seemed disjointed at worst, and Martin Amis-ish at best.

Then Winston thought of his third problem, the omnipresent shadow on the lung, called Tony. Sans Palm Pilot, Winston picked up his special Lobby Force pen and started to write. For a celebrated wanker, he was surprised how much it took out of his right wrist. He called the piece 'Cowardice'. He thought about changing names to protect the innocent, but then thought, fuck it. He wrote in an old exercise book in which Cindy had started to note low-fat, low-sodium meals. The last was chickpea and fennel bake. He turned the page. After three attempts to start, he began.

Tony went in first. Legs disappearing through the broken window like a rag doll. A gap of baby skin flashed between T-shirt and jeans, so white I was scared it might reflect headlights driving past. Then he unwound himself and beamed his chipped-tooth market boy's smile. The one that, with his hands wedged deep in his pockets, made old ladies buy an extra metre of binding. Then Jacob the Ladder dived in, ripping his trademark black-hooded sweatshirt on a nail, and me last of all. Even though I was the eldest and it had been my idea. But Tony was like that, brave to the point of simpleton. No noise now, just the wind blowing out the lining of silver birches. We didn't speak, just made our way through the house, expertly, not like they did it on TV.

In those days we divided the rooms. I was electrical; Jacob the Ladder stole the ornaments and CDs; Tony, because of his tailor's eye for detail, was the incidentals man. Jewellery boxes, backs of drawers, plastic in airing cupboards. It was amazing what people kept under piles of polyester cotton. First up he'd strip the master bedroom of its four pillowcases. Swiftly, like a cleaner. Four makeshift swag bags. Tony, kind Tony, the housewives' favourite, liked to disembowel the house, rip it apart, intense and gangly like a madman. That night he was even more agitated, which was why he didn't hear the car. Jacob the Ladder was in my ear like a shot. Shouting because there was no reason not to. Tony was in some bedroom or other, footsteps thudding, making the door frames vibrate. I was halfway up the stairs when Jacob the Ladder grabbed my collar so hard I thought the zip would garrotte me, making me sick to my Adam's apple. His liver breath, Bacardi and BO clinging to my nostrils. Tony still searching, pulling the place apart.

No headlights because the police were there on a tip-off. The Dawsons, squeaky Welsh Methodists, with fish eyes and piecrust faces, had seen the torch bouncing off the ceiling and called because they knew the Joneses were in Florida. Not that we knew that then. The reasons for our downfall only came out at the committal hearing with the Dawsons lined up smugly, in clothes that looked like they'd been made out of spat-out spinach.

Winston put his pen down and wiped his hand over his forehead. It was a start. But of course the robbery hadn't been the painful bit. Nor had worrying whether Tony, caught as they'd made off over the back garden fence, would grass them up. The stomach-gnawing part had been the two years Tony had spent in a Suffolk borstal. A stark quadrangle of buildings built in the nineteenth century as a school to teach English gentlemen how to run the British Empire. And all that time Tony never breathed a word, just kept his secret between Winston and Jacob, and any fixative he could get his hands on.

XI

Of all the routes she could have driven to Hertfordshire, Patti chose the most tortuous. Her mid-afternoon departure at least meant she'd return in the twilight commuter hour. Patti was the only person she knew who loved traffic jams. (Maybe there were others but how people loved to feign business, wearing their exhaustion on their dry-clean-only sleeves like a badge of self-importance.) To Patti, bad traffic meant one thing: a delicious sense of community. Shiny-suited executives shaking their heads into mobile phones, bonding through the medium of Capital FM to seen-it-all-before HGV drivers, lofty and superior in their treetop cabins. She loved the make-believe depression and the thrill of not knowing whether the Cinquecento, with its temperamental Italian engine cooling system, blowing hot and hotter, would make it. And better still the sympathy it evoked when you arrived ashen-faced at your destination. It was like a motoring Munchausen's syndrome.

At just after three, she'd left the Russian in the lock-up with a packet of custard creams and a selection of out-of-date celebrity gossip. To make her feel at home she'd even sorted them so the one with Anna Kournikova in a baby-doll nightie on the cover was on top. Though what pink chiffon had to do with tennis was anyone's guess.

The line of traffic seized up joining the North Circular and then again close to the junction with the M1, which she'd been banking on, what with the closing days of the Ikea January sale. At 4.05 p.m. she called her mother to tell her she'd be late.

'Traffic bad, dear?'

'Chocker.'

Her mother said, '*Shocking?*'

It was near enough.

Mother: 'You know you shouldn't have bothered coming.'

Patti thought, yeah, right. She said, 'Don't be so stupid. I always do, don't I? Look, I've got to go, the lights are on green and there's a police car behind me.'

'All right then, dear, but be careful.'

Nominally Patti was going to see her mother to help re-lay a sliver of carpet under the bay windows in the sitting room. Though her mother didn't know it, Patti had for the last two months (egged on by Elaine) been conducting a ten-step plan to having a better relationship with her. The idea came from an article in the centre pages of *New Year New You* which had come free with *Celebrity*. She was on step seven, 'If you find your mother difficult, confront the issues that divide you.' The article began, 'No matter how difficult we find our mother's behaviour, remember it is not her behaviour per se causing us emotional distress; it is the way we feel about her behaviour.'

Patti didn't understand that bit but then the piece had been written by a woman called Chesley-Anne Burrows, so what could you expect? She parked the Cinquecento a couple of spaces down from the house to stop her mother nagging her over the L-Ability mutilation, as if that had been her fault. (Tell it to the hand, as Elaine might say.) She walked up the path with the usual feelings of guilt. The front flower patch was overgrown and paint was flaking off around the damp course. Patti wondered who put the bins out.

She put her key in the lock, using the same keyring with a silhouette of Paul Weller that she always had. To her, the issue had been crystallised listening to *Desert Island Discs* late last year, a few weeks before Christmas, when Geoff still occupied the two feet three inches of bed to her left (even though he'd gone for a run). He liked Radio Four, she preferred Five Live. The castaway was Beryl Bainbridge or Margaret Drabble or some other grande dame of fiction, maybe A.S. Byatt. Nobody that Patti had really heard of.

Sue Lawley got her onto relationships in that probing way of hers which was nothing more than an ill-concealed attempt to find out if they were being shagged. The castaway was talking about children, her children, when she said, straight out, that she preferred boys to girls. Not just preferred in the bringing up sense but thought they were better than girls. It was just the way she'd been brought up, she said.

Her mum had the television on. A docusoap about the veterinary police department at Gatwick Airport. 'Hi,' said Patti airily. The house smelt of day-old lamb fat and boiled vegetables.

'In here,' she called out from the dining room. She didn't get up like she did when her sons arrived. She was riffling through an old family-sized ice-cream tub marked 'Black and White Photographs'.

'What are you doing?' Patti said accusatorily.

Her mum said, 'Just trying to make some order out of this lot.'

There were some other scraps of family waste in the tub – foreign currency receipts, an old building society book, petrol rationing coupons from the seventies – too official looking to throw out, too serendipitous to know what else to do with. The scene caused Patti a cattle prod of alarm – old people went through their belongings as a prelude to death. During this time their internal heating system failed them and they switched the heating on full.

'Christ, it's hot in here,' said Patti and turned the gas heater off, as if it would make her mother young again.

'How's Geoff?' her mother asked.

You see, thought Patti. There you go. There's the problem.

She said, 'He's fine. Why do you ask?'

Her mum looked her up and down. 'Why shouldn't I ask? Why do you have to be so defensive all the time?'

Patti picked up a picture of her and her two brothers on a swing. They both went so high that at the peak of the swing's arc, she could almost feel the weight of the wood disappearing from under her. No matter how fast Patti rowed her legs in and out, or how hard the chain cut into her bare elbows, she never got that high.

Her mother started telling a story about a family holiday on the Norfolk Broads. Then she asked if Patti wanted a cup of tea.

Patti said, 'Mum, I have an issue.'

'Tissue, dear? On the side.' She put a photo on the table face down. She was wearing a white shirt with a bow at the neck and a straight blue skirt. She always wore outdoor shoes in the house, even if she didn't go out.

They drank their tea. Mrs Moss talked about a dispute with a neighbour's cherry tree and bumping into Mrs Peroni in the library.

Then she said, 'Well then, shall we go and do that carpet? I've moved the bed.'

'On your own?' said Patti. Why didn't you get Richard to help?'

'You know how busy he is.'

They were both on all fours pushing the air bubbles to the skirting board when Patti asked. 'You know boys, Mum.'

'Yes, dear.'

Patti spoke away from her mother, towards the wall. 'Well, you think they're better than girls, don't you?'

Her mother thought for a split second, but really no longer than that.

'Yes, I suppose I do. Why do you ask?'

Patti sat on her haunches. 'Do you think all women your age think that?'

Her mother stopped pushing air bubbles. 'I imagine so. Why?'

'Well, don't you think it might have had a negative effect on me?'

'Like what, dear?'

'Made me feel, I dunno,' she felt embarrassed to say it, 'inadequate.'

'I shouldn't have thought so, dear. Could you pass the Stanley knife?'

Patti was wearing a bottle-green skirt with a kick pleat and knee-length woollen socks; the Axminster prickled her legs. She shook her head, unconsciously fingered the Stanley knife, and thought to herself, this isn't the way a 32-year-old is supposed to get carpet burns.

XII

Beaver Ciriano looked at the cardboard nameplates by the buzzer. One was for a video production company, called Arthouse, written in spindly Gothic font, another was handwritten, The Chocolate Magazine. Two others were indecipherable, and one said Women Trust.

Beaver said to himself, women trust what? In his experience women trust men in surgical masks with an unlimited supply of Novocain. His finger hovered above the buzzer and he had one of those feelings that if he applied just a fly's weight of pressure, his life would never be the same again. He hesitated but the doorway smelt of urine. What made up his mind was a Mediterranean man with a patchy beard and knee-length pale coat bundling in behind him. He said, 'You want chocolate?'

'No, mate,' said Beaver, fake pally. 'I want the women's place.'

The man nodded and let him into a long corridor made up of mirrors. It looked partition-flimsy as if the whole building was a crush of half-divided rooms.

Beaver knocked at a door on the second floor. The corridor was windowless and airless, he worried he might faint. Then the door opened. Tracey McCloud was wearing La Perla matching underwear with a balcony-style bra, a Calvin Klein chemise, a Prada tank top and a functional Karen Millen skirt. She was barefoot, having kicked off her slingbacks for an impromptu shiatsu foot massage. All this technical detail was lost on Beaver who was only aware of her gleaming choirboy's bob and faintly rose-scented perspiration.

'Can I help you at all?' she asked. 'If you want the chocolate mag, you've come up one floor too many. If it's Arthouse, they're on the fourth.'

Beaver said, 'No, actually, it's you I wanted.'

Tracey peered at him over half-moon glasses. 'Do I know you? How did you get in anyway?'

'A chocolate bloke let me in.'

From the corridor to his left, they heard squeals of women arguing, then the heavy thud of boots as one of them came towards them. She was wearing fishnets and a furry bikini.

Tracey said, 'You'd better come in. Strippers, they change here – there's a corridor through to Madame Jo Jo's.'

Beaver said, 'I thought that place closed down last year.'

'It's opened again.' She said it slowly, weighing up how he knew that and why he would care. 'New management.' She turned to face him. 'I'm on my own. But I must warn you there is a rape alarm, linked to every police station in the West End, dotted at secret locations around this office.'

Her figure was statuesque but she had a long graceful neck. Her shins petered out into delicate ankles. She sat behind a desk with a photograph of what Beaver thought was a ball of white wool on her desk. When he looked closer, he saw it was a cat. When she saw him looking at it, she turned it away, not embarrassed, more proprietorial.

'Kitten,' she said.

'Evidently,' said Beaver. He put his hand out, 'James Ciriano, publisher.'

Tracey's little finger rose like a twitch. 'Tracey McCloud, women's issues.' She smiled. 'How can I help you?'

Beaver said, 'Nice office you've got here. You really get to see what's going on.'

Tracey snorted. 'If you mean what's going on in smut and tackiness, then yes, you're absolutely right.' Tracey waved her left arm over her shoulder. 'So, tell me, Mr Ciriano, what kind of publishing are you involved in?'

Beaver's publishing house was called Voyeur; it was a small outfit with a typesetters on Canvey Island that relied heavily on images downloaded from the Internet.

'Well, it's pretty specialist,' he said. 'What you might call niche. You know, pictures, art, contemporary.'

Tracey said, 'Francis Bacon?'

Beaver said, 'Got it in one.'

There was silence in the room. Outside you could hear the electronic beep of a pedestrian crossing and a man shouting, 'Pizza a pound a slice.'

'Miss McCloud—'

'Please, call me Ms.' She was saying it to be friendly.

'It's like this, Ms McCloud. I've read in the paper about your campaign to clean up Soho. Make it more, sort of, family orientated.'

Tracey nodded. She said, enthused, 'That's right, more Covent Garden-esque. As you may know, there are a tremendous lot of very fine women's designers in Covent Garden. They seem to clean up an area immediately. Lend it some sort of cachet.'

Beaver spotted that her excitement had made the channel between her cleavage blush.

'Exactly,' he said. Personally, Beaver hated Covent Garden with its Bavarian Christmas markets and street artists. He once told a string-thin juggler on a unicycle where she could stick her balls. But this was different, this was love. 'Well, put it this way, I'd like to offer up my services.' Beaver put his briefcase on her desk, on top of a shallow pile of papers. He opened it and dragged out two handfuls of fliers. 'And this is just from today.'

Tracey smiled, clasped her hands together and called him, 'You dear sweet man.' Then she said, 'Wherever did you get them all?'

'Here and there,' said Beaver, beaming a shy crusader's smile. What Tracey wouldn't have noticed among the coloured handouts was that there were none for the Mile High Club. Well, reasoned Beaver, there was being in love and there was being a complete prick. After five and a half hours' work, his club was the only one left advertised in any phone box within a two-mile radius.

Tracey beat a 'New in town, 42F will make your dreams come true' card against her ringless left hand contemplatively. Then she said to Beaver, 'Really, this is too much.'

Beaver nodded.

She went on, 'To think men care about this sort of stuff.'

'It was the least I could do,' Beaver told her bashfully.

Tracey said slowly, weighing it up, 'As a businessman who cares passionately about his community, I was wondering if you'd ever thought about getting into politics?'

Beaver looked abashed, then he imagined stuffing campaign leaflets and watching that tongue lick envelope after envelope. It was as if something red had momentarily eclipsed his brain. Within three seconds of the question, he found himself saying, 'Well, it's funny you should mention that . . .'

XIII

Wycliff Secondary School was no exception to the rule that all educational establishments made Patti feel sick and that was before the offal-based incident. If the man who, for want of a better name, she was calling – in line with the Russian's instructions – *Winston*, was attending the evening class, she was sure she would recognise him. She remembered a tall man in a leather jacket had approached the car after she'd been disturbed. He was what girls' magazines of her youth would have called 'mega-tasty'. Not that it was about that.

Patti didn't want to get too close to the school in case she was recognised by one of her former classmates who then took her to be some sort of resentful stalker. The last person she wanted to see was Mrs Griffith gliding along as if she had a tent pole stuck up her back. Car Maintenance came out first in oily boiler suits carrying cans of oil with antennae funnels. They looked pretty jubilant, like marathon runners given water bottles after a race. Patti put their good spirits down to petrol fumes. Next up were Tai Chi, a dozen or so too proud to change out of their padded suits. A thin straggle of serious Ikebana ladies, who looked as if they thought they weren't getting their money's worth.

From her hiding place beyond the corner of a Portakabin she could only see the students by the time they started to fan out across the car park. She was hoping Winston, carless, would be walking to the tube. So far he hadn't emerged. Shit, said Patti and then hung back while her cookery class trooped out, looking defeated. She was just about to give up when she saw him. The leather jacket was a tailored sports coat, fashionable but trying to be timeless. He was on his own, checking messages on a mobile. Patti waited for the coast to clear and darted out. So far she hadn't scripted what she was going to say. She was hoping it would come to her. He was walking towards the road, fast paced, she was behind him so she had to tug on his coat to stop him. He spun round quickly, not expecting his assailant only to come midway up his chest.

Patti panted, 'Are you Winston?'

The man said cautiously, 'Why? Who are you?' He had a five o' clock shadow, or maybe hadn't shaved that day.

She said, 'I think I've found something that belongs to you.'

He said, 'Really?' His eyes were black. All black so you couldn't see where the pupil started. Or maybe it was the light. Traffic was pulling up onto the pavement while a police car with its siren blaring shot down the middle of the road. At the Wheatsheaf pub opposite, a couple of drunks, oblivious to the commotion, sparred ineffectually.

Patti said, 'Well, it's not so much a thing, as a person. I know it might sound funny. But you couldn't come with me, could you? It's probably better if you looked in person. It's important.' She ended the sentence out of breath.

Winston frowned, then nodded. Under the orange glow of the street light he noticed the woman had a heart-shaped birthmark under her left eye like a purplish beauty spot.

Chapter Six

I

Patti weighed up her options. As she saw it, they were: one, initiating a conversation with the stranger; two, getting a cab. Trouble with option two was, by this time all the cabs were heading south. She didn't give up on the idea, though, and every couple of minutes, or when a stream of traffic overtook them, she'd shoot a glance behind her. Then she stopped. It was making her look as if she had an elaborate nervous tic. She had also come within six inches of walking into a lamppost with the number 83, via Tate, bus route nailed on it, and a West Indian man eating a bag of chips.

'Easy, lady, you watch yourself,' he said.

'Sorry,' she muttered.

'Are you all right?' The man, Winston, gave her a sideways glance. Patti knew he didn't mean it in any casual sense but was she all right in the head. For the first time she noticed a rolled-up exercise book in his pocket.

'Yes, of course I am.'

She reckoned he was taller than any other man she had ever walked with. He took giant astronaut's steps that kept his head bobbing so high that, like HGV drivers, he looked down on everything.

Traffic surged past them in frenzied bursts. They walked, Patti's two strides to his one, in and out of food smells, first a chip shop then an Indian takeaway. Halfway to the lock-up, a billboard loomed out of the darkness with Claudia Schiffer writhing around in her underwear. Winston's gaze lingered on it a whole lot longer than it did on the advert with the Ka on it.

OK, thought Patti, spelling the letters slowly in her head. Here is a man who likes to look at beautiful women in underwear. She noticed things like that. He also had the biggest feet of anyone she'd ever met, sloppy like a baby seal's.

Patti asked, 'So, what are you studying?'

'Sorry?'

'At the evening class. You do go? I mean, you're not a teacher or anything?'

'No, God, no. It's a writing course.'

'That's nice. You know. I used to study there too. Small world, hey?'

'Really?' He was uninterested. 'Which A levels are you doing?'

Patti slowed down to make sure he caught her look of bewildered astonishment.

He said, 'Oh, I'm sorry. Which GCSEs are you taking?'

Patti shook her head and thought, what the fuck? She said, 'No, no, not A levels. An evening class, like you.' He must have taken her for a schoolgirl. She knew she shouldn't have worn the cagoule. She was also wearing an old school tie, the type that used to be fashionable in the eighties and were making a comeback on the catwalks of Milan. Those ones might be Dolce e Gabbana, hers was St Albans High School for Girls. But that was the thing about fashion, you had to adapt it. Then she thought, no wonder he'd come with her so easily, he must have thought it was some sort of Girl Scouts bob-a-job week.

'It was cookery actually,' she explained. 'Offal and that. Really useful. Steak and kidney pies, cheese straws, a fricassee with sheep's hearts.'

Patti continued listing recipes until Winston said, 'Look, why am I here?'

Before that there'd seemed to be some tacit understanding that neither of them would mention it.

Patti said, 'It's a bit complicated. It really is best if I just show you. Honestly, we're nearly there.' She nodded gravely in a way supposed to make her look trustworthy. Half a block more and she said, 'What sort of writing?'

He said, 'Creative. You write stories.'

'What about?'

'I don't know. Yourself, emotions. You know. Things that happened in childhood.'

Patti didn't have any supplementary questions other than, 'Does it help?' and if she asked that he really would have her down as a self-help nutter. Not only that but a nutter who watched too much daytime TV. So she speeded up to a half-jogging sort of scamper ahead of him.

The lock-up was just beyond the Vauxhall Tavern, underneath a railway siding. It was terrain that the Lambeth Team Cleansing Department rarely got to. Winston kicked a beer can out of his path. Patti's feet got wound up in a thin red and white plastic bag of chip wrappers.

She said, with a half flourish, 'So then, here we are. Watch the dog dirt.'

Winston looked round sceptically as if it had occurred to him for the first time that it might be some sort of heist. He said, 'Where are we exactly?'

'At the lock-up.'

Patti fumbled in her cagoule for the key. Winston hung back. Patti was anxious to let him know there was nothing to worry about. Her ideal scenario was: foreign girl and tall man are reconciled, in a brother-sisterly sort of way, and then leave fairly swiftish. So that Winston shouldn't recognise his stolen car, Patti had taken the precaution of covering it with the tarpaulin.

She started speaking before she swung open the double doors. She felt unaccountably pleased. It was rare that one of her plans went so well.

She called into the lock-up, 'Hello there. It's me. Didn't I tell you I'd—'

The bare bulb was on and the air had that just-breathed feeling that meant it hadn't been abandoned for long. The empty packet of custard creams were on the bench next to an undisturbed pile of magazines. The radio she'd brought her specially from home was still on, playing 'Rock the Casbah'. Patti felt as if the white board on the far wall, where Fahmy outlined the shape of his tools in black paint, should have an outline of the hunched missing foreigner on it.

She turned to Winston with her palms out and a deliberately

shocked expression. 'Listen, I swear, she was here. A lanky girl, blonde, Russian. She kept asking for you.'

Winston stopped dead still. 'Me?' he said. 'How the hell did she wind up here?'

Patti wasn't listening. 'The bloody little madam, she's gone and done a flaming bunk.' Winston held back by the door. 'And fuck me,' said Patti, exhaling heavily and leaning on the workbench, not even caring where the oil stains went, 'if she hasn't taken the fucking Niva as well.' Then she looked at Winston with round, scared eyes.

He said, 'What fucking Niva?'

Patti said, 'Whoops.'

II

Beaver said, 'OK, just sit there and tell me there's not something weird about what that woman's doing.'

Ben shrugged. 'Other than coiling a live snake up her leg?' The main part of the club was dark, with all eyes on the stage.

Beaver had never understood the snake thing; no matter how hard he tried, he couldn't get reptile and erotic in the same sentence. He thought for a while and said, 'Hey, yeah, you know, maybe that's it. Snakes eat chickens, don't they?'

'What are you talking about?' Ben was at the other side of the bar, cleaning down the counter with a beer mat.

Beaver said, 'I thought maybe a couple of them were doing a St Trinian's thing with a pillow fight. That would have maybe explained it.'

Ben looked up. 'Explained what?'

'The feathers, on the stage,' Beaver told him excitedly. 'Now I get it. It must be that snake. The snake must be eating chickens.'

Ben said, 'Boss, are you sure you're not working too hard?'

By clubland standards it was still early but there were already clusters of men with chairs scooted away from tables towards the stage. Three was the number for a strip club outing, Beaver figured, unless it was a solitary punter, or a stag do. Men, he reckoned, found it uncomfortable being turned on if it was just two of them or even four. Odd numbers were the thing.

WHITE MEAT AND TRAFFIC LIGHTS

Beaver ignored Ben. He said, 'Which one of them does the snake thing? What's her name?'

'Helena, I think,' replied Ben. Then he turned away from the stage. 'Come on, boss, you know this isn't my kind of gig.'

Beaver was impatient. 'I'm not asking you to sit through the Nuremberg trials. You're an art student, aren't you? You study the female form, just tell me what you think.' Now he'd said it, Beaver was wondering if the Nuremberg trials might not be more of Ben's thing after all. That dyed blond hair, erect posture and unforgiving attitude did lend a Hitler Youth-ish look to him.

Helena was on stage massaging chunky thighs and wobbling her backside onto her palms. Early evening only one dancer was on stage, but as the evening pulsated on she was joined by another or, at weekends, two. It never ceased to amaze Beaver how the presence of another dancer could gee up a lacklustre performance. It was primeval, as if they were competing for a mate. Beaver looked around. Not that you could call the current crowd of flabby no-hopers exactly Darwinian.

Out of the dry ice, Snake Woman was joined by a tall thin blonde with triangular peaked breasts. She was more casual in a G-string, rotating her hips in large wide circles and then banging herself against a chrome pole. Beaver preferred it that way; the less gimmicks, the less there was to go wrong. He knew of boa constrictors that had escaped, ping-pong balls that had been lost, tassels that had got stuck. He was never convinced the punters preferred it to an honest-to-god striptease. Eye contact was what punters really liked and for the women to look as if they were enjoying themselves. As he told them time after time, moody they can get at home.

The song was 'Girls On Film' which Beaver had heard in so many strip joints up and down the land he'd got to wondering if Simon Le Bon hadn't been, at one time, on the pay list of Peter Stringfellow. True, the beat was jerky – personally Beaver preferred something flowing, one of them did a dance to a U2 track that he quite enjoyed – but was that enough to explain those movements?

'Right then,' Beaver said. 'Out go the buttocks, little shimmy. Then turn round, out go the tits. Then goes the head and then the bum again—'

'Shut up, can't you? You sound like David Attenborough.'

'Sorry,' said Beaver. 'But do you see what I mean?'

''Fraid not. She looks like your run-of-the-mill bog-standard stripper to me. What're you worried about, anyway? Look at 'em.' He gestured carelessly at the crowd with his arm.

Beaver had to agree. Whatever he thought of it, the new-style dance was whipping the crowd into a beer-sodden frenzy. The girls had reported bigger tips.

'Takings are up,' said Ben.

'True,' said Beaver. Maybe he'd just become oversensitive to the whole naked issue. Especially since he'd agreed to help fund a clean-up Soho campaign (the way he saw it, the less competition for the Mile High, the better). Maybe he was taking things a bit too far. Losing his head. And losing his head was the last thing a man in the porn trade could afford to do. He ought to learn to sit back and just enjoy the show.

III

Patti and Winston ran out of the lock-up at the same time. Patti knew he was angling for a scene of angry confrontation. So she kept telling him, 'Shhh, I'm trying to think.' Winston was looking at his reflection in the window of the tile shop next to the lock-up. Not in a vain way, more in a what-the-fuck-am-I-doing-here sort of way.

She couldn't understand why she hadn't noticed it straight off, the way the tarpaulin was spread out like a picnic rug. What she couldn't get was how the girl had escaped from behind a padlocked door which had been re-locked. What was she, some sort of Russian Uri Geller? Actually, now she thought of it, Patti had a suspicion Uri Geller *was* Russian. She thought some more. She was the only one with a key and, of course, Fahmy.

She pulled out her mobile. She was impressed at how quiet Winston was keeping. She thought he must be used to difficult women. The sudden burst of adrenaline had caused a flash flood of perspiration inside her cagoule.

'VIPS. How can I be of service?'

'Fahmy, it's Patti. You can be of service by letting me know why you let her out.'

There was a five-second delay while Fahmy went through a Rolodex of excuses. Then he said, in a hands up sort of way, 'I never let bonkers girl out. I gave her key. Moss, she has to go to the loo. I will not have Russians peeing in my lock-up. It's health and safety as well as immigration.'

Patti was plaintive. 'Why couldn't you let me deal with it? I was taking her to the loo at the Wheatsheaf.'

'What, you going to keep her there for ever, like little pet?'

'No, of course not. As it happens, I was just returning her to her,' she looked at Winston, 'rightful owner.' He scowled back at her.

'I don't think so, Moss,' said Fahmy.

'Besides that, she's nicked my car.'

Fahmy said, 'Tough cheese. Now get off the line. I got fares coming in.' He hung up.

Winston and Patti half-heartedly started to follow the tyre marks. The chunky trail of the four-by-four veered off the road towards a green slab of scrubby grassland opposite. Clods of earth were dug out where the car had wheel-spun at the edge of the muddy playing field.

'Not much of a driver,' said Patti by way of weary consolation.

'Evidently,' said Winston. Patti kicked at a couple of sods with her plimsoll. Winston said, unexpectedly, 'You're not on your way to a fancy dress party, are you?'

'*No. I am not*,' she screeched. 'Why, are you?'

Winston made at sound between his teeth.

Patti said, 'Look, don't take it out on me because someone's stolen your car. It's not my fault.' Winston's eyebrows winched themselves into overturned L shapes in a look of non-comprehension.

The tyre marks had taken them past an under-fives playground, skirted around an urban farm locked up for the night, and then over a small hillock. After five minutes they were back on the road and it was impossible to tell if the Niva had lurched to the left or right. When they looked up, they were opposite a pub called Raffles.

Winston looked at his watch. 'Come on, we'll get last orders. I need a drink and you've got a lot of explaining to do.'

Patti said acidly, 'Yes, master. Who do you think you are, the Sunhill Bill?'

He ignored her and walked towards the pavement benches of the pub. One was loaded with empty Bacardi Breezers. Patti couldn't believe anyone would sit out in this weather.

She jogged after him sheepishly, swerving to avoid a dog turd and landing half-cocked on a manhole cover. She swore to herself but enjoyed the sensation of being in someone's wake.

IV

Pretty early on in the evening, Bates had become aware that opening conversations in West End bars with the words 'I'm after a woman' was going to get him into a heap of trouble by morning, not to mention an STD clinic. He'd asked at three places. One had a door made up of long strands of multicoloured plastic hanging to the floor that he'd only ever seen before in greengrocer's. The techno music thudded in time to the beat of his migraine which had started halfway through the second act of *Starlight Express*.

'Not just any woman, though,' said Bates to the Middle Eastern man behind the counter. He spoke slowly, fearing a language problem. 'She's tall, blonde, thin as a pole. A Russian, I think, and she's carrying a plastic bag about so big.' He sketched the dimensions of the bag carefully on the counter.

The man told him they didn't do live acts and were strictly imported Dutch videos. He told him to try Medway Street. 'Loads of Eastern Europeans down there, mate, if that's the bag you're into. Personally, I prefer a Brazilian. Know what I mean?' To clarify, he added, 'No pubes whatsoever. Clean as a whistle.'

Charming, said Bates to himself as he left.

Half an hour later, in a swirling mist of dry ice and cigarette smoke, he and Herbert found themselves a hundred quid down. Not that Herbert had paid for much. The only time that one put his hands in his trouser pocket was to scratch his balls.

WHITE MEAT AND TRAFFIC LIGHTS

Then Bates thought that someone had recognised him. They'd pointed over at them and then done a chicken walk which was the traditional sign he'd been spotted. The last thing he needed was the paparazzi on his tail. That's why they'd taken refuge in the Hamster and Hand.

'Funny name for a pub,' said Bates as they swung through the saloon-style doors. He looked round and went on, 'But, by Christ, it's nice to get away from all those women. Come in here to a man's pub where you can have a pint in peace.'

He ordered two bottles of cider at the bar, tutting when the barman told him they didn't have cider on draught.

'Flaming hell, look at the muscles on him,' said Bates as he wiped the back of his hand over his mouth. 'I reckon he'd be an asset to any production line.'

Herbert nodded, and changed the subject. 'Selwyn, we're getting nowhere fast here. You had an address. What say we try there?' Herbert's leatherette trousers creaked against the vinyl bar stool. He drained a packet of spicy cashew nuts into his mouth.

Bates said, 'I told you, I'll be blowed if I can remember it.'

'I bet you will.'

'You what?'

'Be blowed if you remember it.' Herbert pushed his tongue into his cheek to mean fellatio.

Bates replied icily, 'I suppose you think that's funny?' He regretted ever telling Herbert about his Butterballs dream. Though having said that, Herbert had a point. Bates thought about the sealed package of ICBINB in his case. He'd always imagined his Butterballs girl to be a lusty country type. There was no reason why she shouldn't be urban. City girls, with their haughty expressions and stuck-up faces, were more prone to bad habits, after all.

He supped on his cider which he always drank from a glass. Until they'd come into the Hamster and Hand, Bates had been of the opinion that Herbert was about as bumpkin as you could get. He thought back over the day. Take the theatre, for instance. Herbert had used his opera glasses to roam around the audience, flicked sweet wrappers at young mothers and then ripped the cardboard bottom out of his popcorn cone so that when Bates reached into it, well, it didn't bear thinking about. But the cider was starting to weave its calming magic and he was feeling back to his usual charitable self vis-à-vis his old retainer.

'You know, Herbert, I really thought you'd lost the plot walking around in those blasted shiny trousers, but now I'm starting to see they're all the rage—' He turned to find Herbert still wasn't back from the loo. What the devil's he doing in there? he thought to himself. Then he remembered. Italian food sometimes took him that way too.

'Two more bottles, please, barman,' he said, getting into his cider groove. He hopped anxiously from foot to foot while he waited. 'By golly,' he said as he handed over a tenner, 'you're a good-looking boy.' And friendly too, thought Bates, the way he gave his palm a little squeeze. Once you got away from those women, maybe London wasn't so bad after all. He sat down opposite an open-faced lad in denim and waited for Herbert. Then he thought about where they were going to stay. He wondered if he should inquire about them having any rooms out back.

V

'They only had these.' Winston returned to the palm-fringed table with two dense red cocktails.

Patti said, 'What are they?'

'Singapore Slings.'

'But they must do lager,' Patti protested.

'Apparently not, it's Raffles theme night on Thursdays.'

'But I saw some Bacardi Breezers outside.'

Winston said, 'Look, I'm not the fucking manager, all right?'

Patti took a swig of her drink. She grouched, 'I only said.'

Even under the up-light bamboo lampshades, Winston could see she was older than he'd first thought. He didn't expect any grown woman to be that small. She didn't wear make-up, which didn't help him. He found it impossible to age women without make-up, they all seemed to have that pudgy-cheeked infant look. The cocktail tasted surprisingly sour. She used a straw to suck it up, leaving the glass on the table like a milkshake.

So, what's your name?' he said.

WHITE MEAT AND TRAFFIC LIGHTS

She hesitated as if it was a trick question. 'Patti.' Then she added, 'Moss.'

'Really? That was Stirling Moss's wife's name.'

'You're joking.' She didn't mean it as a question.

'No, why would I joke about the wives' names of race-driving champions?'

'No,' Patti told him eagerly, 'it's just I'm in the motor business too.'

'What, like Arthur Daley? That explains the lock-up.'

'No, actually, I run my own driving school. It's called L-Ability. I specialise in getting the over-fifties back behind the wheel.'

Winston cocked his head slightly. 'Is that why you steal cars, then?'

'I'm sorry?'

Next to them the cigarette machine choked out change. The bar showed no signs of slowing down. Actually the reverse – it was getting busier. Winston wondered if the Raffles night wasn't so they could keep Singaporean licensing hours. He was about to repeat the question when his mobile went off. He rooted it out of his jacket pocket. It was a number he didn't recognise. For one demented second he thought it was Mr Jaycroft telling him that on the strength of his opening chapter he'd secured a two-book deal and six-figure advance for *Cowardice*. Winston kicked a small bar stool aside and headed towards the door past two plump girls with underarms squeezing out of sundresses.

'Hello?' He prayed it wasn't Poppy.

He didn't recognise the voice. 'Hello, Mr Freely?' It was old and female. At first he thought it was his mum, but even she was yet to call him 'mister'.

'This is he.'

'Hello there. This is Mrs Tomkinson from upstairs. Do you remember we met during that crime prevention neighbourhood meeting? You gave me your number to liaise about the sign?'

'Yes, of course. What can I do for you?' He thought, not the bloody neighbourhood watch sign again. Not at this time. He went outside where it was quieter.

She said, 'I'm rather afraid it's what we can do for you. Or rather, what my husband has already done for you.'

'What's that, Mrs Tomkinson? Don't tell me he's put the plaque up?'

'Oh, I'm afraid it's nothing like that.'

'What is it?'

She said confidentially, 'Well, it appears you had some visitors earlier.'

'Ye-es.' He said it slow and sarcastic, because the Tomkinsons watched the comings and goings at his flat as if it was a KGB safe house.

She went on, 'My husband was putting the milk out when he saw them. It must have been that French couple on the ground floor, they will leave the front door on the latch. Anyway, your visitors didn't look very nice.'

'Don't worry, Mrs Tomkinson,' said Winston, shivering. 'It was probably my brother Tony, he's like that.'

'Oh, I don't think it was,' she paused, 'unless he uses a crowbar when he visits.'

'I'm sorry?' Winston felt his bowels drop into his ankles.

'Yes, dear, that's what I've been trying to tell you. They were trying to force the lock.'

'Force it?'

'That's what I'm saying,' she told him.

'What did your husband do?'

'Well, nothing. When they saw him they made a dash for it.' She said it proudly because her husband had Parkinson's disease or some muscle spasm thing.

Winston asked, 'What did they look like?' It had to be Tony. But Tony would never break into his flat.

'You know how that hall light plays up. By the time Dennis got there, they'd gone, he hardly saw a thing.'

'How many?' asked Winston, efficiency taking over from panic.

'Now that much he knows. There were two of them.'

'But if it was dark,' protested Winston, 'maybe he got it wrong. They might just have been visitors carrying, I dunno, a bottle of wine or something. How could Mr Tomkinson tell?'

'I don't think so, Mr Freely.'

'Why not?'

'Because they dropped the crowbar on their way out. I'm

looking at it. Don't worry, Dennis used a Marks and Spencer bag to pick it up. It'll only have their prints on it.'

Winston spent the next four minutes persuading her not to call the police. Even if it didn't turn out to be Tony or one of his associates, what were the police going to do? Then he ran through his list of possibles. Chances were, he kept telling himself, it was a random break-in. What else was it going to be, Cindy in a revenge attack? Surely not the turkey men, Bates and his trusty sidekick? Halfway through the call Winston sank onto a bench. He absent-mindedly reached out for an empty bottle and clasped it. Whatever he told himself, he didn't fancy his chances back at his flat. What he really needed was another drink.

VI

Tracey McCloud flicked her hair into a ponytail and, for the third time, went through her wardrobe, mix and matching outfits for the campaign trail. Her *mots de campaign* were feminine and ruthless. She didn't want to come across as one of those female politicians who only do it because they can't get laid, e.g. Anne Widdecombe et al. Goddammit, she wanted to be *desired* in her opening address, and what was wrong with that? Why should men be the only ones in charge of their sexual presence? Since getting home she'd eaten a bowl of brown rice with broccoli and half a packet of pork scratchings that she'd snatched from the kitten's cat feeder. She had, naturally, rinsed the scratchings. She had steam-cleaned the carpet in the hall and vacuumed the remainder of the flat. Then she'd scrubbed three lavatories, two of which hadn't been used, to her certain knowledge, for more than a year.

She had an open bottle of Laphroig on her bedside table, which she drank neat, and was humming happily 'Flower of Scotland'. When she got to 'Proud Edward's Army' she sang out loud using an Egyptian cotton pillow as a pair of bagpipes. The unaffected Prada shift would do to start with but she didn't want to come over as completely utilitarian. Next day would be fluffier. Maybe the Ben de Lisi floral number.

Then she got on to thinking about her election policies and

refilled her tumbler. Ban phone boxes, that one was easy. Campaign for restricted licensing hours, although she wasn't sure how popular that one would be. Besides, wasn't that Tony Blair hell bent on extending them? Third up, ban sex shops. Well, maybe not ban them, maybe for every sex shop you had to have one decent designer. She refilled her tumbler – this happened when she adhered to her Scottish roots and refused to add water to a single malt – drinks went down much faster.

She plodded into the kitchen and ferreted for a notebook and pen. Finding neither, she used a black-and-white DKNY catalogue and an Yves Saint Laurent lipstick.

1. Ban boxes.
2. Sex shops only allowed if come with Ghost (absolute minimum) opposite.
3. Get Elaine to hand over Russian immigrant for blanket media campaign.

By ten forty-five she felt slightly wobbly but at the same time highly desirable. The TV in her room was switched on to *Newsnight* with the sound down because she liked to check out what Kirsty Wark was wearing. Kirsty Wark, though she'd never admit it, was her number one role model. She lay back and stared at the overhead fan

She ran her fingers from her throat downwards. She knew one man who would love to hear from her. She riffled through her crocodile skin clutch bag and dug out a red and black card. James Ciriano, purveyor. Or at least she thought it said purveyor. She held it closer and scrunched up her eyes. It might say surveyor, but that made no sense at all. She stabbed in a mobile number which, from what she could make out, was the only number on it. A voice told her the call could not be connected. When it beeped she purred, 'Hello, James, this is Tracey. I just called because I wanted to tell you how pleased I am to have you riding the campaign trail with me. We're going to whip their asses and lick the opposition. See ya.'

She only hoped it was suggestive enough. She'd got ride, whip, ass and lick into one message. Not bad after a third of a bottle of Scotch. Then she reached over to her bedside cabinet and pulled out a seven-inch vibrator with additional rotation drive and an add-on clitoral stimulator. She adopted her ready-to-be-satisfied pose and thought to herself, why should men be the only ones in charge of their own sexual stimulation? Then another voice in her head told her to shut the fuck up and press the 'on' button.

VII

When Winston returned to the fug, the bar seemed to have notched up to a whole new level of drunkenness. Patti had finished her drink and bought another round. It was gone eleven but there was no suggestion the lights were about to go off over the pool table or that the jukebox was slowing down. The two pudgy girls in sundresses were arguing over selections from the *Best of Wham!*.

Patti said, 'Looks like Harry's.'

'Harry's what?'

'Harry Rafters. Afters. It's a lock-in.'

Winston said, 'Oh, right.'

Patti moved her face towards her drink. 'What's up with you? You've gone all pasty.'

'Thanks.'

'I got you another drink.'

'So I see.'

'So what's the matter? If it's the car, I can explain that.'

'Really.'

'Yeah, course.'

'Well, it's not the car. I mean it is the car. But it's my flat. Someone's tried to break into it.'

'Jeez,' she said, 'what else can go wrong?' She made it sound as if she'd been the one put out by the call.

'That was the upstairs neighbour,' Winston told her.

Patti bit into the complementary pineapple ring that came with the drink. 'Shouldn't you call the police?'

Winston said, 'It's complicated.'

Patti looked at him. Winston polished off his drink in three needy gulps and lit a Camel. She had one of those faces that could either be very beautiful or very ugly depending on how she played it or how others judged it. Out of context, without a mate to say whether she was fanciable or not, Winston couldn't tell. The mouth was downturned, which made her look permanently angry. But something about the birthmark set her face off in a mildly erotic way. The same hint of something to come that he got when Cindy told him she wasn't wearing any underwear.

She smiled at him and the heart-shaped birthmark dimpled upwards. 'You're not having much luck.'

Winston said, 'What do you mean?'

'Well,' she started slowly, finishing her drink. 'I nick your car and then someone breaks into your flat. And,' she pushed her drink towards him, 'it's your round.'

He looked at her, annoyed. 'So you did steal my car.' His reflexes were dulling, comfortably. 'Why the hell would anyone want to take a Lada?'

Patti sank further into her bamboo chair. 'It's complicated.'

Winston went to the bar. When he walked past the Wham! girls one of them nudged the other and giggled. The barman wasn't using optics, just sloshing drinks from open bottles. The round came to seven eighty-three, which Winston thought blankly couldn't be divisible by two.

When he sat down, Patti asked, accusingly, 'What's that?' The drinks had gone from red to amber.

Winston said, 'Straits sling. It's the same as the last one but it's got Benedictine in it.'

'What was in the last one?'

'Gin and cherry brandy.'

She pulled a face that emphasised her broad forehead, making her look foetal. Winston wondered if her mother had drunk a lot during the first three months of pregnancy. She'd given up on the straw and picked up the glass with both hands, drinking quickly. Her nails were short, not bitten but not manicured, and she wore no rings.

She said, 'So then, who is she?'

Winston said reflexively, 'Who?' For a minute, Winston thought she meant Cindy.

'Who?' she repeated sarcastically. 'The girl in the lock-up, who do you think?'

'Oh, her. If it's who I think it is, then she's a friend. Well, a colleague. An acquaintance, sort of. Friend of a friend.' He thought that covered all bases.

Patti nodded. 'What's she doing then?'

Frankie Goes to Hollywood sirened out of the jukebox. The pudgy girls had been joined by two male adolescents who sat on stools next to them, knees spread, with pool queues in their left hands, like chargers.

'*Doing?* She's not doing anything.' Winston had been curious as to how Xenia had ended up in a south London lock-up but he wasn't going to tell her that.

'How did she get here?' Patti asked in that nagging register that Winston believed was issued to all women on birth.

'I don't know, fly?' Winston said. 'How do any foreigners get here?'

Patti frowned. 'I'm just saying it's weird. Her with my business card. What is she, a student? I mean, where the hell's she disappeared to now? Your "friend" has stolen my car. I need that car.'

'Oh great,' said Winston sarcastically. 'You need the car.'

'Well, come on there,' said Patti, 'I stole it fair and square. From what I remember, the driver had even left the keys in it.'

'You're unbelievable. You steal my car and now *you're* pissed off.'

'How do you think *I* felt, some Russian bird turning up unannounced in the middle of the night with Fahmy blaming me for his sperms being up and then her eating all my custard creams.'

Winston had had enough. He stood up. His lowest shirt button caught the edge of a beer mat and flipped it into the ashtray. 'I'm off,' he said.

Patti, who was sulkily making origami shapes out of prawn cocktail-flavoured crisp packets, didn't look up. 'Good,' she said.

Then Winston's shoulders sagged, as if the day had replayed in his head, and at the end the most he could do was limply wave a white flag. He fumbled inside his jacket pocket for his wallet and added, 'To the bar.' He looked at her. 'Do you want another one?' Suddenly it seemed to Winston he had absolutely no reason to go home.

'Same again,' Patti said without looking up. He set off towards the bar. The main body of the pub was in darkness now, with only the counter illuminated. 'Oh, Winston,' she called, sniggering in a nasal way that made Winston think she was going to snot herself, 'can I have some more crisps, please?'

Christ, thought Winston, what does she want? Jam on it? 'Yes, of course,' he said, and smiled his market boy's smile that was the one thing he'd learnt from Tony. Admittedly, she was about as far from his type as it was possible to get, but you never did know.

VIII

Alfie Appleton had never been kidnapped before. The last thing he felt was the dull blow to the back of his head while he was bent over, fumbling with the code of his cycle lock. He remembered the slow-motion split-second of realisation as he fell. He even remembered catching his eye on the handlebar as he keeled over and the sharp jabs of gravel on his palms as he fell.

It was a testament to his cub reporter's instincts that his first thought, after he'd checked for broken bones of which there was none, was how to get the story out. It was only when he heard a voice beside him in the darkness, when he came round groggy and stiff as an anvil, that he thought he might be on to the scoop of the century. Alfie knocked on the wooden floor with his knuckles. Underneath the straw it sounded hollow. Somewhere was the staccato sound of turkeys, scraping and clucking. Alfie imagined himself on a stilted platform. The trapped air smelt thick with straw dust and the chemicals of fertiliser bags that lined the walls. Even at his height he couldn't stand up. He felt like a dog shut in a kennel, or a coffin. For a nanosecond of panic, he worried he couldn't breath and would die a lingering airless death inhaling the sour gritty straw dust. Then he felt a draught blowing underneath him. He rolled to the other wall. Three rotations. What would that be? One and a half metres.

When he awoke again it was to a voice coming from beyond the creosote black wooden wall.

'Who is it?' The voice was young, male and scared.

Alfie said, 'Alfie Appleton, *Eastern Angle*. Who are you?'

'How did you get here?'

Alfie said, 'I don't know, someone grabbed me.' Alfie wasn't interested in his own story, he knew all that. He said anxiously, 'Who did you say you were?'

'Me,' replied the voice, as if it had forgotten, 'I'm Alan Raynham.'

Despite everything, Alfie's tiny stomach back-flipped with excitement. He still had his duffel bag with him. Now the only question was, could he do shorthand in the dark?

IX

Winston groped for his jacket, pulling it up by the tail. 'Come on, I think we should make a move.'

Patti said, 'Whassa time?'

Winston steadied himself and looked at his watch. 'Three thirty.'

'It can't be.'

Winston ignored her. A group of three men were still sitting with their backs to them at the bar, polyester shirts straining over fat backs. They were drinking tumblers of whisky, looking like co-conspirators. Winston said, 'Where do you live?'

Patti said, 'In the lock-up.' Then she started to laugh.

'No, seriously.'

Patti repeated, 'No, seriously.' Then she slipped further down into the bamboo chair and her head flopped back. After ten seconds, though it could have been longer, she started dribbling snores. It was only then that Winston realised she had a piece of kiwi fruit stuck underneath her chin.

The barman sauntered over as if he was immune to the effects of alcohol. 'Time we were having you.' He looked at Winston. 'Is she with you?'

Winston said, 'Kinda,' and tried to pull Patti's cagoule over her head. He removed her school tie in case of asphyxiation and put it in the zip pouch at the front. Along with a wrapper for a Freddo the Frog chocolate bar, and half a packet of Fruit Polos, was the key she'd used to unpadlock the garage.

'Looks like she's had a bit too much, mate.' The barman's

fringe fell on his forehead in a half-moon so perfect it looked as if it'd been painted on.

'Yeah, well, she's not very big,' said Winston.

'You'll have a job getting a taxi to take her in that state.' He collected glasses by pushing four sausage fingers into them.

'We live close by.'

By the time he'd bundled her out, a fine drizzle had left a greasy layer on the pavement. It smelt of blocked drains. Somewhere to their left he heard the hollow twang of a car lock being activated. She was an easy weight and height to manhandle, even with eight measures of gin and cherry brandy inside him. He did it by maintaining a constant pressure under his armpit as if he was carrying a plank. He set off across the park, hauling her like a soldier returning from the front. His choices were, leave her on a park bench or deliver her to the lock-up.

'Whaddya doing?' She turned her head so the words muffled into his chest.

'Taking you home,' said Winston.

He propped her against the door, keeping her up with his free hand while he unlocked the door. She'd left the light on; the radio had moved onto mood music for lovers. He stretched the tarpaulin out and swaddled her limp body in it. It reminded him of lifting his grandma from chair to chair just before she died. It was the same yielding sort of flesh, all too happy to be handed over to someone else. He had been cold but after five minutes of parcelling her, he was running a sweat.

He leant against a workbench and looked at her. When she exhaled, a bubble of saliva inflated and deflated over her mouth. It burst and she opened her eyes with a start. She said to the moss-covered ceiling, 'Fuck, Beryl Bainbridge' – at least that's what it sounded like – and fell back into a semi-coma.

X

Because he used a pencil, it didn't matter if Alfie wrote upside down. But the back of his head had come up like a lead balloon, which made lying on his back painful. For no particular reason he could think of, the backs of his legs hurt, as if he'd been playing football. He put his bag under his left ear (the graze over his eye where he'd clipped his handlebars felt as raw as a cut of his uncle's meat) and turned to face the wall.

'Alan,' he said, 'can you hear me?'

'Yeah.'

'What time do you reckon it is?' A good newspaperman dated his piece exactly.

'Sometime after midnight, the moon's halfway over.'

'How long have you been here?'

'Ten days.'

'How can you tell?'

'Well, it's not difficult, and I haven't got a hell of a lot on at the moment. I put a piece of straw in my sock every day. And I can count it by the Butterballs siren.'

'Do they feed you?' Alfie had no idea who the 'they' were.

'On and off they push a bowl of something through the hatch. One time it was a slice of pizza.' Then he said, puzzlement tinged with annoyance, 'Anyway, who are you? What happened to you?'

Alfie didn't know how much time he'd got. He said, 'I'll tell you later but now I've got to ask you some questions.' He waited for it to sink in. 'Do you mind?' It was important to win the interviewee's trust.

'Why the hell would I?' He sounded annoyed and sceptical. That was to be expected.

Alfie said, 'How old are you, Alan?'

'Fifteen.'

'And can I check that's Alan with one l or two?'

'What the f—'

'It's just that the news editor's a stickler for that sort of thing.'

Alan told him, 'One l.'

Alfie said, 'Pupil of St Joseph's in—'

'Yes,' he snapped.

'Studying?' Alfie left it hanging.

'Look, my name's Alan Raynham, one l, one h. I'm in year eleven at St Joseph's in Sudbury. I'm sitting GCSEs in maths, English, French, RE and design. I play football for a five-a-side team once a week on Tuesdays. My mum works at Butterballs and my dad's a dosser. I have a peanut allergy, for which I don't need to carry adrenaline, and my favourite TV programme is *Buffy the Vampire Slayer*. I smoke Rothmans and drink rum and Coke. I'm an only child. I had a pet rabbit called Giles but it got eaten by a ferret four summers ago. I'm the only boy in my class who's never been laid and I dress to the left. Is there anything else you need to know?'

Alfie couldn't believe his luck. His pencil skimmed excitedly in the blackness across page after page until he thought he had everything down. When he finished he breathed in so hard he sucked up a piece of straw that made him cough. Background detail was everything in proficient journalism.

'OK then, Alan, if I may stop you just there.' Alfie paused.

Alan said, 'Have you got any fags?'

Alfie ignored that. 'So, Alan. How do you find yourself to be here?'

He said caustically, 'Well, Alfie, it's like this. Some bleeder hit me on the back of the head—'

'No, before that. Can you start at the beginning, please?'

Alan sighed. 'I want to be a gamekeeper when I leave school. I know this area, ever since me and me dad used to poach rabbits off Bates's land.'

'That'll be Selwyn Bates, turkey multimillionaire?' clarified Alfie.

'Yes, it would,' said Alan, patient but sarcastic. 'Mostly I knock about on my own, going round the pheasant traps, bagging a few rabbits, nothing much. But occasionally I go out with Herbert – that's like his foreman.'

'Herbert Long,' said Alfie.

'Yeah, Herbert Longshot's what we call him.'

'Why?' asked Alfie.

'It just means he's got a long shot. It's what the kids in the village call him.'

'I see,' said Alfie, although he jotted down a question mark on his pad.

'Anyway, one day, I dunno, a week ago, I'd arranged to meet him. Loose arrangement, it was, and I'm knocking about at the back of these sheds when kerpow, wham bam, someone grabs me from behind. Clobbers me on the head and the next thing I know I'm in this turkey coop.'

'Is that it?' asked Alfie.

'What else were you expecting?'

'I dunno.' Alfie thought he'd be hard pushed to take the news agendas on five continents by storm with this one. He scratched his ear with his pencil.

Alan said, 'What about you? How come you find yourself in this shithole?'

'It was similar. I came up to interview Bates about the reward.'

'What reward?'

'Bates has put up a ten grand reward to get you back.'

'Well, I'll be buggered,' said Alan. 'Crafty sod.'

'Do you think he knows about it then? You being here?' Outside an owl hooted.

'Fuck knows. One of them must. That or there's an abductor doing the rounds.'

Alfie shivered. Then he piped up, 'You know, I saw something before they knocked me out.'

'Oh yeah, what?'

'It was in a shed. I was looking through a hole in the wood. It was, I dunno, weird, all bright inside. Like a spaceship, or a fridge but with people inside. And there was this hum, like a freezer makes.'

Alan said, 'Actually, now you come to say, maybe I saw something like that too. Yeah, but these days, I don't know, I can't remember. My whole head seems to have turned to rat shit. You know, like when you've done too many mushrooms.' He was a Suffolk boy but his accent was more Essex, as if it came from an island, Canvey or Hayling.

Alfie thought, good job I cancelled the pic of Eleanor Raynham weeping over the lad's teddy bear. He said, 'Course.'

There was silence for a couple of minutes, or longer.

'There's something really weird going on here,' Alfie said.

'Don't tell me, and you're going to get to the bottom of it,' said Alan. 'You know what you are? A cross between one of the Famous Five and Alan Partridge.'

'Thanks,' said Alfie graciously, even though he knew it wasn't really a compliment.

XI

Bates was in his favourite position – legs akimbo at the far end of a single bed.

'Come on, little darling, don't be shy. Spread it all over.' She was chunky and dark, with the faint hint of hair on her upper lip. She also had the hairiest nipples of any woman he'd ever seen. But her breasts, low slung in a nursing bra, were large enough for him to forgive her that. Besides, he'd always been partial to a hairy nipple. She also had a no-nonsense way about her which he appreciated. Strutting about the room in a quaint unaffected way, as if she was used to her own company, with her lower back arched and her dimpled buttocks sticking out. Getting the money beforehand and fragrant babywipes by the bed were both touches that he liked, maybe even showed she cared.

Bates and Herbert had ended up in the only club of ill repute they'd seen advertised after they left the Hamster and Hand. Herbert had returned from the gents red-faced and anxious to get going. It was called the Mile High Club on Parkway Street. The theme seemed to be getting laid at altitude, even though it was in a basement club. 'These London folk think they're too clever by half,' Bates had said, loud enough to be heard as he paid the twenty quid admission.

After they'd watched three or four so-so strippers, about on a par with an Ipswich strip joint, Bates had inquired about extras and been guided upstairs. At first the room had smelt of lavender spray freshener which he imagined masked the smell of the previous incumbent. Now it was back to the acrid smell of stale sex and Bates's aftershave.

'Really smear it. Christ alive. Must I show you? Must I do everything?' Bates took a dollop of I Can't Believe It's Not Butter, held it in the palm of his hand and then dipped his testicles in it.

He said, 'Now you lick.'

English might not have been her first language, so Bates mimed the action, all the time thinking, she'd looked a lot smarter on stage when she'd been manipulating that damned serpent between her legs. Now what was the matter with her? Without uttering a syllable, the woman neatly limboed her rear down, like a chicken, to sit on her haunches. She positioned herself between his legs, moving her head from side to side in a motion that he found about as erotic as going through Mrs King's knicker drawer.

If this was the way these city girls carry on, then you can stick them, he thought, or rather he started to think. He gave the back of the girl's head a pat, really no more than a light prod of encouragement but she started off like a woodpecker, jabbing and stabbing at his genitals like he didn't know what. At first he took them to be tender pecks but then the pain got plain excruciating.

'Christ alive, girl, what the hell do you think you're playing at?'

He got the sentence out a split second before she sank her teeth into his balls.

'My god you've taken my dick off,' yelped Bates and sank back onto the bed screaming and moaning. Blood spurted hard and fast, reaching as far as the wall, not that the girl seemed to mind. She was still bobbing up and down when the paramedic arrived.

XII

Patti woke up to the Eurostar, due to arrive at 5.10 a.m., clunking overhead. Despite the cold and lack of comfort, she managed to prolong her fuddled doze until the clatter of an early morning delivery at the tile shop. Then she rolled over and saw Winston lying three feet from her on top of a flap of tarpaulin, under a travel rug. He opened his eyes at the same time. A white crust had formed in the crease of his lips.

She jumped, yelped inside, and said, 'What the fuck?'

Winston said, 'Look, I had to take you somewhere.'

She said acidly, 'What about home?'

'Oh, silly me. Maybe it was because you couldn't remember where you lived and when I asked you where you lived you told me the lock-up.' He sat up and ran his hand over his face.

'Great, so if I'd told you I was the Duchess of York you'd have taken me to . . .' Patti didn't know where the Duchess of York lived only somewhere big and tasteless.

Winston wondered if he'd ever met anyone so ungrateful. He said, 'I could have left you on a frigging park bench.'

'Oh, thank you very much. Now I get it.'

'Now you get what?'

Patti rolled onto all fours and pushed herself onto her knees and ignored him. She said stridently, 'So what are you doing here?'

'I couldn't lock the door with you in here.'

'Yeah, right.'

Winston shook his head. 'Why are you being like this?'

'Like what?' Patti said.

'Jesus,' said Winston, standing up. He towered over her. He said, matter-of-fact, 'In any case, I've come to a decision.' He looked around the oily chaos of the lock-up.

'Yeah?' said Patti. 'What would that be?'

Winston ran his fingers through his hair. 'I've got a lot riding on that car.'

'Really?' said Patti, not sure if she meant it as a joke.

He went on, 'I'm going after that Lada and, as you're the one responsible for it going missing in the first place, you're coming with me.'

'That's what you think.' Patti, rising, stumbled towards the bench, supporting herself with her arms as if she was exercising her triceps.

'No,' said Winston tiredly, 'that's what I know. Unless, of course, you'd like to get a legal opinion.'

Patti scowled at him. She said, 'Fuck off.' But they both knew she didn't have a leg to stand on. As she said it, her feet slid out from under her and she slumped inch by inch to the floor.

XIII

It was late enough for the sun to be coming up when Nevski, who hadn't slept all night, sat down to write a memo to his colleagues in the Institute of Molecular Science, Dnepretrovskaya Ulitsa, Moscow. The operation was getting more fraught every day.

WHITE MEAT AND TRAFFIC LIGHTS

Bates seemed to have as much security about the place as a zoo park. Casualties, though, were the inevitable result of the pursuit of scientific endeavour. Nevski was quite Mengelian in that belief. What worried him more was the fear that his calculations would go astray. Fall into the hands of a competitor or the scientific authorities. He calmed himself in the knowledge they would mean next to nothing to the casual onlooker in this ill-educated wasteland of a country.

Now, despite the teething problems, they had to be quick. Hadn't he read just the other day that they were conducting tests in the Czech Republic, with only months left before they rolled out the hop formula?

He wrote: 'Stage two trials are now close to completion and the anticipatory start date for the formula is the end of February. Internet sales alone of the drug we put at an estimated four billion US dollars annually. The licence to a major pharmaceutical company could be double that. Gentlemen, we should congratulate ourselves on a job well done.'

Nevski put down the memo, sat back in the swivel chair, and relaxed his shoulders. He felt a current of wellbeing surge through him as, outside in the dawn-lit rain-soaked farmyard, the roosters began to crow.

Chapter Seven

I

At 4.45 a.m. triage nurse Beryl Evans was the twelve-stone carer covering the night shift at UCH's A&E department. She had reasons of her own for grading her patient's injury, on a scale of one to three, a low-priority three. The longer he was kept waiting, the more doctors, housemen and nurses got to know of it. Nurse Evans was short of a date for the Valentine's dinner and she supplemented her lack of looks by her currency of stories. Ever since the Paula Yates thing two years ago, she had been running on empty. This one might just give her a chance with the new anaesthetist in obs and gynae. Bates was unaware that, ever since the Ford Mustang Publicity, his face was as well known on campus as George Clooney's. Lowly nurse or not, Beryl Evans would always be the one who admitted Selwyn Bates with his foreskin hanging by a thread.

Bates sat low down in the bulb of his plastic stackable chair. He was in the first row, even though the queuing system didn't seem to work in a sequential way. Didn't work in any way, if you asked him.

He shouted towards the desk, 'How long will this take? Christ, woman, take a look at me. I've practically bled to death here.' Bates had no idea a penis could bleed so much. He was on his third towel and had finished the paracetamol from Herbert's travelling medical kit.

The nurse had a flat featureless face as unyielding as a bedpan. 'Please take a seat, I have assessed your case and I assure you that you will be seen as soon as possible,' she said.

The desk beneath her was a patchwork of immunisation posters.

Another warned of HIV. Bates shuddered, he had clean forgotten about that one.

'I don't know why I pay my taxes,' he said crabbily.

The nurse sent him a look that meant she'd heard it all before. Was it his imagination or was there the shadow of a smile there too? She picked up the phone.

He turned to Herbert. 'The old bush telegraph. You just see if I'm right. I'll be the laughing stock.'

'Well, pray no one recognises you,' Herbert said. 'At least you've used my name.'

Bates half spat. 'By God, I'm going to sue that harlot for every penny she's got.'

'I wouldn't reckon on her being well off,' Herbert said. 'Chances are she wouldn't be doing that sort of thing if she were.'

Bates didn't need to be reminded of what had got him there in the first place. 'Thank you, Mother Teresa,' he snapped. 'My Christ, that nurse didn't even give me no painkillers. Just some gauze swabs. I mean, I ask you.'

Herbert was biting the lip of a plastic cup. Bates had a copy of *Chat* magazine opened at the centre pages on his lap. The feature was a ten-step guide to maximise your fella's sensual pleasure. A bitter irony, thought Bates, and flicked the page to the TV listings.

Herbert said, 'So tell me again what happened.'

'I've told you. The girl just went mental.'

'Mental how?'

'Mental attacking my dick, like a fucking pneumatic drill.' Bates hushed his voice.

Herbert shook his head. 'What I can't figure out is why.'

'*You* can't figure it out?' Bates was incredulous. 'What's for you to figure out? I'm the one here trying to figure out if I'll ever use my knob again. Christ alive, I come into London with my organ intact and leave with it mutilated like a—'

'Mr Long.' The nurse called him from behind the desk. 'If you'd like to make your way to cubicle three, the doctors will see you now.'

Bates said, 'Doctors, what do you mean, *doctors*? How many of them are there?'

'Please, Mr Long, hurry up.'

Bates jack-knifed himself out of the chair. 'Herbert, fetch a wheelchair.'

When Bates looked back at the nurse, to insinuate he needed professional help moving, she was on the phone, chuckling.

'What wheelchair?' asked Herbert.

'Christ, boy. I'm sitting here with my dick dropping off and I still have to do everything.' Bates needed one hand to hold his trousers up and another to cover himself with *Chat* magazine. By the time he'd shuffled towards the door where he imagined wheelchairs, like supermarket trolleys, would be kept, he said, 'Fuck it,' and decided he might as well shimmy all the way to the cubicle.

'Wait here,' he told Herbert.

The casualty department had been quiet, without the helter-skelter activity you saw on the TV. Apart from a couple of drunks who seemed to be asleep, and a woman with a leg up on her boyfriend's lap, it'd been empty. Which was why Bates had been confident he'd be seen by one half-asleep medical professional, preferably an ample-bosomed motherly type who would smile understandingly and ask no questions. But what he got was a UN-style medical convention – three blue-uniformed female nurses, one white, one black and one Asian. In front of them stood three doctors in white coats, two men (one Arabic and one black) and one white woman. In the background, silhouetted against the blue partition, were two porters of indeterminate sex in green. The atmosphere was on the slightly subdued side of party.

The woman doctor stepped forward. She was taller than six foot, in her late twenties, with long blonde hair scraped back from a suntanned face free of make-up. Bates would have described her as an uncompromising outdoor type, which, of all variants of the female species, was his least favourite.

'All rightie, Mr Long, let's be having a peek at you.' She was also Australian. She jammed her bony hands under his armpits and hauled him onto the bed.

'I wasn't expecting the entire hospital to turn out,' Bates said moodily. He winced as he sat on the bed. 'I thought there would only be one of you.'

'Well, I'm afraid this is a teaching hospital.' She looked round. 'And we're all here to learn.' She looked at the eager faces as she spoke. 'Isn't that right?'

The black one said, 'We just want to gobble up information.' He sounded posher than a newscaster. One of the porters started to cough.

'That's right,' said Bates, 'have a good old laugh at my expense. It wouldn't be the first time a man had an accident, would it?'

'No, of course not.' Her gloved hand removed the towel and the gauze. 'Now let's have a look at the little pecker. It's amazing how sensitive an area it can be.'

There were gasps, Bates liked to think in wonderment at his organ, damaged as it was.

The doctor said, 'Oh, I say.' She looked up. 'Whatever it was has gone all the way through to take a nick out of the glans.' She looked up from crotch to eye level. 'That explains the loss of blood. The penis is very vascular, it can bleed like hell.'

Bates thought: tell me about it. 'It is going to be all right, isn't it?' he demanded, scared. 'What about my balls?'

She spoke to his crotch. 'All rightie, you have a cut in the foreskin that's gone through to the glans. Would anyone care to have a look?'

'Christ alive, woman,' Bates said, 'I'm not a freak show.'

'Yes, please,' said both doctors, two of the nurses and both porters. Ten seconds later when Bates looked down he saw the crowns of six heads swaying over his belly and felt a collective exhalation of hot breath on him.

The black doctor said, 'It's truly amazing the vividness of the tear. It's almost as if he'd been bitten by something.' Others murmured grave assent.

Yeah, yeah, thought Bates. To signal the end of the show he clenched his buttocks together suddenly, causing his penis to shake the onlookers off.

The woman doctor said, 'All rightie then, the choices now are a lignocaine injection to give a local anaesthetic, but I'm wondering if that's not going to be as painful as just stitching it up. What do we think?'

The question wasn't for Bates. Stitching his foreskin without an anaesthetic was making his eyes water.

The Arabic doctor (Wasn't he a bit old to be a student? wondered Bates) said, 'What about a ring block?'

'Ordinarily, yes', she told him, 'but that runs the risk of loss of sensation. I take it you do want to be able to feel your penis again, Mr Long?'

Bates said bitterly, 'What do you think?'

'The injection it is, then. All rightie, I'll warn you, it's going to hurt like hell. Then it'll be a course of one-a-day beta blockers, I'm afraid. To stop you getting any erections while the stitches are in.'

Inwardly Bates shrivelled. 'How long will that be?'

She said, 'Six weeks.'

Then one of them (Christ, if it wasn't a porter) piped up, 'Doctor, I think there's some sort of pus.' Back went the heads. The porter said, 'Around the testicles.'

'Oh, I say,' said the doctor. 'Whatever can that be? This may call for a swab.' She fixed Bates in a level, school-ma'am stare. 'Have you any reason to suspect any infection down there?'

Bates said, 'Um, no. Not as such.' Beyond the cubicle, the clatter of a trolley echoed his confusion.

She peered again. 'Most odd.'

Bates said, 'Well, do you know, I think it might be butter, or actually, if it makes any medical difference, I Can't Believe It's Not Butter. The thing was,' he looked around the faces boldly, 'I was making sandwiches this morning and because I was in a rush I didn't have any clothes on.'

Faces around him nodded, though no one, not even the Aussie woman, was looking at him.

He went on, 'You see, my table is at waist height. Like tables are. I forgot you can spread I Can't Believe It's Not Butter straight from the fridge so I dug into it hard with my knife. The knife missed the butter and, well, you see the results.'

'Course we do,' said the doctor. 'Honestly, Mr Long, it could happen to anyone.'

'Yes, that's exactly what I thought,' said Bates and through the pain even managed a smile. He thought to himself, these doctors really aren't so smart.

II

'Don't you need to go home for anything?' Patti spoke out of the corner of her mouth as she drank water from a pint glass, the dimpled type you only get if you steal them from a pub. She chugged down two adult doses of Ibuprofen. Her sentiment was kind but the tone was hostile.

'You're not supposed to take those on an empty stomach,' said Winston and put his hand out for the packet.

'Sorry, oh wise one,' said Patti, swaying her head like an eastern mystic. 'For your information, I've already had half a Sherbet Dib Dab.'

'What, for breakfast?'

'Certainly. It's a sugar boost.'

'That's vile. What can I have?'

'How about fruit salad?'

Winston said, 'Excellent.'

Patti handed him a small bag as big as her fist. 'Fruit Salads or Black Jacks. You choose.'

'I didn't think you meant the penny chew.'

'Suit yourself, I'm having a shower.'

Because there was a hygiene issue about sleeping on a filthy tarpaulin, Patti washed her hair and went as far as to condition it. She took a change of clothes with her into the bathroom so that when she re-emerged she was fully dressed, even down to her shoes.

'Good God,' said Winston. 'That was quick.'

Patti didn't reply. She picked up her mail and put it on the kitchen table unopened. There was one answerphone message, from Rory asking about the car. She played it while Winston was milling around in the kitchen, not acting like an uninvited guest at all.

'Why do you eat all this crap, anyway?' he called through to her. 'I thought you said you did a cookery course.'

'I've got an eating disorder,' Patti told him.

'Like what?'

Patti appeared in the doorway, her hair still wet. Winston was skimming through the local paper uninterestedly.

'Like, I'm addicted to sweets from the seventies.'
'Why?'
'Why the seventies, or why, why?'
Winston looked up. 'Why, why?'
'It dates from a childhood incident that I'm not comfortable talking about,' Patti told him.
'Fair enough,' Winston said, and went back to the classifieds. Patti wasn't sure about her past being discounted so quickly.

She sat down opposite him and propped her chin on her elbows. She thought, in the sober light of day, Winston wasn't really all that great. The skin on his face where it met the crease of his nose was red and, close up, his lips were quite dry, even yellowish. He seemed unnaturally large in the flat. On the other hand, she liked the shape of his thighs and the way he stared straight at her when he spoke.

'Don't you need to shave or something?' she said.
'Nah,' said Winston. 'I'll be all right for a couple of days.'
'*Couple?*'
'Well, we'll see how we get on,' he added pleasantly. 'I wouldn't mind a shower, though.'
'Help yourself,' said Patti grudgingly. Then she said, 'I've got a lesson at eleven.'
'Great,' he called from down the corridor. 'I'll come too.'
Patti repeated what he'd said with a screwed-up scowl like a schoolgirl. Then she said, 'What about your job?'
'I'm off sick.'
'What's supposed to be the matter with you?'
'Just sickness,' said Winston as he closed the door. Patti nodded, as if she knew how he felt.

III

Xenia had only driven a tractor before. She thought that was the reason she found herself so naturally drawn to grassland – and that included verges. Roads were a different thing altogether with their straitjacket lanes and traffic flying at you from all different angles. After she'd left the lock-up she'd lumbered across a park, randomly going up and down the gears until, faced by an oncoming boy on a bicycle, she'd swerved down a back alley. It ended in a cul-de-sac of disused office space. Looking back, she'd gone no further than half a kilometre from where she'd started. Suddenly exhausted, she slept self-compacted on the back seat. Every time, in the eight or nine occasions she'd shuddered awake, she'd regretted more bitterly that, in the split second it took to decide to take the car, she'd forgotten the travel rug. She used an old newspaper as a buffer between her head and the frozen metal interior.

In the murky half-dawn she'd woken herself up for good, started the engine and flicked on the heater. She sat staring straight ahead for hours listening to the rattle of the heater and the hum of far off traffic. She was thirsty and her belly ached from hunger. More painful than that was not knowing what to do next – the hollow panic of abandonment. Maybe she ought to go back to the garage; even though that little spiky girl had locked her in, she'd at least fed her. It must have been around nine or ten o'clock when office workers passed her, making their grim-faced trip to work.

Xenia sank further onto the back seat, hoping no one would see her. Most of all she feared being reported to the police. She had no passport and no papers in a foreign land. God alone knew what they would do to her. She wanted to be around her own people. Russians would look after her. But where were they? Maybe they lived in one area, like Chinatown in Moscow. She'd met only one and that had been at the strip club and she'd been Ukrainian. She couldn't go back there. Maybe she could get Helena and they could drive back to Russia together. She pushed herself through the gap in the seats and into the front and then rested her head on the steering wheel. In the rear window she saw uniformed children ambling to school so slowly that the kids on bicycles tottering alongside almost fell off.

She thought of the club and wondered if she'd be able to find it again. At least from what she remembered from her long walk the roads towards the centre were straight with very little in the way of grassland.

IV

Churches and hospitals always gave Beaver what his mother called

WHITE MEAT AND TRAFFIC LIGHTS

the heebie-jeebies. For years, and because she was so prone to them, Beaver thought they were an actual complaint like chilblains. He imagined them as red sores in invisible grown-up places. His mother got them when the rent man was due, when she couldn't pay the catalogue and every time the phone rang and his father wasn't at home. In Beaver's case, what more than compensated for it, in hospitals at least, was the cleanliness and number of women whose entire job it was to clean and be clean. He sometimes thought if he was ever blessed with a daughter he would call her Sterility. Sterility Ciriano had a nice ring to it.

The flower-seller had just opened when he arrived. He was hawking bunches out of an old-style wooden barrow with Nell Gwyn on the side in old-fashioned writing.

'I thought she was oranges,' Beaver said.

The flower-seller had a weather-tanned face and open pores you could drive a fence picket through. 'I used to do fruit and that but there's no call for it these days.'

'Really?'

'All that peeling. All them pips. People'd prefer to take a vitamin pill. I can't stand all of that. Maternity, is it?'

Beaver said, 'Sorry?'

'You, maternity. You're all edgy like an expectant father.'

'Not exactly,' Beaver told him.

'Only you don't want to be giving her them lilies, that's more of a tragic flower.'

'That'll do fine,' said Beaver and bought a bunch of half a dozen.

He bought the bouquet more to hide his unease than as a gift. Besides, he didn't think the short-stay principle of the casualty department would encourage flowers. Beaver was peering over the reception desk trying to read an upside-down log book when the duty nurse caught him.

'Can I help you? It's no good looking there, we're on the computer data base now.'

'Oh, right,' said Beaver, blushing. 'I'm looking for a bloke that was admitted earlier this morning, around five-ish.'

She said nothing.

'He had a problem with his,' Beaver looked down. 'You know, his thing.'

The nurse said, 'Cubicle three. He's waiting for the doctor to stitch him. Take a seat. You are?'

'James Ciriano.' Beaver's eyes met blankness. 'Er, his brother.'

'But he's Long.'

Beaver thought it was a dig at his height. He said, 'Not all of us can be.'

'No,' she said. 'His name is Long.'

'Oh yeah, I'm his half-brother, cousin sort of thing.'

The nurse shook her head and flicked her eyes to the row of chairs, meaning he should take a seat.

Beaver sat down and thought. He'd guessed something like this had been on the verge of happening. Annoyed as he was, he was partly relieved to know his nose as a sex industry professional hadn't let him down. Something weird was happening to the girls. When he'd talked to the one who'd carried out the assault, she'd said nothing. Literally nothing. Just stared at him with popping eyes, shrugging her shoulders up and down in little pulsing movements and blowing her cheeks in and out.

Beaver told her, 'I'm not sure you know the trouble you could be in, young lady.'

No reply.

Beaver carried on, 'That customer would be well within his rights to bring a charge of grievous bodily harm.' She looked at him blankly. 'Do you understand?'

Then she said, 'Book.'

He said, taken aback, 'Pardon?'

'Book,' she repeated.

Beaver agreed. 'Exactly, he could throw the book at you. You could end up in jail.' He wiped his hand across his brow. 'I mean, for crying out loud, what were you thinking of?' But she just turned away from him and barrelled off down the corridor, flapping her arms in impatient little twirls.

'Mr Ciriano, you can go and see Mr Long if you wish,' the nurse on reception desk called to him. 'Second on the right past the double doors.'

The corridor smelt of lemon squash and urine, with floor tiles that shushed the sound of his feet. Outside the cubicle, he coughed and struck his heel on the floor by way of a knock. The flowers went in first to show he came in peace.

The man in bed was older than he'd thought. He looked defeated. He also looked like a man who ought to be in a casualty department for something dignified, like a pulmonary embolism from sitting too long on a flight to Sydney to visit his grandchildren. Not because a Ukrainian whore had half gnawed his dick off. Then he spoke.

'And who the blummen hell do you think you are?' He was looking washed out, with a bruised expression, but not so much that Beaver didn't clock that it was a face he recognised.

'Hang on a minute,' he said. 'You're that turkey geezer. Selwyn something, Selwyn Bates. The guy from East Anglia.'

'And what's it to you?' Bates was guarded, but couldn't resist a flutter of flattery. 'I am Selwyn Bates, head of the Butterballs empire in Suffolk.' He hated to be confused with his Norfolk rival.

Nothing, really. Beaver couldn't help smiling. It was a cheesy simpleton's smile that could do nothing but inflame. But so what? He could have saved himself a tube fare. There was no way the man in the bed in front of him was going to take this any further.

Beaver cleared his throat. 'Sorry. I'm James Ciriano, the owner of the Mile High Club. Where you had your . . .' Beaver glanced respectfully at the bedpan on the bedside table. Not admitting liability was one of his maxims. '. . . setback.'

Bates tried to lever his upper body off the pillows. 'My Christ, boy, you call this a setback? I would hate to see what you call an all-out disaster. What the bloody hell is this then, some sort of after-service care plan?'

A waft of disinfectant billowed in. Beaver instinctively put the lilies in front of him. 'Not in so many words.'

Bates spluttered, 'One of your employees very nearly cost me my manhood. And you call that a blummen setback. Christ alive.' He shook his head from side to side. Beaver loitered. Bates said, 'What I want to know is, what are you going to do about it?'

'What's the state of play now then?' Beaver's eyes flickered down the bed. 'I mean that in the spirit of innocent inquiry.'

Bates face flashed like a beacon. 'I'll bloody bet you do. For your information my foreskin is hanging on by the skin of its teeth.' A gobbet of angry spittle landed on the sheet. He looked Beaver hard in the eye. 'And, by Christ, I mean that quite literally. My whole dick is only there by the grace of God. If you think I'm going to let that,' he stopped, looked round and lowered his voice, 'that *mauler* get away with this, you've got another think coming, my boy.'

Beaver laid the flowers on the bed and stuck his hands in his pockets. A dusting of amber pollen puffed onto Bates's trouser leg. He said, 'OK then, let's talk turkey.' Beaver chose his words deliberately. 'What are your plans then, in that department?'

Bates said, 'I'm going to bring charges of assault.'

'Now, come on,' said Beaver.

'I don't intend to be disfigured for life without some compensation.'

Beaver, cautious, 'Like what?'

'Like,' Bates told him, 'cash.'

'You mean you'd be prepared to testify in a court of law that some woman had a go at your dick?' Beaver had read somewhere the word testify derived from testes, meaning that only men could go in the witness box. He wondered if there wasn't a legal loophole somewhere. He went on, 'Think about the publicity, man. How many mothers want to give their kiddies turkey nuggets made by Captain Thirdeye? I'm only thinking of you.'

Bates was sarcastic. 'Yes, and I thank you for your concern. But you're forgetting one vital detail.'

'Yeah, such as?'

Bates spoke reverentially. 'Mine is not the only dick.' At that moment a crimson-faced man in vinyl trousers batted his way through the curtain with two styrofoam coffees in his hands. In the sterile overhead light his ruddy face was deepened by a frame of dyed black hair. In four seconds flat his scent of citrus burst and menthol cigarettes had engulfed the cubicle.

'Herbert, this is Mr Ciriano. Mr Ciriano, meet my retainer Herbert Long. Herbert will do just about anything for me. Won't you, boy?'

Herbert grinned with Labrador-loyalty, happy to be of help, but as nervous as the last contestant on a Japanese game show.

V

Because of the fortuitous placing of a couple of mini roundabouts and the general veering anticlockwise to the north, Patti was confident that Emily Fricker would be up to the journey.

'I promise you won't have to take a right-hand turn, ever,' Patti assured her expansively. When that didn't convince, she went on, 'It's all lefts, even at the traffic lights.'

'But I don't understand why we even have to go into town,' protested Emily, even smarter than usual in a Max Mara two-piece. Her complexion glittered copper in the light; she'd discovered bronzing balls.

Patti said, 'Emily, it's like your passing-out parade. If you can do this, it means, it means, well, it puts you in the premier league of refreshers, like James Hunt.'

'Michael Schumacher,' said Winston from the back seat.

Emily flicked her head up to indicate the back seat and said petulantly, 'And why's he got to come?'

'Ignore him,' said Patti. 'Treat him like an examiner.'

Emily was plaintive, edged with panic. 'But I keep telling you, I'm not sitting a test. All I have to do is drive around Bexleyheath. When am I ever going to need to drive into the West End?'

Patti said, 'Well, there's the shopping. Just think of what you'd be able to buy. Selfridges, Liberty's, John Lewis.' Patti ran out after three designer retail outlets without getting a nod from Emily. The car was silent apart from the death rattle of the heater. They were parked in a bus stop beyond the lock-up. Patti was anxious to get moving.

'It's always good to stretch ourselves,' said Winston.

Patti looked at him in the rear mirror. 'Yes, thank you, Vanessa Feltz.' She put a reassuring hand on Emily's forearm, which was slumped limply along the handbrake. 'If it gets too much, then someone else will take over.'

Emily said, 'Tell him to get his knees out of my back then.'

Patti turned to the back seat and the large edition *A–Z* slipped onto the floor. 'Can you remove your knees from Mrs Fricker's back?'

Winston nodded. 'There's not a hell of a lot of room in the back of a Cinquecento.'

'Diddums,' said Patti. Then, annoyed, 'Why do you have to sit like that in any case?'

'Like what?'

'With your legs spread three foot apart. Like some he-man porn star. Sit properly.' She turned to face the front and spoke without looking towards Emily. 'Right then, Emily, I'd like you to start the car, slowly pull away in your own time, looking and listening. Then I'd like you to take the next available right turn.'

'Left,' corrected Emily and accidentally activated the windscreen wipers.

'Sorry, said Patti, head down, fixing the route in the *A–Z*. 'My mistake.'

In the back seat Winston drew his legs together, not bowing to Patti's request so much as adopting the crash position.

VI

Tracey had been up since six, when she'd woken with the beginnings of a dehydration headache, making the spirit level in her brain go dangerously out of kilter. Her eyes looked like a 1980s Benetton puffa jacket. She tapped on some La Prairie bag reducer with the middle finger of her right hand. The woman at Harvey Nics had said that the pressure should be lighter if she used her middle finger rather than her forefinger. If she used her forefinger she could 'seriously damage the nerve endings'. Tracey could still hear the doom in that sales assistant's voice. As if she was blinding herself. She checked her cheeks for broken veins and, after a series of fifty chest presses and fifty lunges on both legs, rewarded herself with three Advil and a carrot and ginger smoothie.

She kept her first-aid box along with anything medical, including her special seven-inch battery-operated stress relievers, in her bedside cabinet. 'Typical,' she scoffed when she saw that her ex-lover Gregory had tidied her panty liners into the bandage section of the medical kit. 'Men,' she said. 'Simply no idea.' Gregory was a spare parts specialist from the Kennington branch of Kwik-Fit, who shared her pride of precision. He was the last man to fleetingly share her two-bedroom West Ken mews cottage. And even then she suspected it was only because it allowed him easy access to the car shows at Olympia.

She took the tube to work direct to Leicester Square. Most days throughout the year, Soho was more buzzing at four in the morning than five hours later, which was why Tracey started her rounds at nine. It was too early for the Soho Square habitués. This was the secretaries' hour with underweight women trussed in cheap Hennes macs, bustling from bagel outlets and sucking on double espressos. The only men in sight were those on their way home. 'Typical,' tutted Tracey.

She was down-at-heel chic today, Gap combats and trainers set off by an LK Bennett red leather bag. Make-up was a Versace natural glow, but for daytime wear she'd rather outdazzled herself on the aquamarine eye shadow, causing her to grab a pair of Aviator shades on her way out.

After fifty minutes of patrolling the phone boxes, Tracey had started to smell a rat. She knew olfactory discomfort was not unusual, but this was different. True, Mr Ciriano had put in a tiptop performance denuding the booths yesterday. But today only two fliers were visible, one a white laminated A4 from Women Trust, in eight languages including Tadjik, advising immigrant sex slaves that help was at hand and giving a number to call in confidence. Judging by the lack of response, either these women didn't use phone boxes or Elaine's translation had been piss poor. The other poster was for the Mile High Club on lurid green paper with a half-naked female air hostess licking the fuselage of a model Boeing 747. 'Come fly with me, indeed,' tutted Tracey as she yanked the paper in one savage downward movement.

As she tugged she felt the tremor of her mobile vibrating in her pocket. For half a rotation of head spin the sensation made her forget where she was. Faint spots of rain landed on the window. A homeless man with a deep cut on his forehead and greasy blankets up to his eyes lay unmoving outside a bookshop. A Japanese woman furiously smoking a cigarette stepped over his feet.

'Tracey?'

She recognised Elaine's voice, but Tracey still liked people to explain themselves. She said, 'Speaking.'

'It's me, Elaine. Can you come back to the office ASAP? Something's kicked off.'

'Such as?'

'Such as the *Standard*'s been on the phone. It's about a story.'

'Story?' said Tracey, slow and suspicious but slightly querulous.

'Yeah, don't get carried away, it's only the *Clarion*. It's about those Tamils. I'll tell you later.'

'What about my campaign leaflets, have they arrived yet?'

Elaine said, 'No, the printer's been on the phone, he can't do them. Look, I'll explain when you get here. The other phone's going, I'll see you.'

Tracey returned via Maison Bertrand. She was feeling light-headed. She took a seat in the café and ordered chocolate cake and double espresso. The waiter had a long fringe that he dabbed back onto the top of his head when he leant over and it fell into his eyes. He obviously liked the action, or he had a bad back, because he did it a lot. Tracey imagined a girlfriend long ago had told him it looked sexy and now he was stuck with it. He reminded her of an Italian she'd slept with years ago, one Friday, Good Friday as it turned out. He'd been the slim-hipped waiter when she'd had too much red wine. It had to have been Easter because the next day she only remembered his name (Fabio, Flavio?) from the chocolate letters on an Easter egg on his kitchen table. It was the only time in her life that she'd felt grateful to the oppressively patriarchal institution of the Catholic Church.

Tracey drank up and, boosted by the memory as much as the caffeine, hurried back.

As she burst through the door she said theatrically, as if she had been interviewed coming up the stairs, 'Bloody media.' Even before she'd whipped her cape off.

She sat opposite Elaine. 'Now what?'

Elaine, wearing a military-style shirt that had gone out with the Ark said, 'It's those Tamils.'

For three weeks, the wives of fifteen Tamil Tigers had been drawing attention to the Tamils' plight and their own quest for political asylum. According to the *Soho Clarion* reporter who'd called Tracey last week, the women were existing on nothing more than Starbucks' moccaccinos donated by passing commuters. Tracey liked to steer clear of the actual politics of the developing world, but as she told the reporter, 'What they are fighting over is up to them. The trust is only concerned with hardship. It's a question of human rights. We believe the Tamils and all other asylum seekers should have their benefits increased. Twenty-seven pounds a week in vouchers and ten pounds in cash is not enough for anyone.' She added that with regard to the moccaccinos, Asians were well known for their lactose intolerance.

'What about the Tamils?' Tracey asked Elaine.

'Take a look at page three.'

Tracey scrabbled into the paper. The headline read 'Trust Calls For Extra Tiger Tokens'.

'Jesus Christ, it makes us sound like a bloody Esso garage. It's outrageous. Is it some sort of joke? Haven't these people got anything better to write about than a load of—' She stopped, remembering how central a well-conducted media campaign would be to her election. Now more than ever she needed the oxygen of favourable publicity. She looked at Elaine. Non-power structure or not, it was time to pull rank. She said, 'Have you found that bloody Russian girl yet?'

VII

Winston checked his watch to see if he had the tuna nicoise all-clear, meaning Poppy's voice mail would be on. He used no sudden movements in doing so, trying to keep the fluids in his inner ear calm. Rather than lower his head he brought his wrist into his line of vision with tai chi slowness. Winston had only ever been travel sick twice in a car, both times gelatine-related. The first time was aged nine, being driven home after a Silver Jubilee party on the other side of the village when he'd won the greasy pole competition and celebrated on pineapple jelly. The second was when he'd eaten too much vodka jelly at the Lobby Force party when the Blair Labour government had been elected. It wasn't a political thing, he happened to have the red jelly in front of him. Cindy had picked him up in her Tigra just about the time Portillo lost his seat, to find Winston doing the same two minutes later. That was why, in a Venn diagram sort of way, Winston had gelatine and car travel in two large circles with vomiting in between. Now he wasn't so sure. It had been years since his last jelly and he felt sicker than ever. With underwater grace he pulled his mobile from his inside pocket.

On the third ring she answered.

'This is Poppy Blanchard speaking.' Winston held his breath to see if it was a recorded message. 'How can I help?' Pause. 'Hello?'

Winston said, 'Hello, Poppy. It's Winston.' He was angry. He'd timed it perfectly. He said, 'What the hell's the matter? Doesn't that sandwich man come any more?'

'Winston? Is that you?'

'He used to be regular as clockwork. Has he left or something?'

'Er, no,' said Poppy. 'He's still here.'

'What happened to your baguette then?'

'I've got a wheat allergy,' Poppy told him, 'wheat and tomatoes. I can only eat soda bread.' She was quiet. 'Is that why you called?'

'What?'

'To check up on the sandwich man?'

'No, of course not.'

Emily lurched round the Waterloo roundabout, squashed between a Cherokee Jeep and a fly-faced cycle courier. When Winston looked up to steady himself, he saw the elfin gap between Patti's ears and the start of her hairline. Her ears were tiny, slightly pointed and unpierced. Even though her knuckles were clasped to the side of her seat, she seemed tranquil. The noise of the heater cancelled out the conversation in the front but Patti spoke quietly, firm and comforting. He felt like a child half asleep on the back seat listening to parents.

Poppy said, 'How are you feeling?'

Straight off, perhaps too quick, he told her, 'Rough. Really rough.'

'Have you been to the doctor yet?'

'No, yes, I mean I've made an appointment to go. I'm going this afternoon.'

'Do you need anything bringing over?'

'No, no, really. That's kind, really kind, but I've got everything. Can you just hold the fort there for me? I mean I don't want to come in and make everyone sick.'

'You could never do that.'

Winston thought, was she flirting? In front of him Patti's wrist hovered protectively over the handbrake. She was wearing an amber bangle that clanked on the metal every time Emily swerved. For a split second (the time it took the car to cut up on the inside lane of an iridescent old beemer) it reminded Winston of the noise his mother's wedding ring made on the banister when she came upstairs to tuck him in.

Poppy said, 'Are you still there?'

'Of course. Anything up? At the office, I mean.'

'No, it's pretty quiet. No more turkey man.'

'OK, then. Listen, I'll call you tomorrow.'

Poppy said, 'Are you all right? You sound like you're in an echo chamber.'

'No, I'm fine. I'm in the car. I'm popping to the chemists. It's dangerous, my head's gone funny.' Then he hung up. A minute later – the time it took to crawl past a group of Japanese tourists framing a picture to get the London Eye in the background and for the tone in the front to change from mentoring to bickering – his phone beeped a message. He called the answerphone; there were four new messages, none of which he'd been aware of. He breathed in deeply, lifting his rib cage in a quasi Zen way that Cindy had taught him. Then he remembered she'd learnt it in Pilates. He deliberately started to breathe shallowly, almost panting, like a woman in labour.

Patti turned round. 'What the hell's up with you?'

'Panic attack,' Winston told her.

'If anyone's going to get panicky round here,' Emily scoffed, 'it's going to be me.'

'And me,' Patti piped up. 'I'm the one in the front.' She

swivelled round. 'You need a brown paper bag. Here,' she passed him a sherbet dibdab wrapper, 'use this.' Her tiny fist grabbed the neck of the bag as if she was going to blow it up and burst it. 'Breath into it. You've got too much oxygen in your brain. You need some more carbon dioxide.'

'It's all right,' said Winston, 'it's gone now.'

'Didn't last long,' Patti said to Emily.

'Very short,' agreed the old woman, slightly cheated.

By the time he'd got through to his message service, he'd made a note to himself that neither of his co-passengers was a stranger to mental illness. The first message was from Mrs Tomkinson asking if he wanted the crowbar back. The second was Tony. The message had been received at eight thirty-four, which was absurdly early for him. So early it sent a ricochet of fear-signal chemicals around Winston's body. It was a casual inquiry as to whether Winston had had any further thoughts about the money he'd promised. In the back of his mind Winston had been hoping his brother wouldn't remember. He was wrong. Hastily he pressed the cock-crow three on his phone to delete.

The third message was from Bates, more conciliatory than Winston might have thought possible. There was no mention of the car, or the missing bag, or the girl. Bates was just telling him he was in town if he fancied meeting for a drink.

Winston listened to the fourth message as the Cinquecento turned left, juddering up towards Farringdon Road. It struck Winston that they weren't so much driving into the West End as creeping up on it.

'Hello, this is a message for Mr Winston Freely. Allow me to introduce myself.' The voice was the priggish side of don. 'My name is Andrew Doughty and I am a literary agent to whom your manuscript, *Avanti*, has been passed. And I must say I like what I read. I would be extremely interested in reading more. Or perhaps you could pop in and see me the next time you're in town. In either case I would be thrilled to hear from you.'

Winston liked the way he said *thrilled*. It had been some time since he'd thrilled anyone. The agent left a central London number that Winston recognised as Bloomsbury.

'Well, bugger me,' he said. He collapsed on the back seat. In the front seat Patti was tearing into a Curly Wurly. She turned round. 'Do you mind? There are ladies present, you know.'

'Quite right,' agreed Emily. It was only then that Winston realised Patti was wearing nothing under a green school blazer but a Victorian bustier. The tension in the front seemed to have dispersed as they crossed the river.

Winston angled his head between the seats. 'She needs to turn left along Charterhouse Street, towards High Holborn.'

'Excuse me,' said Patti, 'Mr Know-It-All, Sir Winston, Lord Protector of All Things, I am the one in charge of this lesson, if you don't mind.' Winston sat back. Patti studied the *A–Z* and said, 'Emily, I think you should turn left into Charterhouse Street.' She spoke as if Winston wasn't there. 'Along to High Holborn.'

VIII

Xenia had less parked the car than abandoned it. When the streets became like a fairytale maze and the traffic got angrier and angrier, she figured she was best proceeding on foot. She'd dipped into a space behind a red car. Out of the Lada she was stiff and, without the blast of heat on her face, cold. She needed to remember where she'd left the car, so every time she turned off a street she looked back, trying to fix it in her memory. She'd found some coins in the side pocket next to the driver's seat, enough to get her a coffee and a cake – a pastry one that was the nearest she could find to ones Galia used to make. It was the first time she'd thought about her aunt and uncle that day. When she did she felt a bubble of loneliness in the pit of her stomach, cancelling her hunger.

She didn't feel certain enough to eat inside the café. She ate leaning against a lamppost. Her eyes were hot from exhaustion despite the wind being funnelled down the narrow streets. Opposite her a young man and a dog sat on cardboard at the side of the road, begging like a babushka or an army veteran. Everywhere she turned there were gaggles of young people bursting with machine-gun blasts of laughter. A loud, nightmare noise. As if anything could be that funny. She hated these grinning ear to ear people with makebelieve happy faces like old Soviet posters. At least Russians were honest about misery.

She found the club thirty minutes later, after spotting the supermarket with the yellow logo accidentally, when she was looking back to get her bearings. The steps to the club were in darkness and Xenia was struck that even at midday it was too early for any of the girls to be up. Helena might not even leave that day. If she did she would almost certainly have a guard with her. What if she only wanted to go back to the club? No, surely, Xenia told herself, she would prefer freedom. It was too cold to loiter and, besides, if she hung about, she ran the risk of someone from the club seeing her. She looked for a place to linger. To the right of the club, in front of a record shop brimming with sulky dirty youths, she saw a telephone box. A red one just like in the picture of London on her primary school wall. Inside, it smelt of urine, which made her smile. Mrs Yurichova would have died if she'd known that an Englishman could pee in a phone box.

Xenia jingled her loose change and picked up the receiver and pretended to speak every time someone approached her. The record shop played heavy metal music and the door rang every time it opened. Xenia grasped the phone intently, with closed eyes, and made up a conversation with Gleb, telling him not to worry, that she was doing fine and would soon start sending money home. She carried on even after the person had left. It was only on the third conversation when she opened her eyes that she saw the card. In retrospect she couldn't understand why she hadn't seen it earlier. The Cyrillic lettering stood out like a statue, even though the sense was jumbled: 'Helping you. If you are needing the assistance in United Kingdom, woman only, we can do it. Secret will be yours. Call number without payment.'

There were translations that Xenia didn't recognise, including insect skeletons of Arabic script. The grammar was so bad as to make it meaningless but something about its earnest tone made Xenia pick up the receiver. She was shaking as she dialled the 0800 number. What if it was a trap? She told herself she could always hang up. What if they traced the call like they did in American films?

She was still reasoning when, on the third odd double ring, a woman answered.

'Women Trust.'

It was too fast for Xenia to understand but at least it was a woman.

'Hello, I'm Russian citizen. Alone in your country with no money and need to go home.'

'Have you been sexually abused?'

'I'm sorry, please?'

'We can only help victims here.'

'I don't understand.'

Then Xenia panicked and hung up. In the furthest part of her peripheral vision she thought she saw a woman leaving the club.

IX

'OK then. Where's the dick biter?' Beaver wasn't tall enough to stride. His walk was the furious pincer march of a European army. The club was empty but not deserted. Ben was in the back room organising a delivery of Red Bull for the punters who were too old for drugs.

'No idea.' Ben had an open can in his hand. It retailed for three quid in the club and, despite his worries, Beaver couldn't help wondering if Ben had paid for it. 'How is he?'

'Mr Bobbit is as well as can be expected for a man who came this close to losing his dick.' Beaver nipped his thumb and forefinger to within an inch of each other. Then he thought it made it look as if he was insinuating that the dick (any dick, *his* dick) was that size. He widened the span.

'Ouch,' said Ben.

Beaver said in a matter-of-fact tone, 'Yeah, well, there's worse. He plans to sue us.'

'Can he?' Ben put an order form on the bar.

'You can sue your best friend for a dinner party if you get the runs the day after. I might not be the world's leading legal authority, but I'd say he's got a pretty good case. Wouldn't you?'

'I guess.' Ben sat on a bar stool. 'Do you want a drink?'

Beaver looked at his watch, twelve fifteen. 'Yeah, go on. A double Scotch.' He drank it in one and looked up with the trace of a smile. 'But there's one good thing. The guy isn't your average punter. It's that bloke off the telly. That turkey bloke, the Butterballs man.'

'Good God,' gasped Ben. 'The little pervert. Surely he's not going to sue. What about the publicity?'

'You'd have thought so, wouldn't you? But the creepy thing is he's got this weird mate. He's planning to use the mate as a stand-in.'

'What do you mean?'

'Get his mate to have his dick nibbled and then use him to sue us. It's like a pride thing. It's not like he can be short of a bob or too. Doesn't want to feel he's a bumpkin being taken the piss out of. That's why I've got to find the woman who did it. Tell all the girls that there's no more going down on punters until this has blown over.'

There was silence while Beaver waited for the effects of a second whisky to kick in. Then Ben said, 'Actually, you're not going to have to worry about that too much. Not as far as the dick cruncher's concerned.'

'Why's that, then?'

'Well, security was down earlier.' Ben looked at him. 'It looks like she's done a bunk.'

'Christ Almighty, not another one? What's the matter with these women?'

Ben replied, picking up the invoice, 'Must be they can't know when they're onto a good thing.'

Beaver ignored him and made a facecloth of his hand, wiping it tiredly across his forehead. In many ways he was relieved. If the dick biter had done a runner, no matter how hard the turkey man tried to get a replicate job done on his friend's penis, he wasn't going to do it at his club. To be on the safe side, he resolved to make it known to all, no more blow jobs until further notice.

X

Ever since the Tamil Tiger Tokens headline, Tracey hadn't been her usual logical self. Had she known the day was going to pan out this way she'd have called in with a mental-health day. Elaine had already left on a non-specific task, leaving her to carry the can if the *Standard* called again. Added to which, the printers had let her know they couldn't do her campaign literature. One of their Weybridge presses had closed and staff shortages restricted them to existing clients only. Then there was the phone call. Only after Tracey had hung up did it occur to her that the woman might be *her* Russian. Tracey slammed her non-dairy clam chowder on her desk, causing leakage. Since the incoming call, she'd rung the female editor of the *Soho Clarion* who had told her, snootily, to write a letter (so much for sisterhood, thought Tracey) and then Sue from across the road to arrange to have her tarot cards read. But there'd been no incoming calls. Tracey 1471'd the call, made a note of it – a payphone – then pressed '3' to return the call. It had that tinny hollow ring you got when you called a phone box. No one picked up. Tracey let it ring until a BT recorded message, by a woman, naturally (why must they make all harbingers of bad news women?), told her there was no reply. She tried again and on the fourth ring a man answered. Tracey pictured a top to toe Man at Next, advertising sales type. It was an important detail because it allowed her to condescend. He was also slurry drunk.

'Hello, could you please tell me where the telephone box you are speaking from is situated?'

'What is this, Jeremy Beadle?'

'No,' said Tracey defiantly, 'I just need to know.'

'Someone's gonna leap out at me, aren't they?'

'No, you are perfectly safe,' said Tracey. 'Just tell me where the box is.'

'Who is this?'

'BT.'

The man said, 'I fucking hate BT.'

'It's a survey,' Tracey told him. 'Please tell me where you are.'

'I dunno. Hang on.' She heard him open the door and call to his friends, 'Oy, where is this? Some Richard wants to know.'

Ten seconds later another, huskier voice came on the line. 'It's just off of Peter Street, behind Brewer. Why do you want to know?'

Tracey ignored the question. 'Why did your friend call me Richard?' she asked.

'What?'

'Your friend,' said Tracey. 'He called me a Richard.'

'Oh yeah. Richard the Third, bird.'

Tracey hung up, suddenly overcome by melancholy. Had the women's movement really meant so little? She grabbed her cape and left a Post-it note on Elaine's desk, hinting at an important mission though giving no time when she expected to be back. If she could rein in that Russian missy under Elaine's nose, it would end the power struggle once and for all. She might even pack Elaine back to the council, see how she fared under the over-seventies women's transport division. Then she could put in for another assistant. Maybe a man this time, and one who wouldn't question her authority; one with a slouching sexual presence who could perform in a crisis.

Three minutes into the walk and her sensory perception was on overload. Whose wouldn't be, scanning the area for more fliers (a lot were going up on lampposts like pleas for lost dogs, which, in some ways she said to herself sadly, they were) as well as checking out store fronts for hidden bargains of retro chic? Only when she turned into Peter Street did it fully occur to her that, no matter where the call was made from, the chances of the Russian still being there were remote in the extreme. Still, she could loiter. Russians were internationally renowned for their lack of clothes taste, she was sure she could spot one a mile off. Also it gave her a chance, she thought, as she wrenched open the phone-box door, to rip down some of these damned Mile High posters. She said out loud, 'If I could only get my hands on the—'

'Ms McCloud,' said Beaver. 'I thought it was you. Where's your bucket?' The door swung open. Unlike most people Tracey met on her round, she sensed James Ciriano didn't mean the question sarcastically.

Tracey told him, 'It's just a flying visit.' She gave him a girlish smile. 'Where did you spring from?'

'Just in the area,' Beaver said. 'Business. Can I help at all?'

She pointed at the Women Trust poster proudly. 'That's one of ours.'

'Excellent,' Beaver told her.

'But as for these—'

'Filthy, aren't they?' commiserated Beaver. He looked at his watch. He said on impulse, 'How about a lunchtime drink? I mean just a quick one. Go on, I've had a bitch of a morning. You do drink, don't you?'

'A little,' said Tracey. 'I'm supposed to be finding this Russian girl, though.'

'What Russian?' Beaver frowned. 'Who says?'

Tracey thought. 'Well, no one really. Actually there is something about the campaign I need to talk you about. It's a printing thing. You do that, don't you?'

'Look,' Beaver grasped her elbow in a way that caused Tracey to feel weak, 'tell me over a drink.' He checked round the phone box. 'Haven't you got any cleaning stuff with you?'

Tracey thought he intended to carry it for her. He seemed oddly devastated when she told him all of it was back at the office.

XI

It never ceased to amaze Patti how cruel the average driver could be to a car with L plates. She'd once read that you could judge society on the way they treated its mentally sick. Patti thought you could judge society on how it judged its learner drivers. She'd given up yelling out of the window that they'd all been learners once.

'How soon they forget,' she said to Emily as she wound the window up. 'I hope this is an eye-opener to you,' she called into the back seat, where Winston had his eyes shut. Then she said to Emily, 'You're really doing extremely well. Really getting into the swing of it. Isn't she?'

'It's incredible,' said Winston. It had only been the hint that there would be no charge for the lesson that had coaxed Emily round the Holborn Viaduct and then the promise of ten free ones that got her down New Oxford Street.

'For God's sake, I'll drive,' Winston offered.

'You're not insured, brain ache,' said Patti.

Emily said, 'What about you taking over?'

'Drive in central London? You must be joking,' Patti told her.

When they reached the bottom of the Centre Point megalith, she told Emily to turn left.

'It's buses only,' she protested.

'Ignore that,' Patti told her. 'Buses and learners from nine to five.'

'Since when?' asked Winston.

'Look, if you've got nothing constructive to say, will you please shut up?' she said testily. She poked her head between the seats to address him in private. 'It was your idea to come into Soho. You said you knew where this woman would be.'

Winston kept quiet. It had been his idea to go back to the Mile High Club. 'Where else could she have gone?' he'd reasoned at just after eight, slumped on Patti's sofa watching *The Big Breakfast*. She'd replied sarcastically, 'Try anywhere.' Now he was starting to think she could be right.

At the traffic lights outside Charing Cross Waterstones, the car stalled.

'Now, Emily, take your foot off the gas and the clutch and put the handbrake on. Now, I don't want you to panic but once we're off again, I'm going to ask you to turn right at the next traffic lights.'

'Right into Shaftesbury Avenue?' quavered Emily.

'That's the one,' said Patti reassuringly. 'But don't worry, there's a filter on the lights.'

Then her phone went off, trilling to a TV theme.

'Hello, Patti, it's Rory.'

'Hi, Rory. This isn't a great time for me at the moment. I'm in the middle of a lesson.' A man in a suit wobbled along the pavement on a mini-scooter.

'Fine, I just need to know when you can get that car to me.'

'Oh, there's been a slight hitch on the car front,' Patti told him.

'Like what?'

'Like, look I can't talk now. I'm losing the signal.' She hung up.

Winston said, 'You can say that again.'

'Ha ha,' Patti said. Then as Emily eased towards the right-hand lane at the traffic lights at Cambridge Circus, she said, 'Think again, Mr Know-It-All Sir Winston.'

Winston looked up. 'What are you going on about?'

Patti swung round to look at him and follow the car with her eyes. 'Tell me if that's not your precious Lada over there going in the opposite direction.' She faced the front. 'Emily, do a ewie.'

Winston looked behind as the Niva swerved between two lanes, sweeping past a woman walking with a carrier of soup held at arm's length as if it contained a small savage animal. Then north towards Tottenham Court Road.

XII

Alfie Appleton never went anywhere without his Swiss Army knife – a twelve-blader with magnifying glass that his uncle had given him the Christmas before last. It wasn't entirely altruistic. For Alfie's part, he'd hinted that he wanted a kite. But it was his uncle's way of getting him used to wielding miniature blades in the run-up to his joining the abattoir.

He extracted the biggest blade and kicked himself for not remembering it sooner. 'What time would it be, Alan?' he called to the coop next to his.

'Sorry?' Alan sounded dozy.

'I mean, is it afternoon or morning?'

A pause while Alan used his poacher's nose to assess the light. He said, 'I've been asleep. I can't tell. Maybe lunchtime. Did I miss any food?'

'No. Don't worry.' There'd been nothing since two bowls of rice and a Kit Kat the night before.

'Hey, Alan?'

'What?' Considering he didn't have much to do at the moment, the Raynham lad could be awful moody.

Alfie said, 'Listen. I'm going to have us out of here by evening.'

'Yeah, whatever,' said Alan.

'Trust me,' said Alfie and started to hack at the wood with the knife. That was the thing about being so little, people didn't take you seriously. Well, Alfie Appleton was about to show them.

Chapter Eight

I

The car juddered down the gears from fourth to stall in the bus lane just past the end-of-the-world sprawl of King's Cross. Both passengers in the front seat jolted against their seat belts, then fell back and exhaled. On the back seat, Winston had his head down behind the passenger seat.

'Holy shit,' said Emily.

Patti turned to her. 'Well, I, for one, thought you did extremely well. Emily, well done *you*.' Patti hoped that by saying 'for one' she would get some praise from the back seat. Hearing nothing, she shook her head and made a *tsk* noise. Then she reached for a child's exercise book and pen from the dashboard. 'But before you disappear, there are a couple of things we still need to look at.'

Winston hauled himself upright. 'Ladies, I wonder if you couldn't do your debrief at a later time. When the traffic lights behind us go green, we're going to be crushed between two black cabs and have a bus up our jacksy.'

'Charming,' said Emily.

'Isn't he?' said Patti. 'You big baby. Learner drivers have special privileges, in case you didn't know.' Patti swivelled her torso to face Emily and batted the pen onto the notebook contemplatively. She said, 'Actually, maybe we could do this later. It was only one cyclist you got a bit close to.'

'And the pram,' added Emily.

'And the pram,' Patti admitted. Patti didn't count prams, specially not a three-wheeled buggy being pushed imperiously across Tottenham Court Road towards Heals as if it housed the Last Frigging Emperor. Patti said, 'If you're getting the tube from King's Cross, don't forget the Northern Line's not stopping.'

'What, still?'

'You'll need to get the Piccadilly to Leicester Square. Where are you going, back to Bexleyheath?'

Emily nodded and painted her lips with a layer of what Patti took to be lipstick, then noticed it was let-them-have-it lip gloss. 'I've got a date.'

'You do surprise me,' said Patti, not surprised. A bus behind them hooted.

Winston said, 'Ladies, could you hurry it up, please?'

Patti shook her head. 'All right,' she snapped. 'Will you please shut up? Anyway, we're not ladies, we're women, aren't we, Emily?'

'That's right, dear,' murmured Emily out of the side of her mouth. 'Now I must be off. Don't forget that was a freebie.' She nodded to the back seat. 'And say goodbye to your boyfriend for me, won't you?'

'What boyfriend?' Patti said, incredulous. 'Say goodbye yourself.'

Winston warned, 'Watch the door when you open it, there's traffic behind.'

Emily ignored him. Just as she was about to slam the door, Patti leant over the seat, still warm from Emily. She said quickly, 'Emily?'

'Yes, dear?'

'You don't think boys are better than girls, do you?'

A black taxi turned pink by adverts for the *Financial Times* beeped and swerved round them. Emily frowned.

'Good Lord, no. What makes you think that?'

'Nothing.' Patti pulled herself into the driver's seat, straightening her blazer. She gave a half-salute to Emily as she set off round the metal barriers.

Winston said, 'Jesus Christ, I thought she was about to vault them then.'

Patti reached for a pair of sunglasses from the glove compartment. 'Don't be silly, Emily Fricker is seventy-three.' She started cleaning the rear-view mirror. She pulled her seat forward so she could reach the pedals and adjusted the mirror so Winston couldn't see her. She went to undo the handbrake but saw that it wasn't on. She said, 'Now, where to, master?'

Winston said gloomily, 'Well, where do you think she's going?'

She juggled her feet on the pedals. 'Until now she's been stuck in a seventy-three bus lane, so I'm guessing Stoke Newington. Why would your girlfriend be going there?'

Winston shrugged and carried on looking out of the window. Two tramps with their faces encrusted in scabs were arguing outside a kebab shop, unaware of the drizzle. A homeless man with a patchy beard sitting with his back to a wall next to an amusement arcade stared ahead unseeingly. Winston said, 'Wherever it is, hurry up. We've been here getting on for ten minutes.'

'Yes, master.' Patti started the car. She asked Winston to pass her a tissue from a box on the back seat. 'A box of tissues is essential in this line of work,' she told him sagely. 'Driving can be very emotionally charged. It's a veritable roller coaster.' She was trying to hint at professional mystique.

'It's the way you drive,' Winston said.

'Sorry?' queried Patti. 'I missed that.'

'Nothing.'

Patti pulled into a line of traffic and passed a packet of prawn cocktail crisps back to Winston. 'Do you want some?'

'No thanks.'

'Can you open them?'

Winston said, 'They stink. Why do you eat all that crap anyway?'

Patti took them without looking at him. 'It's easier when we're on the road.' She thought she felt him baulk at the 'we're on the road' bit, as if she was implying they were part of an American road film. She said quickly, 'Anyway, why do you have to be so ultra critical all the time?'

'I'm not.'

'You are.' She leant to look in her wing mirror. 'You probably weren't socialised right when you were growing up.' She swerved in front of a Polo. 'Did your father ever read to you as a child?'

'I like that, me, *critical*. I was only trying to save your system from a cocktail of e numbers.'

'That's not what prawn cocktail means.'

The windscreen wipers sliced through the edginess, beating out the backtrack to an endless summer of childhood holidays. Patti nudged the car up the tilt of Pentonville Road. Vehicles crept slowly in the rain as if they were shy of each other. Elegant Georgian houses rose on one side and a ropy seventies office block on the other. On the corner shone the daytime lights of a comfortable local.

Patti switched the radio on. It was a lunchtime nostalgia hour for the nineties. She wasn't sure you could properly be nostalgic about something that ended eighteen months ago. The song was 'You're Too Sexy'. She switched it off pronto in case Winston thought it was referring to him.

In front of them school kids on the back seat of a bus had spotted the Liability sign and were laughing. Patti ignored them.

She repeated, 'Why would she be going to Stoke Newington?'

Winston was looking ahead. 'Maybe she's just lost. She's only a kid and she's foreign.'

Patti thought, that's right, make excuses for her, why don't you? The Russian had been old enough to steal her Niva.

'And who was that with her? There were two of them.'

'Really?' said Winston. 'You didn't say. Man or a woman?'

'Woman, I think,' Patti told him.

Behind them a professional couple argued like lawyers in a blue Audi. He was white, she was black with wrapped-in straight plaits. When they spoke they looked ahead, unfocused. A rangy pock-marked teenager in a yellow baker's van beat out a pop tune with his palms on the steering wheel.

'It looks weird,' Patti told him, 'with you in the back and me driving like some sort of chauffeur. Why don't you get in the front?'

'I feel safer in the back,' said Winston.

Cars in front made the dash to Upper Street, released in spurts by the green light. After three minutes of silence, Patti said excitedly, 'Look. I see them, the Niva. They're just ahead.' She poked her head between the seats to face him. 'Four back after that white Bedford van. Can you see?' The car was steaming up on the inside, denser around the driver's seat. She cracked open an inch of window.

WHITE MEAT AND TRAFFIC LIGHTS

Winston sat up and put his head between the seats so that Patti felt his breath on her cheek. He said, 'Yeah, I see them. Can't you get any closer?' He smelt of peppermint.

Patti looked at him. 'Listen, buster, I'm doing the best I can.' She indicated and jostled in front of a Volvo Estate. 'Now I'm thinking they're not following the bus. That'd go down Essex Road. But they're in the lane to go straight along Upper Street.'

'Try and stick with them,' Winston told her.

'Yes, master,' said Patti and pulled away. Cars bumped for position along Upper Street, moving slowly past a glass-fronted Japanese juice bar where waitresses knocked their white-socked knees against a chrome counter in boredom.

Patti announced, 'Hey, look at that. They're turning off.' The Niva ducked left without indicating.

By the time they reached the car it was parked and locked. Winston and Patti looked in. There was a cardboard box on the back seat.

'Oh, fantastic,' said Winston.

'It's not my fault there was nowhere to park.'

'Did I say it was?' Winston said.

Patti peered inside. 'It really is a nice looking car, this. So much nicer than ones you get these days. Modern cars always look so, I don't know, Down's syndrome to me. Big round faces and slightly bulbous headlights – too curvy.' She looked at Winston. 'Know what I mean? Not that I'm saying there's anything wrong with Down's syndrome, of course.'

Winston ignored her. He said, 'Go on then.'

'Go on what?' She had left her coat in the Cinquecento. It wasn't cold but the rain fell in fat globules.

'Nick it.'

Patti said moodily, 'It's your car, you nick it.'

'I'm not the car thief.'

'Haven't you got a spare set of keys?'

Winston looked at her in a withering way. Two aproned men were watching them out of a shop front called Tie Me Up. Underneath in green it read 'Specialists in exotic jungle plants'.

She said, 'I'm not stealing any car in broad daylight.' She kicked her feet. 'Specially not round here.'

'But it's *my* car.'

'Whatever,' said Patti. 'Look, why don't we just wait for them to come back and then confront them.' She turned her collar up. 'There's a pub we can watch for them from.' Without waiting for a reply she started walking towards an Irish theme pub that advertised midweek Guinness at a pound a pint, champ at two pounds and no entry to workmen. Which Patti considered rich coming from an Irish pub. The pub had a huge glass front, the type you never saw in south London, out of which they could keep the Niva under surveillence.

'What's champ?' asked Winston, overtaking her at the door and holding it open.

'Dog food,' Patti told him.

The place smelt of cigarettes overlaid with chip fat. Patti ordered fries, beans and egg in that order but only if the beans were Heinz. Winston asked for a Cajun chicken baguette.

'Look at you, fancy pants,' said Patti, sitting down with her back to the wall and a pint of lager.

Winston said, 'You eat a lot for a little person.'

'I have a high metabolic rate.' She made it sound official, like an O-level pass. 'Besides, don't say "little person" like that. I'm not a fucking leprechaun.'

Winston lit a cigarette, inhaled and looked as if he was trying to make an effort. He said, 'So, how long have you been a driving instructor?'

For Patti, cars were the ideal surroundings for a conversation. Something about transition, mixed with the fact that eye contact was virtually impossible. Winston, on the other hand, had become chatty out of the car. Next to the bar, a one-armed bandit choked out winnings.

Patti licked her top lip. 'About two years. It's not the only thing I do, I also—'

'Steal cars,' said Winston.

Patti looked at him. 'What is it with you and that car? You make it sound as if no one ever steals cars any more.' Then she said, 'I'm also opening a driving school in Egypt.'

'Really?' said Winston.

Patti lifted her chin defiantly. 'Really,' she said. 'Alexandria, actually. The Corniche, that's the promenade, is twelve miles long. It's very straight, which will be a boon for the learner. Also,' she looked at Winston confidentially, 'no written test.'

'You don't say.'

Patti nodded, impressed that he was impressed. 'I'm going to combine it with a holiday. My partner, my business partner that is, Fahmy, is going to come in with me. He's from Cairo.' She drank some more lager and started to concertina empty packets of crisps which were spewing out of the ashtray. She looked up past Winston's left shoulder to a small portable television by the till, with the sound turned down, tuned to the lunchtime news. She said, 'Phewie, I hate him. He gives me the creeps.'

Winston followed her gaze. The screen was filled with a coloured still of Selwyn Bates. Then it flashed up a school photo of a teenage boy and then a live shot of a bicycle with its front wheel spinning.

Patti said, 'What about you?'

'What about me what?'

'What do you do, dunderhead?'

Winston said, distracted, 'Me? I'm a lobbyist and a writer.'

'Children's books?'

'No,' said Winston. 'Why does everyone always think it must be children's books?'

The waitress dressed all in green carried the food as if her wrists were about to snap. Patti said 'Ketchup' as a reproof when the waitress automatically put her plate in front of Winston.

She lodged a chip between her teeth. 'Dunno, you look the type. Anyway, what does a lobbyist do?' She said lobbyist as if it was the first time she had ever said it.

'I lobby for people's interests in Parliament and in the media.'

'Like what?' Patti picked up the salt.

'Well, for example, that guy on the telly just now, he's one of my clients. I make sure turkeys get a good run in the Houses of Parliament.'

Patti was imagining an actual turkey run with chicken wire.

'What's the turkey man on the telly now for then?' she asked.

'He's put up a reward for some kid who has disappeared,' replied Winston. 'Actually, he's eccentric, but he's not all bad.'

'He gives me the willies,' Patti told him. 'His hair is so white.'

Winston ignored her. He waited for her to cover her chips in a sachet of tartare sauce and said, casually, 'But writing's my main thing. Actually, I'm in negotiations about a manuscript now, as it happens. That's why I can't spend too much time on a wild goose chase.'

Patti put her fork down. 'Listen, buster, this was your idea. I could be at home now,' she ate a chip with her fingers, 'putting together the finance on my new business.'

'Of course you could,' said Winston.

Patti flushed. It was either the red-hot poker of annoyance, hot chip fat or early menopause. In case it was the latter, she recomposed herself.

She picked up her fork and dabbed her mouth with her paper napkin. 'So, what's your book about?' she asked serenely.

Winston sighed. 'It's about a soldier who returns from the war to discover his wife has run off with an itinerant salesman.'

'Which war?'

'Sorry?'

'Which war?' asked Patti. 'The Wars of the Roses, Vietnam, the Falklands?'

'Actually, the war's more of a metaphor.'

'Oh.' Patti picked up her knife and jabbed it into her egg. 'Fiction?'

'Fiction.'

Patti said, 'You can dunk your bread in my egg.' When he blinked, his upper eyelashes enmeshed the lower row, making her wonder if he would be able to pull them apart. 'I mean, only if you want to, obviously.'

'Thanks,' said Winston. He put his baguette down and went on, 'He was jealous, the soldier, even before he went away. He couldn't help himself. He used to watch his girlfriend's pupils to see if they dilated when she spoke to men. If they did, it meant she was attracted to them.'

Patti said, 'I thought it was his wife.'

'Who?'

'In the book.'

Winston said wearily, as if he was explaining it for the millionth time, 'Girlfriend, lover, wife, it doesn't matter. It's a literary device.'

Patti said, 'Right.' A minute later she asked, 'Where is it set?'

Winston was looking past her. He said, 'Shit.' He picked up a napkin smeared with mayonnaise and wiped it across his mouth. 'Come on, they're off.'

Patti twisted her head. Two women with expressions as downturned as the weather were getting into the car. The smaller one, dressed in jeans and a sweatshirt, who Patti didn't recognise, got into the driver's seat. Winston set off, giving the impression he didn't care if she followed or not. Patti picked up a handful of chips and a sachet of tomato ketchup and ran after him. At the door the waitress smiled at her benevolently. Patti imagined how it looked. The tall handsome doctor taking out a bipolar patient. Patti scowled and deliberately trod a chip into the carpet. And just when she'd started to like him.

II

The lunchtime rush at the King of Corsica reached a crescendo at one thirty with the collective euphoria of one pint down and the thrill of another to come. By two it had settled into the dull prospect of an afternoon back in the office. On Fridays it was different. Fridays peaked at three. Beaver looked at his watch. It was 1.12 p.m.

'Drink?'

'G and T, please,' said Tracey.

'Double?'

'Why not.' She took off her poncho and sat at the only free table away from the bar. Because of the way sexual conventions were stacked against women, Tracey had only one rule when it came to sex. Never sleep with a man who weighed less than she did. Tracey was big boned but James Ciriano, as she appraised the body leaning against the bar, was on the heavier side of chunky. Like a Welsh prop forward.

Beaver sat down on a stool opposite Tracey, putting the drinks down first, and flicking his jacket back from his waist like a concert pianist. Aside from the advertising sales people from the magazine round the corner, the bar was mostly full of market traders. Beaver wouldn't normally think of taking a woman of Tracey's calibre here. He had two reasons: one, it was the nearest place to get a drink and, secondly, he liked the contrast of her catalogue cleanliness with the beer-stained tables. More than that, it actually turned him on.

'I got you some dry roasted cashew nuts,' he said. 'They don't seem to have much in the way of food.'

'Thanks,' said Tracey warmly, not picking them up.

'Hoy, Beaver,' the barman called over, 'you forgot your change.' A bearded man in a blue striped butcher's apron put 'Blue Suede Shoes' on the jukebox and started swaying around to the music.

When Beaver sat down again, Tracey said, 'Is this your local then?'

'I've been here a couple of times.' He picked up his drink. 'Cheers.'

'Cheers,' answered Tracey absently. 'Why did he call you that?'

'What?'

'Beaver?'

'Did he?' said Beaver, shaking his head nonplussed. 'It's a nickname. Beaver and Butthead. It's a cartoon. He thinks I look like one of them.'

'But that's Beavis,' said Tracey.

'Exactly,' he said. 'How's the campaign going?' He added quickly, 'Who's this Russian you're after. What is it, a spy?'

Tracey lifted her left eyebrow in contempt. Beaver felt a hand turn of arousal in his loins. 'It's part of my clean-up Soho campaign. I was thinking, if I could highlight one girl's story of abuse and degradation in the papers then it'll make all the difference.' Tracey picked her lemon out of the glass and sucked on it.

Beaver gave her a knowing smile. 'Oh yeah, who says?'

'I say. You're forgetting that media relations are my forte. Not for tabloids, but the upmarket papers. My voters. A thousand women are sold into sexual servitude in this country every week.' Tracey opened the cashews and moved her legs nearer his.

'*How many?*' Where did they all go? Beaver wondered.

'You see, you're shocked.' Tracey gave a jubilant smile that annoyed him.

'As it goes, I'm not that shocked. The women, they know what they'll be doing before they get here. Most of them make a packet and send it all back home. The Thai economy is kept going by foreign sex workers. There would be more misery if they didn't do it. I can't see why you've got a problem with it.'

Tracey put down her drink at the same time the jukebox stopped. She said, 'But I thought you believed in our crusade.'

'Up to a point,' said Beaver. 'The thing is, I don't like to be made to feel like a pervert in a telephone kiosk. Kids go in those places and everything. I don't think it's healthy to see pictures of Brazilian knockers when they make a call, that's all. Now, a tasteful advert would be different. Can I ask you something?'

'What?'

'How do you get your hair so shiny?'

'I'm sorry?' Tracey put her glass down. Another Elvis song went on the jukebox.

'It looks like it's wet but it's just clean. And it smells of coconut oil.'

'Er, I shampoo and condition it like everyone else.' She ignored his gaze, which had a glazed look to it. Then he snapped out of it and picked up his pint of bitter. Tracey was glad about the bitter. It wasn't a hard and fast rule but she found it more difficult to sleep with lager drinkers.

Beaver, embarrassed, went on quickly, 'What's worse for a woman, coming over here to get married to some old sod and having to sleep with him for free, or working for yourself, saving up and being in charge of your own destiny? One chap I knew got a Thai wife over here and then set her up in a takeaway food business. She even had to drive the bleeding van herself. And cook it all. And shag him. Now that's what I call taking the piss. Having your cake and eating it.' He finished his pint. 'In his case, Thai fish cake.'

Tracey said coldly, 'I don't call these women being in charge of their own destiny.'

'You'd be surprised,' said Beaver moodily.

Tracey was suddenly exhausted. 'Do you want another drink?'

'Go on then. Twist my arm. When do you have to be back in the office?'

'Don't mind. My assistant's out.' The jukebox must have had

an Elvis special. It was playing 'Love Me Tender'. 'We can take all afternoon if we want to.'

Beaver swallowed hard and put a fist, knuckles down, on each knee. He said something as Tracey got up to go to the bar. His voice was drowned out by the jukebox; at first she thought he'd said, 'Fuck it,' then she understood he'd asked her where she kept her bucket. It was an odd request but, despite everything, she was attracted to this man with his apparent sympathy with the sex trade. But that was one of the good things about growing old, reflected Tracey as she pushed her way to the bar. Principles, like veins on her cheeks, broke much easier.

III

Herbert finished his fourth pint of cider. They were in the snug bar of the first pub they'd come to out of the hospital. To cut down on bathroom trips, Bates was on shorts but going down the optics like a draughts board, sampling every other bottle, unless it was a woman's drink, like Dubonnet.

Bates hadn't found his drinking rhythm while Herbert seemed to have hit a paranoiac phase. To try to ease his retainer out of it he ordered him a double Scotch.

'Why can't we just go home?' whined Herbert.

'You really are worse than a flaming girl,' Bates told him. 'I cannot, I will not go home with my dick in tatters without some sort of redress. I thought you, of all people, would understand that.' His comment had no grounding in logic but he was appealing to noble sentiment. 'Really, is it too much to ask?'

'She might not do it again,' Herbert said in a dull voice.

'Let me worry about the details,' said Bates. 'Christ, boy, it's not like you use the thing a lot. It might as well be cut off, for all you do with it.'

Herbert flushed. He said, 'Once it's done, then what do we do?'

'Report her to the police, or get a settlement from the club.'

'What about me?'

Bates said, 'You get up the hospital, if needs be, and then we can all go home.' He looked beseechingly at Herbert. 'Don't we share everything, old chum?'

'There's a sight of a difference,' spluttered Herbert, 'between a turkey fritter and having my dick bitten off.'

'Oh, if you must split hairs.' Bates knocked back a Scotch. He eased himself off the bar stool. 'I'm going to the bog. You'd better have made your mind up by the time I come back, my boy. Or else.'

'Else what?'

'Else I might have to do it myself.'

Herbert's head spun as he watched Bates hobble stiffly away. Two boys in tartan shirts were throwing darts over a plastic mat at right angles to the Gents. Herbert prayed for a dart to lurch off target and hit Bates in the back of the head. Three old men sitting erect by the exit were drinking a cloudy spirit like ouzo, with a jug of water in front of them. Herbert smiled at them. He thought, on balance, that if he escaped he hadn't got so much to lose and he had a foreskin to save. He unpegged his coat from the hook below the bar and staggered casually to the exit.

IV

Helena eased the car into fourth gear and said, 'This country is so crazy. In the centre of London the streets are so narrow you couldn't get a pony down them. Now in the outskirts, they're as wide as the Dnieper.'

In Xenia's opinion, Helena was swaying along the Holloway Road like a drunken Red Army major on a May Day parade. She didn't say anything. It hadn't been easy to convince Helena that she wanted to leave the club and risk her chances with her. Helena had told her, 'It's only because I don't feel so good that I'm coming with you. I don't trust these English doctors.' She said she was feeling forgetful and light-headed and was acting in an odd, unpredictable way. 'It's worse at night,' she'd said, when they reached the car. 'You should see my toenails, they're like concrete.' She did look puffy. 'And look at me in this awful country. I've put on weight. Look at my chin and my neck. I've got folds of fat. And my speech. Sometimes it goes.'

Xenia put it down to homesickness or something in the water. She told her not to worry.

Helena chirruped as she drove. Mindless stuff about clients and the other girls. After so long on her own, Xenia liked it. As they sprinted and stopped between the traffic lights, Helena said, 'You know you left a bag in the room, just before you left. One with Arbat Irish House on it. Full of papers.'

Xenia shrugged. She didn't remember any bag like that. 'What happened to it?'

Helena said, 'Nothing. If it was important, you've lost it. I didn't have time to pack it.'

They drove for five minutes in silence. Xenia tuned the radio into a foreign station that played Europop. Suddenly she'd had enough of the sharp scrawly English language. She was dozing off when Helena said brightly, 'So, how did you get to be here?' She turned her head to Xenia. Helena wasn't a pretty girl, her nose was sharp and in profile she had a weak chin which seemed to stretch from her neck. Her bosom was a great shelf, though, settling on her stomach like bags of shopping.

'I was working in this farm with turkeys,' Xenia told her.

'No kidding. Big place with the owner's house down the hill?'

'That's right. You too, huh?'

'Yeah. Eight months ago they moved me and a couple of Latvians to London. And you know the rest.'

Xenia asked her, 'Who moved you?'

'I don't know, it was in the back of a van. They just picked us up and dumped us down.'

'Why didn't you try to run away or go to the police?'

Helena glanced at her. 'Are you kidding? They told us the police here are in league with them. Worse than in Russia, they said. If you make trouble, then your family back home gets it.' She pulled her forefinger across her neck.

Now, though, they were on their way home. First step was getting their documents back. Helena had said that the guards at the club had told them their passports were at the farm.

'And you believed them?' Xenia asked.

'What, about getting them back, or the documents being at the farm?'

'Both.'

Helena looked at her. 'I remember my papers being collected by some woman at the farm. They're more likely to keep passports there than anywhere else. Women get moved around in London so much.'

Xenia sighed and picked at a loose thread on her skirt. 'Does anyone ever get them back?' she asked. 'You know, if they earn all the money they ask for?'

In profile, she watched Helena's scornful scowl. 'What, twenty thousand on top of the two hundred a week board and lodging for staying in that fleapit? Yeah, I heard of some girls who got their papers back, but by that time they were into narcotics and shit and couldn't get it together to go home in any case.'

Helena always sounded so worldly it made Xenia feel like a village girl. It had been the same back in the brothel. A truck beeped the Niva but Helena only smiled and waved, keeping to the lane nearest the pavement.

'Stupid filthy Englishman. To think we grew up thinking they were gentlemen.' She wound down the window and spat onto the road.

Car headlights were being switched on, showing the rain bouncing off the road. Xenia traced the road on their new map in the gloom, too scared to switch the car light on in case they were recognised.

'You don't think anyone will follow us, do you?' she asked, panicky.

'Like who?' said Helena in a reassuring way.

It was too dark to see the route but Xenia remembered the way. Follow the signs for the A1, she told Helena, and they smiled because in any language that meant the best.

V

It took them seventeen minutes and a ten pound fine to get out of the Sainsbury's car park without a shopping receipt.

'I've never seen that before,' said Patti.

Winston said drily, 'Clearly.'

'What a cheek. Bloody supermarkets.'

Winston looked at her. 'I don't know what you're complaining about. I paid it.'

'I said I'd buy some sweeties,' Patti grumbled. She pulled out in front of an Espace people carrier. 'Do you think we'll have lost them?' she asked girlishly. When she went over a series of sleeping policemen he banged his head on the roof with metronomic regularity.

Winston was irritated by her lack of gravity. 'Won't this thing go any faster?'

'It's a thirty mile an hour zone,' Patti told him. Unusually, there was nothing in front of them but when he stretched over to look at the speedometer it read twenty-two miles an hour – apart from the speed bumps when the Cinquecento went faster. Winston wondered if she was doing it just to annoy him, although it hadn't been her fault the Niva had pulled into Sainsbury's.

He ran his hand through his hair. 'Can I just tell you what I've got riding in that car?'

'Sure,' said Patti expansively.

Winston looked straight ahead, counting on his fingers. 'Number one, it's my car. Number two, it's got nearly twelve grand in the boot that I need to prevent my brother being pulped by a South African coke dealer. Number three, there's a bag containing stuff belonging to a client who is so keen to be repatriated with it he's tried to break into my flat. And last, but not least, there's my Palm Pilot in the glove compartment with the only copy of my novel on it.' He looked at Patti.

She shook her head as if she couldn't believe his bad luck, but at the same time confirming that in all likelihood she was the final jinx.

She changed into fourth. 'This brother of yours, how come he's a coke dealer?'

Winston didn't look at her. 'It's a long story.'

'Like what?'

'He got sent to borstal when we were kids. That's when he got into drugs.'

'But that's not your fault,' said Patti. She braked at a zebra crossing. 'I mean, why can't your parents pay the money he owes?'

'Actually,' said Winston, turning to face her, 'it kind of is my fault.' He went on quietly, 'It was my idea to break in places. More for a laugh than anything. But he was the one who got caught.'

Patti was quiet for a moment. Then she said, 'Bummer.' More cheerily she said, 'You know what? I'm guessing they're heading out of town along the Holloway Road.' The speed had dropped to fifteen mph.

'What makes you say that?'

'Feminine intuition.' Winston looked at her profile. It was a shrunken skull like something from an ethnographical museum. She was licking her lips pensively in the half-light. 'I think they're heading for the coast.'

'The coast? They're about as far from the coast as it's possible to get.'

'OK then, brain ache, what's your suggestion? A day out at Alton Towers?'

'I don't know, they could be going anywhere.'

'All right, all right,' said Patti, lifting both hands off the steering wheel. 'You should know, she's your girlfriend.'

Winston ignored her.

She carried on, 'If it was me, though, I would be driving home.'

Winston said, 'Apart from the fact that she comes from Russia, not bloody Royston.' Then he thought, maybe they were heading into the country, maybe to the coast. He had a premonition of the Cinquecento trailing them across Europe. Suddenly he was aware of Patti talking to him.

She repeated, 'So what do you want to do? Because I know what we should do.'

'What?' said Winston with hostility.

She spoke in an odd, flat voice Winston hadn't heard before. 'I am a driving professional, possibly with a gene pool shared with Stirling Moss – though I can't back that up with documentation. I'm going to catch them up.' She slipped the Cinquecento into third and indicated to overtake a Metro in front of them. 'Pass me a Spangle,' she said fiercely, as if she was Hunter S. Thompson asking him to give her a Quaalude. Winston tutted out loud.

VI

'You didn't really think you could get away, did you?' Bates clamped his hand on Herbert's shoulder. Herbert hadn't made it further than the PVC outlet at the end of the street. He was as tall as the model that was wearing a diamanté-studded pouch but not as thin. 'Herbert, my boy,' said Bates wearily, 'you have nowhere to go, don't you understand that yet?'

Herbert readjusted his bag on his shoulder. He said, panicky, 'But I don't remember where the club is. Besides that, they won't be working at this time. It's a nocturnal thing you're asking me to do.'

Bates led the way towards the club. They trudged past the back entrance to a theatre where four down-and-outs were drinking from cans of Tenants. They asked for spare change and Bates told them to piss off. Then they passed an Italian restaurant which was full, despite the time of day, and then a shop that specialised in everything for the left-handed person.

Bates turned to him. 'You think this is easy for me?' He shook his head and looked reluctant. 'It's painful, if you must know.'

Herbert was a bag of nerves. He pulled a half-bottle of vodka from his jacket. When he drank, he cupped his crotch comfortingly. He said, 'What about if I gave you the money that you'd get from the club? I've got something put by, you know. Then we could forget about the whole thing and just take in a show.'

Bates turned to him. In the twilight, shadows fell across the contours of his face. 'You don't get it, do you?' he snapped. 'This isn't about the money. It's the principle of the thing.' Spittle mixed with the drizzle. 'You're doing this not just for me but for all of Suffolk. Think of your ancestors. We don't want these people to think they can make fools of us.'

'From where I'm standing,' said Herbert, 'I think I can live with it.'

'Think of Boudicca,' Bates told him.

'What the hell's she got to do with it?'

'She defended East Anglia from the foe, that's what she did.' Bates stopped outside the Mile High Club and pushed his retainer in the back. 'Herbert, it's a far, far better thing that you do now than you have ever done. Now get in there, and ask for the one with the snake.'

As he watched him go, Bates suddenly thought it might have been a nutritional thing. He delved into his travel bag on wheels, called Herbert back, and handed him his tub of I Can't Believe It's Not Butter. 'Use it as bait,' he said.

Herbert shook his head.

'The next time I see you I want you as clipped as a Jew boy.' He pushed Herbert again. 'Now get in there.'

As Herbert rang the bell, he looked at Bates. His mackintosh was unbuttoned and his shirt hung above the priapic bulge in his trousers.

'And if you go sharpish we can catch the eight thirty and be home in time for *Sex and the City*.' Bates had both thumbs in the air, intended as a sign of jaunty encouragement.

Herbert mumbled that from where he was standing he'd had quite enough of sex and the city. After thirty seconds the door opened and he went in.

VII

'You know, you're the sort of man that gets better looking with age.' They'd caught up with the Niva at the Archway roundabout where it had come to a sort of flummoxed stop outside a twenty-four-hour snooker hall. 'Your brother, is he older or younger?' Now they were cascading round the north circular. When Winston spotted the World of Leather, he knew where the Niva was headed. He relaxed, pushed his legs out in a half stretch and let his head bounce onto the back of the seat.

'Younger,' he said.

He felt her soak up the information. She said, 'Sibling placement says a lot about you.'

'You don't say.'

'I had you down as an elder brother.'

He had a feeling that if he didn't offer any information she'd dry up. Lack of light had made her more expansive or maybe she was nervous with men in dark confined spaces.

'Elder brothers are responsible, conservative, follow their parents' wishes. That'll explain why you dress like a stockbroker on leave.'

'Hah.' Winston sat up. 'What does that make you then? The runt of the litter?'

She took her foot off the accelerator. 'I'm sorry?'

'Well,' said Winston, 'if seniority makes you dress smart, what category does that put you in?'

Patti was haughty, with her foot back on the gas. 'The individual category.'

'Very individual,' Winston told her.

Two minutes of silence later he said, 'I'm sorry. I didn't mean it like that. You do dress in an unusual way, that's all. I mean it's nice, just unusual.'

She overtook a Mini Metro in the slow lane, packed full. It could have been a student returning after the Christmas holidays.

He said, 'What are you then? Middle child? Two sisters?'

'If you must know, I'm the youngest with two brothers.' To clarify she added, 'Older.'

'Oh, I see,' said Winston. 'You mean, over-indulged and thinks the world owes you a living.' He hadn't lived with Cindy for two years without imbibing his fair share of psychobabble. He passed Patti an unwrapped Spangle.

She said quietly, 'Something like that.' In the darkness, above the fizz of the heater, all he could hear was her bangle clattering on the wheel.

VIII

Beaver was beaming. It was his favourite time in the mating ritual. The heart-thumping certainty that sexual intercourse is guaranteed but that sacred moment before the disappointment sets in. After they left the pub, on Beaver's suggestion they'd nipped into the Women Trust office, flushed with alcohol and the promise of cleaning products.

'Let's do some boxes,' he urged her by the coat rack.

'The time's not right,' Tracey told him, giggling. 'It has to be before lunchtime.'

'Who's to stop us?' he panted.

He carried the bucket and Tracey the bleach. Jammed in the

double kiosk on Dean Street in front of a shop that supplied the catering industry, he made his move. He grabbed her round the waist as she straightened up and kissed her on the mouth in an intoxicating blast of Eau d'Issey and Cif. Above him the bare breasts of a buxom Italian new in town dangled before him. He tried to move his hand up Tracey's poncho. He pushed her head against the glass and kissed her neck. She murmured, 'Not here.'

With the proximity of the bucket, this came as a relief to Beaver. Aside from the logistical aspects of having sex in a phone box, there were legal implications. Besides which, it was for kids. Beaver was close to forty.

'What about your office?'

'Elaine might come back. What about your place?'

'No.'

'Why not? You're not married?'

'No, we just can't.' Being close to the Mile High Club made him nervous.

Tracey said, 'Come round to mine tonight. I'll cook.'

'OK.' Beaver leant against the kiosk, watching her straighten her clothes and totter back to her office. For want of anything else, she'd scribbled her address on the back of a flier advertising 'Brand new Thai boy/girl gives spanking good time'.

Beaver sauntered back to the club whistling 'A Nightingale Sang in Berkeley Square', feeling like someone from a 1940s musical. In his head, he was making sideways jumps and clicking his heels together. Ben was the first to greet him.

Beaver said, 'Ben, you know what?'

'What, boss?'

'If you were named after an English port, you'd have the ideal name for a career in porn.'

'Oh, yeah?'

'Yeah, imagine your name was Dover.' Beaver poured a Scotch. 'What is your surname?'

'Higgins.'

'If it was Dover, your name would be Ben Dover. Get it?' He picked up an ice cube and bounced it off his elbow into his drink. 'Maybe I should open a club in Dover Street. What d'ya say? I could call it Ben.'

'Are you pissed?'

'High on life,' said Beaver. 'Just high on life.'

Ben was resting his forearms on the bar. 'Where've you been?'

'Out and about. What's up?'

Ben, who had been filling in the order book, straightened. 'I hate to piss on your parade, but there was a chap round here looking for Helena.'

'So?'

'Helena,' said Ben, 'is the dick biter. He wanted to see her. Asked for her specially. Didn't know her name but definitely asked for the one who did the snake act. He was weird.'

Beaver sat down and tapped his forefinger on his chin. 'What do you reckon, the police?'

'He didn't say. Security said he didn't look like police.' Ben opened a can of orange juice. 'Then I remembered you said he was sending his mate round.'

'Who?'

'The Butterballs guy.'

'Yeah, he did. Half of me thought he was having a laugh, though. Maybe it was the Old Bill.' Beaver frowned. 'In any case, I thought you said she'd done a bunk.'

'She has, that's what made Terry suspicious. When he told him she wasn't on duty, the guy said, "Thank Christ for that." Terry reckoned he sounded weird, like a foreigner.' He took a sip of juice. 'Terry asked if he wanted anyone else but by that time he'd legged it.'

Beaver scratched his head. 'Not to worry. If it was anything to do with the Butterballs guy, she's gone now. It doesn't sound like Dibble to me.'

'Yeah, I guess. I thought I ought to let you know in case.'

'I appreciate it, Ben.'

Beaver pumped a double from the whisky optic into a champagne flute and knocked it back. 'Now, though, I have to make myself ready for a dinner date.'

Ben picked up his pen. 'Get a load of you. Who with?'

'Ah ha,' said Beaver, 'that would be telling.' Walking out from behind the bar, Beaver caught his foot in the handle of a white carrier bag with green writing on it. His foot slid on the plastic. 'What the fuck's that doing there?'

'Yeah, that's the other thing, boss. Terry found it by Helena's bed.'

'Helena?'

'The dick chomper, who did a bunk,' repeated Ben tiredly.

'What is it?' Beaver pushed the handles apart with his foot.

'Dunno. Papers, letters, that sort of thing. Do you want me to sling it?'

'Nah,' said Beaver. 'I'll take it. It'll give me something to read in the bath.'

When he picked it up he thought he was either pissed or had gone turkey mad. He could have sworn he saw the Butterballs logo at the top of the first sheet.

IX

Herbert had arranged to meet Bates in an Angus Beefeater restaurant on Shaftesbury Avenue when he was finished. From there they'd go, depending on the severity of the wound, either straight to the A&E department or the nearest police station. Bates had barely ordered a 12-oz well-done rump with chips and onion rings from a pudgy blonde waitress who, had he not been out of action, he might have given a Butterballs trial to, when Herbert sauntered in. It was the ill-concealed relief mixed with low-level machismo that got his goat.

Bates spat out a mouthful of Jack Daniel's and Coke. 'What the bloody hell do you think you're doing here?'

'That's nice. I said I'd do it, didn't I?' Herbert said.

'So what the bloody hell happened?'

A Japanese family with a Furby on the table made no secret of looking over. Herbert sat down. 'I need a drink.'

'What happened?' demanded Bates.

'Nothing,' said Herbert, rubbing his eyes in the light. 'She wasn't there.'

'Oh, charming,' complained Bates. 'She was probably on a break. Did you ask?'

'Yes,' said Herbert definitely. 'The bloke said she'd done a flit.'

'Great,' said Bates.

The waitress brought over a huge oval platter. She said to Herbert, 'Anything for you, sir?'

'Yes,' interrupted Bates. 'This.' He handed Herbert a hand-held device more often used for snipping the ends of cigars. 'I brought it from a tobacconist's round the corner. I thought you might pull a stunt like this. You can have your meal when you've finished.'

Herbert looked at him beseechingly. 'But, Selwyn, please, come on, be reasonable.'

'The bogs are behind you to your right,' said Bates with a ghoulish smile as he sank his teeth into an onion ring. 'Don't come out till you've done it.'

X

The rain started really hard as they left the M25. Patti had been complaining it was virtually impossible, even with her driving skills, to follow the Niva in the dark. Because he sensed she liked to complain and it stopped her laying into him, Winston let her carry on. The engine first cut out at just gone 5 p.m.

Patti, already in the slow lane, pulled over to the hard shoulder. 'Shit, I knew that was going to happen. This car's crap in the rain.'

'What about the AA?'

''Fraid not.' She tried to smile.

Winston shook his head and reached to see if his phone still had battery power. Lorries sprang past them, kicking out water in high yellow beams.

She said, 'It always cuts out in the rain. It'll be all right when it's dry. It's the spark plugs or transmitter or something.' She moved her body to face the passenger seat. 'Anyway, you're the boy, you should be able to fix it.' She looked at him sceptically. 'Don't tell me, you're a lover not a fighter.'

'You're the car expert.'

'Well, we just wait here till it gets dry.'

'Sometime in May,' said Winston.

'Now you're just being silly,' said Patti. Something about her manner suggested that one misfortune of one kind or another occurred most times she left the house. She seemed to expect it. Apart from the flash of the hazard lights, the car was in darkness, no lights even down the central reservation.

Patti said, 'If I was on my own I could get a man to stop.'

'Why don't you, then?'

'Blokes don't stop if they see you've already got one man with you. They sense it would be too emasculating for you.'

'Why don't you just go ahead and tell them I don't mind?' Winston stared ahead dismally.

She switched the radio on. It was 'Raining Men'. She returned it to Classic FM. Neither of them spoke.

After three minutes Winston said, 'Haven't you got anyone you're supposed to get back to?'

'You've seen my flat, I live alone.' She unwrapped a Spangle. 'Actually, my boyfriend dumped me.' She said it matter-of-factly. 'What about you?'

Winston was going to think of something but he just said, 'Ditto. I mean my girlfriend dumped me.'

'Not the Russian?'

'No, not the Russian.' He lit a cigarette and opened his window.

'Well?' Patti prompted.

'Well, what?' Winston wound the window up when rain splatted on his leg.

'Who was she?'

He held smoke in his lungs for a couple of seconds and then exhaled theatrically. 'Her name was Cindy. She was an aerobics teacher who ran off with a Pilates instructor.' He was staring straight ahead, unseeing, along the hard shoulder.

Patti said, 'A normal tale of twenty-first-century folk.'

'Something like that.'

'Why'd she do it? I mean, she must have run off with him for a reason.'

Winston sighed. 'The usual. Said I was a commitment phobe.'

Patti switched the radio back to a pop station. 'It must have been more than that.'

'If you must know, she said I could only communicate by proxy.'

'What's that supposed to mean?'

He looked at her; if she didn't understand women, how was he supposed to? 'Well, when I called her on the phone she reckoned I wasn't speaking to her, I was talking so the people around me could hear. But if she was there when I answered the phone, I was speaking so she could hear me.'

'Oh,' said Patti, nodding. 'Weird.' She thought about it until Winston finished his cigarette. 'What about when there were no phones?'

'Nothing.'

'Communication problem,' Patti summarised.

'Something like that.' He flicked the cigarette butt out of the window. 'What about you?'

Patti folded her arms. 'The usual.'

'Such as?'

'Lousy cook. No interest in his work.' She started twisting her hair, half tugging it. 'Then he told me on the day he left it was because I was the only woman he'd ever met who didn't collect seashells.'

Winston said, 'Crustacean problem.' She looked at him at the same time a lorry screeched past her shoulder. He added, 'Bummer.'

XI

Beaver's mother wasn't hot on tidiness. Ashtrays in the kitchen mingled with vegetable peel, while copies of the *Racing Post* got dusty in the lounge, stacked under old cups of tea growing a sealant of mould. But Beaver had a mate called Paddy who lived in a brand-new council flat in Camberwell that was as bright as a new pin. In the days when he was still James, he spent a lot of time with Paddy. And every night, in her apron and patent leather shoes, Paddy's mum, cloth in hand, would bend down to check for crumbs or specks of dirt on the brand-new blue melamine worktop, drawing her tight V-neck down to eye level.

'Can you see any specks there, James?' she asked.

'All clear, Mrs O'Casey,' he'd reply, peering down the dark crack of her cleavage and watching her breasts wobble.

Somehow it had just stuck with him. He found women doing

housework erotic. If he stopped and thought enough about it, some days the mere idea of a Dyson could give him a hard-on.

Watching Tracey McCloud flit a squeezy sponge over her work surfaces made his insides groan from deep beyond the trumpet of his belly button. Better still, the open-plan kitchen/diner gave a peeping Tom easy access to his fantasy.

Tracey called, 'I have to have a tidy kitchen before I sit down and eat. Don't you?'

'Absolutely,' said Beaver and dropped a linen napkin on his lap. 'It's a nice place you got here. I like that.' He nodded at a black and white picture on the wall above the *chaise longue*.

Tracey stuck her head through the breakfast bar. She was wearing a flowery 1950s style chiffon dress gathered at the waist. 'Lithogram, it's a Kandinsky.'

Beaver thought lithogram was something schizophrenics took. He had the feeling he was out of his depth.

'Could you light the candles?' Now she was rotating a spatula in her hand childishly.

Beaver half stood. 'Sure.'

'It's nothing special. Pan-fried squid with a pumpkin salsa followed by rack of lamb and a cranberry jus, served on a bed of watercress and giant Spanish capers. Could you open the wine?' She came out of the kitchen slightly flushed. 'I'm no good with a corkscrew. Or would you prefer a gin and tonic?'

Beaver tried to take her hand. 'Look, why don't you sit down. You must be knackered.'

'Well, actually, these kitten heels are killing me.'

'No,' said Beaver urgently, 'leave those on.' He led her to a chair with his open palm in the small of her back. 'I thought all you lot didn't believe in this sort of lark.'

Tracey was suspicious. 'What do you mean?'

'Cooking for men.'

Tracey said tartly, 'People have to eat.'

'True,' said Beaver.

'And I like to cook.' She smiled.

'And clean,' Beaver reminded her. He passed her a glass of white wine. 'Let's drink to the campaign.'

'Cheers. That reminds me. Can you do that printing job? The leaflets, the ones I told you about.'

'No problem,' said Beaver. 'You know, if there's anything I can do to help more in your campaign, you've only got to say the word.'

Tracey said despondently, 'The only thing I'm really going to get short of is cash. I had no idea how much this sort of thing costs. Leaflets, campaign wardrobe, envelopes. If you know anyone who wants to make a political donation to a good cause ... I mean I don't mean Bernie Ecclestone, but anyone in your line of work who believes in morality.'

Beaver swallowed. 'I'll certainly put the word out. As far as I'm concerned, it's just that money's a bit tight at—'

His mobile went off. 'Christ, I'm sorry, I didn't know it was on.'

Tracey crossed the room to change the CD and then went back to cooking. Beaver sat on the sofa to get a better view of her.

'James Ciriano speaking.'

'Ciriano, this is Selwyn Bates.'

Beaver's bowels fell into his boots. 'What can I do for you, Mr Bates?'

'We seem to have a little problem.'

'Like what?'

'Like that little hussy that attacked me has just done the same thing to my friend. She's a menace and this time we are planning to take it further.' He waited for Beaver to speak.

'Are you sure? It's my understanding the lady in question no longer works for me.' Beaver pointed to the phone and shrugged at Tracey, meaning he was taking the phone into the hall.

'In that case, can you explain how come my friend has had a run-in with the mauler on your premises?' Beaver said nothing. Bates carried on, 'We will be filing charges. What have you got to say about that?'

Beaver kept quiet. He wanted to hear all Bates had to say before he waded in.

'You see, Mr Ciriano, you city boys think you're so smart, making fun of us provincials. I intend to show you what happens when you mix with the tractor boys.'

Beaver tried conciliatory. 'Where you come from has got nothing to do with this. What did the police say?'

WHITE MEAT AND TRAFFIC LIGHTS

There was a three-second pause before Bates said, 'That's a matter between them and me.'

Beaver was exasperated. 'Look, are you sure it happened at my club?'

'Would you like to speak to Mr Long? He can verify anything I've got to say, and he'll go into the witness box to prove it if he has to.'

There was another silence. Beaver heard pans clattering in the kitchen and smelt a waft of mint. 'OK, Mr Bates, let's get down to brass tacks. How much?'

'I'm sorry?' Abba was playing in the background. Bates sounded as if he was in a pub.

Beaver said, 'Don't come the innocent with me now. How much to settle this out of court?'

'Fifty grand.'

'*How much?*'

'Mr Ciriano, my friend Mr Long might never have a fulfilling sex life again. It is what we call a very personal injury.'

'You can say that again.' Beaver asked for contact details and told him, 'I'll get back to you.' He snapped his phone shut. On the last stair was a pile of objects waiting to be taken upstairs. It included a matching bra and briefs set that he absently started to stroke, a pair of tweezers, retinol cream in a purple tube and four AA batteries. Beaver sat on the third stair with his head in his hands. When he looked up, Tracey was standing in front of him, offering him his glass of wine. Her face was nervous, like a child expecting bad news. She had a tiny half-moon sliver of orange peel on her cheek. Beaver picked it off.

'Everything OK?' she asked.

'Not really, something's come up.' He sucked in his lips. 'I'm going to have to go back to the office.'

'What, now?' said Tracey. 'What about the lamb?'

Beaver touched her hip. 'I'll try and get back later. Honestly.'

She rested against the pale green wall. 'Can I do anything?' She sounded disappointed and eager to please.

'Cheers but no, not really.'

Then she said, 'Really, it's OK if you go. I mean it, it's fine. Honestly. Just go. It's fine, really.'

It struck Beaver all of a sudden that she was a woman who was used to being let down by men.

Beaver stood up. 'Look, why don't you come with me? I just need to check a couple of things. Then I could take you for dinner.'

'What about the pumpkin salsa?'

'I dunno. Bring it with you. And the lamb. We'll eat it at my place.'

She pretended to think about it.

Beaver said, 'Come on, babe, it'll be a laugh.'

Tracey giggled and flicked her hair over her shoulder. 'I'll get the tuppers out.' She turned and started to unfasten her apron. Had he not been so preoccupied, Beaver might have spun her round, pushed her against the steps, pulled up her dress and taken her on the stairs. But there was work to be done and she was a lady.

'Don't forget your washing-up gloves,' he called after her and followed her back into the dining room, which was steamy from the cooking.

She reappeared without the apron, perplexed. 'Why?'

'To wash up with, babe. I haven't got any.'

Her face was perfectly still while she weighed up the information. For a split second Beaver thought she might explode. Then she said, 'OK then,' and cantered back into the kitchen.

'That's my girl,' said Beaver.

XII

Alfie Appleton rested his wrist. He knew people had escaped from Alcatraz using things less penetrating than the inner tube of a Biro. By rights, a Swiss Army knife should put him ahead of the field. It wasn't working out quite like that. For a start the blade wasn't serrated and then the wood was as thick as hell. And whereas in Colditz they might have been force fed sauerkraut, all Alfie had eaten in the last twenty-four hours was half a Snickers bar and a cold cheese and tomato pizza with a can of Dr Pepper, lobbed soundlessly from a hatch.

All day the gravel at the front of the house had crunched under a succession of vehicles. Alan had confidently identified the car brands, shouting them in the soupy light. 'Sounds like an Orion,' he said. Then, 'That's a Jag. No doubt about it.' Alfie felt like asking him how the hell he could tell but he'd learnt Alan had an answer for everything and it was no time for rifts. Periodically Alan asked how the great escape was going and started to whistle the theme tune. For the first half-dozen times of asking, Alfie ignored him. Then he got used to it and, mid-afternoon, even started to hum along.

At some point when it got dark and rain clonked hollowly onto the corrugated iron roof, Alfie downed tools and dropped off to sleep, using a fertiliser bag to keep the wind off his face. When he woke, it was pitch-black. He took comfort in the gurgling snores from next door. He thought of Alan's mother's face pinched by the dehydration of her tears. He thought of the happiness of reuniting mother and son. But more than that he thought of his uncle's face when he, Alfie Appleton, all natty in his black tie, collected his Scoop of the Year prize, bouncing along on the thick carpet of a swanky London hotel. Then Alfie dusted off strands of hay caught in the knife and started to gouge for all he was worth.

Chapter Nine

I

There were four LCD square clocks on the wall behind the Travel Lodge reception, thumping out the time in Colchester, New York, Paris and Jakarta. Winston handed over his credit card at exactly 7.02 p.m., Essex time. Because of the International Leather Convention and an unspecified sporting fixture tomorrow, all the rooms – with the exception of one double with a foldaway bed overlooking the car park – were full. The receptionist mentioned the car park proudly to show she didn't care if they stayed or not.

'We'll take it,' said Winston.

'I'm not sharing a bed with you,' said Patti.

'No, I know you're not.'

'What about me, then?' she said.

'You'll be sleeping in the child's bed.' He gave her a critical appraisal. 'You're about the right size.'

'Great.'

Sometime before, after pushing the Cinquecento a quarter of a mile along the hard shoulder to shelter under a flyover and waiting two hours for the engine to dry out before it hiccupped its way another eight miles to the services, the mood had changed from confessional to confrontational.

Patti watched the rump of the receptionist as she turned to select a key. A phone rang unanswered and an old man in a pink baseball cap waited for a signature on a clipboard. A notice told residents they had full access to the World Wide Web.

Patti said, 'Do you know how you find out the number of someone's room when the hotel won't tell you?' She didn't wait for a reply. 'You write them a note and see which pigeonhole they put it in. It really works,' she said proudly, as if she'd invented it and not seen it on a James Bond double bill. Winston was signing for the room. His signature was flowing and illegible, just the way Patti liked them.

She said, 'Bags I have the first bath.'

The woman behind the desk said, 'Do you require the services of a porter?' She had a pudgy child's face daubed with glittery green eye shadow. Her name tag said 'Dawn Reception', which made her sound like a spy novel.

'What the hell for?' said Winston. 'We haven't got any luggage.'

Dawn said, 'Keep your hair on, I was only asking.'

'Do you know where I can buy a change of clothes?' asked Winston.

Dawn shook her head. 'Sorry, everything in the town'll be closed by now.'

Patti said, 'What about ordering them off the Internet?'

Winston said glumly, 'Don't be ridiculous.'

'So-rree,' said Patti. 'Don't blame me if your blood sugar levels are low.'

The man in the baseball cap jabbed his clipboard onto the desk and signalled for a signature.

'We've always got a laundry service,' said Dawn matter-of-factly.

'There you go,' said Patti, as if that would be the end of it. 'Look, can we hurry up? I need a bath.' And grabbed the credit card key off the desk. 'Can you wait down here till I've finished?' And she jogged off to the lift. It was only then that Winston noticed she was wearing a pair of tracksuit bottoms under her blazer. Not tight lycra with a go-faster stripe, but baggy grey ones with a cord string waist. The type worn by people who have spent too much time in the hands of social services.

Winston didn't want to be left with Dawn, who was in a vicious debate with the man in the baseball cap over paper towels, so he set off towards the bar. The décor was country house with bold crimson stripes halfway up the wall and a contrasting red above. Swathes of green curtains draped the far wall, even though there was no glass. Winston got a pint of lager and a packet of dry roasted peanuts and sat by a window that was a window. When he flicked back the curtains, he looked out onto a lorry park with a kiddies' playground between it and the motorway. Sales reps released from their suits into their leisure gear of jeans and T-shirts smoked heavily on alternate bar-stools behind their twin badges of success, full tar cigarettes and a mobile phone. One had a pyramid of loose change on the beer mat, from which he segregated pound coins with a finger, expecting the barman to pick them up.

Winston's mood was surprisingly sanguine. Tomorrow they would retrieve his car and he'd be back in London by lunchtime. The mix-up, as far as Bates was concerned, was easily explained. If the Russian didn't have his precious bag then that was her problem. Winston drank more lager and sat back. The room was quiet apart from the knock of pool balls next door and the thud of dance music coming from further down the corridor, with an occasional whoop that sounded like an exercise class. Winston wanted to check his messages but he didn't want to put himself in the same category as the men at the bar. He even hesitated at lighting a cigarette. He picked up an abandoned copy of the *Mirror* and started reading the sports pages. Then he thought of Patti in the eighth floor hotel room hanging and unhanging her clothes, reading the room service menu, trying on the complementary shower cap, bouncing on the bed. He finished his pint and started towards the bar.

'Winston? Is that you?' Winston hadn't been aware of anyone approaching him but that might have been because of the spongy carpet tiles and the state-of-the-art trainers. 'What are you doing here?'

He looked up. Cindy was wearing a pair of blue cotton shorts and a sort of sports bra. While other Travel Lodge residents trudged, Cindy was bouncing along as if suspended by an invisible cord. She said, 'I can't believe it.' She had a faint gloss of perspiration all over her.

'Well, I never.' Alarm spread through Winston's body like contagion.

Cindy beamed and shook her blonde ponytail in disbelief. Surprise was making her over-effusive. He didn't remember her being this happy to see him when they were going out. Especially not the last time they'd met, but he had had his trousers round his ankles at the time.

Cindy said, 'It's a convention. An international Pilates thing. I'm a teacher now.' She shook her head from side to side.

'But I thought you were going skiing,' said Winston.

'No, we had to cancel. That's how come we're here. Like, Hartley had an emergency client. Some sort of lumber thing. It was a pop star. Famous, you'd have heard of her. Of course I can't say her name.'

It was the first time Cindy had referred to her new partner by name. From what he remembered of the wanking incident, there had been no introductions. For Winston it represented a considerable victory. He smiled.

'You mean Hartley, as in Hare?' He paused. 'That's his name?'

'Yes,' said Cindy, frowning. And then quickly, 'Actually, he's just coming. Why don't you join us for dinner?' Without waiting for an answer she said, 'You haven't said what you're doing here.' With disdain, 'What is it, like, some sort of works do? Surely not a weekend break?'

'Actually,' Winston started slowly, not sure how to pare down the events of the last twenty-four hours in any credible way, 'it's complicated.'

'Yeah, it always was with you.'

He said, 'No. Not so much complicated as, I'm on my way to see—' Mid-sentence, something distracted him over Cindy's shoulder. Receptionist Dawn had her forearms extended from her rounded hips in annoyance. Someone smaller was standing almost up against her, shaking wet hair in her face. At first he thought it was a schoolgirl. Then he realised it was Patti. As he made the connection, Patti strode towards him, speaking from ten yards away.

'I can't believe that bloody woman. All I want is a hair dryer. Our one is knackered. Oh, hello.'

Winston's face fell. It was the reference to the joint hair dryer that did it. He said quickly, 'Patti, I'd like you to meet Cindy, she's my ex-partner. Cindy this is Patti, she's my . . .' He left it hanging in the air while Patti shoved a small hand at Cindy.

Patti said, 'Hello. You're staying here too? That's a coincidence. We broke down.' She looked at Cindy and half smiled. 'Why are you dressed like that?'

Winston thought that for someone dressed in a bustier with a green blazer and tracksuit bottoms it was quite a question.

'Like, it's a Pilates convention,' said Cindy, looking at Winston.

'Oh,' replied Patti. 'I'm starving.' She slapped the credit card key against Winston's stomach. 'Hurry up if you're having a shower. Like, there's no hair dryer.' She must have used the hotel shampoo and conditioner because the ends of her hair were drying frizzy, like the fluffballs cats bring up. Even more ominously, she'd twisted a pink plastic gardenia, the type that get stuck in hotel vases, into it.

'Actually, I need to, like, shower and change too,' said Cindy. When she spoke, Winston saw her bare stomach muscles slide over her rib cage. She'd had her belly button pierced with a tiny silver ring. He looked down further to her legs and the curve of her pubic bone.

He said, 'Pilates seems to agree with you.'

'It's so much more than aerobics, it's a whole life thing.'

Patti looked up at them. 'I'll get the drinks in then,' she said.

'Nothing for me, thanks,' said Winston.

'Me neither,' said Cindy.

Patti headed towards the bar. Pushing herself up on the simulated brass foot bar, she watched Cindy and Winston walk to the lift. Was it her imagination or was he using his outstretched palm at the bottom of her spine, just above the curve of her buttock, to guide her?

II

Because, as a bachelor, Beaver never knew his luck, he kept his flat as tidy and as interesting (from a woman's perspective) as he could manage. Since he'd met Tracey and had a positive female quarry in mind, he'd adjusted his coffee table books from *Operation Barbarozza* to *The Making of Tate Modern*. Other factors were neutral. As far as his day job went, there were very few pointers – a couple of matchboxes picked up in the name of research and two Airfix kits of model planes that he'd used for the advertising fliers. His walls were bare and not at right angles to the floor – the floorboards had breathed in too much fetid

London air and been distorted by it. Beaver was starting to know how they felt.

'Another drink?'

Tracey's knees were clamped together primly, ankles crossed like the Queen Mother. 'Shouldn't we eat?' She'd been relaxed in her own place, but here had dried up as if she couldn't trust Beaver's motives.

He turned the heating on full and pulled his only classical CD from its holder. 'Come on, babe, chill out,' he said. 'It's not that bad.'

Beaver's flat was lodged one flight up from the Mile High Club. It was the sort of flat where builders gave up on spirit levels, where only a skilled sort of skewed logic would work. There was a Moroccan jazz club on one side that only opened on a Wednesday. The other side was empty and used as storage for the record shop downstairs. The most noise came from his own joint so he was in no position to complain. Six months ago Beaver had been approached by a property developer with white hair styled like cake frosting. He had a vision for the terrace that involved Beaver clearing out. He wanted to convert it into part of the Comfort Inn chain. He had offered Beaver a six-figure sum to leave. Beaver didn't like being told what to do. Had he come up with the Comfort Inn conversion scheme, it would have been a whole different ball game, but he hadn't, so he'd told fondant hair man to sling his hook and never discovered if it was a high, low or middling six-figure sum. Sometimes, many times, he wished he'd asked.

Tracey smiled. 'Maybe I'll have a small G and T.' In Beaver's experience, only big drinkers asked for small measures. Asking for a small drink, nine times out of ten, meant that they'd been thinking of a large one but ruled it out. Like dieters and small slices. If they hadn't been used to big slices they wouldn't be on a diet. He kept his views to himself.

'Sure thing, doll.'

'And stop speaking like you're a nineteen-seventies pimp.'

'Ice and a slice?' Beaver said, innocent, as if he hadn't heard.

Tracey smiled. 'Can I heat the food up anywhere? Have you got a microwave?'

'No problem, babe. Make yourself at home. I'm going to have

to pop into the office.' At some point in their relationship, Beaver was aware he would have to admit to what he did. He was a strip club owner and she was a female liberationist. But then, he reasoned, didn't they say opposites attract? He didn't have to tell her right now.

'Oh, OK. Is it near here?'

'Not far.' He kissed her on the cheek and inhaled the smell of her make-up. It reminded him of the powder puff smell from childhood when he was rooting around in his mum's handbag. He beamed. 'See you.' When he shut the door he reflected how nice it was to have a woman. Especially one who smelt of Persil tablets and who would still be there, scenting the room like a giant pot-pourri, when he got back.

III

It took Patti one read-through of the cardboard menu to come up with the vegetarian lasagne and onion rings and chips, and no starter. Winston dismally pointed to the mushroom pâté followed by the grilled trout. As far as he was concerned he had two options: remain the wanker Hartley thought he was, or hook up with the woman with the plastic flower in her hair who talked with her mouth full. On balance, he thought, everyone masturbates.

'I never trust a menu with photographs on it,' said Cindy skittishly.

'Me neither,' admitted Patti. She used the prong of her fork to gouge crumbs out of her wicker placemat.

Hartley and Cindy ordered green salad with no dressing to start, followed by the black bean chicken, swapping polenta for brown rice – if they had it. When Cindy asked if the chicken could be grilled, Patti tutted out loud and raised her eyes to the heavens. Because she was shorter and her head several inches closer to the table, no one noticed. The dining hall was a mixture of red-faced businessmen, flaccid and sweaty, contrasted with clumps of hard-bodied Pilates teachers, pensively eschewing the menu. Dumpy dark-haired men and women from the International Sale of Leather acted as a sinewy buffer. Winston ordered a bottle of Pinot Grigio. Patti asked if he thought one bottle, between four, would be enough. He told her, under the circumstances, that it would be. Patti wondered what the circumstances were, but didn't say anything. Then Winston looked at Cindy and asked if she'd like a bottle of mineral water.

'Fizzy, isn't it?' he asked.

'You remembered,' she said.

When the orders had been taken, Hartley asked Winston, 'So how did you two get together?' His face was shiny and open-pored as if he'd recently exfoliated. He was skinny as a marathon runner and looked as if he'd spent his youth outdoors, in a riding and skiing sort of way, not bunking off. He wore a gold signet on the little finger of his manicured left hand. Patti figured the men Cindy went for were wannabe toffs who worshipped her.

'We're not together,' said Winston quickly. 'No, really, the car broke down. We're on the way to see a client. The turkey man in Suffolk. You remember him, don't you, Cind?'

Cindy looked up, bored. 'Like the Butterballs guy, right?'

Winston said, 'Yeah.' He looked touched that she remembered. 'The Butterballs man. My car's sort of out of action, so Patti was giving me a lift. She's a driving instructor.'

'What, like as in a lesson?' said Cindy sceptically.

Patti said sourly, 'Like, as in I only do over-fifties.' A waiter came round with a basket of bread rolls in one hand and individually wrapped butter pats in the other. Winston looked sweaty, either through embarrassment or his closeness to the heated food counter.

One Pilates table had an opened window. Sharp stabs of cold air doused them in bursts. Patti didn't use a knife to scrape butter onto her roll, just smeared the pat over it.

'What about you, Hart?' she said. 'How did you get into this keep-fit stuff?'

He looked at Cindy. They were sitting next to each other and looked as though their thighs were clamped together. Hartley spoke as if he couldn't believe people didn't know this sort of stuff. 'It's actually more medical than that. It's like physiotherapy. Muscle groups. It actually started as a way of getting injured ballerinas back to full fitness.'

Winston looked at Cindy while Hartley was speaking. Then he said, 'It always makes me think of Pontius Pilate.' He waved to the waiter to pour the wine without tasting it. The waiter went straight to Cindy's glass and waited for her to sip. She had changed into a pair of jeans low on the hips with a shirt that knotted under her chest. Her hair was out of the ponytail and fanned out over her shoulders, resting on a prominent clavicle. When he thought people weren't looking, Winston gawped at her, using his fringe as a curtain.

'I read that Carol Vordeman does it,' announced Patti cheerfully, bending towards Cindy. She added quickly, 'It said so in *Heat* magazine.' She took three consecutive gulps of wine and signalled Winston with her eyes for a refill.

'And Elle MacPherson,' added Cindy and made a point of yawning.

Winston had refused a roll. He was examining a smudge on his jacket cuff. 'Can't we talk about something more riveting than celebrity workouts?'

Hartley said expansively, 'Sure, we hate to talk about work in the evenings. Don't we, darling?'

Cindy said, 'Right. It can get really, like, draining.'

Nobody could seem to find anything to say to that. Winston drummed a plastic salt cellar on the table. They busied themselves adjusting cutlery and brushing crumbs onto the floor. After two minutes Patti said, 'I'm going to the loo,' and pushed her chair back into the waiter who swayed Winston's mushroom pâté above her head.

'Ooops. Sorry.' She said it to Winston who had his head down.

'Me too,' said Cindy quietly. At a table to the right of them a mobile phone rang to the 1812 Overture.

'You're sorry too?' said Winston, looking up. 'What are you sorry for?'

'No, I mean I've got to go to the loo too,' said Cindy.

By the time she'd got up, and both men had made vague attempts to remove their napkins from laps while they half stood, Patti had disappeared.

She was halfway through her pee when she heard the wet clickety-click of Cindy's heels on the linoleum. She heard a compact open and a lipstick snap shut. To mask the sound of her urinating, Patti pulled at the toilet roll. Then she heard the bolt of a cubicle next to her and the sound of long nails scratching on plastic.

Patti pulled the chain and walked to the sink, picking at a square of loo paper stuck to her foot. The rota on the back of the door to monitor cleanliness hadn't been filled out for a week. The bathroom smelt hot and unhygienic.

When Cindy burst out of her cubicle, she was smiling and gesturing to Patti. She nodded towards the cistern. Patti thought there was some problem with the flush but when she looked in, she saw a Tesco Clubcard with a line of white powder on it. Next to it was half a straw.

'Care for some?' said Cindy, touching her left nostril absently and sniffing.

Patti looked from side to side. 'Er, no thanks, I don't.' She looked at Cindy. 'But, really, you carry on. Don't let me stop you.' She looked at the cistern.

Cindy said, 'It's a shame to let it, like, go to waste.' She stopped over the cistern and took the straw in one hand and pushed her hair back with the other. One knee rested on the bowl and bent over the cistern with a dancer's spiny grace. Cindy was shaking her head when she came up. She said, 'That's better.' Her great red smile was like a gash across her face. Patti didn't know where to look. Cindy washed her hands and dabbed her face.

'Don't you need to use the loo?' Patti asked meekly.

Cindy ignored her.

'Does Hartley,' Patti looked down, embarrassed, 'you know, does he do it? I mean, does he know?'

Cindy said, 'What's to know? Don't be so naïve. Like I'm not some sort of crack addict. He thinks I'm on a double dose of St John's Wort, that's all. Listen to me.' She turned to Patti with venom. 'You don't stay this fucking thin by stretching for a couple of hours a day.'

Patti said unsurely, 'I'll bet.' She waited while, with jerky movements, Cindy re-packed her vanity case.

'So, do you fancy him then?' Cindy said quickly.

Patti screwed up her face. 'Who?'

'Winston, of course. I can tell by the way you're looking at him.'

'*No!*'

'Look, you can't fool me. I've been there. He has melancholic charm. I'm surprised he hasn't already told you. When he says, "Never underestimate the persuasiveness of charm," that's when you know. He thinks he's a charmer, but it's all a load of bollocks really.' She closed the toilet door. Patti turned towards the sink. The coke seemed to have turned Cindy into some sort of game show host.

Patti muttered, 'Well, he's still better than Hartley Hare.'

'Hartley's in touch with, like, his spirituality,' said Cindy in a way that was supposed to mean Patti wouldn't understand.

Patti said, 'Yeah, right. Telling a lot of overpaid twats how to stand up straight. I don't think so.'

Cindy either didn't hear or ignored her. She was staring at herself in the mirror. Patti waited for her, leaning against the door, out of range of the full-length mirror. She said, 'So why did you and Winston split up, then?'

Cindy didn't look up, just carried on rubbing her forefinger under her nose. 'He had no commitment. I don't mean to me. To anything. His job, his family. He's a loafer, charming but a loafer.'

'What about his writing?' said Patti defensively.

'Yeah, we'll see. It's just part of the Winston Freely you-get-more-than-you-see package.'

Patti thought, at least he didn't need half a gram of coke to get him through a meal. 'Well, everyone I know just bumbles along,' she said. 'Isn't that what it's all about?'

Cindy raised her eyes in patronising despair. 'Shall we get back to the boys, then?'

Patti nodded.

Just past the reception desk, Cindy turned to Patti. 'Do you mind if I ask you something? It's been bugging me all evening.'

'What?'

'Why are you dressed like that?'

Patti said, 'It's for driving.' She paused. 'It's a uniform for my school.'

'Your *school* uniform?' asked Cindy.

'No, not my school uniform, for my driving school,' explained

Patti. Cindy looked twitchy and blank all at the same time. Patti said, 'Oh, forget it.'

What had surprised her most about the encounter had been the Tesco Clubcard. But that was the thing with wannabe toffs, everything was not as it seemed.

IV

With the smell of Joop aftershave masking something stale in the bread bin, Tracey got down to work. She cleared the kitchen table of yesterday's *Soho Clarion* opened at the classifieds, along with a see-through envelope of junk mail. Then she yanked a pair of gardening shears from the far corner of the table, moving them to a ladderbacked chair, and set down the food boxes in order of descending size. She wiped her hands on a smeary tea towel and ambled next door.

The books were standard, three Robert Ludlum novels and a couple of Jeffrey Archers. Underneath them she traced the bent back spines of a series of Jilly Coopers and one Jackie Collins. Drawers spilled with nothing much: a half-filled-in form to adopt a Spanish donkey – in which he'd stated his earnings as in the £40,000 plus bracket – and an unopened Argos catalogue, still in its plastic, a puncture repair kit and a scattering of free samples of shampoo. A spider plant sprouting a satellite of baby plants was turning mouldy on a dried-up saucer and a *Time Out* was neatly folded to Friday's TV listings on the threadbare arm of a once plush chair.

Tracey kicked and prodded in a desultory way. She reasoned simply that if he didn't want her to poke around he wouldn't have left her alone. The bathroom was windowless and painted a deep dark blue, too gloomy for the space. She tugged open the cabinet and wrapped her hands round a couple of pill bottles of drugs she didn't recognise. She rotated a canister of foam aftershave ninety degrees to see its label. Gillette, the worst a man can get, she said to herself sourly.

She was taking her time because she was in no rush to get back to the kitchen. She was on the cusp in this relationship, looking for clues to take her forwards or to retreat. She was looking for a sign to progress – it might be a receipt from Quo Vadis, a Paul Smith jacket, a battered Mont Blanc pen atop a nearly-finished *Times* crossword.

She sank, defeated, onto the hard metal rim of the bath. The free-standing bath with its stylish crow's-feet legs she liked, but was it enough? Stretching her bare arms in front of her, she lazily nipped the wattle of fat hanging underneath her triceps. She sighed and looked up, craning her neck towards the bare bulb clinging to the ceiling. An electric toothbrush on the sink and stains of toothpaste and shaving foam around the basin formed the telltale crust of bachelordom. Apart from that there were no clues to James Ciriano. Tracey rotated her ankle gingerly and considered getting back to the kitchen. He could return at any second and she'd noticed that the pumpkin salsa had separated in a very unsatisfying way.

She yawned as she stood and reached for the sink to steady herself. When she saw the bag, she couldn't understand why she hadn't spotted it before. But that often happened in a flat search; concentrating on the incidentals you missed the big things.

The bag was a well-worn carrier with the logo smudged off. Tracey prodded it with the point of her shoe, listening extra hard to make sure no one was coming. Then she knelt down in front of it and fished into it hesitantly, not looking, as if it was a lucky dip.

The papers were clipped together. At first it just looked like the bureaucratic detritus of any forty-year-old-tax demands, passport renewals and standard letters of threat from credit card companies. She would have stopped there had it not been for the ruff of black at the neck of a plump turkey printed in the left-hand corner. Tracey frowned. It was a stylised turkey such as a child might draw, but it was a turkey nonetheless. Her eyes went automatically to the first sentence. And then to the second and so on and so on, flitting down the page like a secret agent.

Very soon the separated pumpkin salsa was on semi-permanent hold. After five minutes, Tracey McCloud had started to see the world in a whole different light. A light that, if she played her cards right, would illuminate her triumphal propulsion to the chamber of Westminster Council and, possibly, very much further. 'Tiger Tokens be damned,' she said out loud.

V

'Sweetheart, you've hardly touched your food.' Hartley smiled with parental concern at Cindy. Winston didn't know if it was genuine or just a reminder to him that interest in Cindy's welfare had been snatched like a baton from under his nose and passed on.

Cindy leant forward animatedly and took another sip of wine. 'I know, but I get too excited when we've got a demonstration.'

'You must eat,' said Hartley affectionately.

'Exactly,' said Patti. 'Who wants a pudding?' she added quickly. 'I didn't have a starter, which means I can have the crème brûlée.'

'I might head off to bed,' said Winston morosely. 'I'm absolutely done in.'

'Oh, don't go,' said Cindy, making a lunge for his hand. 'It's still early.'

Patti looked at him less persuasively. 'Stay and have a pudding. Besides, I'm only going to wake you up when I come to bed,' she told him, as if she'd already decided on it.

The overhead strip light showed up the blodges of red wine on the tablecloth and the unused cutlery at weird angles like an abandoned game of spin the knife. There were only two tables with people still at them, both businessmen finishing off carafes of wine and smoking hard. From the hall, a cash register clunked out a till receipt and there was a whooping as a taxi pulled up and a couple fell into the lobby. The draught from the open window was frosty. Patti had suggested closing it but Cindy said that it let the smoke get out.

'Darling,' Hartley said to Cindy, 'you've got a big day ahead of you tomorrow, maybe we should make a move too.'

Winston suddenly slammed the salt cellar on the table. 'Christ, will you stop simpering over her. She's not a child. It's pathetic.'

Hartley lifted his left eyebrow, making Patti wonder if it was something you learnt in Pilates. He said in a restrained way that meant he would prefer to shout, 'At least I know how to treat a lady.'

'What's that supposed to mean?'

'Meaning I'm not the one tossing myself off in some sad bachelor pad.'

There was silence for a good five seconds. Winston went red. Then Patti sat up and put her glass down in a determined way. She looked first at Hartley and then at Cindy and said, 'So? What's wrong with that? Everyone masturbates.' Then pointedly, almost proudly, 'Masturbation is not a crime.'

She spoke as the waiter was bringing over the coffee. It must have been louder than she intended because both the businessmen and a delinquent-looking barman gave her a stupefied look.

She flushed. Winston realised that Patti didn't know Hartley was referring to an actual incident. He smiled at her.

'Exactly,' said Winston. 'We can all be wankers, can't we, Hartley?' He stood up and turned with the faintest trace of a bow in Patti's direction. 'Shall we go to bed?'

Patti looked as if she was waiting for the punch line. She glanced from side to side. 'Er, OK.' She smiled at Cindy. 'Looks like we're off then.'

She finished her wine with one hand while Winston grabbed the other.

VI

'Hi, babe, I'm home.'

If he sounded like the dialogue from a 1950s sitcom, Tracey didn't notice.

'Tracey? Where are you?'

She looked up when she heard her name and stuffed the papers back into the bag.

'I'm in the bathroom,' she said, scrabbling to her feet, hoping the loose tile wouldn't snag her stockings. 'I hope you don't mind, it was filthy. I was just giving it a jolly good scrub.' In the time it took for Beaver to cross the flat, she had grabbed the Mr Sheen bathroom spray and a sponge from behind the sink. When he arrived, her elbow was going like a piston.

Beaver kicked the door open as if it was locked. He stood with both hands above him, resting on the doorjamb. There was a tightness round the trousers.

'God, are you a sight for sore eyes,' he said.

Tracey turned round from the sink to face him, flushed from her sudden activity. Beaver looked her up and down and then up again, his eyes moving reluctantly from her breasts to her mouth.

She said weakly, 'How did you get on? Did you sort your stuff out?'

'Lift your skirt up.'

Tracey dropped the sponge. 'It's a dress.'

Beaver said, 'Lift your dress up.'

She was wearing red silky pants with a V of flowers round the crotch . . . Beaver groaned. The suspender belt wasn't matching, though at this stage the details were lost on Beaver. As he crossed the bathroom, Tracey kicked off her shoes to achieve height parity and started to work the cap sleeves of her dress over her arms. When Beaver got to her, he put one hand down the back of her pants and with the other gouged her breasts out of her bra one after the other in quick succession. He kissed her once on the lips and then quickly moved down. Then he told her to turn round so he could watch her breasts in the mirror. Tracey did as she was told. By this time Beaver was as thick and hard as a bottle of Domestos.

VII

'If you think I'm shagging you to get back at your girlfriend's boyfriend, you're very much mistaken.' Patti scurried down the corridor to keep up with Winston.

'She's not my girlfriend.'

'Do you think the mini bar will be expensive?' asked Patti as Winston slid the key over the lock.

Winston said, 'And anyway, I don't want to have sex with you.'

Patti slumped against the door edge, exhausted by the dash and more tipsy than she'd thought at the table. 'Why not?'

Winston said, 'It wouldn't be fair.'

WHITE MEAT AND TRAFFIC LIGHTS

'Actually, then, neither do I.'

Patti went straight into the bathroom to lay claim to the complementary toothbrush. A sign asked residents to put only towels they had used in the bath to be washed. Earlier, on purpose, Patti had dumped them all in the tub. She retrieved one and wiped her mouth. She went into the bedroom and looked at Winston.

He said, 'What about a nightcap?' He was lying on the bed, wafting a cigarette as he spoke.

'This is a non-smoking room, you know.'

'So?' said Winston caustically.

Patti started making up the child's bed, fetching sheets and a purple nylon quilt from the top shelf of the walk-in wardrobe. Winston stared at the blank TV screen.

After three minutes of silence, Patti said, 'Look, what's got your goat?' Winston ignored her. She carried on, 'Is it because you still fancy her?'

'*No,*' said Winston.

Patti said, 'Liar.' She impersonated Winston at the table: '"More water, Cind? Wine OK for you? You look great, you know. Is that a new hair colour?"'

Winston said, 'Fuck off,' and tried to throw a pillow at her. It got stuck behind his head so that when he dislodged it he fell hard against the headboard.

Patti tucked a sheet in. 'Serves you right.' She grabbed the pillow to use on her bed. She went on, 'Go on, admit it, you still fancy her.'

Winston spoke with his head towards the carpet. 'All right, all right, I still fancy her.' He lifted his head and looked at Patti. 'I mean, what's she doing with that plank Hartley?'

Patti hauled the quilt over. 'Some women like planks.' Then she said, 'Some men like plankesses.'

'What's that supposed to mean?'

Patti didn't look at him as she spoke. 'I mean, she's a vapid cow with an eating disorder.'

'*So?*'

'So what's so great about her?'

'She's got a fantastic arse.'

Patti said, 'She's a cokehead.'

'She's got great tits.'

'She talks about, like, muscle groups with the same, like, degree of concern other people have for, like, endangered populations. And take your shoes off when you're lying on the bed.'

Winston said moodily, 'What's it got to do with you? You're not sleeping in the bed.'

'Good,' said Patti, hanging her jacket on the back of a chair. She mooched around in silence.

'You're a fine one to talk.' He finished his cigarette with a smoke ring. 'You're just jealous.'

Patti gave a hollow laugh. 'No, I am not.' She sat in the middle of the fold-out bed and opened a free sachet of moisturiser and smeared it on her face. 'I wouldn't want to be her if you paid me.'

'Good, 'cos no one *is* paying you.' Winston kicked his shoes off, swung his legs onto the floor, and slouched over to the mini bar. He picked up the remote and switched the TV on. It was a flat page of script welcoming them to the Travel Lodge. Winston switched it off. He had four miniatures of whisky in his hand. He unscrewed two and handed her one.

Patti said, 'I've cleaned my teeth,' and took it.

They drank in silence for a while. Patti unscrewed the second drink, which she expected to be whisky but turned out to be Bacardi. She drank it anyway. Then she looked at him. She said, 'I bet you went down on her a lot.'

'*I'm sorry?*'

'Eager-to-please men give a lot of head.'

Winston thought for a few seconds. 'Some men like it.'

'Yeah, right.' Patti went back into the bathroom for a glass of water. Her hair still had the flower wrapped into the crown.

Winston called after her, 'You look like the urchin from a West End musical.' He waited a few seconds. 'The one that doesn't get to have a secret benefactor.'

She said, 'Thanks. Can you switch the light out while I get into bed?'

'Sure.' Implying there was no way he'd want to see her take her clothes off. He leant over and switched off the double lamp above the bed, which extinguished every light in the room. She heard him suck on his miniature while she took her top off and laid it flat out on the writing desk. Outside they heard four car doors slam in quick succession. Inside, the twang of Patti taking her bra off.

Winston said, 'OK then, you seem to think you know all the answers, I've got a question for you.'

Patti said, 'Fine,' and draped her bra over her blazer. She'd decided to sleep in her tracksuit bottoms.

'Do you give good blow jobs?'

'Excuse me?'

'You're the one that brought up oral sex. You women think you're so fucking marvellous. Come on. It's a simple yes or no. Do you give good blow jobs?'

Patti thought for ten seconds. 'Well, put it this way, I've never had any complaints.'

'Hah!' said Winston, jubilant. She heard him sitting up. 'I rest my case.'

'What case are you resting, exactly?' said Patti tiredly.

'Ask any woman if they give good head and they go all smug and say "I've never had any complaints".'

'So?'

'So,' ask a bloke how many good blow jobs he's had, I'll tell you how many. Pretty bloody few. Nine times out of ten, they're crap. On the other hand, women go around thinking they're hotter than fucking Linda Lovelace.'

'So?'

'So, men don't complain. They're grateful for that sort of thing. Women, though,' he paused and she heard him drink, 'that's different. Moan, moan, moan. And not in that sort of way.' He slumped back against the headboard.

'What are you trying to say? That you're crap in bed and Cindy's better off with Hartley?'

'I mean, women complain about everything. I mean everything. They tell you you lack commitment, you put too many tablets in the washing machine, you don't give them enough space, you don't call them enough. You think the G-spot is a type of furniture. Fucking hell. I mean they're not so fucking perfect. It takes two to fuck up a relationship. They give crap blow jobs, but we don't complain.'

Patti didn't say anything for a minute. She could hear Winston breathing. Then she said, 'Glad you've got that off you're chest?'

Winston was silent.

Patti said, 'Look, you've got to have stamina for a high-maintenance bird. Payback for dating a beautiful woman is selfless devotion. I don't see you as the selfless devotion type.'

Winston said, 'Thank you, Dr Raj Persaud.'

'Anyway, I do give good blow jobs.'

'What, you've got a certificate?' Winston said caustically.

Patti ignored him and put the second empty bottle on the carpet under her bed. Without the light, she felt her head sway. She tried to fix the far window in a steady gaze.

'Anyway,' said Winston, sounding drunk, 'what all women tend to forget is that you should never underestimate the power of charm.'

Patti wondered if she shouldn't fetch the waste paper basket in case she needed a sick bucket in the night. She grunted at Winston and fell asleep.

VIII

Tracey never complimented men on their sexual performance, which she considered, in relation to what women had to do, perfunctory.

'Wow,' she said. They had moved from the bathroom to the bedroom under a pale green duvet. 'I didn't think men of your age . . . I mean the recovery rate was . . .' She stroked his chest. 'You're not on Viagra, are you?'

Beaver laughed. 'No, of course not.' He kissed her head. 'It must be you, babe.'

She had her head on his chest. Without the duvet, she would have seen her legs were half a length longer than his, but this was no time to split hairs.

'You were great,' she said.

Beaver smiled. 'What can I say?'

'I mean *really* great.'

'It must have been seeing you in the bathroom like that.'

Tracey picked at his chest hair. 'What, have you got a mirror thing, then?'

'No.' He stroked her hair. 'You looked so, I dunno, *domestic*.'

'Thanks.' Beaver's left thigh was sandwiched between her legs.

She started to stroke his upper thigh higher, coyly, until she found his testicles. Then she remembered. She pulled away quickly. 'Butterballs!'

Beaver released her as if she carried an electric current. 'You what?'

'Butterballs,' said Tracey. 'That stuff in your bathroom.'

'What stuff?'

Tracey was sitting up, her breasts falling in opposite directions along the ridge of the duvet. 'The carrier bag in your bathroom.'

He bent over and licked her right nipple affectionately. Then he scratched his head and frowned. '*That* has something to do with Butterballs? I don't get it. That's from work.'

'You mean your work is to do with all that,' Tracey ran a hand through her hair, 'stuff?'

'I swear, babe, I don't know what you're going on about.'

'Then what's it doing in your bathroom?'

'Honestly, love, I haven't even seen what's in the bag. Someone at work found it and asked me to look after it.'

Tracey looked at him. Her mouth was dry. She reached out for a glass of water next to the bed, thinking. She said, 'You mean, you haven't read it?'

'Babe, I swear.'

'Well, you'd better go and get it then.'

'Hang on.' Beaver got out of bed. 'I don't even remember where it is.'

'By the bath.'

Tracey was too preoccupied to watch his buttocks move in that post-coital alpha male swagger that she loved. He came back and presented the carrier to her meekly. She patted the bed next to her and waited for him to get in. She was being school ma'amish in a way that made Beaver's dick start to feel tight again against the weight of the duvet.

'Right then,' she said, 'we'll start with page one.'

IX

'Helena, will you please get down from there?' Xenia wrapped her coat round her shoulders. The rain had stopped but the night was cold. 'Please, you'll freeze. Come down and tell me what this is all about.'

The last thing Xenia wanted was for someone to report them to the militia. It was half an hour since Helena had decided she didn't feel well enough to drive. She'd been chirpy enough on the way out of London and even down the long dark country roads, until it really started to get dark. At just gone eight, she'd turned off the main road and into a quieter lane and then pulled into a lay-by.

The car was surrounded by silver birches stretching way back from the road. It was creepy but reminded Xenia of home. Helena had switched the engine and the lights off and then twitchily got out of the car. She had climbed onto the bonnet and then pushed herself onto the roof of the car, where she'd been ever since.

Xenia sat in the car. With the engine off and no heater, she rubbed her hands together and then sat on them, trying to keep warm. She opened the door and tried again.

'Come on, Helena, let's talk about it.'

Helena didn't speak. She was kneeling on the roof of the car with her small dark head rotating in tiny safe-cracking clicks, as if she was keeping watch. Xenia was confounded. Maybe it was the stress of the last few months. Maybe it was the full moon.

'It'll be much warmer in the car.'

Then Helena spoke. It sounded like 'book' in English. Xenia did a double take. 'What is it, darling, what book? Is it the map you want?' But she was ignored. As far as Xenia was concerned there was nothing else for it but to stay in the Niva, try to sleep, and sit it out until the morning. She moved the cardboard box from the back seat onto the front, issued a silent prayer for Gleb and Galia and curled up on the back seat. She gave out a long confused sigh and listened to her stomach growl in hunger. The weird thing was, despite everything, she still hoped she'd dream of the handsome dark stranger with the shiny shoes who'd come to the village last summer and started the whole thing off.

X

Bates looked across at Herbert. 'I told you it wouldn't be so bad.' He tried to be chipper. Then he tried conciliatory. 'What about if I bought you a Cornish pasty to make up?'

Herbert said, 'It'll take more than a meat pie to make up for this.'

'Ah!' said Bates. 'That means that at least you're talking to me.'

Herbert ignored him. As a special treat, because the seats were softer, Bates had upgraded the tickets to first class. They were just past Manningtree when Herbert issued his first words to Bates since the Angus Steakhouse. The table was awash with little bottles. Both men were now drinking shorts.

Bates said, 'We'll get you home. Mrs King will cook us up some turkey fritters, we'll watch the *Hollyoaks* omnibus and have a jolly fine time.'

Herbert carried on watching the darkness flit by. Bates watched Herbert's drooping moustache in his reflection in the carriage window. All the contours of his face were sagging downwards. In the next compartment a mobile phone rang. It was two couples rowdy after a night out at the theatre, the men drinking twice as fast to make up for wasted time.

Bates said, 'If it makes you feel any better, you can have all the compensation from the club. All ten grand of it.'

Herbert looked at him. 'I thought you said it was fifty grand.'

Bates said tiredly, 'My boy, you know what these Londoners are like, they're slippery. He's trying to bring the price right down.'

'You can stick your compensation where the sun don't shine,' Herbert told him.

Bates was genuinely offended. 'Well, Herbert, after all I've done for you over the years.' He picked at a corner of his Thai chicken mini-fillet foccacio. 'At least they were nice to you at the hospital.'

'I'm not surprised,' said Herbert in sarcastic wonderment. 'That hospital has got to be in line for a Nobel prize for its work in the field of mutilated foreskins by now.'

Bates said, 'There's no need to be like that about it.'

The trolley service barrelled down the aisle and Bates stocked up on more wine, which was all they had left. As she leant over with the change, the waitress's eyes inadvertently slipped first to Bates's groin and then to Herbert's, who had dispensed with using an *Evening Standard* as a shield at Chelmsford. Her face fell in panic. Bates said he'd never seen an Anglia Rail employee so anxious to get to economy seating.

Herbert drank from a half-bottle of red wine. 'I still can't see what we achieved by the whole trip.' He shook his head. 'Apart from circumcision.'

'Well, the good thing is,' said Bates, sitting back, 'Nevski seems to have shut up about his precious package.' Then he looked at Herbert. 'I'm just wondering when you might do the same.'

'Do the same what?' asked Herbert.

'Shut up about your precious package.'

XI

That night the evening meal, much later than usual, fell into the coop with a message. The hatch went up as usual and in came the pizza and the chocolate bars. Despite their incarceration, both the boys grunted, 'Thank you,' as if it was a waiter service. Only this time there was a voice in the dark.

'Make the most of this one, guys.' The voice was thick and foreign. 'Because it's the last meal you're going to get.'

At first Alfie thought he meant they were being released. Then he thought about it some more and came up with a much more sinister take. Afterwards Alan agreed with him and Alfie thought he heard a whimper in the darkness, above the bubbling brook noise of turkeys roosting. That night, Alfie started hacking at the planks like a woodpecker.

Chapter Ten

I

Patti asked, 'You want to wait to say goodbye to them?' In the watery daylight the Travel Lodge had the flimsy feel of a low-budget porn set. On the clocks behind the reception desk, whether by coup or natural disaster – or the battery running out – time had stopped in Jakarta at 5.48 a.m. In Colchester it was 9.07 a.m.

Winston said, 'No way. I'm settling up the mini bar and then we're off.'

'What about breakfast?' Patti said.

'You want something, go and nick a roll.'

Patti scowled at him. 'You're a real charmer.' She was going to add, 'No wonder Cindy left you,' but something told her the less reference made to last night the better. She said, 'You want anything?'

Dawn had been replaced by Dickie Reception, which was another book title, thought Patti, only this one was set in the tense world of WWII radio communication. Dickie wanted to know if Winston had used the telephone. He looked momentarily bamboozled, as if he'd been asked if he knew how to use the telephone. Winston told him no, definite and calm. Then he yelled, 'Get me a yoghurt.' He spoke to Patti's back as she bounced towards the dining room. 'But not banana.' She was almost out of audio range when he called, 'And something to drink. But not Dr Pepper.'

Breakfast was set out dismally in the bar. It was the complementary value-adding part of the budget double, and Patti felt the thrown-together bitterness of tables shabbily dressed in grease-spotted pink tablecloths and ashtrays hastily removed. It must have been too late for the Pilates people; meanwhile, she smelt the International Leather Convention setting up in the far hall. She loaded rashers of bacon into three rolls, giving Winston an opportunity to offer her the spare one, and stuffed two yoghurts into her pocket. She wrapped the rolls in opened napkins and grabbed three cartons of orange juice and one of Ribena. Halfway to reception she went back for two spoons and picked up an apple, placing it in the crook of her elbow.

Winston was waiting for her at the exit, jamming open the automatic door by leaning against it. He had a lit cigarette deep between the V of his forefingers. Of all the ways of smoking, this was Patti's favourite, better even than holding it between thumb and forefinger. Somewhere under the bacon rolls she felt a stab in her heart, or it might have been trapped wind.

'All ready?' she said.

Winston flicked the butt into the bushes. He tugged the Ribena from her pocket and bit the cellophane off with his teeth. 'That had better not be banana,' he said, his eyes on the yoghurt pots.

Patti looked down. 'Relax, it's natural.'

'Natural,' he said, 'is even worse than banana.'

'Diddums,' said Patti and handed him a bacon roll.

Winston opened the napkin. 'Excellent.' He took a bite.

Patti half-curtsied, making her tracksuit bottoms drag through a puddle. 'Thank you, wise one.'

She was looking round the car park; she always did. No Ladas but that was no surprise, in her experience. They were more of an urban phenomenon. Then again, that might be by dint of the fact that that was mostly where she looked for them. The car park was made up of rows of company-valeted sales rep cars, Mondeos and BMWs. Further away from the centre, parked shyly, were a couple of beat-up vans that must have belonged to the leather people. Then came the sleek slug of a Citroën Diane and a new Volkswagen Beetle that had Pilates written all over them. Patti had parked under a light on the far verge next to a wooden picnic bench. The sky was a bank of clouds that made her eyes hurt. The air smelt of diesel. HGV lorries sluggishly made their way to the slip road back onto the motorway.

'What a dump,' said Winston.

Patti opened her door and stretched over to let Winston in. She dabbed a licked sleeve onto the greasy mark left on her blazer by the bacon rolls. 'Bugger it. I'll have to have it dry-cleaned.'

'I wouldn't bother if I were you,' Winston told her.

'Cheers.'

'No, I mean it's dark, you can't see it.' He slammed the door shut. The car smelt of stale cigarettes and old apple cores. She passed him the bundle of breakfast and went to start the car.

She said, as if it was the first time it had occurred to her, 'Shit, I hope it goes.' She stopped and waited in silence for a few seconds, clenching her buttocks in nervous excitement.

'Go on, then,' urged Winston after half a minute. 'In case you've forgotten, we're in the middle of a high-speed chase.'

Patti looked at him and relaxed. 'You said you knew where they were going.'

'I do, but—'

Patti jumped as her mobile rang out a text message. 'Hang on.' She tried to tug her phone from inside her blazer and the apple fell on the floor. 'You'd better eat that before it bruises,' she told him. Winston had his head down close to Patti's lap, trying to reach the apple. Patti crooked her arm round her mobile to read the message. She said, 'It's from Rory.'

Winston came up, prodding the apple and rubbing it on his sleeve. He said, 'Really.'

Patti stopped looking at her mobile and studied Winston. 'Do you know why you do that?'

'Do what?'

Patti said, 'Rub apples on your clothes like that.'

'Er,' said Winston sarcastically, 'because they've just fallen on the floor of a filthy Cinquecento?'

'No,' said Patti, 'wrong.' She smiled. 'People do it to apples anyway. I mean you wouldn't rub a pear on your jacket.'

'Depends on the pear.'

Patti looked at him. 'It's supposed to represent rubbing away Eve's fingerprints when she handed the apple to Adam in the Garden of Eden.'

Winston bit into the apple and specks of fruit flesh sprayed outwards. He chewed and thought. 'Really? What was that Garden of Eden gig? Doesn't it mean all women are head fucks?'

'Something like that,' said Patti absently. She was reading her text message. 'Rory wants to know where he can—' She stopped dead. 'Oh, nothing, he's just saying hi.'

Winston repeated his question. 'What does it mean, the apple thing?'

Patti replied, distracted, 'I dunno. Temptation, isn't it? The temptation of women.'

Winston held the apple away from him, above his knee, and studied it. He said, 'Probably.' Then changed the subject. 'Look, can we go now, please?'

Patti pulled out the choke and turned the ignition. The engine caught first time. Her face lit up and she adjusted the mirror out of habit. She turned to Winston and said, 'Where to, Grasshopper?'

II

Xenia rotated her neck slowly and stretched her calf muscles by resting her leg on the wheel arch. She said, 'How do you feel now?' She was speaking to Helena through the open passenger window. The car was so cold without the heater on that it made little odds if the windows were open or shut. Helena was sitting in the driver's seat.

'Better, much better. Hungry, though.' Xenia got into the car and looked across at Helena. It was the first time she'd studied her since last night. She was pale and glassy-eyed. 'And quite cold,' Helena added.

Xenia wasn't surprised; she'd spent ten hours on the roof of the car. She said gently, 'Don't worry, we'll soon warm you up, and look,' she lifted her weight off her right buttock and dug deep into her coat pocket, 'I've got some money left. Let's go and find somewhere to eat.' She was trying to cheer her up. 'What do you fancy?'

'Corn,' said Helena straight off.

'You mean kasha,' replied Xenia, calmly looking at the dashboard.

'No.' Helena clung to the steering wheel with both hands. 'Corn.'

'Then you must mean popcorn.'

Helena nodded slowly. A red car drove past them, making an exaggerated point of indicating round them even though there were no cars on the road. The driver was a middle-aged woman in a green anorak who looked like the Queen. Xenia smiled at her as she passed. The woman, lost in her own thoughts, smiled back.

'Popcorn would be good,' said Helena.

'And some coffee,' said Xenia definitely.

'Water'll do me.'

'Whatever you like. Are you sure you feel well enough to drive?' Xenia was trying to shake Uncle Gleb's notion that women shouldn't drive at all. 'They just veer all over the road whenever they see a dress in a shop window or a kilo of tomatoes,' was how he put it.

Helena started the car. The narrow road was banked by steep verges on either side; a cluster of three early daffodils peeped up from the undergrowth. The engine drowned the birdsong that had woken Xenia at five, which had only added to Helena's scratching on the paint on the roof of the car. She'd checked it earlier when Helena was in the car; the paintwork looked as if someone had taken a nail to it.

Helena was shaking her head. 'I don't get it. I feel weird, not myself at all. Do you remember that rumour in Soviet times that they used to put stuff in the water that changed people?'

Xenia frowned. 'You mean it made the women taller,' she said. 'That was all a load of rubbish though, wasn't it?'

Helena's face was worry-worn. 'I guess,' she said slowly. 'I don't know, it's ever since I've been in this country.' She stopped, though Xenia sensed it wasn't the end of the conversation.

Both of them stared ahead in silence. Another car, this time a blue one, passed them, barely acknowledging the black Niva at the side of the road.

Xenia said, 'You didn't take anything in London, did you?'

Helena looked at her. Hurt, but not as though she hadn't thought of it before. 'Like what?'

'You know. You were the one who told me the girls take drugs to keep them awake.' She looked away. 'And to forget about what they're doing.'

'No,' said Helena definitely, 'I've never taken anything like that. I don't want to be a narcomaniac.'

'I didn't mean that.'

They sat in silence and Helena tapped her fingers on the

steering wheel. Her nails were short, with a trace of dirt behind them like a schoolgirl's. She said, 'Though there was one time, at the farm. When they gave us stuff. They said it was regulation for foreigners, to stop the turkeys being contaminated with germs.'

'That's a good one,' said Xenia with disdain. '*Us* contaminate them.'

Helena asked, 'Didn't you ever have to take it?'

'Never,' said Xenia, shaking her head for emphasis.

'That's odd,' Helena said quietly and started the ignition.

III

'Don't you see?' Tracey stared at him with unblinking eyes, her eyelashes knotted with yesterday's mascara and her pupils large dark orbs. 'This would give me exactly the start I need. Think of the publicity.' Since the Russian girl had eluded her, this, she reasoned, was heaven-sent.

'I'm not so sure.' Beaver needed time to think. Tracey had given him all night to sleep on it. But the only thing he'd slept on was a hard-on brought on by the memory of Tracey naked but for an apron.

On the other hand, Tracey had used the five hours since they'd finished going through the mish-mash of papers at 4.40 a.m. to come up with a plan. Mostly, though, she'd just turned the Rubik's cube of possibilities around in her head. 'I'm wondering what the best course of action is.' She scratched her hair. 'I'm thinking the papers first and then the police.' Beaver was lying down, staring at the ceiling. She went on, 'Or the police first, make it official, and then the papers?'

Beaver slowly eased his elbows out and pushed himself up. The duvet was at a diagonal on the bed, most of it on Tracey's side. He said, 'Now, are you sure that's the best thing?'

Tracey tipped her chin back against the headboard, defiantly. 'Of course,' she said. 'And I'll tell you, I intend to go a sight higher up than that rag the bloody *Soho Clarion*. By the time I've finished, they'll be choking on their bloody Tiger Tokens.'

'I'm sorry?'

'Nothing. Have you got anything I can wear?' Underneath the

duvet she was naked. She reached to the bottom of the bed for Beaver's cast-off shirt. The bottom four buttons were still done up; she pulled it over her head and got out of the bed.

Beaver tried to pull her back. 'Come on, babe, come back to bed. It's freezing. Where are you going?'

'Is there anything to eat?' she said, not turning round. 'We've got a big day ahead of us.' She padded towards the door. Beaver watched the way her calves tightened as she walked and the faint blue translucent snake of veins.

'But it's Saturday.'

'All the more reason to be quick, we might get the Sundays with this one,' Tracey called from the bathroom. The door was open and Beaver could hear her pee. He sat up and rubbed his face with his hands.

He said, 'Tracey, can I have a word?' He heard the taps running and squirts from aerosols. 'Trace, babe, can you come here a minute?'

She appeared in the doorway with his toothbrush in her mouth and grunted, making him aware of the inconvenience he was causing her. A flash of music blared into the room from a car stereo driving fast along empty streets. It must be later than he thought.

Beaver rubbed his nose. 'Sweetheart, it's about last night.'

'What about it?' Tracey asked, quick and suspicious.

Beaver looked askance. 'No, no, babe,' he told her, 'nothing like that.' He added quickly, 'It's about those papers. The Butterballs stuff.' He gave her a look that he hoped conveyed the impression of frankness. 'It's just that I kinda know about it, already.'

Tracey frowned so that the ridge of skin above her nose formed an exclamation mark. 'How do you mean?'

'I mean not all of it,' said Beaver with a wry smile. 'It's like I know the – hell's bells.' He put his hand out. 'I think you'd better come over here, babe.'

IV

'By God, that tastes better than all that foreign muck.' Bates, on his fourth tandoori turkey topper, wiped a stringy length of cheese from his mouth on the back of his hand. Herbert was eating toast and peanut butter. To make a point, he'd poignantly lined up two painkillers on the rim of his plate. They followed like ducklings behind the bigger yellow beta blocker. All three stared at Bates in silent reproach. After a night in his own bed, Bates was feeling chipper. He had even suggested a game of croquet, hinting that, as part of the rapprochement, he would let Herbert win.

He pushed his plate away and sat back. 'Did you phone Mrs King to tell her we'd be back last night?' he asked. 'I simply cannot fathom what has got into that woman. She ain't never here no more.'

Herbert said, 'She left a note to say she's still round her brother's.'

'Well, who the dickens will be looking after me then?' Bates belched and used a wetted finger to pick up bits of crispy crumb coating from his plate. 'The heating wasn't on, bed not made, washing-up in the sink, dogs not fed. The whole place is a shambles. That woman. I tell you, I have to do everything round here.' He sighed heavily. 'Who'd be a turkey magnate, eh? I found these in the fridge, past their sell-by date.'

The radio jangled out an advert for Toys B Us, a new toddlers' retailer in the Clacton shopping village.

Herbert licked his knife. 'What time's that copper supposed to be coming round?'

'There's no supposed about it.' Bates looked at his watch. 'He'll be round any minute now. He said half past. And before you throw another moody, your accident is incidental. I need to ask him about the Raynham lad, how the search for him is going.'

Herbert picked bits of peanut from between his teeth. 'What's happened to all that while we were away?'

'It's all in Nevski's hands now.' Bates poured a cup of tea from a Charles and Di memorial pot. He poured milk straight from the bottle, after sniffing it. 'Talking of which,' he said, 'he seems to have done a bunk 'n' all.'

'Maybe he's gone back to Russkiland.' Herbert was drinking a can of Pepsi.

Bates tapped his fingers on the side of his mug. 'Not yet he hasn't.'

A sparky DJ on the radio introduced a Queen song. Herbert picked up a fork and strummed it with his right hand like an imaginary guitar. Bates observed, 'You've cheered up.'

'Yeah, well,' said Herbert. 'I can't be mad for ever.'

'That's the spirit, old boy.' Bates reached over and clapped him on the back. He pointed to the line of pills with his eyes. 'Don't forget your beta blocker. Now, I've got some accounts to do.' He pushed his chair out from the table.

'I'm not seeing that copper on my own,' Herbert said, panicking.

'Did I say you were?' said Bates wearily.

He left the question hanging and then made his stiff bow-legged walk to the door. When he was halfway out, a grey pepper-flecked lurcher lifted an ear and galloped over to the window, yelping and whimpering with excitement. Five seconds later the men heard the skid of tyres on the gravel.

Bates smiled eerily and looked at his watch. 'The long arm of the law, ever punctual.'

Herbert looked at him. 'You've got some bottle bringing him up here.'

'What?' said Bates incredulously. 'I suppose you'd prefer to go to the station, would you? Or have had one of those London coppers eyeing the evidence?' Bates adjusted his trousers and checked the front of his shirt for stains. 'Believe me, it's much better this way. All I need is a police report to send to that club-owning toerag. Make it official.' He switched the radio off as the doorbell rang. 'Bring him into the sitting room,' he said, pulling the napkin out of Herbert's collar. 'When you're ready.'

Neither of them was expecting a woman officer, especially not one in trousers. She carried her hat solemnly under her left arm. Trousers or not, for a second or two Bates had difficulty seeing her as anything other than a strippergram. He knew that women working in male-dominated professions acted as if they had something to prove; it usually made them more bolshie. He'd witnessed it first-hand in the warehouses and seen it second-hand on *Ready Steady Cook*. Besides, he put the woman in front of him, with her cropped hair and lack of make-up, down as a dyke;

didn't even consider her for the Butterballs test. To give him the unquestionable air of authority, he'd moved to the easy chair underneath his portrait. He had made a point of not standing when the WPC came in.

'WPC Marion Peters,' she said, putting her hand out to Bates.

'Pleased to meet you,' said Bates genially. Herbert nodded and blushed.

She sat down on one of the ladderback chairs without being asked, got a notebook out and leant heavily on the table.

Bates said, 'Where's Sergeant Butcher today? He was the one I asked for.'

'The sarge's off today, sir, I'm afraid,' said the WPC, without looking as if she was sorry.

'But we really would prefer,' said Herbert, 'to see a male officer.'

'Well, I'm afraid that's impossible,' said the WPC.

Bates nodded to himself. He said, 'OK then, have it your own way.' He smiled broadly at Herbert. 'Right then,' he said. 'Would you like to describe the crime to the WPC?'

She looked up from the blank page. 'Crime? I thought this was about Alan Raynham. The sarge said you wanted an update.'

Bates was perched on the edge of his chair. He was no longer able to cross his legs and sitting with his knees apart he considered inappropriate. His legs were demurely clamped shut.

'Well, obviously that as well,' he said. 'The lad's never out of our minds, is he, Herbert?'

Herbert nodded.

Bates went on, 'Is there any news?' He looked over at Herbert. 'Herbert, why don't you bring the WPC some tea?'

'Yes, of course.' He padded to the door, glad of the excuse.

Bates turned to the WPC. 'You were saying?'

'There's no update, as such,' she said. 'He's still missing. There were a couple of calls after your appeal, but I'm afraid there's not much I can divulge while the operation is ongoing. It's procedure, I'm afraid.' The WPC stopped, apparently weighing up information before she spoke. Bates waited. She said, 'There is one thing though. Another lad's disappeared. A bit older, a reporter on the local paper. They found his bike over Wickham way.'

Bates didn't answer at first. Then he said, 'Well, I'm jiggered. I guess that's what happens when you go away for a couple of days.'

The officer uncrossed her legs. 'That was one of the reasons I had to come up here.'

'You what?'

'The lad's news editor said his last job was up here.' She looked at Bates. 'We called but there was no reply.'

Bates nodded, unflustered. 'That's right,' he said slowly. 'Herbert and me's been away in London for a couple of days on business,' he smiled, 'in the main, but there was a bit of pleasure. Herbert's a devil for those musicals so we went to that *Starlight Express*. Personally, I can't stand 'em.' He shrugged.

The WPC made a note. 'We had a look round, anyway,' she said.

Bates said, 'Find anything?' almost hinting he'd have been surprised if they hadn't.

'Nothing, sir. The place was all shut up.' Bates noticed she was wearing dark tights under her trousers.

'That's right,' he nodded. 'Mrs King, my live-in lady, she's been away.' He paused and then went on, 'In any case, you say his bike was found Wickham way. Maybe he went on somewhere. Chances are he never came up here at all. You know what these lads are like.'

'No doubt you're right, sir.'

The door opened and Herbert appeared with a tray with one mug on it. 'I was just telling the WPC how we saw *Starlight Express*,' Bates said. 'What a super show it was. Isn't that right?'

Herbert said quietly, 'Roller skates.'

'Then, just after that, that's when Mr Long here became a crime victim,' said Bates. 'Didn't you, Herbert? A country boy at the mercy of an urban crime wave.' He smiled at the policewoman. 'Let me find you a mat for your tea, WPC.'

WPC Peters licked the end of her pencil and wrote the date in the top right-hand corner of her notebook. 'What was it, a mugging? A street attack?'

Bates looked at Herbert and spoke for him. 'Something like that,' he said. 'Now, I'm going to give you some time on your own while poor Mr Long tells you all about it.' He turned to Herbert. 'Off you go, then, boy.'

V

Tracey was cross-legged on the bed with Beaver's shirt lapels dangling in her lap and the duvet pulled up to her knees. Because the room was so cold, Beaver had reluctantly brought in a convector fan from the sitting room. His idea was that if it was cold enough, she'd come back to bed. Instead, he thought he heard the whirr of Tracey's thoughts above the 1,200 revs per minute fan.

She said, 'So let me get this straight.' She stretched her legs out in front of her. 'You don't know where these papers come from, but you think the guy who owns Butterballs may have left them accidentally on your premises when he came to . . .' She looked at Beaver, defeated, 'Now you see, that's the bit I get stuck on. Why was he here?'

Beaver tried to make it sound obvious. 'Babe, I told you. He's a client of mine.'

'A publishing client?'

'Let's just say he uses my services,' said Beaver.

'But then one day, when he was on your premises,' she took a sip of tea, 'he had an industrial injury for which he's suing you.'

'That's it exactly, babe.'

'What sort of injury?'

'A nasty one.'

'Such as?'

'Babe, I can't tell you. Not while the investigation is ongoing.'

Tracey frowned in irritation, put her mug down and picked the cuticle on her thumb with her forefinger. She said, 'And what's that got to do with what's in this lot?' She nodded at the papers scattered around the bed.

Beaver pushed his hair back. 'It means that if you drag me into your plans to take over the world, he's going to throw it all back in my face. And yours.' He tried to edge the shirt collar aside and kiss her neck.

Tracey pushed him away. 'I'm not planning to take over the world.' She went on, 'You mean to tell me that you can know what we now know, be aware of what he's doing and let him get away with it? It's immoral.'

'I think I could live with it.'

Tracey shook her head. 'I don't believe you. I thought you understood my campaign.' She picked up her mug and emptied it. 'I thought you believed in cleaning up Soho. I thought you understood me.'

'Now, babe, please don't cry. Look, I'll try and help. I will, honest. But I can't see—'

Tracey tugged the duvet off and got up, swaying her hips in exaggerated annoyance. Beaver rubbed his eyes, collapsed against the headboard and sighed. It was a familiar pattern.

Two minutes later she reappeared with a glass of water. She leant against the doorframe.

'You know,' she said, 'I don't think your a real businessman at all, are you?'

Beaver lifted his head. 'Er, hang on, babe, what do you mean, I'm not a businessman? What do you think I do?'

'You're no businessman if . . .'

'I'm no businessman if what?'

'You're no businessman if you can't see a way out of this that will get you off the hook and get me a seat on Westminster Council.' She smiled and nodded her head. 'And expose this whole evil scandal.' Beaver thought she even sounded like a politician. She walked towards him. 'What sort of car have you got?'

'A Renault, why?'

'In that case, we'll take mine. Come on, get up.'

Beaver groaned. Tracey started collecting the papers around the bed, scrunching them into fat bunches.

Beaver tried one last line of attack. 'Look, what if the whole thing's a hoax? We could get in a bundle of trouble. Libel, defamation, contempt of court. It could cost a packet.'

'Shut up and get out of bed,' she said. 'We're going for a trip to the country.'

VI

Patti chewed on a Poppet contemplatively, pushing it round her mouth.

'I didn't know they still made these,' said Winston, shaking the carton and rolling them from one end of the box to the other. 'Or sherbet dibdabs, come to that.' Traffic was lighter than the day before, with fewer lorries in the slow lane. The Cinquecento chugged along at 74 mph, sweeping from lane to lane for no apparent reason, while Patti cursed women drivers for clogging up the middle lane. 'I mean, what are they overtaking?' she asked twice an hour.

Winston went on, 'Or Tutti Frutties. Why don't you eat up-to-date sweets?' He looked out of the window, still feeling the contours of the Poppets packet. 'Like a Star bar.'

Patti said, 'I told you, it's complicated.'

'So tell me.'

'It's a compulsion. Why do some people run marathons, or bite their nails? I don't know.' She looked across. 'Why do you smoke Camels?'

The countryside flashed by in a stream of grey. No matter how far they went, there was always one farmhouse or a barn on the horizon, clinging to the road. Or maybe they were just there anyway, no matter which direction the road went. Winston put his head back and said, 'I'll tell you why I smoke Camels. I smoke Camels because they're not Winstons.' To make the point he took the packet from the dashboard, making a smoker's check of how many were left, before taking one out with his lips. Before lighting it, he thumped it on the packet like her father used to do.

'There you go,' said Patti, lifting her hand off the gear stick, missing the point. 'So why don't you smoke Winstons?'

Winston used his free hand to pick at a loose bit of plastic on the ceiling. 'Well, if you must know, it's actually a guilt thing.'

Patti frowned in confusion and shrugged. Her seat was so far forward that when she looked at Winston she had to twist her head right round. 'What, guilty 'cos they're higher tar?'

'No.' Winston carried on picking, determined to dislodge a

triangle of plastic. 'I feel guilty because my brother started me on Winstons when we were little.'

Patti nodded. 'Your brother that's the coke dealer?'

'Yeah, my brother that's the coke dealer.'

'So?' asked Patti. 'What made you switch?'

Winston inhaled and let the fumes linger in his lungs. Then he relaxed and let the smoke burst out of him. He said, 'After I let him down with the break-ins, I felt bad. After a while I got fed up with feeling bad, so I decided not to any more.'

'Not to what?'

'Feel bad any more,' said Winston. 'That's when I started smoking Camels.'

Patti said, 'Did it work?'

'Kind of.' He stubbed it out and flicked the butt out of the open window. 'I should give up, in any case.'

She drove in silence, pulling out without indicating to pass an old X-reg red Ford Fiesta. Every now and then she stretched her arms by straightening them against the steering wheel. She frowned in concentration, and Winston watched her profile and the hairless patch of white skin behind her ear.

He said, 'So go on, it's your turn. What's the sweet thing? What was it, some sort of child abuse with a Curly Wurly?'

Patti kept looking straight ahead and her shoulders tensed. 'Look, can you change the subject? I'll tell you but not now. I've got enough to think about now.' Winston, amused, said, 'Like what?'

She ignored him. Winston sat forward and twiddled the radio knob. He tuned it in and out of local radio stations, tinny with adverts. Patti reached over and switched it off and asked, 'How much further is it?'

Winston leant over to look at the petrol gauge, resting his hand next to Patti's knees, childish shapes in her grey tracksuit. When he looked down he noticed she wasn't wearing any socks and her trainers were scuffed at the toes and moulded to the shape of her feet. Patti unconsciously brought the fasterning of her blazer together.

'Don't panic,' said Winston and sat back, removing his hand. 'We'll be there in an hour.'

'But what if they're not there?'

'Trust me,' said Winston. 'They will be.'

VII

Helena leant against the wheel. 'So now what do we do?' A gold and black sign with the Butterballs logo announced that they had the right place. At the bottom a discarded cardboard placard in red said, 'Compassion in farming'. Xenia thought compassion in farm workers might have been more appropriate, but she knew the British love of animals was legendary. An untarmacked drive led at an angle away from the main road. Each side of the drive was lined with scrubby forest land, pine trees mixed with ash. Apart from the occasional burst of birdsong and the hum of a tractor behind them, the place was deserted and eerily quiet.

'We wait,' said Xenia.

'What for?' asked Helena. Her voice was flat and sad.

Xenia didn't know what for. All she knew was that if they appeared anywhere near the turkey farm and were spotted, they'd be re-stolen. That was how she viewed it. She nervously looked in the rear-view mirror. She'd been kidnapped and sold into slavery. She hated this country. She made a promise that if she ever got home she'd never complain about anything ever again. They were parked in a lay-by, the type found on country roads, to let tractors pass. None of the countryside was familiar. They'd had to ask at a garage for directions to the Butterballs factory.

After half an hour of waiting, Helena fell asleep, twitching and restlessly muttering to herself in the driver's seat. Xenia looked at her with bewilderment and affection. Even if they managed to get the passports, they were still miles from home with no money. If Helena really was sick, the last thing they wanted was to be stuck here. Xenia reached over and tried to pull the bottom of her coat over her friend. Helena was bigger than Xenia and the coat strained to cover her. Every time she moved it, it exposed some other part of her. 'Poor thing,' she said to herself. Now Xenia had the added responsibility of another person to worry about.

She concentrated on the silence. Say they did make it home, then what? Helena would probably still work as a hooker, the only difference being she'd get paid in Ukrainian coupons rather than

English pounds. And where was the glory in working a double shift in the Tolyatti factory and coming home to Aunt Galia and Uncle Gleb?

Suddenly she looked up. Out of the corner of her eye, she saw flashes of yellow and blue between the trees as a car drove towards the road. She nudged Helena. 'Quickly, move down in your seat, someone's coming out of Butterballs.'

Helena nodded, half asleep. Xenia undid her seat belt and pushed Helena's shoulder down. Her flesh was solid and heavy. Absently Xenia picked at a dark feather on her sweatshirt. Then she bobbed down too, listening while the car slowed and stopped and then the crunch as it left the gravel and drove onto the road. It turned right. After ten seconds Xenia reasoned it was safe to sit up. Drops of rain had started to fall on the windscreen, light but definite enough to mean there was more to come.

'Well,' she said to Helena who was still dozing. 'If that doesn't confirm it.' She sounded almost proud. 'You see that?' Helena didn't respond. 'That was a police car leaving. That confirms what they always said to us. The police are in it as well. Now do you see why we can't go to them?'

Now, she thought to herself, they really were on their own.

VIII

Bates didn't see the policewoman to the door. As he pointed out, he couldn't do everything. When Herbert ambled back, Bates was setting out dominoes. Herbert said nothing, he was thinking of other things. Bates was not insensitive to the recent ordeal of his retainer. 'How did you think that went then, boy?' He spoke in a kind, modulated voice. 'I thought she wasn't a bad type, that policewoman. That is, for a police officer. And a woman.' He added, 'A flat-chested one at that.' Herbert stood at the door with his hands in his pockets. His leatherette trousers had been changed for a looser pair of cords, baggy round the middle. Bates didn't know if it was an issue of comfort or association. Chances were his trousers needed a wash, or a sponge down, or whatever you did with leather-effect clothes.

Herbert was quiet and pensive, as if waiting to be asked in. He slouched moodily into the room, sliding his slippers along the carpet, hitching his trousers up at the knees before he sat down. 'I didn't know she was going to have a look,' he said.

'Oh, for goodness' sake,' Bates told him. 'What does it matter? I'm sure it's not the first one she's ever seen.' Then he remembered the black tights underneath the trousers. 'The minx.'

The lurcher mooched in, yawning, with its head down. It lazily circled the rug in front of Herbert two or three times before lying down. 'I still don't see—'

Suddenly the lurcher cocked its ear. Bates said, 'Sssh.' He looked at Herbert. 'What's that noise?' Herbert told him not to worry; it was probably Mrs King. He had his feet up on a golden velour pouf, cradling his balls with one hand and looking at the TV listings guide with the other.

'There's someone at the back door,' said Bates. 'What, are you deaf?' He stopped setting the dominoes out and started to cross the room in short panicky steps. He reached as far as Herbert's chair when the door sprang open. The lurcher yelped and Herbert threw his magazine onto the floor.

'Nevski!' Relief mingled with shock. 'What the dickens are you doing creeping around here?' Bates said. 'I didn't even know you were still here.'

'Gentlemen, I wish you good day.' Nevski was wearing a light brown anorak with its sleeves rolled up to the elbow, revealing forearms matted with hair. On his head sat a flat cap with a peak and a rim of mildew round the top. His trousers had a metallic finish to them, with a streak of dirt below the knee. The overall look was so astounding that neither Bates nor Herbert noticed the handle of a small pistol in his left-hand pocket.

He moved towards them. 'You've been away.'

'That's right,' said Bates. 'We have. To tell you the truth, we've been on the trail of your blasted papers.'

Nevski nodded, weighing up the information. 'What was the result?'

Bates and Herbert exchanged glances. 'No bloody result at all,' said Bates. 'Look, do you still need them, or what?'

'Well, let's forget about that right now,' said Nevski. 'We have more pressing matters to deal with. The boy that was caught snooping around my experiment has been joined by another.'

WHITE MEAT AND TRAFFIC LIGHTS

Bates rolled his head round. 'Don't tell me you know something about that other lad?' he said, finishing the sentence with his head in his hands.

'I had no choice. He was caught red-handed.'

Herbert said, 'You're flaming paranoid is what you is,' wading in on his master's side.

Nevski ignored him. 'I am expected back in Moscow tomorrow and I'm not sure I can trust either of you two to finish the job.' Bates and Herbert looked at each other. Nevski went on, 'I propose therefore to do away with them today. As you know, I've always thought we should have liquidised the first one at the start.'

'Oh, now look here,' started Herbert. 'What's he going on about?' He turned from Nevski to Bates.

'Don't worry,' said Bates. 'He don't mean actually liquidise them, as in soup, do you?'

Nevski said, 'I mean liquidise as in kill them.'

Herbert said, 'Oh.'

Bates said, 'The other one, who was he?'

'No idea,' Nevski said uninterestedly. 'I caught him poking around the laboratory.'

Bates said heavily, 'You know, I'm starting to rue the day I ever got caught up in this caper.'

Nevski snorted and sauntered over to the drinks cabinet. 'And lose all that cheap immigrant labour?' he said. 'Not to mention the extras?'

All of a sudden Nevski was acting as if he was running the show. Bates stood up. 'Now look here, that's as maybe but it's all got out of hand. I mean, I can't condone killing a couple of lads.'

Nevski had poured himself a drink but hadn't put it to his lips. He swilled the glass in his palm. 'That's the problem with Westerners,' he said. 'You're too sentimental. Lives have to be lost in the pursuit of progress.'

Bates sat down and brandished a domino at Nevski. 'What I can't get,' he said, 'is why you couldn't do all this in your own country. Why do you have to drag honest Suffolk folk into it?' He looked at Herbert to back him up. Herbert nodded.

'Honest?' said Nevski. 'Please, you are making me laugh. I don't see you complaining when they work an eighteen-hour shift in your filthy factory. I don't hear you complaining when you send them off to work in London brothels, if they can make you money.'

'Now hang on a minute,' said Bates, shaking his head. 'Them girls could be doing anything in London. They might even be students, for all I know. I don't even know where they get sent to most times. I'm not the one with all the contacts. Isn't that right, Herbert?'

'Course it is.'

The lurcher, sensing excitement, pottered over to Bates, wagging its tail and sniffing his trousers. Bates went on, flinging one hand over his shoulder, 'Why can't you do it in your country?'

'Why do you think?' Nevski gave him a pitying look. 'Money, of course. Girls here can earn thousands in—'

'I'm not talking about the girls,' said Bates. 'I mean the experiment. Why can't you do that in your own country?'

'Money, my friend, money.' His voice hinted at sadness. 'Even here I think you have heard of the Russian Mafia. We are sitting on a potentially multimillion dollar industry. In Russia these days you can't open a shoe shop without someone wanting a slice. Every transaction, from paying a parking fine, requires you to pay someone.' He went towards the door, not to leave, but to lean against it. He turned to the room. 'It's simple economics, Mr Bates. You want our women for cheap sex and cheap labour, I need you for your law and order. Fair is, after all, fair. Wouldn't you agree?'

'No, I blummen wouldn't agree,' Bates said, still sitting. 'At least those women have a choice in whether they come over here.'

Nevski smiled. 'Oh no, they don't, Mr Bates. Please don't kid yourself. Many times they are kidnapped or told their families will be killed unless they agree to go to the West. They are slaves. It is quite simple.' He shrugged. 'But then Russians are used to serfdom. It doesn't shock us much. Me, I studied in the university to be a physicist. Now look at me. We all have to get a little used to prostitution. It's not so bad and the money is wonderful.'

Bates put his chin up defiantly. 'That's as maybe, but those boys don't have a choice in whether you put a bullet in their head.' He shook his head. 'By Christ, Nevski, I know the lad's mother.'

Nevski flung out a guffaw of laughter. 'The lives of those two are nothing,' he said. 'Believe me, if I had conducted this experiment in Russia, there would be a trail of corpses several kilometres long.'

'No, Nevski,' Bates told him. 'I can't allow you to kill those lads.'

Nevski shrugged with his hands and the dregs of his glass of vodka sprayed onto the carpet. 'I'm afraid you have little say in the matter.'

'I'll go to the police, so help me God.'

'I don't really think, bearing the circumstances in mind,' said Nevski wearily, 'that's a viable option. What do you suggest we do with them? Keep them in a turkey coop for the rest of their lives?' He left them time to think about it. Neither man said anything. Nevski stood up from his slouch. 'Now, gentlemen, if you'll excuse me, I have some business to attend to.'

He sauntered over to the drinks cabinet, slowly poured another drink and downed it in one. Then, with exaggerated deliberation, he screwed the cap back on the vodka bottle. As if he really was a man who took care of every detail. Herbert wriggled uncomfortably in his chair. Bates felt pinpricks of irritation prodding the back of his neck. He slammed his open palm on the table and the dominoes jumped and rattled in reply. The lurcher gave a lazy one-off bark. Quietly Nevski pulled the door shut behind him.

Bates stood up to take control of the room again. 'If that boy thinks he's got us over a barrel, then he's got another think coming,' he said. 'No one gets Suffolk boys over a barrel. Isn't that right, Herbert?'

Herbert was adjusting his trousers. 'No, they do not,' he said. 'We'll show him.' But something in the flatness of his voice suggested they both knew they were beat.

IX

Patti had been humming to a tune in her head. She checked and realigned the car closer to the verge. She said, 'Why would she be going to some turkey factory?'

Next to her Winston was asleep, his head lolling in the arch of his seat belt. She poked him in the ribs. If he complained, she'd say she didn't want him to get a stiff neck. She repeated the question.

'I told you, she used to work there.' Winston grimaced as he hauled himself up. He had gluey sleep in his voice.

'So why did she leave?'

He rubbed his neck and tried to push his legs away from his seat. 'How should I know? Fancied a change, I guess.'

'In London?' Patti sounded sceptical.

'Yes, London. Why not?'

Patti drove in silence. Then, 'Don't they have turkeys in Russia, then?'

'How the fuck should I know?' said Winston. 'All I know is I came to visit Bates and he asked me to give her a lift into town. Which I did.'

'Look, don't get shirty with me. I'm the driver, remember?' She braked deliberately hard to jolt him. 'Whoops,' she said and added quickly, 'Then what?'

'Then she got your business card and you know the rest.' He fumbled for his cigarettes. Smoke in the car reminded Patti of her father and the blast of cold air in the back when he opened the window. Summer holiday journeys when the three children in the back seat would persuade him to tell them a story, usually boastful tales of flash Italian cars he'd owned or near misses rally-driving. Looking back on it, her mum never told them a story. Either she didn't have any, or she wasn't telling them. More likely, though, they never asked her. She was thinking this when Winston said, 'Maybe she was only on holiday. Yeah, that'll be it. She's seen the sights and now needs to get back to work.'

'In my car.' She pulled the Cinquecento in a wide arc round a corner.

'How many more times do I have to tell you? Taking and driving away does not count as legal ownership.'

'You would say that.' She braked and slipped into third before accelerating into a corner. It was all bends now. She wondered if Winston had noticed the way she'd braked before the corner rather than on the bend, to save the brake pads. Then she remembered he was a man more readily impressed by firm tanned stomachs.

Winston waggled his head from side to side. He told her, 'If I remember right, it's pretty close to here.'

'There haven't been any signs.'

'No, I know. He likes to keep it pretty secluded because of the animal rights people.'

'What, is he cruel then?' asked Patti.

'Dunno,' said Winston. 'I don't think so. You know what they can be like.'

Patti said, 'Lobbyists, eh?' Then she smiled because she wanted to show him she could be a smart cookie when she wanted to be. The persistent beat of rain was slowing. Patti switched the windscreen wipers off and manually flicked them on when raindrops clogged her vision so much she could barely see the road ahead. She had gone back to humming the tune in her head. The tyres gave a satisfying slosh as she ploughed through puddles.

'Slow up a bit,' Winston told her. 'The entrance is somewhere on this road but it's difficult to see.' He turned to face her. 'I said, slow down.'

'OK, OK, keep your hair on.' Patti went down from fourth to second and drove with elaborate caution.

Winston said, 'Not that slow.'

Patti said, 'Sorry, master.'

They crunched round a sharp corner flagged up by a sign with black and white chevrons and a farm track leading away to the right. Rain was smeary on the windscreen so Patti flipped the wipers.

Winston said, 'Yeah, it's just round this—' He stopped, which made Patti turn to face him. Then he said, 'Well, bugger me.' Patti followed his eyes. 'There it is, look, there's the car. Parked up in that lay-by.'

Patti checked the rear-view mirror. She said, 'Now what do we do?'

'What do you think? I'm going to get it back.'

'Can you do that?' She'd pulled off the road into a gap in the hedge. Next to them was an immense field ploughed with huge furrows. Winston wound down his window to get a better look. The deepest smell in the fresh air was the mulchy earth. 'Is there anyone in it?' asked Patti, her hands still clasped to the steering wheel.

'I dunno,' said Winston. 'I can't see from here.' He opened the passenger door and filled the car with a gulp of cold air that made her eyes water. In Winston's wake she found herself staring out of his window at a cluster of crows or maybe magpies leaving the tallest tree of a clump on the other side of the field. She watched him plod over to the Niva with halting steps, as if he was wearing a blindfold. She could tell from the angle of his head that his jaw was wary: it turned and rotated to the left. She kept the battery running so she could use the windscreen wipers. The body of the Niva was just out of sight, shrouded with an unruly mesh of shrubbery. She figured there was someone in the car because Winston was knocking on the glass. She must have been holding her breath because she exhaled noisily. In her head a voice said, 'Damn.' Competition in the shape of a shapely Russian in distress was the last thing she needed at this stage of the game. Then another voice in her head, an older one and male, urged her to see the bigger picture. Not for the first time she tried to remember it wasn't all about her.

X

'Babe, I'm not even sure we should be travelling into the country.' The car was heading out along the M11. He went on, 'It might set off my agoraphobia.'

'Listen,' said Tracey savagely, 'if you don't stop whining you'll get my foot in your mouth.'

'Babe,' said Beaver sounding hurt, 'please.'

Tracey was head-to-toe Burberry for an out-of-town trip. She was wearing tartan trousers and a pale cashmere jumper. She had decided a waxed jacket was too eighties and had stuck with her poncho. Next to her, Beaver was more ageing urban terrorist than Farmer Palmer, with his combat trousers and hooded sweatshirt.

Beaver was nothing if not persistent, only he didn't want her to think she could get away with talking to him like that. 'I mean, what about the telephone?' he said. 'He might not even be there.'

'He is there,' argued Tracey. 'I called earlier.'

'And spoke to him?' asked Beaver. 'In person?'

'Not as such, no,' Tracey admitted, 'but I got through to the factory and asked if I could speak to him.'

'And?'

'They said he doesn't work on a Saturday but I should try at the house.'

'And you tried that number?' In profile he saw faint lines of crow's feet when she talked and when the sun burst into the car from the driver's side the hairs of a downy moustache covered in powder.

She gave him a withering look. 'I am a PR professional,' she said. 'They didn't *give* me the number. I got that off an animal rights website.'

'And you spoke to him, right?'

'No,' she said tiredly, 'but I spoke to a chap at the house who said he was there.'

They drove in silence. 'Are you sure about this, babe?'

She turned to him. 'Honey, trust me.'

Beaver smiled because, one: his tactic had worked, and two: no one had ever called him honey before. Maybe things weren't going to turn out so badly after all.

Chapter Eleven

I

Xenia had her elbows folded and her hands tucked under her armpits. It was for warmth and a way to defy and dismiss the scene in front of her. She was curved into the curl of the seat so that her shoulders were stooped to face her pelvis. When she heard a knock on the window her body flipped apart. The noise of her scream woke Helena.

Winston said, 'Can you get out of the car, please?' Typical, Xenia thought, the idiots were still polite even when you stole their cars. It was no later than early afternoon but the light was fading and when he spoke his breath blew steam.

Xenia shook her head and checked that the door was locked. 'No.' She indented her shoulder towards the passenger seat, acting as if Winston was a nuisance, like someone selling newspapers at traffic lights.

'Please, I need to speak to speak to you.' He looked up and down the road. 'It's urgent.'

Xenia's back didn't move. Helena, for her part, locked on to Xenia's face with puffy eyes, hoping that if they ignored him he'd go away.

'At least wind down the window.' Winston's mouth was so close to the glass it left condensation after each urgent burst. He knocked on the window again. Then he tried the door. He must have been murmuring something, because Helena saw milky clouds of breath when he moved. He had his hands fixed above the knees as if he was talking to an unruly child or a pet.

He spoke slowly. 'Look, it's OK, I'm not going to hurt you.

I'm trying to help. But I need to talk to you.' He eased himself up, resting a hand on the roof and feeling like an idiot. Inside, the women were talking in rapid bursts of constrained conversation. After the hothouse temperature of the Cinquecento's heater blasting at his feet and face, the cold felt like liquid ice. He walked to the boot and tried the lock.

'Hello,' Patti said blankly. 'What's up?' He hadn't heard her come towards him with her schoolgirl creep, deadened by the muddy verge.

'Nothing,' said Winston. 'They won't open the door.'

'Well, dunderhead, what do you expect? They're in a stolen vehicle.'

'Look.' Winston pushed a hand through his hair. 'I know they're in a stolen car. It's *my* stolen car, remember?'

She handed him the box of Poppets and walked up to the driver's door. She'd buttoned her blazer and turned the collar up. To stop her tracksuit bottoms dragging in the mud, she'd rolled them up, showing brittle white calves. She walked with both hands on her hips. On a grown-up woman it would have come across as angry defiance, but on her he thought it looked like a put-out toddler.

Winston turned away, leant against the slope of the boot, crossed one ankle over the other and lit a cigarette.

He felt the deadened ripple of Patti's confident knock on the glass.

'Hello, Xenia, it's me, Patti.' She sounded like she did when she was being a driving instructor, calm and persuasive. Against the metal of the car, Winston felt the mood inside change, sensed the women looking towards the window. 'From the garage.' She waited ten seconds, not pushing it, acting as if she didn't care about the outcome. 'I tell you what, though, it's freezing out here. Do you mind if I sit in the back?'

He heard the door open from the inside. He turned round; he could hardly see Patti's head above the roof of the car. When she caught him looking, she shrugged and looked deliberately baffled. Winston thought that was a nice touch. When she clambered into the back, the Niva didn't bow to her weight at all. Winston flicked his cigarette butt towards a clump of trees, thinking of forest fires and then reasoning it was too cold. Then he pulled his coat around him and walked back along a muddy furrow towards the Cinquecento.

II

Herbert put his hand on Bates's shoulder to steady himself while he pushed his foot into the cold cavern of a wellington boot. Then he waited for Bates to do the same. A couple of dogs sniffed around their trouser turn-ups, tails beating hard in expectation of a walk, but the men singlemindedly ignored them.

'Are you sure this is a good idea?' Herbert said.

Bates's face moved up from his feet to Herbert's face. His breath smelt of tandoori spices from his last turkey topper. 'I can't see how we've got a helluva lot of choice in the matter.'

'He'll be as mad as hell when he finds out.'

'We'll worry about that when it happens,' said Bates. With his head bowed, Herbert could study the shock of white hair on the crown of his head. Bates's voice was wheezy. 'You know, I'm starting to think that I wish I'd never set eyes on that blasted little toad. It's no secret that I prefer a woman with an ample bosom, but if I'd have known where this was going to end up, I never would have done it.' The strain of tugging his boot on left him red-faced. 'And I swear that on Mrs King's life.'

Outside, the forecourt was empty except for the detritus of the outdoors; a deserted roll of chicken wire looked as if it was waiting to be taken somewhere and a rusty, saddleless old man's bike leaned against the nearest outhouse. The wind must have been from the east, blowing into their faces the acrid smell of animal dung and chemicals.

'Are you sure you need me?' asked Herbert. Bates had noticed that whenever Herbert was trying to get out of something he cupped his genitals in his right palm by way of reproach.

'Yes, I bloody do. There might be some aggro. They might be like caged ferrets, those little buggers,' said Bates. 'You're the one with the gym membership and the muscle power. Allegedly.'

Their shoulders tightened in the wind. Bates kicked at a milk bottle that had blown into his path. 'And after I've performed this humanitarian act I'm going to have a glass of cider and prepare my case against that club man.'

Herbert had to think for a moment who he meant. 'Oh, the Mile High guy.'

'Who the dickens did you think I meant?' He smiled at Herbert sourly so that he had three distinct lines down both cheeks. 'Then we'll have to start thinking about how we can get that five grand in compensation.'

Herbert was going to speak but instead kicked at the barn door moodily. The squabble from the turkeys distracted them from the coops to the left.

'Now hush, my darlings,' said Bates. 'Daddy's not here for you.'

Herbert tugged at the bottom of his jumper. 'Er, boss.'

'What is it, Herbert?'

'Well, take a look.'

The boarded doors to two coops were open, pushed back as far as the hinges would allow. The doorways spewed a trail of hay like an old sofa splitting its sides.

Herbert said, 'Looks like if we wanted to let them go we're too late.'

'Christ alive,' said Bates, his face drawn, 'you don't think Nevski's gone and done it, do you?'

'Well,' said Herbert, 'put it this way. I wouldn't put it past him.'

III

'OK,' said Patti, 'this is the deal.' Winston was slumped behind the wheel. Patti sat in the passenger seat without comment on the reshuffle.

'What did they say?' interrupted Winston.

'Hang on,' said Patti, out of breath from her sprint between the two cars. 'I'm about to tell you.'

'Anyway,' said Winston, 'how come they let you in the car?' He turned to her. 'It's my car.'

'So what?' said Patti. 'The girls have come up with a deal.'

WHITE MEAT AND TRAFFIC LIGHTS

She sat with both her hands under her legs like a child trying to contain bubbles of excitement.

'And?'

'Well, it's like this.'

Winston said, 'Look, will you stop spinning this out? It's not frigging *Tales of the Unexpected*.'

'So-rree,' said Patti. Her voice had gone flat. 'This might be a good time to point out that I have nothing to lose by turfing you out of this car and driving home.'

Winston looked at her. Because the driver's seat was so far forward he had to rotate his whole body. His left hand was fiddling with the seat belt. 'No, sorry,' he said. 'I'm just anxious, that's all.'

'Anxious because you're not the one in charge, you mean?' asked Patti in the same flat voice.

'No,' said Winston with a laugh that sounded like a drum.

'Have another sweet,' Patti told him. Then in a flash she went back to normal. 'Anyway, the girls, that's Xenia and her friend Helena, both used to work here. I mean at the Butterballs factory. Terrible work, eighteen-hour shifts, can you imagine? Anyway, when they started they had their passports taken away from them, apparently for safekeeping. Then they got sent to London to work there.' She broke off and looked at Winston, whose feet were drumming on the pedals. 'She didn't tell me what as. Did you know anything about that?'

'No, course not,' said Winston too quickly. '*No*, no, seriously. Now go on.'

Patti rocked forward slightly as she spoke. 'Xenia escaped – that's when she went to the lock-up – and now one of them, not the one I had in the lock-up, the other one, Helena, well, she's ill.'

'What's wrong with her?'

'Some sort of mental thing. Stress,' Patti told him. 'She keeps sleeping on car roofs.'

'I'm sorry?'

'Yeah, I didn't understand that bit either.' Patti unwrapped a sweet. 'Is it lunchtime yet?'

'Can't you think of anything but your stomach?'

'I don't operate well when I've got low blood sugar levels,' Patti told him. 'That's official.'

Winston waited for her to finish her sweet. She spoke with her mouth full, her tongue mangling the toffee like a Magimix. She said, 'What they want, all they want, are their passports back so they can go home.'

'In my car?'

'No, dough brain, calm down. They don't know how they're going to get home.' She looked at her lap while Winston assimilated the information. 'Besides, how important is that car anyway? I thought you only wanted some dumb package and, of course, your opus.'

'Well, call me old-fashioned, but I wouldn't mind getting my car back as well,' said Winston caustically.

Patti looked up. 'OK, then, so the deal is we get their passports and then they return the car.'

'And how the fuck are we supposed to do that?'

'Listen, buster, I did the negotiation bit. You're the one who's supposed to have all the so-called brains. You think of something.'

They sat in silence while Patti smoothed out sweet wrappers and folded them into triangles. After four minutes Winston said, 'All right, then, I'll go and get the passports.' He released the catch on the door but showed no signs of getting out.

'How are you going to do that?' asked Patti.

He smiled in a way that flattened out his eyes and made his eyebrows meet in the middle. 'Come with me if you fancy seeing the master in action.'

Something in the casualness of his approach made her say, 'OK, then.'

IV

Alfie Appleton was going nowhere until he'd worked out what it was that was so important that it was worth killing two people for. Alan wasn't quite as keen. Seconds after he'd dug out his escape hatch, Alfie had nipped round the front of the barn and released his co-captor. At first sight Alan was much weightier than Alfie had been picturing him. Not just taller but somehow more substantial. The media had described him as a kid, but standing next to him, dusting the hay from his clothes, he found himself looking up at Alan. He also had considerably more beard than Alfie, which made Alfie talk with one hand over his face.

'Pleased to meet you,' said Alfie and offered his free hand.

'Likewise,' said Alan, ignoring it. 'Now let's get the fuck out of here.'

'Don't you want to have another look?'

'Are you kidding? I wouldn't have another look in that barn if it contained Courteney Cox and Jennifer Aniston mud-wrestling.'

Alfie sighed. One thing was clear, he was going to have to do a lot of what his news editor called 'writing round' the real Alan Raynham for his piece to make *Look East*, never mind the Sundays.

'I suppose that's all the thanks I get for rescuing you,' said Alfie.

'Look, mate, no offence and I really do appreciate it, but when all's said and done, we're not exactly rescued yet and we're not likely to be if you go poking around like a fucking inch-high private eye.'

'There's no need to get personal.'

'Sorry.'

'Apology accepted,' said Alfie. They'd made it out of the barn and were crouched with their backs against a creosoted shed fifty metres away. Neither of them spoke for a couple of minutes. Then Alfie said, 'In any case, you'd be better to wait till it gets dark before you make a run for it.' He hadn't spoken much in the last seventy-four hours and his jaw ached.

'Yeah, well,' said Alan, 'I'm not planning on going out the front gate.' Alfie smelt his stale breath and felt it on his cheek. 'I'm gonna nip out the back across the fields. I know a path.'

'You can't go without me,' Alfie told him.

'Why's that then?'

''Cos it's me who got you out.'

Alfie heard him sigh. He raised his knees in front of him to try to warm the back of his thighs. Wet pinpricks of dew had started.

Alan said, 'OK, then, I'll wait for you to poke about.' He threw a clod of earth aimlessly in front of him. 'But I'm only waiting till the siren goes off at four. If you're not back by then I'm going on my own.'

'Thanks,' said Alfie and reached across with his right hand to try to show his appreciation by a clamp on Alan's upper arm. 'It's good of you.' All the time he was thinking it was a whole lot less than James Garner would have done in *The Great Escape*.

V

The door creaked open no more than twelve inches. Winston smiled and put out a hand. 'It's Herbert, isn't it?' Winston said it more as fact than query. He was on the top step, Patti trailing him on the third, her right foot nervously pawing a wrought-iron shoe-scraper. She clasped a carrier bag to her chest, holding it like a shield. In the gloom of the interior, the contours of the face at the door were soft with a small feminine chin. Then she spotted the black moustache that looked as if it'd been made with two burnt corks.

Winston went on, 'Is Mr Bates at home, please?' He waited five seconds before adding, 'We've got some urgent business.' Then he said, 'About the documents he left in my car?'

The door opened in a wide arc. Herbert said, 'Is that them there?' nodding towards Patti.

'I'd really prefer to talk to Mr Bates,' said Winston officiously. Patti thought, prick, but jogged after him, knocked out by the pungent smell of dog biscuits and decaying meat turned into dogs' breath.

Bates met them in the hall. 'Good God, Freely, you've got a nerve showing up here.'

'What do you mean?' asked Winston innocently. 'I thought you wanted this stuff. If not, I can always . . .' He turned with deliberate slowness, expecting to be called back.

'Now, you just hang on a minute.' Bates sized up Patti as if he hadn't noticed her before. He turned to Winston. 'Who's she?'

Winston had his back to the door. He said, 'My chauffeuse.'

Patti moved half a step forward, dangling the carrier limply by her side. 'Well, hang on, that's—'

Bates ignored her. 'Why's she dressed like that?'

WHITE MEAT AND TRAFFIC LIGHTS

'That's the way London drivers dress these days,' Winston told him.

All four of them stood in silence. Patti opened her mouth to object but closed it again. A beige-flecked dog with a coat like wood-chipped wallpaper sniffed Patti's tracksuit bottoms, yawned and mooched away with its head down. Patti couldn't help thinking glumly that she couldn't even sustain the interest of a hound.

Bates watched the dog and then put his hand out towards Patti. She scampered forward to shake it. Bates looked at her quizzically. 'No,' he said. 'Give me the bag.' Patti flushed.

Winston moved forward and stood between Bates and her. 'I'm afraid not.'

Bates looked at Winston. 'Freely, that bag belongs to me. Hand it over.' He glanced over at Herbert, summoning him with a nod and a quick jerk of the head.

'Mr Bates,' said Winston, I've got a deal to make with you. You get the bag when I get some documents that don't belong to you.'

Bates frowned. 'What the devil are you going on about, boy?'

'You get your precious papers back when I get a couple of passports.'

'*Passports?*' said Bates.

'That's right,' said Patti. 'Passports.'

Winston glared at her. He went on, 'Two of your employees, your working girls,' he added so there could be no confusion, 'want the return of their passports that you confiscated.'

Bates gave a ghoulish, mirthless grin. 'Now, why don't we go somewhere we can discuss this in a civilised manner? Not a draughty old hall.' He extended both hands in the style of a host and rounded them into the sitting room.

'Please take a seat,' said Bates.

Patti looked at Winston who remained standing.

Bates had moved to lean against the mantelpiece, country squire style.

Winston said, 'We can't stay long. You've heard my proposal and I think it's fair.'

'From what I recall of our dealings, Mr Freely,' Bates said, 'I pay your wage. Isn't that right?' Bates's face lit up an oxygen-starved red. He added, 'So don't tell me what's fair.' He motioned for Herbert to close the door. 'I'm the one who decides what's fair.' He smiled at Patti. 'Now, please, why don't you and the little lady sit down?'

Patti and Winston edged towards the door.

'I told you to sit down,' Bates said. Patti's knuckles were white as she held on to the bag. Bates went on convivially, 'Now, you two, what about a drink? Herbert, could you get our guests a tipple of whatever they fancy. I'm sorry, young lady, I didn't catch your name.'

'Patti.' As she replied he turned to the fire and placed a log on it. She smiled and perched on the rim of a wooden chair. 'I'd like to say how much I enjoy your turkey fritters—'

'Mr Bates,' Winston cut her off, 'we're really not here to socialise. I've brought back your papers and—'

Bates turned round. 'All in good time, Freely.' Then he reached for a conker-bright pipe and started tapping it slowly on the mantel. 'I'd like to know if you've had time to read my documents.'

Patti and Winston looked at each other. 'No, of course not,' said Patti. 'They're private.'

'Exactly right,' Bates told them. 'But I can't imagine a couple of nosy London folk like yourselves wouldn't have had a good delve into my personal bag.'

'Mr Bates,' said Winston indignantly, 'I can assure you I have done nothing of the sort.'

Herbert padded around like an apparition, placing a gin and tonic in front of each of them and handing Bates a glass of cider. Under the table Patti petted the ear of one of the dogs nervously.

Winston said, 'Look, give us the passports and you can have them back.'

Bates drank his cider in one and then wiped the back of his hand across his mouth. 'The trouble with you London folk is that you think you're all so damned smart. We don't agree, do we, Herbert?'

Herbert had retreated to the drinks cabinet by the door and half-heartedly nodded his head with damp enthusiasm. Patti had her head down and was studying the grease splodges on the table. Only Winston was staring at Bates.

Bates's face seemed to have lost its contours. He spoke in an even flat tone. 'We think it's time you were taught a lesson. Don't we, Herbert?'

Herbert said, 'Well, I . . .'

Winston said, 'All we want is the passports and if you're so keen on taking this further, I might just decide to expose your illegal workers operation.'

'And lose your job,' said Bates.

'So what?' said Winston.

Bates stamped his foot and a log in the fire fell against the grate, issuing a cavalcade of sparks. 'Don't you tell me what you can and can't do, boy.' He waved the pipe at Winston. 'And don't ever threaten me. I'm the one in charge now. Herbert, will you lock that blasted door, please?'

Herbert spun on his heels and then turned back. 'There is no lock, boss,' he said.

Bates hid his annoyance with exaggerated calm. 'OK, then, well, why don't you go and fetch my twelve-bore? I believe it's in the shed.'

Air left Winston's body, turning it limp, making his chin rise. 'I'm sorry? What did you say?'

'My gun,' said Bates as Herbert pulled the door to. Winston flicked his fringe nervously.

Patti said, 'Look, why don't you keep your bloody bag and we'll just go.' She pushed the bag away from her on the table, stood up, pulling at her tracksuit bottoms, and looked at Winston. She was moving as if momentum on its own would be enough. Fronds of her fringe were damply pasted across her forehead.

Grabbing a fistful of her blazer, Winston bundled her towards the exit. Bates didn't move to stop them. The lurcher lifted its head to bark twice, more to show that he was there than in protest. Another log slid in the grate. Patti and Winston pawed each other towards the door – Patti in front then Winston, toing and froing to safety. Halfway across the room, they heard the creak of the main door opening and felt the air in the room being dragged out of it.

Winston glanced over his shoulder at Bates who stood stock

still by the fireside, his face frozen like a gargoyle's in malevolent surprise. Then he heard a gasp from Patti. He looked at the door. It wasn't Herbert but a much shorter man in a brown anorak roughly holding a small boy by the scruff of his neck.

'What the devil?' Bates sighed more to himself than anything.

Winston, holding Patti by the arm involuntarily exhaled. 'Fucking hell, I know him. It's that Russian.'

The man in the anorak ignored Patti and Winston. He was standing at the door, showing off the boy like a poacher might a hare. He spoke past them to Bates. 'You look what has happened now. I catch this boy out of his cage and in the laboratory and you tell me I'm wrong to kill him. What do you think I should do with him now? Nominate him for a Nobel prize in science?'

'Who the dickens is he?' said Bates. Winston and Patti were edging their way round the men's field of vision. What about the Raynham lad?' he added quickly.

Winston forgot himself and said, 'What do you know about Raynham?'

Bates hissed at him, 'Don't get out of your pram. I don't know anything about him.'

Nevski laughed. 'I hardly think so. One day you want to kill him, the next day you tell me, save him. Now you pretend you don't even know who he is. It is your legendary sense of British humour, no?'

'Kill him?' said Winston. 'Jesus Christ, Bates, what in hell have you been getting up to on this farm?'

'All I'm trying to do is run an honest business, that's all.'

Nevski said, 'Don't make me laugh.' He pushed the boy into the room. His eyes were bulging from the rough grip at his neck, seeming, Patti thought, to gulp in information with huge, deliberate blinks. The man holding him kept his eyes barely open, blinking often, as if hoping to filter out as much of the world as possible. For several seconds of silence no one seemed to know what to do. Patti and Winston let their eyes roam from table to fire to chair to floor while a wall of resentment bristled between Bates and the foreigner.

Then as the last dregs of information percolated into Nevski's brain, he looked at Bates. 'Who are these two?'

'Mr Nevski,' Bates said, 'You have already met Freely. Freely organises my representation in the House. This is his,' he looked at Patti, 'chauffeuse.' There was another pause. Bates had started to fill his pipe with tobacco, compressing it with a fat thumb. He added, 'You should be thanking Mr Freely, he's brought your documents back to you. Isn't that right, Freely?'

Winston wriggled. 'Well, in a manner of speaking.'

Nevski dragged the boy further into the room. Patti saw that his fingernails were long and manicured like a woman's. 'Where the hell are they?'

Bates pointed to the table. 'In that bag.'

Patti and Winston looked at each other and unconsciously shuffled backwards. Winston said, 'When I said documents, what I really meant was . . . How can I put it?'

Nevski pushed the boy to the table and held his collar tightly while he upturned the bag with his free hand. Out tumbled two toilet rolls, sixteen tampons, a can of hair spray and a mesh-effect cosmetics case full of make-up.

He said, 'Is this some kind of joke?'

Winston and Patti looked at the table.

Bates roared, 'Freely, you wanted two passports in exchange for all these feminine accoutrements?' A slug of tobacco stuck to his lip.

Patti looked up innocently. 'Gosh, we must have brought the wrong bag.'

Nevski shook out the empty carrier, jabbing at the cosmetics in angry stabs, knocking them onto the floor. The lurcher yelped but didn't move. Bates, Patti and Winston were so transfixed by the display of temper that they missed Herbert appearing at the door. He coughed to grab their attention. A burst of sunlight illuminated a smoke screen of dust motes before a cloud scudded into its path.

'Sorry, boss, I couldn't find the twelve-bore. Something tells me it's in one of the outhouses.'

Bates waved his hand. 'Oh, don't worry about that now,' he said. Then Nevski tugged a pistol out of his anorak pocket and pointed it towards the fireplace. His tiny fist seemed hardly strong enough to hold the blue-black butt.

'You are right. Listen to your boss. Don't worry about the

twelve-bore. One gun is enough. But you might like to bring some rope.' He flicked the muzzle around the room.

Colour drained from Herbert's cheeks as if he'd been garrotted.

Nevski went on, 'And don't think of any funny stuff or your boss gets a bullet.'

Bates's sigh was more resentful than scared. 'Go on, Herbert, you'd better do as he says.'

As ever, his friend turned to do his bidding.

VI

'The man and the woman have been gone a long time.' Helena turned to Xenia. 'What are we going to do, wait for ever? In Xenia's opinion, in the two days since they'd been together, Helena had been more hindrance than help. 'I don't know, what do you suggest?'

'Wait, I guess,' said Helena.

Then Xenia asked quickly, 'Why, you're not starting to feel funny again, are you?'

'Who, me? No.' She shook her head in a violent whinny.

Xenia looked in the rear-view mirror and told her, 'Ssshh, bob down. There's a car behind us turning into Butterballs.' They both shrunk in their seats as a royal-blue Audi indicating to turn right swung out of vision.

VII

Tracey pulled over just past the entrance. It was a sudden decision reflected in the jolt.

Beaver rubbed his neck. 'What's the matter, babe?'

Tracey spoke to the windscreen. The woodland was matted and dense. 'Nothing. I'm wondering if this is safe. If we wouldn't be better to continue on foot.' She glanced over.

Beaver was reluctant to get out of the car. To him the countryside represented a genuine, uncharted threat. 'Listen, sweetheart,' he said, 'I don't really do nature. This is freaking me out.' He jumped at a jagged crow's caw and the rustle of trees.

Tracy turned to him. 'You big baby. Come on, get out of the car.'

'Babe, I will not get out of the car.'

'Get out of the car.' She pushed him hard with her elbow. 'You can't expect me to go up there on my own.'

'Listen, honey, it was your idea. You're the post-radical post-militant post-everything feminist.'

'I am not a feminist.'

'Whatever,' Beaver said sarcastically.

'I am a promoter of women's rights.'

'Course you are.'

'Get out of the car.'

'No.'

'Fine.' Tracey started doing up her coat buttons. 'If that's the way you see it, I'll go on my own.' She started to bundle herself noisily out of the car. She turned to the back seat and dragged the carrier bag off it. Beaver stared up at the ceiling. He had zero interest in confronting the man who was suing him for loss of foreskin. A fact with some relevance, he thought, no matter what information Tracey had unearthed. Tracey's hair lashed his cheek as she turned back. He inhaled his annoyance and tasted a mouthful of her fragrance. He shook his head and *tsk*ed as she slammed the door.

'Hang on, babe, I'm coming.'

VIII

'Your wrists are the thinnest, can't you slip the knot somehow?' Like all of them, Winston's hands were crossed and tied behind him to the chair. The rope was made of nylon, which cut into his flesh, making it burn.

'No, Mister Know-It-All Houdini, I can't,' replied Patti stubbornly. 'Besides, what about the kid's?'

'I'm not a kid,' said Alfie. It was the first time he had spoken since he'd been dragged into the room. His voice was wavering but defiant.

'Sorry,' Patti said. 'Anyway,' she was talking to Winston even though she didn't mind if they all heard, 'it's worse for people with little arms. They can't stretch round the back like yours. I'm in agony.' An out-of-season fly buzzed down the length of the chairs. Winston turned his head in sharp rotations.

'This is absurd,' he said.

'Christ, boy, *you* think it's absurd.' Bates's chair was the furthest from the door. 'This is my bloody house. I swear, as God is my witness, I'll kill that bloody foreigner. Coming here and making a mockery of me.'

Patti said, 'Where's he gone?' Her chair was next to Winston's and she could hear frustrated puffs of exhaustion as he writhed. Patti's thighs hardly covered the wooden seat but as Winston rolled and rocked, she felt the effect. So he couldn't accuse her of not making an effort, she swayed impotently alongside.

Winston said, 'Bates, don't you think you should let us know what's going on?'

'I think I know,' said Alfie in a low voice that no one heard.

Bates called down the line, 'What can I say? The man's a lune.'

'But what are these papers he needs to get hold of?' Winston had stopped squirming.

'Christ knows,' Bates told him. 'We haven't got a clue, have we, Herbert?'

'Clueless,' said Herbert on a chair sandwiched between Bates and Alfie.

'He kept me locked up in a turkey coop,' protested Alfie. 'With the lad that had disappeared, Alan Raynham.'

Winston said, 'Did you know anything about that, Bates?'

'Good God, no. I tell you, the man is deranged.'

'Morally bankrupt,' added Herbert. Outside, the Butterballs hooter blasted out the end of the day shift. The smell of different people was overlying the doggy odours. Nevski had left an hour ago, carefully piling logs on the fire before he went. Every so often when the wind changed direction a blast of smoke came down the chimney.

'What do you think he's going to do?' said Patti quietly to Winston.

'Dunno.'

She locked on to his eyes and stared up at him. A tuft of his hair had fallen over his eyes. In usual circumstances he would have swept it away, separating his fingers and shaking his hand over the crown of his head. He tried to dislodge it by shaking his head, but that only caused a further hank of hair to collapse onto his face. He had no choice but to leave it there.

'That thing you do with your hair,' she said, 'that flick. You do that because you don't like hair in your eyes, don't you?'

'Er, yes,' he said, more irritated than perplexed. 'Why else?'

'I thought it was just a bit of a pose. You know, for other people's sake.'

He looked down at her. She thought he was going to be angry, but when he spoke it was with concerned amusement.

'Patti, you've really got to understand that not everything in this world is done for your benefit.'

'*I* know that,' said Patti, meaning that he didn't.

'Good,' said Winston and resumed writhing as if he'd spent too long away from it.

IX

Beaver's heart soared at the shut-up look of the house; the curtains were drawn as if it was dozing and a length of guttering leaned askew. 'Come on, babe,' he said, 'there's obviously no one at home.' He was a few paces behind her, using a weird cosmonaut's walk to muffle the sound of his footsteps on the gravel. Tracey, on the other hand, was striding. He went on, 'If we leave now, we could be back by evening. I'll take you out for a meal – what do you say?'

'Ssssh,' said Tracey. 'Will you stop blithering on? I can't concentrate with you prattling in the background.' She turned towards him, away from the house, when she spoke. Beaver put her sharpness down to nerves, not that he objected overmuch. The house was more grey than red with an untamed wisteria half-heartedly clinging to it. Upstairs windows stared out blankly from the cataract of flimsy curtain lining. Downstairs windows were veiled in thick netting bearing triangular scorch marks from ironing.

'Babe,' he said, 'I don't think you should ring the bell.' Tracey reminded him of a politician canvassing for votes – unabashed and unable to countenance failure. She didn't only ring the bell but knocked as well and when her knuckles made little impact, she kicked the door with the pointed toecap of her slingbacks.

The door swung in on itself with exaggerated deference. Tracey started speaking before it had moved more than a quarter of its arc.

'I'm here to see Mr Selwyn Bates, managing director of Butterballs plc.' Beaver hung back like a tuneless carol singer. The man who opened the door wasn't Bates but some sort of oddly dressed servant. Tracey had him down as a stable boy because of his size. When he spoke he sounded Eastern European.

'How you English do love to pop in on each other. Do come in. Let me take your coat.' Tracey flashed Beaver a nothing-to-be-scared-of smile and followed the man's ushering arm. Beaver crept after her. The man added, 'And, please, your bag.'

He closed the door after them. A staircase led away to their right, between a corridor to their sharp left and one opposite leading into the house. The hallway was lit by a bare bulb hanging low from the centre of the ceiling. Tracey's eyes roamed for a couple of seconds and she said, 'No, I'd prefer to look after that myself, if you don't mind. This bag is very important.' The house was cold and the man was in shirtsleeves. 'Now, if you could just tell Mr Bates that Tracey McCloud, prospective candidate for Westminster Council, is here.'

'I think you might tell him yourself.' Tracey and Beaver turned to the man to see a pistol pointed at them.

X

Alan Raynham gave it till well after four before he decided to go. After the Butterballs siren he'd recited every lyric he could think of and been through his most-like-to-sleep-with inventory eight times, refining it to start off with Britney Spears before going on to Phoebe Bright in year ten (ahead of Emma Bunton) because, when all was said and done, Phoebe had accessibility on her side. When he stood up and dusted the clods of cold earth from his backside, it was dark. That funny little newspaper reporter might have wanted another look, but he'd had enough. By his calculations it was Saturday. He'd be back in time for fish fingers, chips and *Blind Date*. He stretched his legs and then looked left and right before sloping off into the woods.

Chapter Twelve

I

The lurcher was acting as if it'd never had so much fun. That was loyalty for you, thought Bates miserably. When the door opened, the dog scampered over, barking and groaning between barks. The line of chairs faced away from the door but Nevski walked his latest captors in front of them; first Tracey, then Beaver. Neither of them spoke.

Patti whispered to Winston, 'I know her.'

Ten seconds later, from further down the line, Bates piped up, 'Christ alive, it's the bloody man with the amazing dick-eating women. What the hell are you doing here?'

Nevski corralled them to the space left of the fire between a log basket and the wall. Then he unwound a length of rope, trapping one end under his foot and the other in his mouth while he cut it one-handed with the serrated edge of a bread knife. He sliced two lengths off and passed one to Beaver, the gun in his hand fixing them in a malevolent line of fire. 'Tie her up,' he said.

'What to?' said Beaver. All five dining-room chairs were already being used.

Nevski said, 'Just tie her hands behind her back.' Then he added, 'This shouldn't take long.'

'Sorry, babe,' said Beaver, tugging Tracey's arms behind her. 'I'll try not to hurt you.'

The five others watched in fascinated horror.

'Sit her on that chair when you've finished,' Nevski told him. 'But let me see the knot first.' He tugged at it with one hand. 'I don't want any of your funny stuff.' Then he pushed Tracey onto a fireside chair. She sat slightly off balance. He turned to Beaver. 'Now you. Put your hands behind you.'

Beaver had once read that in crime scenes the criminals were most times more scared than the victims, but the unlaboured breaths on his neck and the unhurried way he was being tied up suggested different.

The man kicked him in the back of his knees, making his legs buckle, and then pushed him onto the chair opposite Tracey's. There was a pile of *TV Times* on the table next to him and three unwashed teacups.

'Now look, Nevski,' Bates said, 'it seems to me that things are getting a little out of hand here. Nobody wants to see anyone get hurt.' He looked down the line. 'There are women here, for goodness' sake. I'm sure if you were to let us all go, we would all just forget it ever happened.'

'Hear, hear,' said Herbert.

Nevski wasn't listening. He was emptying papers and envelopes from the carrier bag onto the table behind them. There was quiet while the documents slid around on the table, more noise when Nevski pushed aside a plate and the metallic clink of cutlery as it fell. The gin and tonics smashed to the ground.

'I suppose you've read this?' He was speaking to the two in the fireside chairs. 'You, woman, what is your name?'

'My name is Tracey McCloud and I am a female liberationalist.'

Patti craned her head towards Winston. 'That's how I know her. She works with my friend Elaine on some barmy women's project.'

Tracey went on, 'I intend to expose the horror of what you are doing to the world at large,' she said, her chin raised and her head tilted back.

'Well, now, babe, hang on,' said Beaver. 'I mean, there's always room for negotiation.' He looked down the line of faces opposite. 'How would it be if you let us go and we agreed to say no more about it?'

Tracey tried to wriggle into an upright position. 'Absolutely no way.'

Bates said, 'And if you think you're getting out of my compensation you're sadly mistaken.'

'Shut up, all of you,' Nevski shouted. He was drumming a finger on the wooden table. A bluster of wind outside drove a volley of rain at the windows.

Alfie asked politely, 'Do you mind telling us what's in the documents?'

Nevski gave a mirthless laugh. 'Sure, no problem.' He stood up and walked in front of the fire. 'It doesn't matter who knows now because in the event you are all going to die.' He gave Bates a sour look. 'Maybe you'd like to tell everyone what we've been up to.'

'*You've* been up to,' said Herbert, 'more like.'

'That's irrelevant,' said Nevski. He cocked the gun and pointed it at Bates. 'Please, we are listening.'

Bates was flushed from the heat of the fire. Three of his shirt buttons had come undone, revealing tufts of grey hair and two rose-pink nipples. 'For some years,' he said, 'Dr Nevski here has been working on a formula for breast enlargement that doesn't rely on surgery.' He was looking at the floor. 'A successful formula would be worth billions worldwide. After some time he decided to synthesise the hormone which we farmers use to increase the flesh on our turkey breasts.'

'Fucking hell,' said Winston to himself. 'That's why he wanted a good GM show in Parliament.'

'Blimey,' Patti said.

'In return for a ready supply of cheap labour from Eastern Europe, I let him work on his experiment here at Butterballs. And I might say we've had some success—'

'Until the last batch,' interrupted Nevski. 'When things started to,' he paused, 'how can I say,' he looked hard at Bates, 'unravel.'

Bates tried to turn his head. He said indignantly, 'What the dickens are you talking about, boy? You never said nothing about that to me.'

Nevski told him, 'Why do you think I had to come back to this godforsaken place? What did you think those papers were all about?' Bates's face was blank. Nevski explained, tapping his right forefinger absently on his temple, 'The formula was starting to produce unexpected side effects.'

II

'I can't leave you here,' Xenia said. 'You might go on the roof again.' It was usually at this time in the early evening when

Helena's behaviour started to deteriorate. 'Come on, we'll just go up to the house to have a look.' Xenia had decided they couldn't wait in a lay-by for ever.

'What if it's dangerous?' said Helena with a staccato shake of her head.

'Well, in that case we'll take Boris.' Xenia turned to the cardboard box on the back seat. She added, 'Only you carry him, because they give me the creeps.'

Helena said, 'What good's he going to be?'

'I don't know,' Xenia said, exasperated. 'He's better than nothing.'

'Oh, OK, then,' said Helena. 'Come on.' She got out of the passenger side and undid the back door. She opened the cardboard box and delved into it with a scooping embrace. Xenia watched in the rear-view mirror until she could bear it no more. She got out of the car, her jaw slack and shivering in the cold.

'Ready?' She turned to Helena. 'Follow me. And keep that bloody snake under control.'

III

'You mean women were actually taking the hormone?' asked Alfie innocently.

'Of course,' replied Nevski, 'how else could we see the results of our labour?'

Patti said, 'Wasn't it dangerous?' Winston felt a jolt against the wooden chair frame as she struggled with the knot.

'For the women? Of course,' replied Nevski, warming to the topic. 'But individual cases concern me less than the result. Process is nothing.'

'So what good will it do if you kill us?' asked Beaver.

'As I said, individual cases matter little. Reluctant as I am to close down this branch of operations, tomorrow I return to Moscow. Any teething problems I can work out there. In theory I have a marketable product. I will refine it in countries that are less litigious than your own.' He looked at each of them and shook his head. 'No one knows of my involvement here.

Police will be confused by the bodies, but they are unlikely to suspect a Russian scientist on the other side of the world.'

'Mrs King will know,' said Bates.

'Indeed she does, but I'm afraid Mrs King is on my payroll now, she has been for some time.' He smiled an eerie leer. 'In fact Mrs King is already in Moscow waiting for me.' He cocked his head to one side. 'We are what you might call an item.'

'Well, I'll be jiggered,' said Bates. 'Moody mare, I might have known she was up to something. Bugger me.'

'Me 'n' all,' said Herbert.

Alfie said, 'Alan Raynham, the boy I was locked up with, he knows the full story.'

Nevski shook his head pityingly. 'I think I can get around the testimony of one teenage boy. Especially when all the evidence has been destroyed.' For extra gravitas Nevski had been standing on the granite hearth. He stepped down and said, 'Now, can I trust you ladies and gentlemen to do this honourably? Who wishes to go first?'

They all stared down at the floor, except Patti who twisted her neck in line with Winston. She whispered, 'I guess what with us all staring death in the face and everything, I can say something.'

'What?' Winston moved his eyes from the swirls of the carpet to the crown of Patti's head.

'I have feelings for you.'

'What sort of feelings?'

'Sexual feelings.'

'It takes the prospect of imminent death for you to say that?'

'Pretty much,' said Patti. She waited for five seconds. Down the line, Bates was arguing with Nevski. Then she said, 'Well?'

'Well, what?'

'You could at least say you fancy me.'

'I fancy you,' said Winston.

'Is that it?

'What else do you want, a proposal?'

'Say something nice,' said Patti.

'Snake.' Winston's head jerked to the right.

'Excuse me?' said Patti.

'Snake,' he yelled. 'There's a fucking great boa constrictor coming towards me.'

Nevski leapt away from Bates and turned towards it. It was as thick as an arm and rippled towards them, iridescent skin contracting and relaxing. As Nevski aimed the gun at it, Patti leapt from her chair, grabbing the poker before hurling herself from the hearth and smashing it across Nevski's head. The gun went off in the direction of the door as it flung open.

'Boris!' a woman screamed. 'Please don't shoot my snake!' A dark-haired woman ran into the room and grabbed the snake by the head. Patti landed another blow on Nevski's head.

'Well, blow me, if it isn't the dick-biter,' said Bates. 'What the devil's she doing here?'

Patti was sitting on the side of the hearth with her head in her hands. A trickle of blood came from Nevski's head; his legs were splayed flat behind him, twisting outwards. Patti looked at Winston. 'Do you think he's dead?'

Winston said, 'No, I don't think so.' He smiled at her. 'Smart move.'

'Skinny wrists,' explained Patti.

'What about undoing us all then?' said Tracey. She looked at Patti for the first time. 'Hang on,' she said suspiciously, 'you're Elaine Peroni's friend, aren't you?'

'Yeah,' said Patti, 'and this is Xenia, the Russian you were so anxious to meet.' Xenia stood at the door behind Helena. She walked forward as if expecting an introduction.

'Sod that,' said Tracey, 'this has become a whole new ball game.' She looked at Patti. 'Come on, undo me sharpish, I can't waste any more time here. I've got a campaign to start.'

Winston said, 'Someone should call the police. That guy looks like he needs an ambulance.'

'Now hang on,' said Bates, 'there's no need to start bringing the police into this.'

'What?' cried Winston.

'Well, he's a criminal for a start.' Bates nodded at Beaver. 'And I've got the police statement to prove it.'

Beaver glanced anxiously at Tracey.

No one noticed as Xenia glided across the room and bent over Nevski as if out of concern. She stooped gracefully and reached for the gun. Even then she had to cough twice to get everyone's attention.

'Please.' She walked back towards the door to get everyone in range. 'My friend is very sick, this is my big concern. Then I have others. She and I have been treated very badly by this country. We come to work and then end up in brothel. That man is a criminal. In my country he would be in jail.' She spoke to Helena quickly in Russian.

Bates said, 'Now who the devil is she?' Beaver and Tracey gave each other bewildered stares. Patti went back to sitting next to Winston though she made no attempt to untie him and he didn't bother to ask. Helena had sunk to the floor, kissing and stroking the snake.

Xenia turned back to the group. 'Now I have a gun and I have a proposal. This is how we do business in my country.' She walked over to the table, keeping the pistol steady at waist height. She shook a piece of paper free from a binder and checked nothing was written on it. Then she handed it to Bates with an uncapped Biro and gave him an *Illustrated Sporting Guide* to lean on.

'Who the dickens are you?' asked Bates. 'And what the devil's this pen for, young lady?' He shook his shoulders. 'Will you stop messing about and undo these blasted ropes?'

Xenia pointed the gun at Bates's head. 'It's simple. I have the gun and you have the business,' she said. Still holding the gun to his head, Xenia undid the ropes binding Bates's hands. 'Now you sign paper to give me the business.'

'Good God, girl, you mean Butterballs.' He tried to twist his head to look at her. 'Listen, your argument is with Nevski, not me.'

'No, you sold me as a slave,' she said. 'Now I want something back.' She pressed the barrel of the gun harder at his head. 'You sign the factory for me.'

'For heaven's sake, girl. You'd never use that gun, you're just a tiny slip of nothing.' Bates stared at the blank paper. His hand twitched. The space where a finger should have been hovered above the pen. 'In any case, there's no law in the land that will say it's binding.'

'In my country it is and yours too, I think,' she glanced round. 'We have people here.'

'Indeed we do,' said Tracey. 'And I'll make sure this whole thing is exposed, don't you worry.' She half smiled. 'Men.'

Bates started to write in childish capitals. Just as he added a scratchy signature, they heard police sirens screeching up the drive and the quick double thud of two doors slamming shut.

'That'll be Alan,' said Alfie proudly. 'He must have called the police.' He pushed himself up in the chair. 'Now, if someone will let me out of here, I've a feeling I might just make the Sundays.'

'You're a journalist?' asked Tracey sceptically.

'Certainly,' replied Alfie.

She turned to him and smiled. 'Do you mind if I speak to you alone? On the record?'

'Be my guest,' said Alfie.

Chapter Thirteen

I

'I don't ruddy well believe it,' said Winston. He stood at the end of the Butterballs drive in the lay-by where the Niva had been parked. Instead of taking them in for questioning, the police had interviewed most of them at the house. Only Bates and Herbert had been taken in for more questioning, demanding legal representation as they were led away. Nevski had been ambulanced to Hadleigh Cottage Hospital to be released to the station when he had recovered. Xenia and Helena had stayed at the house, pending an immigration inquiry.

'Will they get the factory?' Patti asked.

'I don't know,' Winston told her. 'Anything's possible if they get the right publicity.' He turned to face her. 'Where the hell can it have gone now?' In the darkness he couldn't see Patti's face. He went on, 'Is this anything to do with you?'

'*Me*? In case you've forgotten,' she said, 'I've been with you for the last eight hours.'

'So where is it?'

'Mini-crime spate?' she suggested. 'I read somewhere that criminals come from the city just to target villages.'

'I don't think so,' he said morosely. 'What about my manuscript, what about the money?'

'Shit,' said Patti. 'I forgot about that.'

'What do you mean, you forgot about it?'

'Nothing.' Patti skipped on ahead. 'It's just as well they didn't take the Cinquecento, then,' she said. 'Come on, let's get something to eat. I'm starving.' The lane was a dense dark you didn't get in the city. Drops of rain fell hollowly from branches onto mud. 'We passed a village about ten miles back, they must have a pub.' She unlocked the driver's door and reached over to open the passenger side. 'Can you do it again, the manuscript?'

'I guess so,' said Winston. 'To be honest with you, it wasn't all that great.'

'That's the spirit,' Patti told him, 'and let's face it, the less stuff that links you with Bates, the better.'

'I s'pose.'

She drove slowly with the lights on full beam, flicking the wipers on when gusts in the overhead trees caused a shower. 'Weird that McCloud woman being there,' she said, slipping the car into third before a sharp bend.

'She was the one who brought the papers.'

'Where did she get them from?'

'Her boyfriend found them.'

'What was all that dick-biting stuff?' asked Patti.

Winston yawned. 'No idea. All this hassle and I'm still down a car, twelve grand and my manuscript.' He pinched his eyes with his thumb and forefinger. 'And it turns out one of my biggest clients is the Mr Big of illegal refugees with a plan to turn every woman on the planet into Pamela Frigging Lee Anderson.'

'Oh well.' Patti shrugged. The Bell was the first building they came to, before even the village sign. On the right about a hundred yards up, lights shone back from the road. She said, 'At least you got the girl.'

The car lit up suddenly under the watery orange sodium light of an olde worlde pub lamp. Winston's face fell.

'Joke,' said Patti and slammed on the brakes inches from the low wooden fence of the pub garden. She tugged up the handbrake and didn't wait for Winston. A second before she slammed the door, she heard his mobile ring. He jolted with the surprise of its unexpected jarring noise.

'Hello, Winston?'

'Hi.' He kept his voice deliberately flat.

'It's Tony.'

'Yeah, I know,' said Winston. 'Listen, I've got some news.' He went on quickly so Tony couldn't interrupt. 'That money I promised to give you. It turns out I can't.' He held his breath.

Tony said, 'What money?'

WHITE MEAT AND TRAFFIC LIGHTS

'The money to stop you getting mashed by some South African.'

'What South African?' Tony didn't wait for a reply. 'Look, I need to tell you something.' He was breathless but in an excited, not drug-related, way. 'I've got a job.'

'I'm sorry?'

'A job. A mate saw one of my designs and now they want them for a sci-fi film set. Actually the clothes weren't sci-fi but that's not the point.' Winston was about to speak. But no comment seemed necessary. Tony went on, 'I fly tonight.' For Tony it tripped off the tongue pretty well.

'Fly,' asked Winston. 'Where to?'

'LA,' said Tony proudly. 'Look, I've got to go.'

'But what about the drugs?' said Winston limply.

'Hey, man, they were just a phase.'

By the time Winston got into the pub, Patti was sitting on her own with her back to the door. She was folding crisp packets in front of an untouched pint of lager.

'Do you want anything to eat?' Winston called over to her.

'I've already ordered.' Patti spoke to him without moving her head. The room was empty. The bar led through to a snug, in the middle of a pub quiz. It made him think Patti must have deliberately chosen the silent side. Winston caught the end half of a question on the Corrs. He looked at the pumps and asked a dark-haired barmaid with a midriff hanging over her jeans for a pint of Adnams. He looked at the board and ordered steak and kidney pie, then he divided his change between a collection tin for the North Suffolk Blind Association and a plastic ship for lifeboats.

'Mind if I join you?'

'It's a free country,' said Patti, halfway down her lager. Winston wondered if she intended to drive.

'What's up with you?' he asked.

'I've got a post-adrenaline low,' said Patti. The barmaid was stacking ashtrays noisily on the bar.

Winston said, 'We should be over the moon. I mean, we could have been dead by now.'

'Exactly,' said Patti. She looked at him, forcing her lips into a smile that came across as a grimace. Winston pulled a cigarette from its packet using his mouth, at the same time scouting round for a machine and unconsciously tapping his jacket for change.

'I did appreciate what you did in there,' he said, thumping a Camel on the table. 'It was really brave.'

'Yeah, well. It wasn't Cindy, was it?' said Patti. 'Cindy would have shagged her way out of that room, flashing her cleavage and her legs.'

Winston considered it, in Patti's estimation for ten seconds too long. 'I don't know about that,' he said. 'But I'm pretty sure she wouldn't have leapt on him from behind with a poker.'

'Exactly,' said Patti. She stood up. 'Do you want another drink?'

'No thanks.' He put his hand on her arm as she went for her purse. 'You know I do think you're really,' he took a drag of his cigarette and looked towards the window, 'nice.' The door opened and a well-dressed middle-aged couple bunched together against the cold staggered in from outside

'Thanks,' said Patti and went to the bar. She waited for the man to be served a pint and a dry white wine, then ordered a lager.

She sat back down at the table and pushed the ashtray away from her. 'It might take a near-death experience for me to admit to my feelings but at least I do,' she said as if she'd been rehearsing it at the bar. 'What are you going to do? Keep chasing Cindys because you know you're safe because she's got nothing for you to get involved with?'

Winston didn't speak. 'That's the way I like it,' he told her after ten seconds.

'Fine,' said Patti.

'Fine,' said Winston. 'But if you're going to give me all that *scared of real women* stuff, you might as well just pass the sick bucket. You're better off finding a woman you're always going to want to shag, because all of them are going to drive you up the wall sooner or later. And don't tell me it's any different for women.'

'You don't really think that.'

'Oh no?'

'No, because if you were such a prick you wouldn't be trying so hard to get your brother off the hook.'

'Oh, wouldn't I?'

WHITE MEAT AND TRAFFIC LIGHTS

'No.' Patti was pulling a beer mat apart. She said, 'Men in their thirties, it's a revenge thing. They spend their whole lives being given the run-around by women. They hit thirty and suddenly they are the ones calling the shots. The power goes to their heads.'

'So you're saying my not wanting to sleep with you is revenge.' Patti looked haughty. 'Yeah.'

'Not because you speak with your mouth full, dress like a charity shop and hum tunes by Simply Red?'

'Well,' said Patti, 'we can all be tossers, can't we?'

'What's that supposed to mean?'

The barmaid arrived with Patti's plate of egg, chips and beans. She asked for two rounds of white bread and butter. The girl told Winston his steak and kidney pie would be ready in ten minutes.

Patti stared at the pattern round her plate. The chips were microwaved and the beans not Heinz. 'You can have some of my chips,' she said.

'Gee whiz,' said Winston, slightly breathless, staring towards the Gents door as if he was on the verge of a big speech.

'I'm trying to be nice,' Patti told him pointedly.

'I know,' said Winston. He poured salt onto a chip but then put it back on her plate. 'I'm sorry.' He finished his drink holding his elbow at a perfect right angle to his body, pushed himself away from the table with one hand and went to the bar.

'Can you get me another lager?' shouted Patti. Winston stopped in his tracks, his glass midway up his chest. 'Aren't you driving?'

Patti gave a big-eyed innocent smile. 'It's all right, they do rooms.' Winston looked at her and his glass dropped a couple of inches. She said, 'Don't panic, I've booked a single.' She squashed three chips into her mouth and went on, 'Jeez, it used to be young ladies who had to protect their reputations in country pubs.'

Winston returned with the foam from his pint on his upper lip. He slurped it off with his tongue. Patti was scooping up beans when the waitress bustled towards them with Winston's pie.

'Sorry for the delay,' she said, 'the microwave's on the blink.'

'Oh, right,' said Winston.

Patti waited for him to start. She said, 'Anyway, we should be talking about what happened this afternoon. We've probably contracted post-traumatic stress syndrome.' She was rolling a line of chips into a buttie. 'The cure for that is talking about our experiences. I read that,' she added proudly.

'I don't want to talk about them,' said Winston. 'I'm knackered.'

'Suit yourself. I wonder if we'll be in the papers tomorrow.'

Winston stuck his knife into the pie and watched brown goo seep onto his plate. 'Maybe,' he said. 'Didn't that lad say he worked for the local paper?' He took a mouthful and said, 'They'd better not mention me, though.'

'Why not?'

'Well, Bates was my client, it'll look bad. I'll probably get the sack if they find out about this, anyway.'

'Good,' said Patti.

'Why?'

'Because you hate your job.'

'How do you know?' asked Winston.

'Feminine intuition,' said Patti. 'Everyone hates their jobs.' She forced a mouthful of beans into her mouth. 'Anyway, it means you can give up and do your writing.'

'And live off what, exactly?'

'Everyone's got to take a chance sometime,' Patti said.

'You sound like a fortune cookie.'

'Thanks,' said Patti.

'What about you?' asked Winston. 'When are you going to take a chance?'

'I told you, I'm going to open a driving school in Egypt.' She dabbed a line of mayonnaise onto her buttie and waited for Winston to take a mouthful of his pie. Then she said, casually, 'You can come with me if you like. I mean, there was that book, *The Alexandrian* something.' She looked at him. 'You might not have heard of it.'

'Quartet,' said Winston.

'There you go,' said Patti. 'You could do another. Make it a quintet or something.'

Winston put down his knife and fork. It was obvious this wasn't the first time Patti had thought of this. He said, 'But we've only just met.'

Patti put down her pint. 'We shared a life-changing experience.'

He put his hands on his knees. 'But we don't, I mean we . . .' He paused. 'We haven't even slept together,' he told her.

'Listen, buster,' said Patti. 'Your sexual hang-ups are your own affair.'

'I don't have any sexual hang-ups.'

'Whatever.' Patti pushed her plate away from her and absently squashed one of Winston's peas onto the table. She finished her drink and stood up. She said, 'Anyway, I'm going to bed.'

'*What?*'

'I'm pooped.'

'What about a nightcap?'

'No, sirree.' She turned towards the stairs and under the sign that said Exit in bright green lights, called, ''Night.'

Winston didn't reply. He looked at the congealing slivers of kidney on his plate, and thought of offal. Then he looked at the couple in the corner silently watching the room as if they were part of an experiment.

Winston caught her up on the eighth step. 'Patti?'

She looked down at him. In the darkness all she could see was a rough outline of his face.

He said, 'Can I come with you?'

Patti said, 'Where to?'

'Bed.'

'It's a single.'

'We'll manage.' Then he followed the whites of her heels bouncing out of her trainers and lighting the way like drunken cat's eyes.

News of the World, Sunday, 1 February 2001.

Turkey King Behind Evil GM of Women

By Alfie Appleton, staff reporter

Butterballs turkey millionaire, Selwyn Bates, was last night being questioned by police over an alleged reign of terror that included the genetic modification of women and the traffic in foreign prostitutes.

Bates, 47, was also behind the alleged abduction of plucky teenager Alan Raynham, even though it was Bates who put up the £10,000 reward for the lad's safe return.

Bates and his deputy Herbert Long, 47, are also believed to be at the heart of a multimillion-pound operation to import illegal immigrants to work in his factory, many of whom were sold on as prostitutes to work in London brothels.

Tracey McCloud, 34, candidate for Westminster Council and self-described women's liberationalist, said: 'I have been on the trail of this evil man for years. What he is doing is nothing short of slavery. This evil traffic must end.'

It was Raynham himself who called police to Bates's four million pound luxury mansion in Suffolk yesterday after escaping from the turkey coop where he was held in miserable incarceration for a week.

Raynham is believed to have rumbled the Butterball King's evil plan to inject women with a growth hormone used on turkeys to increase breast size.

One Ukrainian woman, Helena Maskalenko, 19, who fell prey to the evil drugs cocktail, is recovering in Ipswich hospital. Doctors last night said her chances of recovery were extremely high. Dr Bob Fairweather, 56, Hadleigh's premier genetic specialist, said: 'It's an astounding case. But the girl is strong and responding well to treatment.'

Dr Mikhail Nevski, the Russian doctor behind the medical scam, is also facing his second day in police custody.

Lawyers are looking into Bates's last business transaction as a free man which saw him sign over his empire to Russian-born Xenia Malakova, 18. Diss-based solicitor and expert in turkey business law, Harry Scales, 39, said: 'On paper her case looks good.'

See inside for full story including: 'My terrifying ordeal at the hands of the monster' by NoW staffer Alfie Appleton.

12 March 2001

At 6.13 p.m., Gleb Malakov sat down opposite his wife Galia. She nervously flicked her hands over her flowery housecoat, distractedly pushing lengths of hair back into her bun and jiggling her slippers up and down on the kitchen linoleum.

'Tell it to me again,' she said. She never drank but this evening to calm her nerves she had a small tot of Russian cognac in front of her. The bag waited for them outside like an uninvited guest whose identity was still in some doubt.

Gleb sat back on his stool, resting his back on the painted kitchen wall, taking his time. 'Well, it's like this. I was three hours into my shift at the Tolyatti plant. We'd been moved off the production lines for the day because the foreman wanted me and two other guys to strip a consignment of cars that had arrived overnight from Germany.' He added for clarification, 'For spares.'

'No, this is too detailed,' complained Galia. 'Tell me how you found it.'

He rotated his chewing gum around his back teeth even though Galia never let him chew gum in the house. 'I'll always remember it.'

Galia sighed and raised her eyes. 'It was only three hours ago.'

'I know,' said Gleb. 'But I'm just saying. There was a lovely warm wind blowing up from the Volga and first to roll down the tailgates was this four-by-four black Niva. Nice one, a new model. It was much too good to strip down for parts.'

Galia tutted. 'Go on,' she urged.

Gleb said, 'There'd been this horsefly whirring around my head all day. You know, the sort that you can't shake off. It wasn't even my car, but I called to my line manager for a set of keys just to move away from this horsefly.' Gleb took a gulp of tea. 'Then I opened the boot and there it was.'

'What exactly?' said Galia, just to hear it again.

'That bag with all the money in it,' said Gleb.

'And then what?'

Gleb laughed. 'I told you already. Then in the front, in the glove compartment, I found one of Xenia's handkerchiefs.'

'And a computer thing.'

'Yeah,' said Gleb dismissively. 'But I threw that away.'

Galia sighed and made the sign of the cross across her chest, still clutching Xenia's white hankie with her initials monogrammed in Russian in each corner. 'She must have sent it to us,' she said.

'Doesn't have to be her handkerchief, though,' said Gleb. 'Does it?'

'Who else's?' said his wife, shaking her head delightedly. 'She said she'd send money. And she has.' She touched her husband's sleeve. 'Looks like we can get that washing machine after all.' A burst of early evening sunlight lit up the dusty net curtains and bounced off the silver handle of the fridge.

'Or a new telly,' said Gleb. 'Only this time a German one.' He rocked himself back from the table happily.